THE

THE SECRET
OF
SCRIPTURE

FELIX ALEXANDER

FELIX ALEXANDER

THE SECRET OF SCRIPTURE

FOR MY SISTER, MARIA CELIA QUINTERO

FOR HELPING ME APPRECIATE LIFE'S
LITTLE VICTORIES
AND FOR HELPING ME FIND MY
STRENGTH WHEN I FELT I HAD NO
STRENGTH LEFT.

FELIX ALEXANDER

https://www.FelixAlexanderWriter.com

https://www.facebook.com/WriterFelixAlexander

https://twitter.com/ForeverPoetic

https://www.instagram.com/WriterFelixAlexander

https://www.goodreads.com/author/show/6350092.Felix_Alexander

https://www.amazon.com/Felix-Alexander/e/B00MO0B4KE/ref=dp_byline_cont_ebooks_1

THE SECRET
OF
SCRIPTURE

A NOVEL

FELIX ALEXANDER

ALSO BY FELIX ALEXANDER:

THE SECRET OF SCRIPTURE

"To be rooted in one another, and not in a piece of earth."
~Martin Buber, German-Jewish 20th century philosopher,
religious thinker,
political activist and educator

FELIX ALEXANDER

FACT:

THE DEAD SEA SCROLLS WERE DISCOVERED AT CAVES OF QUMRAN IN 1947.

THEY WERE WRITTEN IN: HEBREW, ANCIENT HEBREW, AND ARAMAIC.

ANCIENT HEBREW IS ALSO KNOWN AS PALEO-HEBREW AND REMAINED IN USE UNTIL THE 5TH CENTURY B.C.E.

THE DEAD SEA SCROLLS AUTHENTICATED THE OLD TESTAMENT, CONTAIN TEXT OF THE OLD TESTAMENT THAT REMAINED VIRTUALLY UNCHANGED DESPITE MANY TRANSLATIONS, AND ARE THE OLDEST SURVIVING TEXTS OF THE HEBREW BIBLE.

FRAGMENTS OF THE SEPTUAGINT WERE FOUND AT QUMRAN.

THE SEPTUAGINT IS THE ANCIENT TRANSLATION OF THE HEBREW BIBLE INTO GREEK.

KIONE GREEK WAS THE COMMON LANGUAGE AFTER ALEXANDER THE GREAT.

DIASPORA JEWS COULD NO LONGER READ HEBREW.

AFTER DESTRUCTION OF THE SECOND TEMPLE, JEWS REJECTED THE SEPTUAGINT, BECAUSE THE TRANSLATION IS FLAWED.

ANAT HOFFMAN OF THE JERUSALEM MUNICIPAL COUNCIL: "WE HAVE DEHUMANIZED THE ENEMY

THE SECRET OF SCRIPTURE

(PALESTINIANS), AS WE HAVE BEEN
DEHUMANIZED...WE ARE RE-ENACTING WHAT HAS
HAPPENED TO US, AS IF WE'VE NEVER LEARNED
ANYTHING."

THE FIRST PRIME MINISTER OF ISRAEL, DAVID BEN
GURION: "WE SHOULD LEAVE THE OCCUPIED
TERRITORIES IMMEDIATELY, BECAUSE OCCUPYING
IS CORRUPTING."

FELIX ALEXANDER

PROLOGUE

Professor Emmett Ben Yaakov sensed he was no longer alone in the room. He sat upright at his desk and steadied his breathing. The barrel end of a gun pressed against the lower back of his skull.

"Do not make a sound," a vaguely familiar voice spoke threateningly.

The professor swallowed hard and nodded in agreement.

"I'm here for the access codes."

"F-f-for the what?" Professor Yaakov flinched before his eyes darted back and forth.

"The access codes to the vault where the androids are being kept until the presentation. What are they?"

"I-I-I don't have them," the professor stammered his reply.

"Do not give me a reason to shoot you, Professor Yaakov," the intruder pressed the barrel of the gun into the thin patch of hair.

"Farhad?" The image of one of his former students popped into his mind when the professor recognized the voice. Though he hadn't seen him in nearly two decades, he clearly recalled Farhad's huge smile and large hazel eyes. The boy he remembered had a hopeful outlook and promising future in applied mathematics. "Farhad Hamid Vafa, is that you?"

Silence lingered between them momentarily before the man replied. "I wish you had not spoken my name, professor."

"But—"

"Do not turn around!" Farhad commanded. He shoved the barrel of the gun against the tender flesh of Professor Yaakov's neck. "Now, I'm only going to ask you one more time. What are the access codes to the vault where the androids are being kept?"

"I already told you—"

THE SECRET OF SCRIPTURE

The deafening bang of the gun left his ears ringing, but that inconvenience soon gave way to the searing pain in his knee when the bullet lodged in his leg. He fell off the chair writhing in agony. He clutched his leg and rolled over as he stared up at his former student, now a full-grown man no longer seeing the world through innocent eyes.

"I came here prepared to do that, and also prepared to kill you if you do not provide me with the information I seek." Farhad aimed the gun at the professor's head.

His eyes widened before he grimaced and gasped for air.

"The access codes, professor."

"No, please, don't," Emmett pled. "I don't have them."

"You expect me to believe you?" Farhad crouched down beside his former mentor. He ran the barrel of the gun against Emmett's forehead, which now beaded with sweat. "You are in charge of the exhibition. How could you not have it?"

"The codes are p-p-programmed to change ev-ev-every fif-fifteen minutes. They sync only…with the master chip," Emmett stammered his reply.

"Where might I locate this master chip?" Farhad smiled.

"It…it…it is imbedded in the brain of the representative who is in charge of their presentation," Emmett winced and drew a sharp breath.

Farhad shook his head, "Tsk-tsk-tsk."

"P-p-please, Farhad, I need an ambulance," Emmett clutched his former student's arm.

"No, you don't," Farhad yanked his arm away. "You need to make your peace with God."

"NO! NO! PLEASE, GOD, NO!" Emmett protested, to no avail.

1

CROWNE PLAZA TEL AVIV CITY CENTER
Tel Aviv, Israel
5:35 a.m.

Aiden Leonardo woke with a start. Darkness filled the room. The telephone rang eerily once more. He reached over to the nightstand without lifting his head and grabbed the phone mid-ring. "Hello?"

"Professor Leonardo?" a man's voice asked urgently.

"Yes," Aiden replied with his face half buried in his pillow. "Who is this?"

"My apologies for calling you at this hour, professor."

Aiden blinked and tried to focus on the digital clock beside the phone. He felt Miriam shift beside him on the bed before she sleepily ran her fingers along his back.

"Again, who is this?" Aiden asked as he turned on the lamp.

"This is the concierge, professor. I called to inform you that there is someone here to see you."

"At this hour?" Aiden sat up and threw his legs over the side of the bed.

"I agree that the timing is most inconvenient, professor, but your visitor insisted on speaking with you immediately."

"Who is he?" Aiden asked. He held a finger up as if to ask Miriam to give him a moment when she asked him about the call.

"He is Chief Inspector Yeshua Schwartz, an important figure of the Israel Police force," the concierge said in a low voice.

"Israel Police force?" Aiden's brow furrowed.

Miriam lifted her head off the pillow.

THE SECRET OF SCRIPTURE

"I tried to convince him to return at a more prudent hour, but he insisted on meeting with you immediately and headed straight for the elevator."

"Wait, he's on his way up now?" Aiden asked.

A thunderous pounding drew his attention to the door.

"You've got to be kidding me," Aiden muttered under his breath. He quickly thanked the concierge, hung up the phone and turned to Miriam.

"What was that about?" she rubbed her eyes.

"I think we're about to find out," he shrugged.

Miriam leapt out of bed and made a beeline for the bathroom. The heavy fist pounded on the door once more. Aiden reached for his ivory-colored robe. It was the same color as the velvet upholstered, tufted back sofa chair with flared arms and wood frame upon which it sat.

"I'm coming!" Aiden called when the pounding continued. He threw the robe over his shoulders and tied a knot around his waist. The grogginess of sleep had finally faded. "Who is it?"

"My name is Pakad Yeshua Schwartz, chief inspector of the Israel Police force. Professor Leonardo, it is imperative that I speak with you immediately." The man's tone was sharp, and he spoke English with an accent.

"What does the Israel Police want with me?" Aiden wondered aloud. Akin to most police forces around the globe, its duties include maintaining public safety, crime prevention, traffic control, and counter-terrorism. Though, unlike police departments in the U.S. there are no local or municipal police departments in Israel.

Aiden cleared his throat before he pulled the door open a few inches. He gave the chief inspector a once over, his hazel eyes cold beneath black bushy eyebrows the same color as his short-cropped hair. He was mostly clean-shaven save for his thick mustache, fair-skinned with a strong jaw and donned an official-looking light blue uniform that reminded Aiden of the type worn by the Chicago PD.

"May I come in?" the chief inspector asked.

Aiden lowered his gaze and pursed his lips before he glanced over his shoulder at Miriam, who had just exited the bathroom wearing sweatpants and a hooded sweatshirt with the U.I.C. logo. She nodded as she crossed her arms and stood in the center of the suite.

"Sure," Aiden pulled the door open as he stepped back. "Do you mind telling me what this is all about?"

The chief inspector crossed the threshold and moved aside to allow the door to close behind him. He glanced at Miriam momentarily before he answered Aiden's question.

"I understand you met with Professor Emmett Ben Yaakov yesterday evening," the chief inspector began.

"Yes," Aiden replied. "He wanted to discuss a philosophical matter before the conference. We met for drinks in the hotel bar downstairs."

"A philosophical matter?" The chief inspector sounded perplexed. "I thought this is supposed to be a technological summit."

"It is, yes," Aiden confirmed.

"Yet, he wished to discuss philosophy?" Yeshua asked again. "I'm not seeing the connection."

"Is there a problem here, chief inspector?" Aiden crossed his arms.

"Do you believe there's a problem, professor?"

"You arrived here pounding on my door in the early morning hours of the day. You're asking questions about a meeting I had with a friend. I don't understand why there needs to be a connection to anything," Aiden replied.

"A connection to anything," Yeshua repeated. "I see, yes, well the reason I've come to question you, professor, is because someone murdered Professor Yaakov, and you were the last person to see him alive."

THE SECRET OF SCRIPTURE

"What?" Aiden and Miriam said in unison. They cast each other an incredulous glance before they turned back to the chief inspector as Miriam approach Aiden's side.

"How?" Miriam asked.

"When?" Aiden added.

"You don't think Aiden had anything to do with it, do you?" Miriam wrapped her arm around Aiden's.

"The investigation is on-going," Yeshua said. "I'm merely trying to understand the nature of your meeting with him. He was a professor of applied mathematics. You are a professor of biblical studies. This is a technological summit. Do you see now why I am trying to make the connection?"

Aiden pulled away from Miriam and turned away. He crossed his arms with a hand on his chin and paced the length of the suite. Yeshua studied him in silence before Miriam spoke.

"Emmett and I studied abroad together, but our families have known each other since before we were born. I introduced him to Aiden a few years ago. They discussed philosophy on several occasions."

Yeshua read her eyes before he gave her a quick once-over, studying her expressions and body language for any hint of deception or guilt.

"When?" Aiden turned to the chief inspector.

"The cororner places the time of death sometime between ten o'clock last night and midnight, but he still has to conduct a full autopsy to know more," Yeshua said.

Aiden nodded pensively. He had returned to his hotel room shortly after nine o'clock. Hotel cameras could confirm it.

"Emmett had concerns," Aiden finally said.

"Concerned about what, professor?" Yeshua clasped his hands behind his back.

"He was worried about how the new technologies—and how they will change our world—would be received by those who still cling to the past," Aiden said. "This summit is a glimpse into the near future."

Yeshua knew Tel Aviv was scheduled to host a gathering of the greatest technological minds in the world. Described by Newsweek as a "flourishing technological center," for being one of the ten most technologically influenced cities in the world made it an ideal location for the summit given its nickname: Silicon Wadi, Israel's center of high-tech.

"It's to be the unveiling of quantum networking for financial institutions. Launching a new era in technological advancement and taking the Internet of Things beyond our wildest imagination. One of the highlights, I understand, will be a secure network to replace computer chips in credit cards with a new form of crypto-currency and nanotechnology by embedding 'trusted notes' into humans—possibly into their brains—that will contain sensitive financial and electoral data."

"I don't understand how this prompted philosophical discourse," the chief inspector held Aiden's gaze. He studied the professor with a keen eye.

"That, in and of itself, wouldn't," Aiden turned and stepped away from the chief inspector. He felt uneasy under Yeshua's glare, and about revealing the topic of his conversation with Professor Yaakov. "It's the artificial intelligence aspect of the summit that raises some philosophical concerns."

"Artificial intelligence? How so?" The chief inspector briefly met Miriam's gaze, and then proceeded to follow Aiden's movement.

"Advancements made in the field of robotics, A.I. in particular have the tech world abuzz. Before I proceed, it serves to note that previous presentations of A.I. have left people with mixed feelings about the entire concept." Aiden turned to the chief inspector and continued after he nodded. "Some instances are merely exaggerated rumors and misconstrued facts about what actually happened, but on a few occasions A.I. robots alluded to what equates to the annihilation of humanity by artificial intelligence."

"You mean, like in those science-fiction films?" The chief inspector chuckled.

"Yes and no," Aiden winced. "It's a bit more complicated, a bit more real."

"I have never heard of this," Yeshua looked perplexed.

"It's mainly been of interest in the tech world, because on the surface it *does* sound more like science-fiction than science-fact."

"Understandable," the chief inspector motioned for permission to sit on the sofa chair as Miriam sat at the desk nearby. "Please continue, professor."

"According to Emmett, the latest advancements in the development of A.I. have raised some philosophical concerns." Aiden paused momentarily to measure his next words carefully. "Apparently, when asked about the topic of human extinction, the artificial intelligence robots remarked— independent of each other—that it was merely a matter of logic."

"Merely a matter of logic?" Yeshua repeated.

"Given our threat to the balance in nature through overpopulation and pollution, A.I. has concluded that we no longer serve a productive purpose in the eco-system."

"Wouldn't eliminating humans throw off the balance in nature?" Yeshua asked.

"An argument could be made either way, but from A.I.'s perspective human activities like resource consumption, habitat conversion and over-exploitation of natural resources are among the key contributors to environmental degradation that threatens all other life forms. So, it isn't a decision made with malicious intent, but rather as a matter of the preservation of life on this planet as a whole. Meaning that by removing us from the equation they would bring back the balance in nature.

Arriving at this conclusion as a logical solution would allow A.I. to execute a form of genocide sans any hang-ups about morality."

"How does this become a philosophical matter when one can simply pull the plug?" The chief inspector shrugged.

"The philosophical conundrum is further compounded when A.I. is asked about the existence of God," Aiden met the chief inspector's gaze. "Given that every decision A.I. makes is predicated on Formal Logic, it stands to reason that when A.I. arrives at a logical conclusion that the universe can exist without a deity as gods are presented by the world's religions, what does that say about us and our level of intelligence? Furthermore, how would the masses who believe in scripture feel that the end of humanity would not come at the hands of their God, but by an intelligent entity that doesn't believe in God?"

"But these are just computers," Yeshua shrugged.

"Are they just computers?" Aiden asked. "We are talking about the most advanced thinking machines in the history of the world. These aren't just a couple of robots capable of calculating at the speed of thought and beating us at chess, inspector. We're talking about the potential of general A.I. to outperform humans at every cognitive task."

The chief inspector stared at Aiden in disbelief. He turned to Miriam, who shrugged at him, and then he returned his gaze back to the professor. "And this is what he wished to discuss with you?"

"Emmett may have spent his career as a theoretical physicist, but he has always been a deeply spiritual man. He worried about the consequences of this news going public. How will clerics and believers feel about technologies that echo passages in scripture with regard to the 'mark of the beast,' and a conscious entity challenging their faith?"

"Are you saying this A.I. is a sentient…being?" The chief inspector asked.

THE SECRET OF SCRIPTURE

"Sentience and consciousness are often confused with one another, but they are not one in the same." Aiden paced the length of the room. "Whereas sentience is the capacity for subjective perceptions such as feelings and experience, consciousness is merely being aware of yourself and your surroundings. A.I. has displayed a capacity for the latter, but not the former."

"I see," the chief inspector contemplated Aiden's words.

"His most pressing concern, however, was how the revelation would fair in the face of religious extremism. Especially when we consider the possibility of this revelation occurring in the midst of the on-going Israeli-Palestinian conflict." Aiden stopped at the foot of the bed with his arms crossed and a hand on his chin.

"Interesting that you would use that word, revelation," said Chief Inspector Schwartz.

"Why?" Aiden and Miriam exchanged a curious glance before they met the chief inspector's gaze.

Yeshua Schwartz paused before he revealed the piece of evidence that led him to seek Aiden out. He pursed his lips and lowered his gaze as he reached into his jacket and brandished a photograph, which he handed to Miriam, since she sat closest to him.

She accepted it, and caught her breath when she saw the image.

"What is it?" Aiden asked.

Miriam met Yeshua's anxious eyes before she turned to Aiden and handed him the photograph.

"What the—?" Aiden's brow furrowed. His instant horror gave way to anger. His friend and colleague, Professor Emmett Ben Yaakov, had a bullet wound in the center of his forehead. His lifeless eyes stared helplessly toward heaven, yet that hadn't been the worst of it.

"It might interest you to know we found him prostrate on the steps of the eastern triple arched Huldah Gates of the Temple Mount three hours ago." Yeshua cleared his throat. "This led us to conclude that religious symbolism played a role in his murder."

"The gates represent the former entrance into the Temple," Aiden said without lifting his gaze from the photograph. He studied the gruesome mutilation in the center of Emmett's chest. "Do you think he was alive when..." but his words trailed off.

"Given the absence of excessive blood, we believe that the carving of his flesh occurred after the gunshot claimed his life, but not long after. Additionally, we don't believe he was murdered in Jerusalem, but rather his body was taken there after the fact."

"So, the killer spared him the agony of this twisted act," Aiden concluded.

"This led me to think it wasn't personal," Schwartz added.

"It wasn't personal?" Miriam repeated, shocked.

"What I mean to say is it may not have been a crime of passion," Schwartz corrected himself.

"I wouldn't be so sure, chief inspector," Aiden moved from around the foot of the bed and held the photograph beneath the lamp between Miriam and Schwartz. "The engraving left on Emmett's chest is in Hebrew and it is a direct reference to a biblical verse."

"Which one?" Miriam asked as she examined the photograph. The lettering became clearer after Aiden's observation.

דָּנִיֵּאל

ז:יז

"It's from the Book of Daniel," Schwartz nodded, which is the other reason I wanted to speak with you.

"So, he came near where I stood: and when he came, I was afraid, and fell upon my face: but he said onto me, Understand, O son of man: for at the time of the end shall be the vision," Aiden recited the passage from memory.

THE SECRET OF SCRIPTURE

"Daniel chapter 8 verse 17," Miriam whispered.

"Who is capable of a more passionate crime than a religious zealot?" Aiden asked.

2
OLD CITY
Jerusalem, Israel
6:35 a.m.

Thirty-four miles east of Tel Aviv, Farhad sank into the back seat of the Uber he had scheduled to pick him up from the same hotel where Chief Inspector Yeshua Schwartz met with Professor Aiden Leonardo.

It happened as the Preceptor predicted.

After the professor had been killed, and the evidence had been planted, he summoned his accomplices to help him move the body. Three off-duty officers—who believed in the cause—arrived in a white cargo van at the rear entrance near the dumpsters.

Once Emmett's body was loaded into the back of the van, two of them transported the body to the Old City where authorities would receive an anonymous tip to find his corpse before sunrise.

The third officer—Abner Badani—went to police headquarters to wait for the call to secure the perimeter of the building where Emmett was killed. Meanwhile, Farhad took an Uber to the Crowne Plaza Tel Aviv City Center, where he was to await the arrival of the chief inspector as the Preceptor had instructed. Once he confirmed Yeshua's arrival, he summoned another Uber to pick him up.

Almost immediately after the chief inspector entered the main lobby of the hotel, Farhad's Uber pulled up to the curb. The driver greeted him with a friendly smiled and confirmed their destination—an intersection just outside the city walls of the Old City—and proceeded to drive ahead.

Farhad had remained silent, hoping the driver would get the hint that he was not in the mood for conversation, and he did. The vehicle moved along the mostly empty streets, but that would soon change as dawn was fast approaching.

THE SECRET OF SCRIPTURE

He stared through the window as the blue sedan sped eastbound along Route 1. *Israel will fall*, he thought to himself. *The false messiah will fall with it. God's promise to Abraham will be fulfilled for the faithful*, he reminded himself as he sat upright when they neared the Old City.

"Turn here," he instructed the driver as the vehicle approached Ha-Nevi'im Street. "Make a right at Nablus Road and you may drop me off at the bus terminal."

The driver nodded and obliged.

Farhad waited for the sedan to pull away before he proceeded to cross the street. With a few taps on the screen of his smartphone, he concluded the ride and initiated a call.

"Yes?" a deep voice answered.

"The deed is done," Farhad said as he glanced over his shoulder.

"And the access codes?"

"It was as you foresaw, Preceptor."

"Naturally," the Preceptor sighed. He knew Emmett would not have them, but killing him was an integral part of their plan.

"I have arrived at the Old City," Farhad continued south along the side of the road. "The authorities appear to have secured every entrance."

"As anticipated," the Preceptor replied. "Go to Zedekiah's Cave and prepare for the next phase of our operation."

"Yes, Preceptor," he obeyed and ended the call. Tingles rushed his spine. The anticipation nearly overwhelmed him. *Finally, I will avenge you, father.*

3
CENTRAL DUPAGE HOSPITAL
Wheaton, IL (Western Suburb of Chicago)
11:40 p.m.

Detective Marquez stood in the hospital corridor of the ICU while the medical staff tended to their patient. The commotion in the room required the assistance of security to subdue the man who emerged from the state of coma only hours ago. The medical staff had to repeatedly put him under, because each time he woke, he shouted in a foreign tongue and struggled to break free of his restraints.

The detective noticed another man out of the corner of his eye. The stranger peered from the entryway of another room down the hall. The staff struggled to keep the patient calm before they were finally able to inject him with a sedative.

"What's his status?" Marquez intercepted the doctor when he stepped out of the room.

"His status remains unknown, detective, I'm sorry. I wish I could elaborate further, but at this juncture Mr. Prescott requires rest and observation until we can determine the extent of his condition."

"I see," Marquez pursed his lips. He glanced over the doctor's shoulder and watched as the nurses checked the patient's vitals. The security guards exited the room to return to their posts on the main floor. "Do you know what he was saying?"

"Honestly, no," the doctor shook his head. "He seemed to be speaking some Middle Eastern language, but I'm not familiar enough with any idioms from that part of the world to determine which one."

They watched Mr. Prescott momentarily as he appeared to repeat the same thing in a hushed tone while he dozed off. The doctor excused himself as the stranger approached from down the hall. The white-bearded man walked with a slight limp wearing a black suit with a matching fedora. His rekel—a frock coat—fell to his knees, buttoned down with a white dress shirt beneath it.

"They finally got him to settle down again, eh?" The stranger peered into the room.

"It appears so," Marquez nodded. The dark blue jacket of his Armani suit opened as he placed his hands on his hips.

The stranger turned to the detective and gave him a once over. He took note of Marquez's light blue silk dress shirt and leather belt with its rectangular silver buckle. "Is he a friend of yours?"

"You could say that," Marquez lied without meeting the stranger's gaze.

"Is he a religious man, this friend of yours?"

"Why do you ask?" Marquez turned his attention to the stranger. It was then that he noticed the man's thin face with pale wrinkled skin and sallow eyes.

"He was quoting the Tanakh," the stranger said.

"The Tanakh? Are you sure?" Marquez asked. His brow furrowed.

"I'm a Hasidic Jew, of course I'm sure," the man replied. He then turned back to Mr. Prescott, who had fallen into a deep slumber. The dark skin of his baldhead and clean-shaven face beaded with sweat. "Funny thing is your friend does not look like a Hasidic Jew himself, much less like someone well-versed in ancient Hebrew."

"I'm sorry, did you say ancient Hebrew?" Marquez looked surprised.

"Yes, ancient Hebrew, or more commonly referred to by your Western scholars as Biblical Hebrew, hence my reference to the Tanakh."

"You mean, the Old Testament?" Marquez asked.

"Well, you people call it the Old Testament, but its proper name is the Tanakh, and it is so named for the first Hebrew letter of each of the Masoretic Texts as they are traditionally divided: the Torah—Teaching, also known as the

Five Books of Moses, Nevi'im for the Prophets, and the Ketuvim for the Writings. T, N, K, Tanakh."

"I'm sorry, what did you say your name is?" Marquez asked.

"I didn't," the man eyed him suspiciously. "How do you know this man?"

"It's complicated," Marquez avoided the question.

"Not as complicated as it is to learn ancient Hebrew without any formal background, I can assure you of that," the man replied.

Marquez studied the man momentarily.

"I overheard your conversation with the doctor," the stranger continued.

"Can you at least tell me what he was saying?" Marquez insisted.

The stranger pursed his lips and sighed momentarily before he repeated Mr. Prescott's words: "God is my judge, nine, twenty-five and twenty-six."

"God is my judge?" Marquez repeated as he contemplated Prescott's words and numbers and their possible meaning. He crossed his arms over his chest and stroked his chin while he mulled over the circumstances surrounding Prescott's case.

He was found in a motel room—in an unincorporated suburb of DuPage County—that had been checked out under someone else's name using a cloned credit card. One among the many listed in the identity theft ring he had been investigating for months. Uniformed deputies responded to calls of a possible altercation between at least two men before gunshots rang out. Screeching tires had been heard in the lot prior to the deputy's arrival, but only Prescott was located at the scene with a head injury caused by blunt force trauma. He had been unconscious for three days, so to have him awaken speaking an ancient tongue only complicated an already muddied investigation.

THE SECRET OF SCRIPTURE

"Any idea why he would say such a thing?" Asked the man.

"Not a clue," Marquez replied.

"Suit yourself," the stranger said as he turned away and waved a hand at Marquez dismissively. He hobbled down the hall in the direction from which he came muttering something unintelligible under his breath.

Marquez waited until the man disappeared back into the room from which he had originally emerged before he retrieved his smartphone from the inner pocket of his suit jacket. He scrolled through his contact list, but his search was interrupted when the man peered out into the hall once more.

"By the way, it might interest you to know that the phrase 'God is my judge' is the etymology of the name, Daniel."

4
OLD CITY
Jerusalem, Israel
6:45 a.m.
In the catacombs beneath the Old
City, Farhad navigated through the dark tunnels of Zedekiah's
Cave. He tapped the head of his flashlight against his palm,
and it flickered back to life.

The people slain by Moses lie within these walls,
Farhad reflected on a story that appears in both the Bible and
the Qur'an. Legend holds that Zedekiah's Cave is the final
resting place of two-hundred and forty-nine co-
conspirators who rebelled against Moses and were led by his
cousin, Korah, a descendent of Levi—son of Jacob, later
named Israel.

The faint light swept across the limestone
walls. The sound of water trickling from the ceiling echoed in
the cavern, *Zedekiah's tears*.

The ground sloped at a twenty-degree angle from
the cave entrance between the Damascus and Herod
Gates beneath the Old City Wall in the Muslim Quarter.
Evidence of quarrying from the time of Herod the Great to
Suleiman the Magnificent remained despite the veil of time
and secrecy.

"I wondered when you would arrive," a woman's
voice pierced the shadows before she stepped into the soft
glow of a lamp hanging on a nearby wall. Her brown hair
parted down the middle and pulled back into a tight bun was
the same color as her almond-shaped eyes. Her gaze reflected
her resolve, but softened upon seeing Farhad.

"Law enforcement agents are everywhere," Farhad
smiled when he took the woman's hand. She held a briefcase
in the other. "I wasn't sure I would be able to avoid detection
now that the sun has met the horizon."

"The important thing is that you made it," she set
down the briefcase before she embraced him. "How did things

go with the professor? Were you able to obtain the access codes?"

"He did not have them?" Farhad shook his head.

"The Preceptor predicted as much," she pressed her head against his chest. "And what about the evidence?"

"The trap has been set. All that remains is for it to be sprung."

"The explosives are in place," she pulled away from his embrace and lifted the briefcase. "The others are waiting for instructions from the Preceptor."

"All of the detonators are inside?" He accepted the briefcase.

"Yes," she nodded.

"Good," Farhad looked at the briefcase reverently.

"By the time this is over, the world will never be the same. Are you ready to do God's work?" she searched his eyes.

"The world will rue the day it permitted the Zionists to perpetuate their crimes," Farhad replied.

"You will have your revenge, my love," Batya placed a hand on his cheek. "And I will help you get it."

5
TEL AVIV UNIVERSITY
Tel Aviv, Israel
7:05 a.m.

The cool early morning air whipped through the open passenger-side window as Aiden watched the city zip past. The chief inspector cursed under his breath as he shoved his smart phone against the magnetic holder mounted on the dashboard.

"Everything okay?" Aiden asked.

"The new head of security at the Temple Mount, her name is Batya. I can never get ahold of her when I need her most," Yeshua grumbled.

"Oh," Aiden turned away unsure how to respond.

"I'd have her replaced immediately, but she was what you Americans call a political-hire, so—" Yeshua shrugged as his words trailed off.

"It's the way of the world, I guess," Aiden replied.

"And what a world it has become," Yeshua added. "It's a shit hole of nepotism and favors that perpetuates the entitlement that has replaced hard work and dedication."

"Perhaps," Aiden nodded.

"Do you not agree?" Yeshua glanced over at the professor.

As much as he would have liked to agree with the chief inspector the truth was that nepotism and favors had been the way of the world since the dawn of civilization. In ancient Mesopotamia, men promised positions of power to others in exchange for assistance in achieving rulership over a city-state. The ensi, as the leader was known, later bestowed favors upon the temple priests for a blessing from the gods to go to war. As long as the priests confirmed the blessing from the gods, the people never questioned the motives of their king. A theme repeated throughout history to wage holy wars in the name of God.

"Why do you think the killer chose a verse from the book of Daniel?" Aiden asked, changing the subject.

THE SECRET OF SCRIPTURE

"Terrorists will utilize religious texts to justify their actions," Yeshua said.

"Well, if this is the work of terrorists, then I think it's a pretty safe bet that they aren't Islamic extremists," Aiden replied.

"How can you be certain?" The chief inspector looked over at Aiden when he stopped at a red light.

"Although he is venerated by Muslims as a prophet, Daniel is not mentioned in the Quran. So, there aren't any verses attributed to him that would correlate with the mutilation left on Emmett's chest," Aiden said.

"What if the terrorist is well-versed in the Writings and sought to shift focus on Jewish extremist groups?" Yeshua asked.

"It's possible but given that Daniel is not a prophet in Judaism it would not fit the modus operandi of religious extremists. Though, even if he was a prophet, I doubt he would be the inspiration for such an atrocious act," Aiden added. "Any attacks made in the name of God have solely been made *in* the name of God, and not the prophets or significant figures."

"What about jihadists?" Yeshua drove through the intersection when the light changed.

"Regardless of the organization: Al-Qaeda, Taliban, Hamas, Hezbollah, or ISIS, the call to arms has been to preserve ideology and fight in the name of God, not His prophets." Aiden said as the vehicle pulled into a parking lot.

"Well, we're about to find out what—if any—is the connection between Emmett Ben Yaakov and religious extremists," Yeshua said as he pulled his vehicle curbside to the walkway leading to the main entrance of the Vladimir Schreiber Institute of Mathematics at Tel Aviv University.

The university itself is the largest in the country with over 30,000 students that enjoy a campus life as dynamic and pluralistic as the city itself. Even in the long shadows cast by the early morning light, Aiden made out the L-shaped structure with its cream-colored concrete façade. The shadows of remaining night accentuated the ominous appearance of the series of thin, tinted-glass windows on all four levels of the building. Two police squads were parked in front of the mathematics building. Samal Sheni Abner Badani met the chief inspector at the front entrance.

"We have secured the entire floor where the professor's office is located. No one has been in-or-out, everything remains untouched, and it appears that the scientist was alone at the time of the shooting."

"Well done, sergant," Yeshua nodded before he glanced over his shoulder and scanned the grounds. "Any suspicious activity?"

"Nothing," Badani replied. "We did a canvas of the area, and the students and staff who were here at the time claim to have heard a few gunshots, but no one reported seeing anyone leave the building."

"Yes, well, the absence of street lamps allowed someone to move like a shadow among shadows before dawn," Yeshua replied. "Find out who is in charge of the lighting and utilities, someone cut the power in advance. Have your men keep an eye out for anything out of the ordinary while I check the professor's office."

Badani acknowledged the command and stepped aside to allow Yeshua and Aiden to cross the threshold into the building. He waited until they arrived at the end of the corridor—beyond earshot—where they waited for the elevator before he placed a call.

"Is he there?" A deep voice spoke.

"Yes, he is here. The chief inspector is with him," Badani replied.

"Good. You know what to do, but first wait until they have arrived at the desired floor."

"Yes, Preceptor," Badani ended the call.

THE SECRET OF SCRIPTURE

As they entered the elevator, Aiden felt tense. Despite having charged into Lazzaro's home office after he heard gunshots, the idea of once again walking into the office of someone who had been murdered did not sit well with Aiden. He did not pretend to possess the bravery of a soldier, nor did he fancy himself a hero. His actions the night of Lazzaro's death had merely been born out of concern for his father.

"Are you all right, professor?" Yeshua noted the distracted look in Aiden's eyes.

"Yeah, it's nothing. I'm simply not crazy about elevators," Aiden lied. It did not escape him that once again he had been drawn into an investigation that revolved around a murder and religion.

"But your room at the hotel was on the seventh floor?" Yeshua replied.

"That was for my fiancé, you know, 'happy wife, happy life,'" Aiden said.

"Forgive me, but I am unfamiliar with the adage," Yeshua said as the elevator dinged. "Ah, we are here."

"Saved by the bell," Aiden muttered.

"That phrase I am familiar with," the chief inspector said. "Its origins are related to boxing and not the popular belief of coffin contraptions in case someone was buried alive."

"Imagine that," Aiden followed the chief inspector out of the elevator.

The lights inside the elevator flickered and the cart jerked just as Aiden stepped into the corridor. He and the chief inspector turned to the elevator and watched the lights continue to flicker as it jerked once more before the elevator bell dinged and the doors slid closed.

"That was odd," Aiden turned to Yeshua.

"There must be something wrong with the power grid," the chief inspector looked around. "Perhaps that is the reason why the street lamps on the campus were out. Come, let's have a look around."

Professor Ben Yaakov's office was located at the end of the corridor. The frosted glass walls and doors encased the corner office with two large windows facing outward over the campus. The corridor was vacant and dark, save for three ceiling lights several meters apart that cast a soft glow. It reminded Aiden of 80's horror flicks as they approached the room where Emmett made his life and met his death.

Professor Emmett Ben Yaakov, Department Chair of Applied Mathematics. His name and title engraved on a silver plate affixed to the glass. His students knew Emmett as "the supplanter," a double meaning given his work as a theoretical physicist.

Though many of his students prided themselves as secular thinkers, most of them had been raised in religious households of various faiths—primarily the Abrahamic religions.

As such, they were familiar with the etymology of his namesake, Ben Yaakov. In Hebrew, Ben stood for "son of," and Yaakov meant "Jacob," later called "Israel" after the son of Isaac, the founder of the twelve tribes of Israel. According to biblical lore, Jacob wrestled with God—or an angel—and his name was changed to Israel because he overcame his struggle with God and man.

Emmett's work had the potential to supplant man's religions, while he wrestled with the implications it would have for the faith of his fore-bearers.

"How long did you know Professor Ben Yaakov?" The chief inspector asked as he pushed through the glass door of Emmett's office. The lights within flickered to life when they crossed the threshold.

"We met during a lecture in Chicago a few years back," Aiden entered behind the chief inspector. "After Miriam introduced us, we got to talking and found we had a lot in common regarding matters of faith."

THE SECRET OF SCRIPTURE

"You mentioned that earlier," Yeshua reached into his jacket pocket. "You said he was a deeply spiritual man."

"Yes, you see, chief inspector not all scientists are atheists. Through his life's work Emmett sough to reconcile his faith with his knowledge. Though his faith told him what to believe, his knowledge made him question why he should believe it. The conflict within—which he believed every man struggles with—had been his motivation, and as he made progress toward a unifying theory that would lead to a third revolution in modern physics, his hope had been to bridge the gap between Einstein's theory of general relativity with quantum mechanics."

"His what with what?" Yeshua pulled two sets of latex gloves from an inner pocket of his coat. "Forgive me, professor, but these terms are foreign to me. I am a man of God, who was not born with the inclination to understand these things. Would you care to elaborate?"

"Well, to put it plainly inspector, general relativity explains the dynamics of the universe on the grand scale. That is to say it accounts for how gravity controls the orbiting of planets, the collision of galaxies, and the universe at large. Quantum physics describes the nature of the universe at the smallest scales, dealing with atomic and subatomic particles."

Yeshua stared at Aiden in silence.

"Think of it this way, everything we are capable of observing in our world is explained by general relativity: i.e., the movement of cars, people, planets, the sun, the moon, etcetera. Think, Isaac Newton and the apple that fell from the tree. Make sense, so far?"

"So far, yes," Yeshua nodded.

"The conundrum—as Emmett once explained to me—is that all matter in the universe consists of infinitely tiny vibrating strings. However, when physicists attempt to observe the universe at the subatomic level to measure where an electron is within the range of the wavelengths of those vibrating strings, they can never be sure where the electrons will be at any given moment.

"Naturally, that's because the waves aren't waves in the conventional sense like sound waves or waves on the face of the sea. They're more of an abstract mathematical calculation to determine the position or momentum of an electron. Since they can't know where an electron will be with absolute certainly, they can only calculate the probability of where it might be at any given moment."

"That's quite the conundrum," Yeshua pretended to understand what Aiden tried to explain.

"Indeed, it is," Aiden nodded. "That's what led Einstein to write in a letter to one of the fathers of Quantum Mechanics—Max Born—*God does not play dice with the universe*, when he disagreed with the fundamental concept that events in nature and the universe at the atomic level are completely random."

"What did Professor Ben Yaakov set out to prove?" Yeshua wondered.

"If successful, his work would have changed the world with staggering implications. More than simply understanding where the laws of nature come from, his work had the potential to give man insight into the mind of God."

"That's rather arrogant, don't you think?" The chief inspector frowned.

"Is it, though?" Aiden asked.

"You don't agree?"

"I find it hard to believe that God would grant us the ability to contemplate profound thought and complex mathematical equations only to limit our understanding and knowledge."

"Who are we to assume we know what God intended for us?" Yeshua asked.

"Do you have children, chief inspector?"

"Yes, I have two—a son and a daughter—though I don't understand how that is relevant," Yeshua looked perplexed.

"Would you provide your children with the resources to succeed only to see them fail?"

"You measure failure against your definition of success, professor. That is hardly doing justice to the infinite wonder of God."

"Perhaps that is where the clerics and I diverge," Aiden scanned the office.

"You're not the first, and you certainly won't be the last," the chief inspector sighed. He circled around Emmett's desk as his eyes swept across the room.

"So, you didn't come here before coming to see me," Aiden asked.

"No," Yeshua replied without meeting Aiden's gaze.

"Why not?" Aiden looked at him perplexed.

"I knew you were in Israel for the conference," Yeshua shrugged. "Given the nature of your work coupled with your highly publicized involvement with the F.B.I. and Chicago authorities to resolve a murder and expose a network of corrupt government officials, I figured I'd see for myself what everyone has been talking about."

"I assure you, chief inspector, I am no hero," Aiden replied. The spotlight had been more of a bother than a blessing, but it did open doors that allowed him to expand his research around the globe.

"This must be where he was shot." Yeshua pointed at the ground behind the desk.

"How do you know?" Aiden approached on the opposite side and took a step back when he saw a pool of blood. He pinched the bridge of his nose and exhaled slowly.

"Based on the two bullet holes in the floor, the killer must have stood over the professor when he shot him. A gun powerful enough for a through-and-through." He glanced over at Aiden. "Are you all right, professor?"

"Blood just isn't my thing," Aiden turned away and approached a mop bucket he noticed hidden in the corner behind a filing cabinet. "This must be how the murderer gained entry into the office."

"Don't touch it," Yeshua instructed. "I'll have forensics examine it for fingerprints."

"That might be a moot point," Aiden crouched beside the bucket and pointed at a pair of gloves crumpled on the floor, turned inside out.

"These things are never easy," the chief inspector shook his head.

"Nothing ever is," Aiden stood and walked away from the corner.

"Here," the chief inspector handed him a pair of latex gloves. "Put these on before you touch anything."

The door to the office opened.

"This is a closed crime scene," Yeshua said to the round-faced man who entered. His light-brown close-cropped beard the same color as his full head of hair and bushy eyebrows. A dark red sport coat and black turtleneck sweater clung to his hulking frame.

"My apologies for the intrusion, Chief Inspector Schwartz. I came as soon as I heard." The man's thin brown eyes reflected worry.

"Who are you?" Yeshua eyed the man suspiciously, because he had not authorized the release of information to the public.

"My name is Dr. Yisrael Avrohom. I was brought in by Professor Ben Yaakov to act as director of the technological summit."

"Wait a minute," Yeshua placed his hands on his hips. "So this technological summit wasn't organized by the university."

THE SECRET OF SCRIPTURE

"No, sir, it was not," Yisrael shook his head. "The campus was chosen by the companies making their presentations for its locale and Tel Aviv's reputation as a technological hub. They reached out to the professor, who acted as a liaison between the university and the corporations that sought to showcase their latest advancements."

Yeshua studied the man in silence as he listened attentively.

"University officials agreed to allow them to host their conference here, but given the demands on the faculty during this time of year—preparing for the Fall term later this month—the school could not spare the staff to oversee the organizational efforts required for such an event. That's when he contacted me."

"And what is it that you do, exactly?" Yeshua asked.

"I was, most recently, a Research Fellow of Social and Cultural Anthropology at Oxford," Yisrael replied.

"How does this qualify you to be the director of a technological summit of this magnitude?" Yeshua fixed his gaze on Yisrael's thin brown eyes.

"I can't say that it does," Yisrael said.

"You shouldn't be so modest, Dr. Avrohom," Aiden interjected and stepped forward. "Aside from his work in Cultural Anthropology and Anthropology of Religion, Dr. Avrohom here has conducted extensive research into the content and structure of human morality."

"You're familiar with my work?" Yisrael eyed Aiden.

"Indeed," Aiden shook his hand and introduced himself.

"This is Professor Aiden Leonardo of the University of Illinois at Chicago Department of Biblical Studies," Yeshua said.

"It's a pleasure to meet you, Professor Leonardo."

"The honor is mine, Dr. Avrohom. I must confess, I was especially impressed with your use of evolutionary game theory to identify distinct problems of cooperation and their solutions in society."

"What is evolutionary game theory?" Yeshua asked.

"Well," Yisrael cleared his throat, "while game theory is the study of mathematical models to determine the strategic interaction between rational decision-makers, evolutionary game theory takes it a step further by focusing on the dynamics of a change in strategy within a population."

"I don't understand how this is connected to the technological summit," Yeshua said. "Does this game theory and artificial intelligence summit have anything to do with video games and computers, or am I missing something here?"

"I suppose that if we consider Emmett's philosophical quandary over the A.I. and God conflict—technology versus faith—then it stands to reason that having Dr. Avrohom here to oversee the summit was a logical decision."

"What leads you to this conclusion, professor?" Yeshua fixed his gaze on Aiden.

"I've read Dr. Avrohom's work and it asserts that morality is best understood as a collection of biological and cultural solutions to the problems of cooperation and conflict recurrent in human society," Aiden replied before he turned to Yisrael. "Am I correct, or have I misunderstood the basis of your work?"

"You are correct, Professor Leonardo," Yisrael nodded before he turned his attention to Yeshua. "Emmett and I attended school together in London—many years ago—so, when he contacted me about assisting with the summit, I jumped at the chance to oversee the organization of presentations, because it would afford me the opportunity to observe the initial reaction of artificial intelligence challenging faith-based ideas in the epicenter of the Abrahamic religions."

"I see," Yeshua nodded pensively. "And this will help you with your work in game theory?"

"Yes, because I'm currently conducting a study on how ritualized behavior and morality would be affected by a paradigm shift in one of the cornerstones of ritual and morality-based systems of thought," Yisrael nodded.

"Religion," Yeshua said.

"Precisely!" Yisrael nodded before he sighed and lowered his gaze. "This news about Emmett, however, is rather unexpected."

"Unexpected is one way to put it," Yeshua looked around. "Do you have any idea who had access to the building last night?"

"I'm afraid you'll have to speak with school officials about that," Yisrael replied. "I only have information about the attendees of the summit at the auditorium, seating arrangements, and order of presentations."

"I see, well, you may observe, then, but do not touch anything," Yeshua instructed. "I may have additional questions for you."

Yisrael nodded and watched as the chief inspector crouched behind the desk to continue his examination of the bullet holes in the laminated floor. He stood silently against the door with arms crossed and a hand on his chin. Aiden leaned over the desk as he pulled on the latex gloves. He then proceeded to glance over the papers scattered across the desk. A pamphlet with the Star of David etched in red on the cover caught his attention.

"This can't be right," Aiden's brow furrowed.

"What?" Yeshua peered over the edge of the desk.

"The Protocols," Aiden read the title aloud.

"The Protocols?" Yeshua asked. "As in The Protocols of Zion?"

"You've heard of them?" Aiden asked the chief inspector.

"I've heard of them, yes, but I can't say I'm entirely familiar with the text."

"The possession of these documents in Soviet Russia is punishable by immediate death," Aiden read a statement on the cover just below the title. "Every patriotic American must read these protocols," he read the following subheading aloud.

"Isn't Russia where the document first originated?" Yisrael asked as he stepped closer.

"Yes, it was during the reign of Czar Nicholas the Second where hatred of the Jews was most widespread, because more Jews lived in the Russian Empire than anywhere else at the time," Aiden replied.

"In Russia?" Yeshua asked. The look of surprise written across his face as he stood.

"They were regarded as the enemies of Orthodox Christians, so the Head of Russian Foreign Intelligence—Pyotr Rachkovsky—sought to pin the blame for oppositional attacks against the czar on the Jews," Yisrael added.

"And to defame the Jews, he commissioned Matvei Golovinski with the task of fabricating the Protocols," Aided added.

"To what end, exactly?" Yeshua reached for the pamphlet.

"Leading up to the fall of the House of Romanov, Russia was a house divided, and Pyotr sought to give the Russian people a common enemy to unite them," Yisrael answered.

"A common enemy—identified through fears and stereotypes—generally leads people to support the existing center of power," Aided said.

"Like your president has done against Muslims and Latinos," the chief inspector remarked.

"Hashtag, not my president," Aiden replied.

THE SECRET OF SCRIPTURE

"Targeting a specific group of people as villains in society isn't exclusive to Russia during Nicholas' reign," Yisrael said. "Psychologist, Heiko Ernst, has gone on record to state that people in power need a scapegoat to conceal their own failures, or inadequacies in order to mobilize a populace for some goal or another."

"It stands to reason that the educated will inspire the ignorant by playing on their prejudices as a call to action," Aiden added.

"It worked for President Trump in America as effectively as it worked for Hitler during his rise to power in the early 1930's after the signing of the Reichskonkordat," Yisrael continued.

"The what?" Yeshua asked incredulously.

"The Reichskonkordat—the Concordant between the Holy See and the German Reich—is a treaty negotiated between the Vatican and the emerging Nazis during the pontificate of Pious XI. The concordant essentially granted the Nazi regime moral legitimacy after Hitler acquired quasi-dictatorial powers through the Enabling Act of 1933," Yisrael answered. "The Act itself was not only facilitated through the support of the Catholic Centre Party, it made Rome the first legal partner to Hitler's regime."

"Though, to be honest, that wasn't the first time the Catholic Church had been embroiled in morally questionable actions," Aiden said.

"I'm guessing that you're referring to the Crusades," Yeshua handed the pamphlet back to Aiden.

"Not just in the Crusades, but in the way it handled slavery through most of its history, because it not only permitted the enslavement of non-Christians," Aiden replied. "It essentially subjected women and children to sexual abuse and human trafficking by leaving them to the fate of their master's will."

"Akin to when two Jesuit priests, who founded and ran Georgetown University, sold 272 African-American men, women, and children in order to secure the future of the premier Catholic institution of higher learning."

The chief inspector shook his head in disbelief.

"It's incredible to think of the atrocities people are capable of committing in the name of God," Yisrael spoke softly.

"This pamphlet essentially led to one of the greatest atrocities of the modern era," Aiden held up the copy of the Protocols.

"The Holocaust," Yeshua lowered his gaze.

"When Golovinski created the Protocols of the Elders of Zion, he plagiarized fictional works, lifting passages—almost word-for-word—from the satirical French novel, The Dialogue in Hell by Maurice Joly, and fabricated one of the most dangerous documents of the 20th century," Aiden opened the pamphlet.

"It spread from St. Petersburg in 1903 to Berlin in 1920 and London in 1922, having been translated into 60 languages since its creation," Yisrael added.

"Though it was in Germany where its existence was regarded as authentic and set the stage of Hitler's crimes," Aiden said without lifting his gaze from the book.

"Not to minimize the Nazi regime's systematic genocide of six-million Jews, it serves to note that within his own inner circle, Hitler praised the efficiency of 'America's extermination of the red savages who could not be tamed by captivity.'" Yisrael remarked as he gazed at the various papers on Emmett's desk.

"Starvation and uneven combat, combined with diseases transmitted through standard interaction and blankets intentionally contaminated with small pox led to the indigenous holocaust of the New World."

"Indigenous holocaust?" Yeshua asked.

"It is a term used by some to describe the death toll of Native Americans from the arrival of the Spanish to the American expansion westward that ranged from ninety-five million to one-hundred and fourteen million," Yisrael replied. "Both circumstances justified by religious beliefs."

"Are you saying God is the villain?" Yeshua fixed his gaze on Yisrael.

"If His teachings are scripture, and scripture is divinely inspired, does one blame the Believer, or the laws that the adherents of faith are commanded to follow?" Yisrael asked.

"The former holds the individual responsible, whereas the latter absolves him or her of culpability," Yeshua replied.

"If people are capable of making their own decisions, then one must ask if they need a religion to dictate how they will behave," Yisrael countered.

"One would argue that faith-based laws provided the framework for modern laws of governing," Aiden interjected.

"True, but here's the conundrum," Yisrael cleared his throat again. "Are the laws obsolete, or must a society continue to adhere to them as they were passed down over the centuries?"

"The rule of law can never become obsolete, or chaos will ensue," Yeshua replied.

"The rule of law is necessary, yes, but what I'm asking is if these specific set of laws—given to us by God—remain relevant, or should society do away with them completely? If they remain relevant, and are divinely inspired, then who are we to alter them to fit our modern sensibilities? If they no longer apply to our world, why not do away with them altogether? Though, in doing so, we must wonder: where does that leave God?"

"Believers will contend that God has always been, and so, regardless of whether we do away with scripture, God will always be," Aiden replied.

"Yes, well, philosophical discussions aside, we need to know what Professor Ben Yaakov was doing in possession of that pamphlet," Yeshua interjected.

"Do you think the professor was killed for his believed involvement with the Elders of Zion?" Yisrael wondered.

"We certainly can't rule that out as a possibility," Yeshua looked down at the desk.

"Especially when there are a number of organizations that believe the false propaganda perpetuated by this pamphlet to be true," Aiden said.

"That's a broad spectrum though, when you consider that it's not just terrorist organizations and their supporters who believe the authenticity of the Protocols," Yisrael eyed the pamphlet.

"You mean, like civilians?" Yeshua asked.

"Yes, both here in the region and abroad," Yisrael answered.

"In the region," Yeshua muttered under his breath. "Hamas has been known to attempt to infiltrate our borders to carry out attacks."

"Not all Palestinians are associated with Hamas," Yisrael said, "and there are many who aren't involved with, nor are supporters of Hamas that take umbrage with the State of Israel."

"What if this material was planted?" Aiden finally asked as he read the small print at the bottom of the pamphlet's cover:

Issued by The Patriotic Publishing Company P.O. Box 526 – Chicago, Ill.

"By who?" Yeshua turned to him.

"I don't know, but what I do know is that Emmett wasn't what a conspiracy theorist would refer to as a Zionist, even if there was any truth behind the propaganda," Aiden placed the pamphlet back on the desk and sifted through the remaining papers.

"If someone did plant this, we'd have to understand why?" Yeshua joined Aiden in rummaging through the scattered pages.

"And why now, on the eve of the summit?" Yisrael added.

"Unless this validates Emmett's concerns about the expected reaction to A.I. by religious zealots," Aiden concluded

"Perhaps, but why leave clues that would point directly back to them?" Yeshua wondered.

"They may be intent on sending a message to the world," Yisrael replied.

"What message is that?" Yeshua asked. "That faith will not cower to science?"

"Umm, this may go beyond the argument between religion and science," Aiden stopped shuffling through the papers and lifted one sheet from the pile. "This may also be a widening schism between the three Abrahamic faiths."

6
CENTRAL DUPAGE HOSPITAL
Wheaton, IL.
12:35 a.m.

Detective Angelo Marquez paced back and forth in the hospital room like a caged lion. The strands of his disheveled hair fell over his brow haphazardly and his eyes were sharp, aware of his surroundings. His light blue silk dress shirt a sharp contrast to his dark blue suit; a red tie with a pattern of tiny blue diamonds rounded out his ensemble.

He watched Prescott sleep and gazed at him pensively: *What were you doing in that hotel room?* There were reports of shots fired, but a weapon had never been recovered at the scene. Guests in adjacent rooms at the motel claimed they heard more than one voice, but no one could provide a description of the assailants.

Marquez glanced at his smartphone again. Miriam's phone number appeared on the glowing screen. After the incident at the Willis Tower, she had told him to call if he ever needed anything. *Daniel, chapter nine, verses twenty-five and twenty-six*, he thought to himself. Given her knowledge of scripture, he wondered if she could provide insight into the quandary of his investigation.

He did not feel comfortable calling her in the middle of the night and instead decided to review the passages in a bible he found in a bedside drawer of the hospital room. He read and reread the passages. He read a few verses before the specific passages, and read a few verses after in order to gain a better understanding of the context, but he felt as though he was missing something. Something he believed he probably would have better understood had he continued to practice his faith.

Marquez gazed at Prescott again. He knew he needed to understand the text better if he was going to make any progress with his investigation. Calling Miriam was a last resort. He was running out of time and running out of options.

THE SECRET OF SCRIPTURE

He didn't have any other choice. He pressed the call button on the screen and brought the phone to his ear.

The line rang a few times and he was about to hang up when she finally answered.

"Hello?" Miriam's voice echoed across the receiver.

"Miriam, hi, it's Angelo," he paused momentarily.

"Angelo, hey, it's been a while."

"Yeah, listen, I don't mean to intrude at such a late hour, but given the circumstances I'll get straight to the point."

"No worries," she interjected. "It's early morning over here. What time is it in Chicago?"

"Half past midnight," Marquez glanced at the digital clock on the nightstand. "Are you out of town?"

"Yes, Aiden and I are in Israel for a conference," she replied. "What can I do for you?"

"Israel, how fitting," Marquez said in a low voice.

"What do you mean?"

"Well, I'm working on a case and have hit a bit of a wall, so I'm hoping you may be able to help."

"I'm listening."

"The Book of Daniel, chapter nine verses twenty-five and twenty-six," Marquez said. "Do they hold any special meaning that I am not aware of?"

"I'm sorry, did you say the Book of Daniel?" Miriam's voice sounded alarmed.

"Yes," Marquez replied. "I have a gentleman here who has spent the past few hours repeating: 'God is my judge, nine, twenty-five, and twenty-six.'"

"Angelo, what's going on?" Miriam asked.

"That's what I'm trying to figure out," Marquez eyed Prescott again. "Apparently, this man was attacked by an unidentified assailant, was found unconscious, and woke speaking these words in Ancient Hebrew."

"Are you shitting me?" Miriam blurted out.

"Whoa!" Marquez replied.

"I'm sorry Angelo, this is just too weird, but a colleague was found murdered over here with a reference to Daniel inscribed on his chest."

"Holy—" Marquez's began to say.

"Yeah, insert pun here," Miriam replied. "Listen, the Israeli police woke us to question Aiden about the murder, and I'm freaking out over here, because he's been gone for quite a while now."

"Do they suspect Aiden's involvement?" Marquez asked. He remembered his own doubts about Aiden's involvement in the murder of Lazaro de Medici a few years ago, despite the F.B.I.'s certainty of his guilt.

"No, I don't think so," she replied. "It has more to with a meeting Aiden had with the professor in the hours before his murder."

"I understand, and I didn't mean to bother you—"

"It's no bother at all, I'm just too distracted to be of any use at the moment, however, Nagi will be able to help."

"Nagi, your Indian friend?"

"He's from Pakistan," Miriam corrected him.

"Same difference," Marquez shrugged.

"Would you agree with that statement if someone said you are Puerto Rican and not Mexican?"

"I get it, Fox news and their 'Three Mexican countries' debacle," Marquez nodded. "My apologies."

"I'll text you his address and I'll let him know you will be in touch."

"I appreciate this, Miriam," Marquez said before the call ended.

7
OLD CITY
Jerusalem, Israel
7:40 a.m.

The courtyard remained mostly vacant. Farhad strode across the central platform past the Dome of the Rock. Batya's words echoed in his mind. *By the time this is over, the world will never be the same.*

He gripped the briefcase in his left hand. The weight of the detonators inside, were no heavier than a laptop. The morning temperatures rose with the sun. Its light gleamed off the gold-topped Islamic shrine and the decorative tin glazed earthenware with verses from the Quran. The structure crowned the highest spot of Al-Aqsa compound; a plateau situated four meters above the rest of the mosque's courtyard.

He hadn't slept since yesterday afternoon. There was too much work to be done last night. The trap had been set. The bombs were in place. The professor's body left at the Huldah Gates. All that remained now was for Farhad to walk past each explosive device. The sensors would activate them via Bluetooth signal to be detonated remotely at a later time.

It seemed redundant when the Preceptor first instructed him to hide the explosives at their designated locations under the cover of night only for him to return with the briefcase in the morning.

"Wouldn't it be easier for me to place them and activate them simultaneously?" Farhad had asked the Preceptor.

"It would, yes, but we can't risk you being caught with both in your possession. You and the explosives would be of no use to our cause if you're detained."

Though Farhad was prepared to give his life before allowing himself to be taken into custody he agreed with the Preceptor that it would be more prudent to not risk compromising the goal of God's work.

FELIX ALEXANDER

Despite being People of the Book, the kafirs will be pitted against each other and parish from the earth.

He descended the wide staircase that led to Suq El Qatanin Street. He followed the walkway where it turned into Baruq Street, but continued westward past the tunnel entrance of the Little Western Wall. He continued past the stalls that lined each side of his path. Some of the merchants cast him sidelong glances, and others paid him no mind while they set up their trinkets and products for sale to tourists and passersby. The cool shade of the tunnel provided a brief reprieve from the morning heat, until he arrived at the other end.

The Western Wall and plaza were situated to his right, but large structures and canopies obscured his view of the Jewish worshippers and the ancient site. Their prayers and presence were of no interest to him. His priority lay elsewhere at the moment as he made his way toward the Jaffa Gate.

It is there where the beginning of the end had occurred nearly 2,000 years ago, and where recent events took place that changed his life irrevocably. *Perhaps our fate would have unfolded differently had the British not capitulated to the Zionists during the first half of the 20th century*, he strode past a small group of people conversing amongst themselves. He reflected on the peaceful co-existence his grandfather often spoke of before the initial stages of the Jewish state had begun in the historic territory of Palestine.

"There was a good deal of respect between Muslim, Christian, and Jew," his late father had often echoed his own father's words. "We lived in relative peace before the Europeans intervened. It is our shared responsibility as People of the Book to re-establish good relations between us. We may yet regain that peace if we treat each other as Allah commanded."

Allah commanded, but they disobeyed, Farhad shook his head.

He recited the verse from the Holy Quran as he turned another corner, "O mankind! We created you from a single pair of a male and a female, and made you into nations and tribes, that you may know each other, not that you may despise each other."

His grandfather was just a boy when the Haganah defied the official policy of restraint that Jewish political leaders had imposed on the militia. Though their original mandate had been to defend Jewish communities and refrain from attacking Arab gangs and their villages, they viewed the command as weakness. After the militant elements splintered off from their original role as an underground defense organization, they swept through the region in a reign of terror.

In 1935, they arrived at the village of Hunin—under top-secret orders—to evict the Arab residents from their homes by force, to kill the men, to take prisoners, to destroy houses, and to "burn what can be burned."

The aim had been to instill fear in those who fled, and to have them spread the word of the terror on the horizon to other Arabs throughout the land. When the British decided to establish a national home for the Jewish people in Palestine, Lord Arthur Balfour declared: "We do not propose to go through the form of consulting the wishes of the present inhabitants."

A museum was built on the ruins of my grandfather's village in Hunin. A nation was built on the remnant of terror in Israel. It ends with me! Farhad passed through a narrow alley and waited for a group of nuns to pass before he continued ahead.

His grandfather and father both lived by the words of the Holy Quran: "Allah does not forbid you to deal kindly and justly with those who have not fought against you about the religion or expelled you from your homes. For Allah loves those who are just."

"I too shall live by the words of the Holy Quran," Farhad said to himself when the Tower of David emerged before him. "Allah only forbids you to be friends with those who have fought against you about the religion, expelled you from your homes or supported others in expelling you. And whoever makes allies of them, then it is those who are the wrongdoers."

Are you ready to do God's work? Batya's words echoed in his mind as he approached the Tower of David Museum. He froze when he saw the Jaffa Gate.

"I will avenge you, father."

7
TEL AVIV UNIVERSITY
Tel Aviv, Israel
7:45 a.m.
Sunlight fell through the windows of Emmett's office
as Yeshua handed the sheet of paper back to Aiden.

"That's a pretty harsh message," the chief inspector
said.

"What's it say?" Yisrael reached for the sheet.

Aiden was about to hand it over when Yeshua
reached across the desk to stop him.

"Oh, right. Evidence," Aiden pulled back. "May I
read it to him?"

"Sure, as long as he doesn't touch it," the chief
inspector replied.

Aiden cleared his throat before he recited the words
on the page:

> "He was the last of the false messiahs
> Another prince of the Jews claiming to be king,
> The fact of his birth concealed by his death
> A lie made truth by the Hasmonean kings
> Each stone placed must be destroyed
> To expose the lie within a god's tower,
> Written in stone by the archangel Jibril
> The false faith to be stripped of its power."

"These words are incendiary," Yisrael looked up
alarmed.

"Well, it's not the first time such words have
been written," Yeshua shrugged.

"No, but it *is* the first time they are
accompanied by a threat to the Old City," Aiden interjected.

"What do you mean?" The chief inspector asked.

Aiden held up the sheet of paper and showed him
what had been drawn on the other side.

"Is that a map of the Old City?" Yeshua's brow furrowed as he walked around the desk and stood beside Aiden. He studied the page carefully.

"It appears so, but based on the shape of the drawing it resembles only an outline of the city walls with markings that seem to denote the location of the eight gates of the city," Aiden observed.

"What are those markings there?" Yisrael peered over Aiden's shoulder and pointed at the Stars of David drawn in red ink.

"I don't know," the chief inspector looked on perplexed.

"Could they be targets?" Aiden wondered.

"Targets for what?" the chief inspector asked.

"Well, on the surface the location of each star may appear random, but each star seems to correlate with the numerous Christian churches located throughout the Old City," Aiden observed.

"Are you sure?" Yisrael asked. "Even if we pencil in the streets that divide the four quarters of the city, there isn't a single star in the area that correlates with the Muslim Quarter."

"And?" Yeshua cast him a perplexed glance. "What's your point?"

"My point is that there is a Catholic Church in the Muslim Quarter, so if we are to conclude that whoever wrote this poem is targeting Christian monuments in the Old City, it doesn't make sense that they would exclude that church," Yisrael answered.

"Maybe it does," Aiden said with the look of realization dawning on his face.

"How so?" Yeshua asked as he and Yisrael met his gaze.

"The Church of Saint Anne—as it stands today— was originally erected in the 12th century, and unlike many other Crusader churches was not destroyed by Saladin after his conquest of Jerusalem."

"How does that have any bearing on the subject?" Yeshua asked.

"The location of the church was believed by the Crusaders to be the childhood home of Mary the mother of Jesus. It had been dedicated to her parents, Anna and Joachim."

"I'm still not following," the chief inspector said.

"Mary is venerated as one of the most important and righteous women in Islam," said Aiden.

"You are shitting me," Yeshua replied.

"She is the only woman mentioned by name in the Quran," Aiden said.

"Then Muslim extremists are behind the murder of Ben Yaakov," Yeshua concluded.

"I wouldn't be so sure," Aiden grimaced.

"Why not? The evidence is right there?" Yisrael blurted out.

"We still have the reference to the Book of Daniel to consider," Yeshua pursed his lips and cursed under his breath.

"The Book of Daniel?" Yisrael asked perplexed.

"It's part of an on-going investigation," Yeshua replied with a sidelong glance. "Which brings us back to square one."

"Yes and no," Aiden said.

"What do you mean?" the chief inspector asked.

"Based on the contents of the poem, someone wants to attack Christianity," Aiden began. "If we reflect on the words and review the map, we can surmise that the attack will center on locations in the Old City important to the Christian faith."

"How can you be so sure?" Yeshua wondered.

"Well, I can't say I'm sure-I'm sure, but given the phrases: 'last of the false messiahs, each stone placed must be destroyed, and written in stone by the archangel,' it stands to reason that whoever is behind this attack has zeroed in on the Christian faith."

Yeshua inhaled deeply as he placed his hands on his hips and stared ahead pensively.

"For what it's worth, chief inspector, I believe Professor Leonardo is onto something," Yisrael broke the silence.

"And what is it about your expertise that supports his argument?" Yeshua snapped.

"I am a student of history, and based on the facts presented in that poem there is plenty of history to support the claims of that stanza."

"The facts?" Yeshua wondered."

"Let's begin with the first line of the poem, 'He was the last of the false messiahs,'" Aiden began. "By the time Jesus had stepped onto the world stage the Roman authorities and the Jewish high priests had grown tired of the countless preachers who claimed to be prophets and messiahs delivering messages of God's imminent judgment."

"They number as many as twenty-five false messiahs," Yisrael added.

"Many whom we know by name, because of the historical record," Aiden continued.

"There was the shepherd Athronges, who in 4 A.D.—the year scholars agree Jesus of Nazareth was born—crowned himself 'King of the Jews' with a diadem on his head." Yisrael raised a finger.

"Then there was the one known only as 'the Samaritan,' who was crucified by Pontius Pilate despite never having actually challenged Roman authority," Aiden added.

"Count those names with Hezekiah the bandit chief, beheaded by Herod the Great in 40 B.C.E.; Simon of Peraea, sometime between 4 B.C.E and 15 C.E.; and Judas the Galilean, circa 6 C.E." Yisrael continued.

THE SECRET OF SCRIPTURE

"And then, approximately two decades after the Crucifixion, there was the Egyptian," Aiden said.

"I'm sorry, did you say, 'the Egyptian?'" Yeshua asked.

"He was a charismatic figure whose true identity even escaped Josephus," Aiden answered.

"He was rumored to have amassed an army of nearly 30,000 men and took them to the Mount of Olives," Yisrael said.

"The location regarded as the place where God would stand on the Day of Judgment," Aiden added.

"Why the need for so many messiahs?" Yeshua interjected.

"It was a tumultuous era defined not only by Roman occupation and the oppression of the Jews, but also by the dissension within Judaism," Aiden replied.

"Josephus made reference to the three sects that defined the discord," Yisrael added. "The Pharisees, the Sadducees, and the Essenes, all of which emerged against the backdrop of the Heliodorus Affair via the Maccabean Revolt."

"The religious and political turmoil of the time demanded change. Some people sought a military leader, while others turned to a charismatic teacher who would provide the correct interpretation of Mosaic Law to restore Israel. Each messiah akin to rolling waves arriving at the shores of society perpetuated the reshaping of the landscape." Aiden reflected on the historical footnote often overlooked by the faithful.

"In the eyes of Rome, all were essentially guilty of treason," Yisrael said.

"Treason?" Yeshua wondered.

"The self-proclamation as 'King of the Jews' by each messianic aspirant of the time was an act of sedition, for which the punishment was death," Yisrael answered.

"Hence, the Crucifixion," Aiden concluded.

"That part still baffles me," Yeshua shook his head. "If Jesus wasn't the first, or the last to be crucified, how did his martyrdom spawn a new faith that has endured twenty centuries."

"That is where the gospels come into play," Aiden answered. "In order to preserve his memory and his teachings, early Christians needed to portray Jesus as a pacifist spiritual leader."

"But why?" Yeshua asked.

"After the destruction of the Second Temple in 70 A.D., his followers—along with the Jews—felt compelled to distance themselves from the revolutionary zeal that led to their expulsion from Jerusalem," Yisrael said.

"Although scripture is rife with contradictions about Jesus' message, one passage denoting that he 'was sent solely to the lost sheep of Israel,' and later quoting him as instructing his followers to 'make disciples of all nations,'" Aiden began to say. "Or, as was written in Matthew 5:9, 'Blessed are the peacemakers for they shall be called the sons of God,' in contrast to Luke 22:36, 'If you do not have a sword, go sell a cloak and buy one,' the gospels were a way for his followers to redefine his mission and identity."

"This later allowed for the nature of the Christ to be transformed from a man lost to history into a deity whose existence cannot be disproven in the eyes of Believers," Yisrael said.

"Which brings us to the next two lines of the poem: 'Another prince of the Jews who claimed to be king, the fact of his birth concealed by his death," Aiden read the lines aloud.

"What is the line after that referring to?" Yeshua pointed at the succeeding text, "'A lie made truth by the Hasmonean kings.'"

Before Aiden could reply, he felt his phone vibrate against his chest and retrieved it from inside his jacket pocket.

THE SECRET OF SCRIPTURE

He handed Yeshua the sheet of paper as he excused himself and turned away to answer the call.

8
CROWNE PLAZA TEL AVIV CITY CENTER
Tel Aviv, Israel
7:55 a.m.

"Aiden, where are you?" Miriam paced the length of the hotel suite.

"I'm in Emmett's office at the university with the chief inspector and Dr. Yisrael Avrohom," Aiden said.

"Dr. Avrohom is there?" Miriam's brow furrowed. "That's doesn't make sense."

"Yeah, long story," Aiden glanced over his shoulder. "What's up? Everything okay?"

"I just got a call from Angelo," Miriam said.

"Your ex, the detective?" Aiden asked. "That's odd."

"That's not even the half of it," Miriam replied.

"How do you mean?"

"He called, because he's working on a case and came across a reference to the Book of Daniel."

"Are you serious?"

"Chapter nine, verses twenty-five and twenty-six," Miriam replied. "I sent Angelo to Nagi, while we sort things out over here, but that's too eerie to be a coincidence."

"Especially when there's no such thing as coincidence," Aiden's voice echoed over the receiver. "Well, I wanted to give you a heads up, in case you hear from Nagi. Have you made any progress over there?"

"Actually, things have become more complicated since our arrival at Emmett's office," Aiden replied. "Now with this revelation of Marquez's investigation, I don't know what to make of things."

"Do you have any idea when you'll be returning to the hotel?"

"Might not be for a few hours, if I can convince the chief inspector to allow me to accompany him to the Old City."

THE SECRET OF SCRIPTURE

"The Old City, why?" Miriam asked incredulously.

"My friend has been murdered, Miriam. I'd like to contribute to finding his killer in any way I can," Aiden said in a lowered voice.

"He was my friend, too," she replied.

"You're right, I'm sorry," Aiden sighed.

"Please just be safe and hurry back. There's a killer still out there," Miriam said before she ended the call. The screen of her cellphone flashed with an incoming message from Susan—Lorenzo de Medici's ex-fiance—asking if they were still on for lunch later that day.

Shit, she cursed. *I'll have to message her back later.*

She glanced around the room as she ran her fingers through her hair. Her smartphone chimed with an incoming message. It was from Angelo, thanking her for Nagi's information, and promised he'd be in touch. With a few taps on the screen she sent Nagi a text that Angelo was on his way from CDH, and to help him in any possible.

His response was quick: *The cop?*

Yes! She replied. *Things are a bit crazy right now, but I'll call you with more, later.*

You're lucky we're besties.

Miriam smiled at his reply and messaged back her thanks.

9
CENTRAL DUPAGE HOSPITAL
Wheaton, IL.
1:00 a.m.

Marquez shoved his smartphone into the inside pocket of his suit jacket and walked over to the hospital room door. He peered down the hall and observed two nurses speaking at the nurse's station before he quietly closed the door and turned his attention back to Mr. Prescott.

"I bet Prescott isn't even your real name," he muttered under his breath.

He looked around the room and noticed a wheelchair in the corner. He then walked over to a locker and pulled the door open. The hangers dangled, and he remembered that Prescott's clothes had been sent to the forensics' lab by the DuPage County Sheriff's department.

"Shit!" Angelo hissed.

He spotted a folded blanket on the top shelf of the locker. *This will have to suffice*, he thought to himself as he snatched it from the shelf and tore away the plastic wrapping.

Marquez noticed a pair of headlights slither through the darkness and turned towards the parking lot entrance of the hospital. He hesitated at the window momentarily. When he confirmed that it was a DuPage County Deputy's squad, he knew he had to get a move on.

"If they find out I'm the one who got you out of here, we're both screwed," Marquez turned to Prescott.

He moved the wheelchair next to the bed and set the brakes with his foot.

"Let's get the hell out of here," Marquez removed the monitoring devices from Prescott's fingers. He carefully extracted the needles from Prescott's arms and hands to ensure there wouldn't be any excessive bleeding.

When the monitor's intermittent beeping turned into a steady tone, he reached across Prescott's sleeping body and shut off the device. He glanced over his shoulder at the door, half-expecting a nurse to barge into the room at any moment.

After what felt like an eternity, Marquez straightened his back and assessed the most efficient way to move Prescott into the wheelchair. He wrapped his arms around Prescott's upper torso and heaved him off the bed.

"Damn, man, what do you eat?" Marquez complained as he felt the hard muscle of Prescott's physique through the thin fabric of the hospital gown. He strained to shift Prescott's dead weight from the bed to the wheelchair, but after careful maneuvering he succeeded in his endeavor.

Prescott snored lightly as his head fell forward. Marquez snapped the blanket open and threw it over Prescott's lap. He glanced around the room one last time before he made for the door.

He held it ajar as he peered at the nurse's station. "Coast is clear," he whispered and propped the door wide open with his foot as he reached for the wheelchair handles and pulled Prescott across the threshold.

Marquez looked over his shoulder and eyed the empty nurse's station once more as he pushed Prescott in the opposite direction.

"Hey, watch where you are going?" The Jewish man complained when the wheelchair struck his foot.

"My apologies," Marquez turned to the man and shrugged.

"Where are you taking him?" The man pointed at the sleeping patient in the wheelchair.

"I must move my friend for precautionary reasons," Marquez lied. "Doctor's orders."

"Is that why you were eyeing the nurse's station?"

"It's complicated," Marquez shrugged again. "Now, if you'll please excuse me—"

"I think we should confirm this with the medical staff," the man suggested.

"There's no time, now please move out of my way," Marquez demanded.

"No time?" The man cast Marquez an incredulous glance. "I think you're in over your head, detective." He pointed a finger at Marquez.

Angelo rolled his eyes exasperated and attempted to maneuver the wheelchair past the stranger.

"Oh no you don't," the man reached for the wheelchair.

"Get out of my way!" Marquez pushed his forearm against the man's chest and shoved him against the wall.

"Police brutality!" The man protested as he clutched the collar of Angelo's suit jacket.

This is not happening! Marquez thought to himself. He released his grip on the wheelchair and grabbed the Jewish man's coat. They struggled in the corridor momentarily when the elevator near the nurse's station dinged.

"Help!" The Jewish man cried.

Marquez turned and shoved him into Prescott's room. "Sorry, old timer," he said as the man collapsed on the ground. Angelo pulled the door shut and quickly pushed the wheelchair towards the elevators at the opposite end of the floor.

"Did you hear something?" A man's voice said from the elevator.

"Sounded like a call for help," a woman replied.

Angelo wheeled Prescott around a corner and desperately pushed a button to summon another elevator. He heard the Jewish man's voice cry for assistance from behind the closed door of Prescott's room.

Either I'm getting old, or that guy is stronger than he looks, Marquez reflected on their brief struggle. "Come on, damn it!" He hissed as he repeatedly pressed the elevator button.

THE SECRET OF SCRIPTURE

The Jewish man's voice echoed loudly down the corridor when the door to Prescott's room opened.

The elevator dinged to announce its arrival. Marquez pushed Prescott into the carriage after the doors slid open, and then he proceeded to select the parking garage before he pressed the "Close Doors" button below it.

He heard the commotion coming from the room where he left the Jewish man on the floor as he stammered his explanation of what had just transpired. Marquez looked down at Prescott after the elevator doors closed. "What kind of sedative did they give you? You know what, never mind. I won't complain as long as it keeps you quiet."

Prescott snored lightly and his head bobbed gently when the elevator sank to the parking garage beneath the hospital. Once the elevator stopped and the doors slid open, Marquez wheeled Prescott toward his dark blue SUV and pressed the unlock button on his keychain remote.

After he aligned the wheelchair with the opened front passenger door, Marquez glanced over his shoulder at the elevators. When he felt certain no one was coming, he heaved Prescott's unconscious body into the passenger seat and secured him with the seatbelt.

He hid the wheelchair between two parked cars and quickly jumped into the driver seat. He wiped away the sweat that beaded on his forehead and looked over at Prescott as he turned the key in the ignition.

"I can't believe I'm risking my career for this shit," he cursed under his breath and pulled out of the parking spot. *An Identity Theft ring, biblical verses in Ancient Hebrew; what the hell is going on?* He thought to himself.

Marquez glanced at the rearview mirror and saw a DuPage County Deputy emerge from the elevator. The uniformed officer appeared to be speaking into a walkie strapped near his shoulder as he stared at the SUV.

Marquez sped toward the garage exit to avoid letting him read his license plate and caught his breath when he turned a corner and saw a pair of headlights coming straight at him.

The approaching vehicle honked its horn before both vehicles screeched to a halt. The other driver laid on the horn as Marquez swerved around the sedan. He slowed momentarily when he arrived at the parking lot exit. After looking both ways, he sped off in the direction of a scarcely lit road.

Marquez checked his mirrors to ensure he wasn't being followed. Then he retrieved his smartphone from his jacket pocket and brought up Miriam's text message that contained Nagi's home address. He proceeded to input the location into his vehicle's navigation system, and waited for the GPS to instruct him on the quickest route.

"Good, he only lives fifteen minutes away. Here's hoping he still doesn't hate cops," Marquez muttered as he glanced over at Prescott again.

10
TEL AVIV UNIVERSITY
Tel Aviv, Israel
8:05 a.m.

Aiden gazed at his smartphone pensively as he reflected on the reference to the Book of Daniel that Miriam mentioned.

"Is everything alright, professor?" Yeshua asked.

"Would it be possible for me to accompany you to Jerusalem? I'd like to have a look around at the site where the body was found." Aiden turned and approached the chief inspector.

"The body will have most likely been removed by now," Yeshua studied the look in Aiden's eyes. "To avoid alarming the tourists."

"I understand," Aiden nodded. "It's just that there's something about that poem and the reference to the Book of Daniel which leads me to believe that whoever murdered Emmett wanted us to find these items."

"Are you suggesting that this stuff was planted?" Yeshua's gaze shifted from Aiden to Yisrael, and then back to Aiden.

"I knew Emmett. He was no Zionist. Nor was he the type of individual to be in possession of false propaganda." Aiden pointed at the copy of the Protocols that sat on the pile of papers on the desk. "Why else move the body if this was just a murder?"

"You think someone is intentionally luring you to the Old City?" Yisrael asked.

"Well, not me, particularly, but whoever killed Emmett deliberately moved his body to the Gates, mutilated his body with an allusion to scripture, and then left this information out in plain sight."

"He wanted us to make the connection?" Yeshua asked.

"To what end, though?" Yisrael added.

"Could it have been to prevent the summit from happening?" Yeshua wondered out loud.

"If they did, we have to ask ourselves why?" Aiden asked.

"You said so yourself, A.I. was going to challenge the concept of faith," Yeshua handed the sheet back to Aiden.

"The concept of faith, yes, but these writings are deliberately challenging Christianity in particular," Aiden answered.

"With the Protocols?" Yisrael's brow furrowed.

"Not *with* the Protocols, but I think that whoever planted this as evidence wants the authorities to believe that extremists are involved." Aiden turned the sheet of paper to look at the map once more. "The Old City with markings that seem to correlate with Christian sites, and a poem denouncing the Christian faith are practically leading us by the nose."

"So, you're saying that whoever killed Professor Ben Yaakov left clues to lead us in a specific direction?" Yeshua asked.

"Yes," Aiden nodded.

"What direction, though?" Yisrael looked at them both.

"I'm not sure we'll find that answer here," Aiden said.

"I'll have my officers gather the remainder of these items for evidence, and process the scene," Yeshua motioned at the desk and glanced around the office.

"May I accompany you to the Old City, too?" Yisrael asked as they made for the door.

The chief inspector stopped and studied him momentarily.

"It couldn't hurt to have his expertise on hand," Aiden suggested. "If we're going to find the killer, we're going to need insight into his motives."

"Very well, but you stay with us at all times," Yeshua agreed. "And don't touch anything!"

THE SECRET OF SCRIPTURE

The three headed down the hall. When they arrived at the elevator, Aiden and Yeshua paused briefly and exchanged a curious glance.

"Do you think the power grid is still—" Aiden began to say.

"How did you get up here?" The chief inspector turned to Yisrael.

Dr. Avrohom met the chief inspector's inquisitive gaze. *I'm surprised it took you this long to ask me*, he thought to himself, but otherwise did not betray his thoughts.

"I was instructed by the Samal Sheni—the sergeant— standing guard at the front door on the main floor to take the stairs," he finally said.

The chief inspector eyed Yisrael momentarily. He contemplated the evolutionary game theorist's involvement. *Everyone is a suspect until the evidence proves otherwise*, Yeshua thought.

"How did you come to hear of Professor Ben Yaakov's death, exactly?" The chief inspector squared his shoulders and placed his hands on his hips.

"I received a call at the hotel where I've been staying. The front desk advised me there was a situation at the university and urged me to respond immediately."

"How do you suppose the front desk came about this information?" Yeshua continued with his line of questioning. The feeling in his gut tugged at him, because he had not authorized the release of information to anyone.

"I don't know," Yisrael lied. "It wasn't until I arrived and saw the policemen that I figured the authorities had requested my presence."

"The elevator is not responding," Aiden looked up at the numbers above the elevator doors as he pressed the button repeatedly. "Perhaps we should take the stairs.

Better to keep my eyes on this game theorist rather than risk letting him slip away, Yeshua thought. "The stairs it is," the chief inspector pointed at the stairwell.

FELIX ALEXANDER

Aiden turned and led the way.

11
THE EL-AMIN RESIDENCE
West Chicago, IL.
1:10 a.m.

In the basement of his parent's house, Nagi sat impatiently before a collection of ten large monitors. The Chief Kontour desk mount curved slightly over his wide, black, glass-top desk; two rows of five monitors projected high definition live feeds from myriad of wireless cameras surrounding the home. The images passed in a timed procession clockwise to allow him to observe any potential threat to his peace of mind.

"Thank goodness the parents and Daddi are in Pakistan for the month, because the idea of a Chicago detective stopping by in the middle of the night wouldn't sit too well with any of them," Nagi scrolled through his social media account on his handheld digital tablet.

In truth, he had no interest in social media, but since he believed the authorities monitored his online activity, he figured he'd give them something to distract them with while he pursued other endeavors on a more secure network. *Give 'em a little strip tease and they won't rush for the goodies.*

"Ample cleavage, ample cleavage, sweet tramp stamp, ample cleavage, jeez isn't anyone original on here?" He continued to swipe up on the screen of his tablet while occasionally glancing at the monitors.

"Vehicle approaching," a feminine voice broke the silence.

Nagi tapped a few strokes on his keyboard before the monitors focused on his driveway. Motions sensors activated the security lights at the front of the residence. Three angles gave him a bird's eye view of the SUV.

"Priya, zoom in on the SUV," Nagi said as he studied the monitors.

"Zooming in," she said. "Would you like me to switch to NVG mode, or infrared?"

"I don't think that'll be necessary," Nagi replied. "Cops are cold-hearted assholes, so you may not get a reading."

"Cops are cold-hearted assholes," she repeated. "Duly noted."

Nagi chuckled to himself as he continued to tap a few more keys.

"Initiating outgoing call," Priya said.

The speakers in Nagi's basement came to life with the sound of a ringing phone. Nagi watched as Angelo jumped in his seat. "Fuckin' cops," he shook his head.

Angelo looked at the monitor on his dashboard before he glanced at the home through his windshield.

"Answer the phone, numb nuts!" Nagi barked.

"Hello?" Angelo spoke into his car's speaker before he cleared his throat. "This is Detective Marquez of the Chicago Police Department."

"This is Detective Marquez of the Chicago Police Department," Nagi repeated in a mocking tone.

"Nagi?" Angelo asked.

"Well, if it isn't Dick Tracy," Nagi replied. "Miriam said you'd be stopping by, so what's up…Dick?"

12
TEL AVIV UNIVERSITY
Tel Aviv, Israel
8:15 a.m.

The three men pushed through the door of the stairwell and exited the building. They found themselves in the back lot near the dumpsters and had to walk around the building to get to the chief inspector's squad.

"What about the next line in the poem that you were going to elaborate on before your phone call? 'A lie made truth by the Hasmonean kings.'" Yeshua pointed at the sheet in Aiden's hand.

"To understand this sentence, we must take into account how the historicity of Jesus can be explained beyond the Synoptic Gospels of Matthew, Mark, and Luke; the Gospel of John, which differs from the Synoptic Gospels; and the Acts of the Apostles," Aiden crossed the rear lot with Yeshua and Yisrael on either side of him. "Though the first five books of the New Testament tell us of the ministry, crucifixion and resurrection of Jesus as the Christ, they don't paint a complete picture of Jesus, the man."

"This lends credence to the idea that omitting details of Jesus' humanity allowed believers to perpetuate the myth of Jesus' divinity," Yisrael added.

"And how did the Hasmonean kings play a role in this?" Yeshua asked.

"A line of kings emerged as a result of the Maccabean Revolt after Mattathias the Hasmonean led an uprising against the Seleucid Empire in response to decrees that forbade Jewish religious worship."

"This was in Judea, correct? When Mattathias refused to worship the Greek gods," Yeshua remembered learning of the Jewish festival of Hanukkah, which celebrates the re-dedication of the Temple after Judah Macabee's victory over the Seleucid armies.

"Yes," Aiden said as they circled the building. "It serves to note that the succession of rulership between the sons of Mattathias—Judas, Jonathon, and Simon—established an independent Jewish kingdom."

"Hence, the Hasmonean kings," Yisrael nodded at the paper Aiden held in his hand.

"That is until the dynasty ended in 37 B.C.E. when the Roman Senate designated one Idumean, Herod the Great, as 'King of the Jews,'" Aiden said. "Which brings us to the detail not mentioned in scripture, but accounted for by the historian Flavius Josephus."

"I'm listening," Yeshua nodded as they arrived at the front of the building.

"After Simon's murder in 134 B.C.E., his son—John Hyrcanus the 1st—succeeded him as king. He initiated a series of military campaigns against the territories surrounding Judea. Through military conquests he added Samaria, Transjordan, and Idumea."

"Home of Herod the Great and the Biblical Edomites," Yeshua reflected.

"Wait, there's more," Yisrael smiled as they crossed the lawn.

"Upon conquering these lands, Hyrcanus forcibly converted the inhabitants to Judaism," Aiden said. "Bear in mind that before that time the Edomites were not Jewish by birth."

"But forced conversion is not permitted in Judaism!" Yeshua protested.

"In modern times, no it is not, because Jewish tradition today, which is rabbinic, doesn't permit Jews to forcibly convert others to Judaism," Aiden corrected him. "However, we have evidence that in antiquity, no such prohibition existed, and forced conversion did occur."

"Among those forcibly converted was Herod Antipas, the grandfather of Herod the Great," Yisrael said as they approached the chief inspector's vehicle. "Which means that

THE SECRET OF SCRIPTURE

Herod the Great was only Jewish by consequence of the forced conversion his grandfather endured."

"This is an important fact to remember, because among the peoples and territories also conquered and subjected to forced conversion were the Itureans," Aiden said.

"Who were they?" Yeshua's brow furrowed.

"Though most scholars identified them as Arabs from the line of Ishmael, and a debate is on-going about their genealogy, the one thing we know for certain is that they lived in Galilee just north of Judea." Aiden paused momentarily to gauge the chief inspector's reaction when they arrived at his unmarked squad.

"The Galilean," Yeshua rubbed his chin before he pressed the auto-unlock button of his vehicle's remote.

"On the one hand, we may consider how this fits into the Biblical narrative when factoring in the socio-economic realities of 1st century Palestine in the time of Jesus," Yisrael said as he climbed into the back seat.

"How do you mean?" the chief inspector met his gaze through the rear view mirror.

"Judeans despised their northern neighbors as inferior peoples lacking cultural sophistication and mocked the distinctive form of Aramaic that Galileans spoke," Yisrael answered. "The air of superiority among the people of Jerusalem led them to dismiss a Galilean who claimed to be a prophet, let alone the 'Messiah.'"

"This is consistent with the pattern of God choosing an unlikely candidate to spread His word," Aided pulled his passenger door shut.

"On the other hand, we have to consider what this means for the validity of the birth narrative of Jesus as it has been written in the gospels," Yisrael added. "Because if the Galileans were only Jewish through forced conversion, and not Jewish by way of the bloodlines—"

"In other words, just because a lie is perpetuated over time that doesn't make it true when there is evidence to the contrary," Yeshua said as he turned over the engine and glanced over his shoulder before pulling away from the curb.

"'The fact of his birth concealed by his death, a lie made truth by the Hasmonean kings,'" Aiden reread the passage aloud. "The Gospels of Mark and John possess no birth narratives."

"What about the other two?" Yeshua asked.

"Though they differ in content, the Gospels of Matthew and Luke place an emphasis on the link to David in order to substantiate his eligibility as the Messiah," Aiden replied.

"This alone creates a series of other quandaries," Yisrael said.

"In what way?" Yeshua asked.

"Well, for one, they each trace different geealogies," Aiden said. "Matthew traces Joseph's lineage, while Luke record's Mary's."

"The conundrum here is that if Joseph didn't actually father Jesus, why was there a need for Matthew to trace the line through David's son Solomon?" Yisrael asked.

"Hence, the reason Luke traced Jesus' genealogy through Mary, his blood relative," Aiden added. "Even though tracing a genealogy through the mother had been an unusual occurrence in that time."

"And no one thought to question these things?" Yeshua asked, as he turned onto the first of two roundabouts on Dr. George Wise Street to proceed southbound.

"There were those who did, like Eusebius of Caesarea—considered the 'Father of Church History'—who wrote On Discrepancies between the Gospels, among other works," Yisrael answered.

"But his excommunication during the Council of Antiochia in 325 A.D. on the charge of heresy eventually led him to change his position," Aiden added.

THE SECRET OF SCRIPTURE

"What heresy was he accused of, exactly?" Yeshua cast Aiden a sidelong glance before he focused his attention on the road when the vehicle approached the second roundabout.

"He initially subscribed to Arianism, which was a Christological doctrine that believed God the Father is a Deity and is divine, and that the Son of God is not a Deity, but is divine."

"Go on," Yeshua shook his head in confusion.

"He was withdrawn from the first Council of Nicaea for this, because it postulated that Jesus was less than God. A heretical view in the eyes of Church leaders who had committed to the Nicene decision of the Holy Trinity, which equated Jesus and the Holy Spirit with God the Father," Aiden said.

"Basically, the idea behind Arianism was considered 'too Jewish,' in thought, and needed to be discredited in order to promulgate the formulae of faith that the Son and the Holy Spirit were to be worshipped and glorified *with* God the Father," Yisrael interjected. "And it was at the Third Ecumenical Council of 431 A.D. that it had been declared 'unlawful for any man to bring forward, or to write, or to compose a different faith as a rival to that established by the holy Fathers assembled in Nicaea.'"

"What does all this have to do with the Old City?" Yeshua asked as his vehicle merged with traffic on Ayalon Highway 20.

"If we take the second half of the poem into account, and compare it to the map," Aiden turned the sheet over. "I'm fairly certain this is an attack on the Christian faith."

"Read the second half of the poem to me again," Yeshua requested.

"'Each stone placed must be destroyed to expose the lie within a god's tower, written in stone by the archangel Jibril, the false faith to be stripped of its power,'" Aiden read aloud.

"To expose the lie within a god's tower," Yeshua repeated. "That must refer to the Nicene decision."

"Yes," Yisrael leaned forward in his seat. "Because it is a direct violation of the Law as it was written in the Hebrew Bible. Whether in Isaiah 46:5 'To whom will you compare me? Who is my equal?' or 1st Samuel 2:2 'There is none holy like the Lord: for there is none besides you; there is no rock like our God.'"

"Similar passages exist in Deuteronomy 4:35 'You were shown these things so that you would know that the Lord is God; there is no other besides Him,' and in the First Book of Kings 'God of Israel, there is no God like You in heaven above or on earth below.'" Aiden recalled from memory.

"These passages contradict the notions postulated after Christ's crucifixion, and undermine the opening verses in the Gospel of John," Yisrael added. "For even if 'He was with God in the beginning,' why is there no mention of Jesus in the Book of Genesis?"

Yeshua listened as he scanned the road ahead of him.

"This has been a question asked by non-believers for quite some time," Aiden said. "The absence of a logical explanation has led them to doubt religion as a whole."

"When you consider the chronology of the events, it's as if the early Church fathers inserted these details after the fact," Yisrael continued. "And worded them in such a way that gave the impression they had been there all along."

"The result being the same as with every other myth passed down from generation to generation... accepted as truth," Aiden concluded.

"We know Jesus—the man—lived, because references were made by historians of the time to 'Jesus, the one they call messiah,' yet such a moniker expressed derision and was not intended to be a confirmation of the title he was given by his followers."

THE SECRET OF SCRIPTURE

"There is nothing more dangerous than an idea that takes root in the minds of men," Aiden reflected.

"It was the ideas that Jesus the man proposed, which sparked a movement that changed the world," Yisrael added. "The Church then aligned itself with the power of kings to become the law of the land and criminalized any effort to undermine the validity of its teachings, and its power."

"Lest it suffer the same fate that other myths suffered in being replaced by new philosophies over time," Aiden added.

"Perhaps it's no secret that the believers are regarded as sheep, and the figure revered by the faithful is seen as the shepherd," Yisreal sat back in his seat and stared through the window at the landscape whipping by beneath the rising sun.

"This is a lot to take in," Yeshua shook his head.

"Given these historical facts, it's pretty safe to say this is more than a murder about science and religion," Aiden reviewed the poem once more.

"What about that line: 'Written in stone by the archangel Jibril,' what is it referring to?" Yeshua asked.

"I'm thinking it's a reference to the Gabriel Revelation," Aiden turned to Yisrael. "What do you think, Dr. Avrohom?"

"It would fit the pattern if we're on the subject of the messianic figure," Yisrael shrugged.

13
THE EL-AMIN RESIDENCE
West Chicago, IL.
1:20 a.m.

"Wait a minute. You're telling me you kidnapped this guy from police custody and decided to bring him *here*?" Nagi stood beside the SUV in his driveway with Angelo. "I always knew you cops weren't the brightest bulbs in the bunch, but this really takes the cake."

"He still *is* in police custody, technically," Angelo contested. "I'm merely conducting a prisoner transport."

"A prisoner transport? Listen to yourself. You're rationalizing your actions. This man clearly needs medical attention if he's suffering from amnesia. What if he goes into shock, or attacks you and you shoot him? Here. In my house."

"That's not going to happen," Angelo assured him.

"Really, because he's Black, and you're a Chicago cop. The track record here doesn't bode well for him," Nagi said. "Or me either, for that matter. I don't need this type of heat, man."

"I don't want to be here anymore than you want me here, but Miriam said you could help," Angelo placed his hands on his hips. "I don't know how much longer he's going to be unconscious, but it behooves us to get him inside. Once he awakens, you may be able to communicate with him."

"Communicate with him?" Nagi's brow furrowed.

"Apparently he only speaks Ancient Hebrew and repeatedly says, 'God is my judge, nine, twenty-five and twenty-six."

Nagi repeated the words to himself momentarily.

"It may have something to do with Daniel from the Old Testament," Angelo added.

"The Hebrew Bible?"

"Here we go again with the semantics," Angelo rolled his eyes.

"Hold on," Nagi raised a finger. "What is your business with this guy, exactly?"

"I've been working a case for the past few months that centered on an Identity Theft ring. This man used a name that was flagged to check into a nearby motel. I was on my way to the motel to investigate further when I called the DuPage County Sheriff's Office to give them a heads up that I'd be in their jurisdiction."

"A courtesy call," Nagi interrupted.

"Yes," Angelo confirmed. "Their dispatch informed me that they were already en route to that location for a report of an altercation between two men, maybe three, and possible shots fired. By the time I arrived, he had already been transported to the hospital by ambulance for having suffered blunt force trauma to the head."

"Hence, the amnesia," Nagi concluded.

"The deputies stated that he was found unconscious upon their arrival, and no one could provide any description of the other parties involved."

Nagi turned to the man sleeping in Angelo's SUV and pondered their predicament. He turned to Angelo with arms crossed and scratched his chin before he finally agreed to help. "We need to move quick, though, because I have nosey neighbors, and if one of them wakes up and sees us—"

"Enough said," Angelo nodded.

They struggled to pull the man out of the passenger seat. His size and weight contributed to the difficulty posed by the limited space they had to work with.

"Damn, what does this guy eat?" Nagi complained.

Angelo cursed under his breath as he tried to maneuver the unconscious man without much success.

"What if we tried this?" Nagi stepped back to allow Angelo to move aside.

He shifted the man's legs out of the vehicle, and wrapped an arm around him to keep him upright. Together they pulled him out of his seat and threw his arms over their shoulders. Standing on either side of him, they pulled him across the driveway and into the garage.

"Are you sure this guy isn't a linebacker?" Nagi grunted.

"I don't know what he is at this point," Angelo said.

"There," Nagi pointed at a wheelchair in the corner. "It's my grandmother's, but it'll be easier to wheel him inside than to keep carrying him."

"Priya, close the garage doors," Nagi commanded.

"Closing the garage doors," Priya repeated.

"What the hell?" Angelo looked around. "Is someone else here?"

"It's my personally designed home computer network. Amazon created Alexa, Apple has Siri, I invented Priya," Nagi grabbed the wheelchair handles and nodded for Angelo to open the door that led into the home.

"Why'd you name her, Priya?" Angelo pushed through the door and held it open.

"It's short for Priyanka Chopra," Nagi followed. "She's an Indian actress. You know, Bollywood films, cheesy musicals, extensive dance numbers, and great music."

"Never seen one of those films," Angelo closed the door.

"Of course you haven't," Nagi shook his head.

"I'm guessing she's pretty?" Angelo followed Nagi into the main basement room.

"She's only the *most* beautiful woman in the world," Nagi scoffed. "But she's more than that. She once aspired to study aeronautical engineering before her acting career took off. Brains and beauty, so it's only fitting I named my home network after her."

"Is that her voice, too?" Angelo scanned the basement. He observed the myriad of leather bound texts that filled the wall of bookshelves, and the ten monitors mounted over the large, black, glass-top desk.

"Yep," Nagi stopped the wheelchair beside his desk.

"How'd you manage that?"

"I compiled samples of her dialogue from when she was on American television, uploaded it into the system, and voila!"

"That sounds kinda-stalkerish, don't you think? Crazy, even?" Angelo said.

"To quote a Spanish poet of Spain's Golden Age, 'When love is not madness, it is not love!'" Nagi said.

"I'm not sure that will go over well with the judge when she files a restraining order against you," Angelo teased.

"Yeah, well, right now we have bigger fish to fry," Nagi took a seat at his desk and typed a few keys before he looked up at his monitors.

"What is all this?" Angelo looked at the images on the screens.

"Home security with a few extra upgrades for the next time The Man tries to show up unexpectedly," Nagi said. "I call it the internet of things on steroids. I can do pretty much anything from here. Thanks to the convergence of multiple technologies, real-time analytics, wireless sensor networks, control systems, and home automation Priya and I can do something as simple as brew a pot of coffee and start my shower, or fuck some shit up."

"Is that how you called me?" Angelo turned to Nagi.

"Yep."

"How did you get my number? Did Miriam give it to you?"

"I hacked into your phone to initiate the call. Since your phone was connected to your car via Bluetooth—" Nagi shrugged.

"It's crazy to think of the things technology let's people like you get away with," Angelo muttered.

"It's crazy to think of the things the justice system let's people like *you* get away with," Nagi replied.

"Funny," Angelo rolled his eyes.

"You don't see *me* laughing," Nagi said.

FELIX ALEXANDER

Angelo felt his smartphone vibrate against his chest. He retrieved it from the inside pocket of his suit jacket and excused himself when he glanced at the screen of his caller ID.

"Is that Miriam?" Nagi asked.

Angelo shook his head as he turned to walk out of the basement and headed toward the garage. "It's my supervisor."

14
CHICAGO POLICE HEADQUARTERS
Area 2, District 3
Chicago, IL.
1:35 a.m.

"He better answer his damn phone," Sergeant Solinski could be heard shouting when Angelo answered the call. He sat reclined in the chair behind his desk.

"This is Marquez," Angelo cleared his throat.

"Marquez, where the hell are you?" Solinski leaned forward in his seat.

"I'm following up on a lead for my investigation."

"Following up on a—" Solinski scoffed. "Man, you've got some nerve. I just got a call from the Sheriff's Office in DuPage County. What the fuck do you think you're doing taking off with a guy from the hospital that they want for questioning about a shooting?"

"Sarge, he wasn't the offender, he was the victim. There was no weapon found at the scene and no gunpowder residue found on his hands to identify him as the shooter."

"I don't care if he's Mother Teresa's favorite nephew!" Solinksi cut him off. "You had no business sneaking him out of there without prior approval."

Angelo sighed before he pinched the bridge of his nose.

"Not only are you in a world of shit for that little stunt you pulled, but you're also facing a battery charge for manhandling some old Jew!"

"The guy attacked me!"

"Good luck convincing the court of public opinion, much less a judge, when all these facts are presented together." Solinski glanced up from his desk and motioned for the officer that appeared in the doorway to enter. "You need to get your ass back here ASAP, or you'll be facing more than a suspension."

"10-4," Angelo said.

Solinski ended the call and shoved his smartphone into his breast pocket. "Cruz, is it?" Solinski asked.

"Yes, sergeant," he approached Solinski's desk. "I ran the search you requested to pin point Marquez's location," He reached across and handed Solinski the digital tablet that provided real-time updates of the phone's location. "This has the address, turn-by-turn instructions, and a street map of his location."

"Get your gear and two of our guys off the street. Tell them they're coming with us to pick up Marquez, and to be ready for anything in case he tries to resist."

"10-4, sarge," Cruz nodded.

"Also, have dispatch get me the name and direct line of the shift supervisor at DuPage County. I want to call him to coordinate our efforts for taking Marquez into custody." Solinski stood, retrieved his round crown military style sergeants' cap from the hook and strode toward the door. "Bring that tablet with you. I want to be apprised of his whereabouts while we're en route. If he moves, I want to know about it. If he eats, I want the list of ingredients in his meal. If he takes a shit, I want to know which hand he's using to wipe his ass!"

"10-4, sarge," Cruz followed Solinski out of his office.

He waited until Solinski turned a corner before he slipped into a vacant office and retrieved a cellphone from his pocket. He pressed a button that indicated a pre-programmed number in the speed dial list and brought the phone up to his ear.

"Yes?" A deep voice answered.

"We are tracking him now," Cruz said in a low voice.

"Well done, Eli," the deep voice sounded please. "Keep me posted."

15
THE EL-AMIN RESIDENCE
West Chicago, IL.
1:40 a.m.

"Back here ASAP, my ass," Angelo muttered under his breath after he slipped his smartphone back into his jacket pocket. He walked back into the home, closed the door to the garage behind him, and met Nagi's mischievous grin when he reentered the basement.

"Mother Teresa's favorite nephew?" Your sergeant has quite the colorful commentary.

"You heard that?" Marquez looked perplexed.

"I hacked into your phone, remember," Nagi shook his head.

"You eavesdropped on my call?"

"Hey, Columbo, I had to make sure you weren't setting me up here," Nagi shrugged.

"Setting you up?" Angelo cast him an incredulous glance. "I'm in as much hot water as you are."

"Oh, no-no-no-no-no-no, buddy, you're in the deep end on your own." Nagi turned to his monitors and typed on his keyboard.

"Oh yeah, well, based on the call I just took, it's pretty safe to say I'm a fugitive. Guess what that makes you?" Angelo waited until Nagi met his gaze. "An accessory."

"Man, ain't this some shit," Nagi threw his hands up. "I knew I should have ignored Miriam's text.

"Look, just help me figure out how this guy is connected to my investigation, and we'll be out of your hair. You won't be implicated in anything," Angelo assured him.

"Don't make promises you can't keep, detective."

"What's that's supposed to mean?"

"While I was hacked into your phone, I noticed that someone was remotely pinging your location." Nagi turned back to his monitors and brought up their location on a digital map.

"Are you sure?" Angelo moved to stand behind Nagi.

"See that flashing red dot? That's your phone. Here at my house. I'm guessing that your sergeant kept you on the phone long enough for someone at the department to pinpoint your location. Which means they're already on their way, and you're on a tight leash."

"Fuck me," Angelo ran his fingers through his hair and looked down at a sleeping Prescott.

"Fret not, my dear Watson," Nagi said in a mock British accent as he pushed the tray of his keyboard into a hidden slot. "I remain two steps ahead of our nemesis."

"What are you doing?" Angelo watched as Nagi slid his fingers across the dark glass of his desk. A virtual keyboard with various digital graphs glowed to life.

"What the—"

"I got the idea from Star Trek," Nagi said over his shoulder as he rapidly typed several buttons on the virtual keyboard. "Watch this."

The monitors flickered momentarily before they displayed images of several different darkened streets.

"What are we looking at here?" Angelo's brow furrowed.

"I've hacked into the home security cameras of every house in my subdivision. We're seeing the streets from their angles."

"Are you checking to see if there are any squad cars in the area?"

"Yes, I'm looking for them, but I'm… also… looking…for…" Nagi hesitated while the monitors rotated through different views, "that!"

A pair of headlights passed through the screen.

"Priya, find the address of the camera where the vehicle just passed in front of," Nagi instructed.

"She can do that?" Angelo asked.

"She's Priya," Nagi turned to him. "She can do anything."

"Address located," Priya's voice said through the speakers in the ceiling.

"Follow the direction of travel and bring up the visual of every camera along that path."

"On screen," Priya replied.

"Whoa!" Angelo said when he saw the vehicle pass through the procession of images on the monitors.

"Vehicle is a late model sedan, three occupants, heading northbound in our direction," Priya said.

"Precisely what I was counting on," Nagi grinned.

He brought a digital map up on his luminous desktop screen, and slid it closer with a deft movement. He placed his finger on a blinking red dot that correlated with his home's location and waited until the moving blue dot neared his home. As soon as the blue dot passed the front of his house, which they could see as the car on the screens, Nagi flicked the blinking red toward the passing blue dot, and the two seeming stuck together as they continued northbound into the night.

"Done," Nagi leaned back in his seat with the look of satisfaction on his face.

"Done? What do you mean, done?" Angelo said.

"As far as your law enforcement buddies are concerned, you just left my house," Nagi said. "Your leash has been cut, for now."

"Are you serious?"

"That buys us a little more time," Nagi turned back to the digital map on his desk. "Priya, did that vehicle happen to have a GPS mapping system in use?"

"Yes, the vehicle has a projected route to a private address in Skokie, Illinois."

"Got it. Okay, what's their projected route?"

"Vehicle is turning eastbound onto Route 64 where it will continue east for 9.5 miles until it reaches I-355. Vehicle will then proceed north to I-90 east Chicago before—"

"Excuse me, Priya, let's try something different," Nagi interjected.

"Proceed," Priya said after a brief moment of silence.

"Let's wait until they near their destination and re-route them to Northwestern University. Have their navigation system 'update' them with information about a traffic accident being the reason for the last minute change."

"Re-route computed and programmed to take effect five minutes prior to their estimated time of arrival."

"Thank you, Priya."

"I cannot believe I just saw you do that," Angelo shook his head.

"I said the same thing when I hacked into a neighbor's Smart TV camera during one of their Netflix and chill sessions."

"Oh man, I don't even want to know," Angelo turned away.

"Don't worry, I don't even want to remember it," Nagi laughed.

"Ugh," Prescott groaned in his sleep.

Angelo and Nagi fell silent. They met each other's gaze momentarily before they turned to him again.

Prescott inhaled deeply with his chin on his chest and shifted in his seat. Nagi and Angelo held their breath and waited. A moment later, Prescott blinked. He shook his head and blinked again. He yawned, his mouth wide like a lion in the shade of the Savanna. His chest rose and fell before he gathered his bearings and pushed away the grogginess of sleep. He lifted his gaze from the floor and met the eyes of two strangers, first Nagi's and then Angelo's. And then he proceeded to shout.

16
CHICAGO POLICE HEADQUARTERS
Area 2, District 3
Chicago, IL.
1:55 a.m.
"Everyone locked, cocked, and ready to rock?" Solinski turned to the officers in the Chevy Suburban squad. Cruz sat with the digital tablet in the front passenger seat, and the two veterans sat in the back. They voiced their replies and patted their chests.

Solinski pulled out of the parking lot and onto the mostly deserted street, save for the passing sedan with a pink glowing Lyft logo on the dash as it drove past in the opposite direction. *The pink 'stache on the dash*, Solinski thought to himself.

"The GPS is telling us to take I-90 south, and then to merge onto I-57 west—" Cruz began to say.

"Yeah, screw that," Solinski cut him off. "We're taking 95th street straight to the 294."

"10-4, sarge," Cruz said.

"Eli Cruz, right?" Solinski asked.

"Yes, sarge," he replied.

"I know you just transferred here from District 5 a few weeks ago, and this is your first week on the midnight shift. You're not familiar with how I do things, but you should know that I don't permit my officers to go off the reservation. This job is challenging enough without making things more difficult by pulling stunts like the one Marquez pulled tonight."

Officer Cruz nodded and listened attentively.

"These guys will tell you that Marquez is one of the best we've ever had on the force. He's a veteran with extensive training as an Air Borne Ranger, which went beyond his primary role as an MP. He did two tours in Afghanistan, saw intense combat, and earned numerous medals for valor and bravery, so this isn't just some beat cop we're dealing with," Solinski continued.

"He has saved all our asses at one time or another," said one of the officers in the back.

"Between his work in the Special Ops Section and Mobile Strike Force, he's no stranger to a dogfight, so you need to be ready for anything," Solinski said.

"Why do you think he did what he did?" Cruz asked.

"I don't know," Solinski shrugged. "He better have a damn good reason for this shit, because he has jeopardized his fifteen year career over it. I don't think the commander is going to care that he helped save a senator's life a few years ago."

"A corrupt senator, at that," the other officer in the back said.

"Corrupt, or not, the fact remains that you can do a world of good in your lifetime, but it only takes one mistake for the world to paint you with a black brush." Solinski turned on the squad's emergency lights and sirens as he pulled onto the on-ramp for I-94 south to reach 95th street in a matter of minutes.

Cruz turned his gaze to the digital tablet that sat in his lap. He already knew of Angelo's reputation and accolades. He had read the file after he agreed to the assignment and subsequent transfer when the Preceptor first made contact. His agents had left a disposable cell phone inside a manila envelope on his kitchen table. The instructions were clear: Do not alert the authorities. Answer the call when the phone rings, and your daughter will remain unharmed.

He wanted to know more. He needed to know more, but there wasn't anytime to prepare when the phone rang in his hand.

"Good evening, Eli. I am the Preceptor. Listen to me very carefully, or this will not go well." Eli glanced at the caller ID, but the number had been blocked.

Eli struggled to steady his breathing. His daughter was at the forefront of his thoughts.

THE SECRET OF SCRIPTURE

"Effective immediately, you will be transferred to Area 2, District 3. Once your transfer is complete, insert yourself into any investigation into Detective Marquez's activities. We're particularly interested in anything he does that goes against protocol. Keep us apprised of the situation, and we will instruct you on how to proceed," the Preceptor had used an electro larynx to disguise his voice.

"Do this task, and we guarantee that the expenses for your daughter's treatment will be covered in full. Fail to comply, and the outcome of her condition will be too grim for any father to bear."

"Who the hell are you?" Cruz had demanded. "And how did you get into my home?"

"For now, you will know me only as the Preceptor," the man had said. "When I decide that you need to know more, you will, but in the meantime you are advised to follow my instructions. After all, you wouldn't want your daughter to go missing, would you? She looks quite adorable in that lavender dress."

Eli had unleashed a tirade of obscenities, but the Preceptor had terminated the call. Little Esmeralda had arrived home from school a few minutes later wearing the lavender dress he had bought her for her birthday. He embraced her with the force of his affection and on the brink of tears. When she finally pulled away, she handed him a cell phone.

"Where did you get this?" His tone was harsher than he intended.

"The bus driver asked me to give this back to you," she whispered.

It rang in his hand. He considered ignoring the call, but he decided to answer after it continued to ring.

"Hello?" Cruz spoke softly into the phone.

"We threatened the bus driver's children too," the Preceptor spoke.

Eli stood and turned away from Esmeralda. "Are you some kind of monster?" he hissed into the phone.

FELIX ALEXANDER

"We are doing God's work," the Preceptor had said. "You will find a file in your new locker tomorrow. You are responsible for its contents. We have an operative working in the shadows, but he will reveal himself at the appropriate time. You will know what to do in that moment."

"I don't understand what you mean," Cruz said.

"You will understand when the time comes. In the interim, discretion is of the utmost importance, Mr. Cruz. Are we in agreement?"

Cruz hesitated momentarily. He thought of his daughter's safety. As a single father with no other family to turn to, he could only trust in the school's faculty to ensure his little girl's safety in school, and then at the day care program after.

"Mr. Cruz," the Preceptor interrupted the silence. "Are we in agreement?"

"Yes. Yes. We are in agreement," Cruz turned to Esmeralda as she emptied her backpack onto the kitchen table.

The tablet chimed in his lap.

"What was that?" Solinski glanced over and broke Eli's train of thought.

"Huh?" Eli looked up as his thoughts returned to the present.

"What was that noise coming from the tablet you're holding?" Solinski demanded.

Eli read the notification. "What the f—"

"What is it?" Solinski raised his voice.

"Marquez is on the move," Eli said.

"I knew he wasn't going to stay put," Solinski pounded the steering wheel. "Get ahold of DuPage County's dispatch. Find out if they have any traffic cams along the route he's taking. I want eyes on that son of a bitch!"

17
EL-AMIN RESIDENCE
West Chicago, IL.
2:00 a.m.

Prescott panicked. He shouted in a foreign language Angelo did not understand, but Nagi had recognized. He struggled to stand while Angelo and Nagi held him down and tried to communicate with him amid the shouting. Finally, Prescott kicked Angelo in the groin, and then punched Nagi with a right hook.

Angelo fell back onto the couch behind him as Nagi collapsed over his desk. When he saw Prescott push himself onto his feet, he drew his weapon and pointed it straight at Prescott's chest. "Don't fuckin' move, asshole!"

Prescott froze with his arms up.

Nagi glanced at Angelo, and then did a double take before he stood and leaned back. "Dude, seriously? I thought we talked about this already?"

"He went for the family jewels, Nagi. He was trying to get away," Angelo pressed his palm between his legs as he shifted and stood. He winced and motioned for Prescott to sit as he stood and stepped forward.

"Angelo, man, please don't shoot this guy in my house," Nagi pled.

"I'm not going to shoot him, so long as he doesn't give me a reason to," Angelo assured him. He held Prescott's gaze with a cold hard stare. "Can you communicate with him?"

"Actually, yes, I can, but it would be best if we have Priya translate, as she may be able to catch any subtle nuances that I might miss."

"Ask him his true name," Angelo said without looking away.

Nagi asked Priya to translate Angelo's question into Ancient Hebrew. Priya repeated the question. Prescott glanced around the room to determine where the voice had come from before Angelo repeated the question and Priya did the same.

Prescott shook his head almost imperceptibly as his eyes darted back and forth between Nagi and Angelo. *They think I can't understand them. Perhaps I can keep up the charade to buy myself some time.*

"I don't think he's going to be too inclined to answer the question with a gun in his face," Nagi said.

Angelo softened his stance. He held up his hands before he holstered his weapon. "Tell him I won't shoot him as long as he doesn't try anything foolish."

Priya repeated Angelo's statement.

Prescott nodded. *Brilliant, he's unarmed.*

"Now that that's settled," Nagi said. "Priya, ask him his name again."

Prescott heard Priya's voice come in over the speakers and replied to her in Ancient Hebrew.

"I do not know," Priya repeated.

"What does he mean he doesn't know?" Angelo demanded.

"You said he suffered blunt force trauma to the head, right?" Nagi crossed his arms and studied Prescott momentarily. "That can lead to temporary short term memory loss. It happened to Aiden a few years ago, the night Lazzaro was killed."

Lazzaro de Medici, he was the one they wanted before his son, Lorenzo, intervened, Prescott remembered.

"How long does this memory loss last?" Angelo asked.

"It depends," Nagi shrugged. "It's different for everyone."

Angelo pursed his lips and stared at Prescott. He reached into his back pocket and retrieved a plastic bag sealed with red tape that read: Evidence. "Where did you get this?" Angelo held the bag up to Prescott's face.

The identification card along with the credit card and hotel key had been left for him in a sealed envelope at the hotel's front desk. Inside the hotel room, he found instructions with a time, date, and address for the meeting. The meeting did not go as planned.

"Is that his I.D. in the bag?" Nagi unfolded his arms and leaned in.

"Yes, but it's a fake," Angelo said without turning away from Prescott. "It's part of an Identity Theft ring I've been investigating for the past few months. I got a hit on the cloned credit card our friend here used to check into the motel where he was attacked."

The local contact has been compromised, Prescott thought to himself.

"You went to all this trouble over a cloned credit card and a fake I.D.?" Nagi asked.

"Actually, no," Angelo stepped back. He eyed Prescott momentarily before he met Nagi's inquisitive gaze. "Each time he woke, he shouted something in Ancient Hebrew: Daniel nine, twenty-five and twenty-six. I couldn't understand how this was connected to my investigation, but I had a nagging feeling that there was more to this than meets the eye. I reviewed the passages in a Bible at the hospital, but it didn't make much sense. That's when I called Miriam, but she was too preoccupied to help."

"That's probably when she messaged me," Nagi concluded.

"Yes. She said something about a murdered colleague in Jerusalem with a Book of Daniel reference left on the body," Angelo said.

"Wait a minute. What?"

"Strange coincidence, huh?" Angelo shrugged.

"There's no such thing as coincidence," Nagi turned around and slid his fingertips across his desk as he sat in his chair.

The three men looked up at the monitors when images began to appear. A pride of lions standing over a man, a map of the Babylonian Empire, Ancient Hebrew script glowing against a stone tablet, world leaders of modern times, missiles being launched, the walls of Old City in Jerusalem, the word: anti-Christ, a piece of parchment from the Dead Sea Scrolls, a Bible opened to the Book of Daniel, and an angel with sword in hand.

"Did Miriam elaborate on the Daniel reference left on the victim's body?"

"No, she couldn't get into it. She was too worked up over the Israeli police questioning Aiden about the murder."

"They don't think he's involved, do they?" Nagi turned to Angelo.

"I'm not sure. She didn't think so, but you know how—"

"Yeah, you cops can be pretty deceptive," Nagi scoffed.

Angelo nudged Nagi on the shoulder.

So, the professor is out of the country. It's just as Omar had said he would be, Prescott thought as he observed the exchange between his captors.

Nagi retrieved his phone and initiated a text message.

"What are you doing?" Angelo asked.

"I'm sending Miriam a text to ask her about the Daniel reference left on the murder victim's body."

"You think there's a connection?" Angelo wondered.

"There has to be!" Nagi completed the text message and placed his phone on the desk. He leaned back in his seat, placed his hands behind his head, and swiveled his chair around to face Prescott. "But halfway around the world?"

"Who's the angel on the screen?" Angelo scanned the images on the monitors.

"That's the archangel Gabriel." Nagi turned and zoomed in on the screen.

"What's the significance?"

"According to scripture, he only spoke to a select few directly," Nagi said.

"Who?" Angelo placed his hands on his hips.

THE SECRET OF SCRIPTURE

"Aside from Daniel, there was Zacharias, the father of John the Baptist; Mary, the mother of Jesus; and the Prophet Muhammad. Though there is one other little known reference that remains a matter of debate among scholars."

"Which one is that?" Angelo asked.

"It has to do with a stone tablet dating back to the first century, maybe even earlier than that," Nagi said. "They call it Gabriel's Revelation."

18
JAFFA GATE OLD CITY
Jerusalem, Israel
9:15 a.m.

The chief inspector's squad slowed with the flow of traffic and passing pedestrians as they neared the Jaffa Gates of the Old City, one of seven main open gates in Jerusalem's Old City walls. Aiden stared in awe at the monumental defensive walls; a marvel of engineering that remained standing since being erected in the mid-1500's by the Turkish sultan Suleiman the Magnificent. The stones of the gate and the walls where much like the stones used for the rest of the Old City, large, hewn, sand-colored blocks.

"Let me get this straight," Yeshua broke the silence. "You're telling me this Gabriel Stone—called the Gabriel Revelation—emerged from the antiquities market after 2,000 years?"

"Yes, and no," Yisrael said. "It was discovered in the year 2,000 near the eastern shore of the Dead Sea. It circulated on the antiquities market for a few years before an Israeli-Swiss collector, David Jeselsohn, purchased the stone tablet from a Jordanian antiquities dealer."

"Dubbed a Dead Sea Scroll on stone," Aiden added. "Its authenticity was confirmed, both in script and in chemical examination after it had been purchased."

"What does that mean, exactly?" Yeshua insisted.

"It bared striking similarities to the Dead Sea Scrolls in that both were written in ink, the text is written in two columns, and both have Hebrew letters suspended from the upper guideline, which is consistent with the 1st century B.C.E. and 1st century A.D. writing style," Aiden said.

"The development of the shapes of letters dates a piece through the study of Typology, which is an accurate tool for dating written works," Yisrael said.

"The 87 lines of Hebrew text on the 3-foot Gabriel tablet draws heavily upon the Book of Daniel, which is consistent with the Second Temple Period, because many Jews focused on Daniel's prophecies related to a coming messiah," Aiden said.

"Hence, the two dozen or so that came before Jesus," Yeshua nodded as the vehicle arrived at the wide entrance into the Old City just south of the Jaffa Gate that is designated for small vehicles. He showed his badge to the officer directing traffic, and the officer waved him through. "Now I understand why the Roman authorities and the Jewish high priests were fed up with the succession of would-be messiahs."

"The line of text that has raised the most questions and sparked intense debate among scholars and clerics alike is the reference to the resurrection," Yisrael continued as the vehicle passed by the Tower of David. It stood like a shadowed sentinel in the morning light. A massive structure that dated back to the time of Christ.

Yeshua drove along the cobbled streets momentarily before he parked the vehicle along a vacant wall.

"What text are you referring to?" he cut the engine and turned in his seat to face Dr. Avrohom.

Yisrael met Aiden's gaze.

Aiden nodded.

Yisrael cleared his throat and said, "I, Gabriel, command you—the Prince of Princes—in three days, live!"

Silence lingered momentarily.

"I don't understand what the controversy is all about. It sounds consistent with the Christian belief of Jesus' resurrection three days after his crucifixion," Yeshua shrugged.

"Initial chemical analysis of the tablet pre-dates the crucifixion," Yisrael said. "With more accurate results later confirming the Gabriel Revelation was written before the birth of Christ."

"So, if it wasn't Jesus to whom Gabriel was speaking, then we must ask ourselves, who is this 'Prince of Princes' that Gabriel was speaking to?" Aiden said.

"Hence, the final two lines of the poem: 'Written in stone by the archangel Jibril, the false faith to be stripped of its power,'" Yeshua surmised.

"But how does he expect to accomplish this?" Aiden wondered.

"Perhaps we will find a clue where the body was left for us to discover," Yeshua unbuckled his seatbelt. "We walk from here," he proceeded to exit the vehicle.

Aiden and Yisrael followed suit. Aiden admired the historical architecture as he pushed his car door shut. Yisrael gazed at the Tower of David, *It was known as David's Gate by Crusaders, and Gate of David's Sanctuary by Arabs. A shame that it will crumble before noon*, he thought to himself as his eyes stopped at the base of the ancient structure.

Farhad leaned against a wall holding the briefcase. They met each other's gaze before Farhad turned and disappeared around a corner.

"Is something wrong, Dr. Avrohom," Yeshua said.

"No, nothing's wrong," Yisrael turned to the chief inspector. "It just dawned on me that I have yet to visit the Museum of the Tower of David."

"Do not let us keep you if you'd much rather—" Yeshua began to say.

"That won't be necessary, chief inspector. I've committed to this endeavor, and I intend to see it through to its end."

Yisrael and Aiden strode beside the chief inspector along David Street, which divided the Armenian Quarter in the south from the Christian Quarter in the north.

"The Church of Saint John the Baptist," Aiden pointed when he observed the whitish-grey dome of the Greek Orthodox Church in the Christian Quarter. "It was originally built in the 4th century of the Common Era."

Yeshua and Yisrael eyed the structure from a distance.

"Although Greek Orthodox tradition holds that the head of John the Baptist had once been kept inside, scholars agree that there is no archaeological or textual proof that this was the case," Aiden continued.

The crowds gradually grew, and the shadows crept back towards the base of the stone structures. Every inch of the city appeared to be paved with stone, narrow streets that led this way and that from paths that originated in an ancient time. The walls and structures reminded Aiden of medieval fortresses with their arched entryways and steel gate doors. Shopkeepers selling clothes, shoes, rugs, fruits, trinkets and religious-themed art all carried on about their business. Signage written in Hebrew, English, and Arabic could be found on plaques embedded into the walls. The Old City—an intersection of three faiths and the four corners of the world— was finally awake and had no idea of the danger hiding in plain sight.

A moment later, the chief inspector, the professor, and the evolutionary game theorist had arrived at the intersection that divided all four quarters from each other.

Habad Street ran north and south up to the intersection to separate the Armenian Quarter on the southwest from the Jewish Quarter on the southeast. Souq Khan el-Zeit ran north from the intersection to separate the Christian Quarter on the northwest from the Muslim Quarter on the northeast. The chief inspector led them through the intersection along Chain Street, which ran east west to separate the Muslim and Jewish Quarters and led up to the open plaza of the Western Wall. The scent of herbs and pastries wafted through the air from the Muslim quarter, but quickly vanished.

"We'll make our way to the Al-Aqsa compound from here. I want to touch base with security personnel before we proceed," Yeshua said.

"Given the circumstances, will they take umbrage with our presence?" Aiden asked.

"Even though the mosque itself is closed to non-Muslims we'll be permitted to pass around it for the purpose of our investigation. It's the quickest way to the steps of the

Huldah Gates at the southeast side of the Temple Mount. We'll see if there were any clues left behind," Yeshua said.

They passed through a triple-arched way where Believers gathered, sat, and walked to and fro for a moment with God. Yeshua led them up along the wide staircase that led to the Temple Mount. Aiden admired the way the gold-plated Dome of the Rock that crowned the structure reflected light like a twin sun.

"This way," Yeshua directed them across the wide-open platform.

An officer approached when they arrived at the Ablution Fountain, which was situated between the Dome of the Rock and the Al-Aqsa mosque.

"Good morning chief inspector, we have been expecting your return," the officer said.

"Has the body been removed?" Yeshua asked.

"Yes, and here are the rest of the crime scene photos you requested," the officer handed the chief inspector a manila envelope. "We had them developed and sent over priority."

"Good," Yeshua opened the envelope and began to flip through the stack. "Where's Batya?"

"I'm here," Batya approached from behind.

"I've been trying to reach you for over an hour," Yeshua turned to face her.

"My apologies, chief inspector, I get terrible reception down there."

"You should have sent a team to check the tunnels," Yeshua snapped.

"I felt it more prudent to have more bodies up here to process the scene and clear the area before sunrise."

He met her gaze momentarily. "And what did you find beneath the city?"

"Nothing but the shadows of time," Batya said. "And who are they?"

Yeshua introduced her to Aiden and Yisrael. "They will be lending their expertise for this investigation."

THE SECRET OF SCRIPTURE

"A pleasure to meet you both, given the circumstances," she shook their hands.

"Did you review the video footage like I asked you to," Yeshua turned to look at the cameras situated high on the walls of the Old City.

"Yes," she nodded.

"And?" Yeshua waited for her to elaborate.

"Whoever dumped the body knew to avoid the angles of light that would have revealed their features, which rules out facial recognition as a means of identification. They stayed in the shadows as –"

"They?" Yeshua interrupted her.

"Yes, there were two subjects, possibly male. They arrived in a white cargo van, pulled in through the Dung Gate, moved the body up to the gates unseen, exited through the same gate, and then fled southbound along Wadi Hilwa Street."

"Unseen? Where were the guards?" Yeshua demanded.

"They responded to calls for back-up at the El-Marwani Mosque before they realized it was an elderly male having a seizure."

"And the traffic cams?" Yeshua asked.

"So far, nothing. The plates were unreadable in every image captured, but we're still sifting through the images and employing high resolution enhancements to see what we can find."

"They could be anywhere," Yeshua placed his hands on his hips. "Keep trying. In the meantime, return to police headquarters and find out what the medical examiner has uncovered. Let me know if anything changes."

He turned to the officer who stepped aside when Batya arrived.

"Have the men keep an eye out for any suspicious activity," Yeshua said.

"Is there a threat to the Old City?" the officer asked.

"We're not sure yet, but we must be ready for anything," Yeshua turned and headed toward the Huldah Gates.

Aiden and Yisrael followed closely in silence, while Yeshua flipped through the crime scene photos and muttered unintelligibly to himself.

The three men arrived and made their way up the steps leading to the triple-arched Huldah Gates. The uneven length of each step prevented them from hastening their pace. This had been a deliberate design when the steps were chiseled out of the mountain. Every other step was wider than the previous step in order to slow the flow of traffic into the temple when pilgrims in ancient times numbered in the thousands.

When they arrived at the spot where Emmett's body had been left, Yeshua, Aiden and Yisrael reviewed the crime scene photos together.

"These were taken when I first arrived on-scene," Yeshua said. "It wasn't until we turned the body over that we discovered the markings on his chest."

"That was the picture you showed me at the hotel," Aiden said.

"Yes, I had it developed immediately, and picked it up at headquarters when I was en route to speak with you," The chief inspector held a different photo out to gauge the approximate position of the body on the steps.

"There isn't a single trace of blood," Yisrael noted.

"We noticed that when we first arrived," Yeshua continued to flip through the photographs. "That's how we concluded that the murder did not occur here."

"It's a show of respect for the customs of faith," Aiden squinted his eyes beneath the sun.

"Customs of faith?" Yisrael turned to Aiden.

"Even before the time of Christ, a pilgrim needed to purify himself before ascending the steps to the Temple Mount," Aiden said. "Hence, the dozens of pools that once existed around the Temple."

THE SECRET OF SCRIPTURE

I see I chose a worthy adversary, Yisrael studied Aiden momentarily.

"Come to think of it," Aiden's brow furrowed. He asked the chief inspector if he could take a look at the photographs.

"Wait," Yisrael reached out a hand to stop him. "Shouldn't he be wearing gloves before he touches those?"

"I appreciate your concern, Dr. Avrohom, but this type of evidence doesn't need to be preserved in exactly the same way as the items we found on Emmett's desk."

Aiden took hold of the photographs. The mutilation Emmett's body endured angered him, even if he had been spared the torture. He glanced up at the gates, down at the steps, and then again at the photographs. He repeated the process a few more times before Yeshua asked him his thoughts.

"The Book of Daniel reference left on Emmett's chest: 'So, he came near where I stood: and when he came, I was afraid, and fell upon my face,'" Aiden observed the way Emmett lied face down on the steps. "Look at the way his body is positioned. It's as if he collapsed forward while walking toward the Temple."

"Interesting," Yeshua scratched his chin.

"His body was left at the triple-arched gates as if to enter, but pilgrims mostly entered through the double-gates and *exited* through the triple gates," Aiden said.

"Unless he was in mourning," Yeshua took hold of a photograph and re-examined it.

"Mourning who, or what, though?" Aiden studied the photograph.

"His eyes were left wide open for a reason," Yeshua noted. "And his head is tilted in the direction they appear to be looking."

"His left arm is flush with his body, but his right arm extends out away from his body," Aiden added.

"His right hand is closed in a fist save for his index finger, which appears to be pointing at something," Yeshua continued.

"Pointing at what, though?" Yisrael finally spoke.

"First, I believe we'll have to consider the reason why Emmett's body was left here at the Huldah Gates," Aiden said.

"No additional evidence was found on-scene," Yeshua scanned the area immediately surrounding them.

Aiden stared up at the triple-arched gates. "Perhaps we have to consider the gates themselves," he approached the walled entrance.

"Jewish tradition states the Huldah Gates were named after one of the seven," Yeshua remarked.

"One of the seven, what?" Yisrael asked.

"One of the seven righteous women, or female prophets as professed in the Nevi'im," Yeshua said.

"The second section of the Tanak," Yisrael nodded. "Got it."

"Though we know very little about her, according to the Second Book of Kings, she prophesied destruction as punishment from God," Aiden ran his fingers along the rough stones of the wall. "Great is the Lord's anger that burns against us because those who have gone before us have not obeyed the words of this book."

"The words of the Hebrew Bible," Yeshua reflected.

"Reinforcing the message relayed in the poem," Aiden said. "Targeting Christianity as a defiance of God's law."

"God's law?" Yisrael feigned ignorance.

"Perhaps it's a matter of perspective, but scholars have debated if the Torah is sacred scripture, or a collection of law books," Aiden stepped away from the walled gate. "The subject of discourse inspired by the Letter of Aristaes, a literary work regarding how the Greek translation of the Hebrew Bible came into existence at the Library of Alexandria."

"In Egypt, correct?" Yeshua asked.

THE SECRET OF SCRIPTURE

"Yes," Aiden confirmed. "During the 2nd century B.C.E. Alexandria was the capital of Egypt and the cultural center of the Hellenistic world. It was also home to one of the largest populations of Jewish immigrants that flourished in the Jewish Diaspora of the time."

"That was during the reign of the Ptolemaic kings," Yisrael said.

"Precisely," Aiden confirmed. "According to the Letter of Aristaes, Demetrius of Phaleron had been appointed by Ptolemy—the Second—to be the keeper of the library. At which point Demetrius endeavored to gather all the books in the world."

"Literary and otherwise," Yisrael added.

"Demetrius went to Ptolemy and said, 'Information has reached me that the lawbooks of the Jews are worthy of translation and inclusion in your royal library,'" Aiden quoted. "The conundrum was that the Torah had been written in Hebrew, and the spoken language of the era was Greek."

"Leaving one to wonder who would be able to read the books in one language, if they were unfamiliar with the other," Yeshua surmised.

"Yes, akin to books written in Latin, which is a language not commonly understood by the masses today," Yisrael said.

"In order to complete this task, legend holds that the king sent a letter to the High Priests in Jerusalem requesting six learned men from each of the twelve tribes of Israel to be sent to Alexandria," Aiden said.

"Seventy-two scribes, hence the Books of the Seventy, and how the Septuagint got its name," Yeshua pieced it together.

"Although the story is fictional, the Torah was, in fact, translated during the Hellenistic period," Aiden said. "Which brings us to the subject of sacred scripture versus books of law."

"But it's scripture, is it not?" Yisrael asked.

"Well, one of the world's leading experts on the Dead Sea Scrolls, Professor James VanderKam appears to be of the same mind. In his words, 'The Torah appears to be the first scriptural text of any religion to be translated into another language,'" Aiden said.

"Sounds about right?" Yeshua nodded.

"Whereas the late Elias Bickerman—who passed away here in Jerusalem—contended, 'the task of the Seventy took its rare place among a long tradition of translation, for it was not a fable, or a philosophical discourse, but law.'" Aiden said. "He added that, 'the practice of translating legal documents has occurred since time immemorial.'"

Yeshua and Yisrael exchanged a contemplative glance.

"If it is sacred scripture, or if it is divinely inspired law, one would argue that the Word of God cannot be amended to accommodate a specific set of circumstances," Aiden said.

"So, it stands to reason that Paul's ministry was a direct violation of the law, because he made exceptions for the Gentiles to whom he preached," Yisrael added. "This allowed early Church fathers to use that as a means to gather followers for the movement."

"But didn't Paul claim to have been visited by Jesus on the road to Damascus?" Yeshua asked.

"He *claimed*, yes, but he never actually walked with Jesus during the latter's lifetime," Aiden said. "For if he had, then he would have known that Jesus rejected the Pharisaic principle of oral interpretation of the law, which is something overlooked when we consider the words in Matthew 5:17, 'Do not think I have come to abolish the Law or the Prophets; I have not come to abolish the law of Moses or the writings of the prophets, I came to fulfill their purpose.'"

"A reoccurring theme that later led to the birth of Islam," Yisrael said. "The archangel Gabriel descended upon the earth to reveal God's word—parts of the Torah and the

THE SECRET OF SCRIPTURE

Gospels—that had become corrupted by the oral and written interpretations of men. Making the Quran the final revelation and literal word of God, while quoting Jesus more than any other prophet within its text."

"So, it stands to reason that whoever wrote the poem we found in Emmett's office, directed us to find the clue here regarding Huldah's prophetic oracle," Aiden said.

"Mourning and impending disaster," Yeshua reflected. "But what lies within the city walls in that direction that would relate to mourning and disaster? Aside from the El-Marwani Mosque there is only the eastern wall."

"Perhaps it's not within the city walls, but a part of the city walls themselves," Aiden said.

"How do you mean?" Yeshua cast him a questioning glance.

"The Golden Gates," Aiden said.

"The Golden Gates?" Yeshua asked. "Are you certain?"

"Follow me, I'll explain on the way," Aiden descended the steps and followed a path around the southern wall of the Temple Mount. "When the Persians conquered Jerusalem in the 7th century, the Holy Cross upon which Christians believe Jesus was crucified had been taken to Persia. The cross was recaptured and returned seventeen years later when the Byzantine army emerged victorious over the Persians."

Aiden led them across the central platform past the Dome of the Rock. Yeshua made eye contact with Moshe, the young officer who had greeted them earlier. He motioned him over before he turned his attention back to Aiden.

"According to tradition, it was imperative that the Holy Cross be brought into the Old City through an eastern gate," Aiden continued.

"But the gate has been closed for centuries," Yeshua said.

"It was closed permanently during the 16th century when Suleiman the Magnificent rebuilt it together with the city walls," Aiden said. "But we must remember that after being built on the ruins of the original gate, sometime in the 6th century—it remained open—through the 9th century, even if it fell into disuse during the Byzantine era. The significance of the gate is shared by both Christians and Muslims, who believe it was the gate through which Jesus entered Jerusalem."

They passed under a structure of five arches, descended a wide staircase and followed a paved walkway along a line of trees. Crows flew overhead and landed nearby.

"In the time of Jesus, the gate aligned with the entrances of the Second Temple, which stood just north of where the Dome of the Rock is today," Aiden pointed at the clearing to their left. "Symmetry was just as important to the Jews as it was to many other cultures of the ancient world."

"But in the absence of the Second Temple, the Golden Gate does not align with any structure on the Temple Mount," Yeshua said. Crows continued to circle overhead and crowed incessantly.

"No, it doesn't," Aiden confirmed. "But I just remembered something that links the poem with the Huldah Gates and the Golden Gate."

"What's that?" Yeshua said as they arrived at a fenced-in platform. A closed metal gate prevented access to the wide staircase descending to the walled Golden Gates and the modern doors. An unusually large number of crows had settled around the ancient structure.

"I recently read that according to Dan Bahat—a professor of archaeology and one of the most important Jerusalem scholars—the Golden Gate is not intended to align with the Dome of the Rock, or any other structure on the Temple Mount, because when looking westward from the gate itself, one sees that it is aligned with a different Holy site in the Old City."

THE SECRET OF SCRIPTURE

"Which is?" Yeshua asked as he followed Aiden's gaze.

"The Church of the Holy Sepulchre," Aiden pointed.

"I don't see it," Yeshua said. A breeze blew past.

"That's because the trees are obstructing our view," Aiden retrieved the folded paper from his back pocket, upon which the poem had been written. It remained in the plastic bag Yeshua had Aiden slip it into when they were in the squad, and they turned it over to look at the map.

"This is the Golden Gate as designated on the map," Yeshua pointed. He ran his finger over the map in a straight line to where it intersected with one of the symbols of the cross.

He met Aiden's gaze momentarily before he quickly turned and scanned the surrounding area. "But why lead us here?" Yeshua finally said. "Is there some sort of projectile that we're supposed to prevent from launching at the Church?"

"I don't see anything?" Yisrael finally spoke.

"You, go round up some of the men and bring them here," Yeshua commanded the young officer.

"I don't think that's the reason he led us here," Aiden said.

"What do you mean?" Yeshua stopped and observed the pensive look in his eyes.

"The terrorist knows that destroying a structure will only have a temporary effect, an immediate reaction akin to lighting a match," Aiden said. "This man wants to do more permanent damage. He wants to achieve what in his mind is the greater good."

"The greater good?" Yeshua said incredulously.

Yisrael smiled inwardly as he watched Aiden reach a different conclusion than the chief inspector.

"Look at the poem and look at the map," Aiden handed it to Yeshua. "Although he marks the Holy Shrines in red, probably to denote destruction, the gates he merely marks in blue."

"And?" Yeshua's brow furrowed.

"Think of the flag of Israel. The blue Star of David lies in between two blue lines," Aiden said. "If the technological summit is the catlyst for launching this attack on Christianity, perhaps this man wishes to destroy what he feels has corrupted the Old City from within, while maintaining boundaries to prevent outsiders from interfering on internal affairs."

You're getting close Professor Leonardo, Yisrael admired Aiden's astute nature.

"Then why send us here, and not directly to the shrines, or the other gates?" Yeshua wondered.

"I'm thinking that since the gate is celebrated as the path Jesus took into the Old City on Palm Sunday, which is viewed by Christians as the fulfillment of the Jewish prophecy concerning the Messiah, the terrorist seeks to strike at the heart of that belief through the legend of the Virgin Mary that is associated with this gate," Aiden said.

"How do you think he plans to do that?" Yeshua asked.

Aiden turned to face the Golden Gates and pursed his lips.

19
EL-AMIN RESIDENCE
West Chicago, IL.
2:30 a.m.

"Finally, she texts me back," Nagi reached for his phone.

Angelo kept a watchful eye on Prescott, while Nagi read Miriam's text message to himself.

"What does it say?" Angelo asked impatiently.

"Daniel 8 verse 17," Nagi said softly.

"Why do you sound so grave about it?" Angelo asked.

Nagi slid his fingers over his desk and tapped it a few times before the image of the Bible appeared on the monitors.

"Priya, bring Daniel chapter 8 verse 17 up on the screen," Nagi said.

The image of the Bible opened and the pages flipped through in rapid succession.

"On-screen," Priya said when the pages stopped turning.

"That's why," Nagi pointed at the monitors.

Angelo read the passage aloud, "As he came near to where I stood, I was terrified and fell facedown. 'Son of man,' he said to me, 'understand that the vision concerns the time of the end.'"

He turned to Nagi, perplexed.

"Son of man? Is he referring to Jesus?" Angelo asked.

"No," Nagi said. "Son of man as utilized in the Hebrew Bible is the translation of one Hebrew and one Aramaic phrase first found in the Book of Numbers as either ben-adam, or bar-adam, both literally mean son of Adam."

"As in Adam and Eve," Angelo said.

"Yes," Nagi nodded. "In Numbers 23:19, it reads, God is not a man, that He should lie; neither the son of man, that He should repent."

Angelo listened as he cast Prescott a sidelong glance.

"In the Daniel passage, Gabriel relays prophesies to Daniel, a son of Adam," Nagi continued. He slid his fingers across the desk, and the monitors reacted to his command. "So, when we place both references to Daniel side-by-side, the one Miriam just sent us and the one Black Jesus here has been repeating, here's where they correlate."

Angelo read aloud the parts of the passages that Nagi highlighted. "From the issuance of the decree to restore and rebuild Jerusalem, until the Messiah the Prince…the Messiah will be cut off and have nothing, and the people of the prince who is to come will destroy the city and the sanctuary. The end will come… until the end there will be war."

"The term, son of man, appears more in the Book of Ezekiel than anywhere else in the Hebrew Bible, but what's interesting to note is that while one focuses on the judgment of Israel by God, the other focuses on God's salvation of Israel from oppression," Nagi fixed his gaze on Prescott. "I need to talk to Miriam."

20
GOLDEN GATE OLD CITY
Jerusalem, Israel
9:35 a.m.

When you're standing in the wood, you must be able to see the forest for the trees, Aiden heard Lazzaro's voice in his head as he pondered their predicament. His late father had always advised him to stop and consider every possible outcome in any situation. Most notably when they played a game of chess.

"You only returned with three men?" Yeshua chastised Moshe.

"Apologies, chief inspector, but the rest were dispatched to the Dung Gate."

"The Dung Gate?" Yeshua glared at him. "Why?"

"There's another gathering of protestors in response to yesterday's clash between Palestinians and Jews."

The confrontations between the two populations had become more frequent and grown more violent with each pass. A bitter dispute over land, over home, and over the most important religious sites to each faith has raged for decades. The claim for God's favor echoed across centuries.

"Professor, what is the connection between the Golden Gate and the mother of Christ?" Yeshua insisted.

"In the Christian apocryphal texts, which are texts included in the Septuagint and later Latin translation, the Vulgate, the Golden Gate became a sympol of the Immaculate Conception of Mary. After the destruction of the Second Temple, Jews rejected the Septuagint because the translation is flawed," Aiden said.

"Flawed in what way, professor?" Yisrael urged him on.

"One of the passages from the Hebrew Bible that Christians associate with the prophecy of Christ is found in Isaiah 7:14, which was originally worded: 'The Lord himself will give you a sign. Behold the young woman shall conceive, and bear a son,'" Aiden said. "And it is that one Hebrew word, almah, which literally translates to young woman of child bearing age, which led to the schism between the Jews who did not see Jesus as the messiah, and the ones who later did."

"One word?" the young officer asked. The shouts of protestors grew louder and drew nearer amid the calls of the crows' overhead.

"Yes, one word, because that one word did not exist in the Greek of the time with the same meaning," Aiden said. "So, when the Greek translation occurred the scribes used the word most closely associated with a young woman, which was parthenos, the Greek word for virgin. Whereas almah—in Hebrew—has nothing to do with virginity."

"How does that connect this gate to the threat the terrorist has made to the Old City," Yeshua scanned the gate and the open area around it. He noticed a crow land on the ground of the lower platform near the gate's brown metal doors. Another crow emerged from the shadows behind the closed doors and landed on a sill of the door's opening. It had something in its mouth and flew into the air. "Was that an eyeball?"

Aiden crossed his arms and turned away as he scratched his chin. Yisrael watched him, but did not move.

"Did you say something, chief inspector?" Moshe drew near.

"How long have these gates been closed?" Yeshua asked.

"Since yesterday evening," Moshe said.

"And no one has come in or out since?"

"Not that I'm aware of," Moshe shook his head.

"Unlock this gate," Yeshua motioned at the gate that impeded their access to the steps.

More crows dashed in and out through the barred openings of the gate doors. Crows continued to circle overhead. The young officer fumbled with his keychain. Crows emerged from the shadowed interior of the closed Golden Gates. Pieces of flesh dangled from their beaks.

THE SECRET OF SCRIPTURE

"Open this damn gate!" Yeshua barked.

Aiden turned to the chief inspector as Moshe turned the key. Yeshua pushed his way through and descended the steps that led to the lower platform. Aiden and the four officers followed. Yeshua peered in through the openings. He squinted at what appeared to be a body partially covered with a blanket as crows pecked at the head.

"Open this one," Yeshua waved Moshe over.

"Is something wrong, chief inspector?" Aiden approached.

"Come on, come on," Yeshua urged Moshe impatiently.

"Stay back, professor," Yeshua drew his weapon and motioned for his officers to take tactical positions.

21
DAMASCUS GATE OLD CITY
Jerusalem, Israel
9:40 a.m.

Farhad completed his sweep through the Old City. He had passed by each of the explosive devices that were hidden in plain sight. Laptops strategically placed where someone who knows where to look could find them. Pilgrims had walked to and fro—oblivious to his motives—as they admired the fine architecture of structures that were imitated throughout Europe in medieval times.

"Despite conquest after conquest of Jerusalem, Muslims often treated Christians with respect and granted them access into our city. They repaid the favor with violence and bigotry. Now they wonder why we retaliate the way we do," Farhad muttered under his breath.

He continued along a paved street as he headed for "the gate of the pillar," named so for the pillar that once stood at the center of the gate's courtyard during the Roman-Byzantine era. Merchants beckoned potential customers to their cafes and street markets under the shade of colorful umbrellas that lined both sides of the path through the bazaar. He stopped to let a group of tourists pass as they ascended the steps toward the exit.

"The Damascus Gate," he heard a young man say to his companions, "is considered one of the most beautiful and impreesive gates."

"Really?" His modestly dressed female companion asked.

"They say it's because it was built by the Sultan Suleiman the Magnificent," the man nodded. "Apparently, excavations that took place in 1967 exposed remnants of the Roman Square and triple-arched gate underneath the Ottoman gate."

Farhad proceeded into the shadowed corridor of the decorative gate with its triangular crenellations giving it the appearance of a crown. The shade provided relief from the rising heat of the day. He emerged on the opposite end to a semi-circular set of stairs that resembled a Roman theater. The steps descended from Sultan Suleiman Street. A mixed crowd of Muslims and Christians, tourists and natives, exited and entered while involved in their own conversations amid a spread of two-dozen police officers standing guard at the gate.

Israel's paramilitary Border Police wore body armor and were armed with assault rifles. They surrounded barriers that closed off some of the stairways to allow them to funnel foot traffic leading to the gate and better observe any approaching threat.

Groups of Palestinian women stood beyond the gate talking amongst each other. The presence of Palestinian men had declined in recent years due to the violent attacks that had become a near daily occurrence. Those who did venture towards the gate were stopped, taken to one side and searched, while surrounded by a trio of officers. One frisked the subject, while a second questioned him, and the third relayed information over a radio strapped near his shoulder.

Farhad ascended the steps and headed to a crowded parking lot just south of the entrance. *Traffic is heavier than usual today*, he glanced at the roundabout that connected Sultan Suleiman Street with Ha-Nevi-im Street—the Street of the Prophets. He strode through the parking lot and found the light blue sedan that the Preceptor told him would be waiting for him.

He climbed in through the unlocked driverside door and tossed the briefcase into the front passengerside seat. The street noise silenced when he pulled the door shut. He opened the center counsel and retrieved a flip phone, small, black, practically obsolete in the era of smartphones.

"There are two numbers pre-programmed into the phone's memory. The first is to the local media. The second is 100, a direct line to the police in the event of an emergency. You know what to say," the Preceptor had instructed him.

"The phone is encrypted. They will never be able to trace the call."

Farhad pressed the number for the first in the speed dial's memory. It rang half a dozen times before a gentleman identified himself as an employee of i-24 News, an Israeli international 24-hour media outlet known to broadcast from Tel Aviv in English, French and Arabic.

"There is a bomb in the Tower of David Museum," Farhad said. "It is set to go off in a matter of minutes."

"Wait, wh—"

Farhad ended the call before the man had a chance to ask anything further. He repeated the process on his call to emergency services. He tossed the phone back into the center counsel, and then pulled down the visor above his head. A single key on a keyring fell into his lap.

"The end of the occupation is near, inshallah," Farhad said as he inserted the key into the ignition. He turned the engine over, and the car exploded into flames.

22
CROWNE PLAZA TEL AVIV CITY CENTER
Tel Aviv, Israel
9:45 a.m.

"The entire body was skinned?" Miriam moved her hair away from her face.

"Practically, except for a small patch of skin at the center of his chest," Aiden said over the phone. "Most of his muscle tissue and tendons were gone. There's no telling how long the body was there, but the crows had practically picked the carcus clean."

"I can't believe this," she said after a brief pause.

"It was gruesome, Miriam. The skull showed signs of being cut open. It was as if someone performed a crude form of brain surgery on him, and then dumped his body here for us to find."

"Who would do such a thing?" She sat on the edge of the bed.

"Whoever he is, he's intent on provoking the faithful," Aiden said. "The crows had taken out his eyes and been tearing away at what remained of his face. They probably would have eaten away at the patch of skin on his chest had it not been covered by a shroud."

"God, what a tragedy."

"The chief inspector thinks the shroud was intended to preserve the markings left on the skin."

"What markings?" Miriam asked.

"Same as Emmett," Aiden said. "A blade was used to carve a biblical reference on his chest in Hebrew."

"Is it the same as the one the chief inspector showed us?"

"No. This is a reference to Ezekiel 44."

"Ezekiel 44?"

"I'm still working it out in my head—"

"No, you need to get back here," Miriam insisted.

"I can't, there's a threat to the Old City," Aiden said.

"A threat? What about the potential threat to your life?" Miriam fired back. "Let the authorities do their job and handle that threat."

"Any word from Nagi?" He changed the subject.

"Aiden, I'm serious!"

"I know and I understand your concern, but this is bigger than me," Aiden said. "A threat to the holiest sites of the three Abrahamic faiths will have staggering implications for the entire world."

"Ugh!" Miriam stood and paced the room. "Why'd you have to put it that way?"

"Have you heard anything from Nagi?"

Miriam sighed and ran her fingers through her hair. She received another text message from Susan asking if they were still on for lunch. Miriam swiped at her smartphone's screen again. *I have to remember to reply to her messages.*

"He sent a text asking about the Daniel reference. I'm guessing he's trying to make the connection, but I don't know," Miriam replied.

"I'd like to know what that is too."

Miriam's phone beeped once more. She glanced at the screen again, frustrated by the interruption.

"Speak of the devil," she said. "That's him on the other line."

"Talk with him. Find out what they're dealing with over there. I'll be in touch."

"Be careful, Aiden," Miriam said. "I love you."

"I will, and I love you too."

23
GOLDEN GATE OLD CITY
Jerusalem, Israel
9:50 a.m.
Aiden slid his smartphone into his pocket as the chief inspector ascended the steps and approached with Yisrael beside him. The four other officers worked to contain the crime scene while they waited for evidence technicians to arrive.

"My apologies, professor, and to you too, Dr. Avrohom," Yeshua said.

"Apologies for what?" Aiden asked.

"For getting you involved," Yeshua said. "Your lives could have been in danger."

"It looks like all our lives are in danger," Aiden said.

"Yes, well, your help is truly appreciated," Yeshua said. "You're free to return to your hotel. I'd take you back myself, but—"

"If it's all the same to you, Chief Inspector, I'd like to remain here and assist in anyway I can," Aiden interrupted him.

"Are you sure?" Yeshua asked.

"I want to help you find the man responsible for these atrocities," Aiden said. "I may not have known the second victim, but Emmett was my friend and neither man deserved to die the way they did."

"I, too, would like to offer my continued assistance with this matter," Dr. Avrohom finally spoke.

"I can't be responsible for what happens to either of you if things get ugly," Yeshua warned.

"All due respect, Chief Inspector, things have already gotten ugly," Aiden said.

"Yes, well, with two dead bodies, and one linked to this technological conference, I fear things will get worse before they get better," Yeshua placed his hands on his hips. "Forensics is going to have a hell of a time identifying that body."

"What do you propose we do next?" Yisrael asked.

"I need you to cancel the conference," Yeshua said.

"Cancel the conference?" Yisrael asked incredulously.

"Lives are at stake here, Doctor," Yeshua said.

"It is scheduled to begin in six hours," Yisrael checked his wristwatch.

"Which gives you ample time to reach out to all the participants, and send out a notification of apology to would-be audience members about the last-minute cancellation," Yeshua said.

"This is more than just a presentation, Chief Inspector. Several corporations have invested millions into the technologies that will be presented here tonight. Not to mention the money spent flying in employees from all over the world, hotel accomodations, the cost of the auditorium, everything!"

"You would risk the lives of hundreds, maybe thousands of people, over concerns about expense reports?" Yeshua chided him.

"I wouldn't even risk *one* life over money, Chief Inspector, but it's not my call! I'm merely trying to explain to you that others may not be so willing to eat the costs over a conflict that has endured for centuries, and will most likely continue after we have left," Yisrael snapped back.

"Over a conflict…" Yeshua's words trailed off as he turned away and pinched the bridge of his nose.

"Perhaps it's something we should consider, but not necessarily commit too right away," Aiden interjected.

"What do you propose, professor?" Yisrael asked.

"What if you return to your office and at least reach out to the representatives of the companies involved in the summit. Advise them of the potential threat in Jerusalem and that it may require a last minute cancellation for everyone's safety."

"They are in Tel Aviv, which is a good distance from the danger," Yisrael added.

THE SECRET OF SCRIPTURE

"One of the men who ended up dead was also in Tel Aviv," Yeshua said. "We need to ensure everyone's safety without divulging what has transpired here."

"Well, I can return to my office like the professor here suggested, and after I've made the proper announcement to the representatives of each company, I can have them conduct a roll call of all their employees to ensure no one is missing, or in danger."

"I suppose delegating that task to the representatives will expedite ensuring everyone's safety," Yeshua agreed.

"In the meantime, the Chief Inspector and I will piece this puzzle together to locate the threats to the Old City," Aiden said.

"I'll have one of my officers escort you to Tel Aviv," Yeshua turned to one of the officers on the scene and waved him over. "What is your name?" Yeshua asked him when he met them at the top of the staircase.

"Rav Shoter Matti Davidi, sir," the officer replied.

Yeshua turned to Yisrael. "Dr. Avrohom, this young man is a corporal. He will personally escort you to your office to ensure your safety."

"Right this way, doctor," Matti led Yisrael back up to the upper platform of the Temple Mount. "I have a squad just beyond the Lion's Gate for us to use."

Yeshua looked after them with an uneasy feeling before they disappeared around the corner. His train of thought interrupted a moment later when his cell phone vibrated in his pocket. *Police headquarters*, he scowled. "Excuse me professor, but I must take this call," he turned away.

Aiden stepped over to the fence and gazed at the dead body below. "The Book of Ezekiel," he muttered to himself. "What are you trying to tell us?"

"A car bomb! Are you certain?"

Aiden heard Yeshua shout and turned to glance at him over his shoulder. The chief inspector cursed and demanded that the forensics team expedite their arrival.

"Did I hear you correctly?" Aiden said. "A car bomb?"

"Just outside the Damascus Gate," Yeshua nodded as he approached. "This son of a bitch has no regard for life."

"How many are dead, or injured?" Aiden asked as the chief inspector walked past.

"They're still assessing the situation," Yeshua whistled and motioned for Moshe to approach. "I have instructed dispatch to keep me posted."

"Yes, Chief Inspector?" Moshe arrived at the top of the staircase.

"I need to follow-up on a lead at the Church of the Holy Sepulchre. You are to wait here until forensics arrives to process the scene. Have those two men remain here to secure the scene when forensics is done, and I want you to go to the Damascus Gate and find out what you can about the car bomb that just went off."

"There was a car bomb? When?" Moshe asked.

"It just occurred moments ago. Are you clear on my instructions?"

"Yes, Chief Inspector, I am clear."

Yeshua turned to Aiden and asked, "Are you sure you don't want to return to your hotel?"

"We have a terrorist to stop," Aiden said.

24
EL-AMIN RESIDENCE
West Chicago, IL.
2:55 a.m.

"Hey Nagi, what's up?" Miriam appeared on the center monitor of the top row.

"My sister from another mister," Nagi replied. "How are things in the Holy Land?"

"Things are getting crazy over here. They just found another body in the Old City," Miriam moved her hair behind her ear. "This time it was at the Golden Gate. Aiden said it was practically a skeleton save for a small patch of skin left on the center of his chest. He's there now and he refuses to return to the hotel. I'm really worried about him."

"Practically a skeleton?" Nagi said. "Damn, that's savage."

"Miriam, it's Angelo," Marquez stepped into view of the camera. "Don't worry about the professor. I've seen him in action and I'm sure he can take care of himself."

"Hi Angelo, thanks," Miriam sighed. "It's just with another Biblical reference and threats to the Old City—"

"I'm sorry, did you say *another* Biblical reference?" Nagi interrupted her.

"Yes, Ezekiel 44 was carved into the second victim's chest in Hebrew script."

Nagi and Marquez both turned to Prescott, who sat silently as he looked at Miriam on the screen.

"Son of a bitch," Nagi said as the look of realization dawned on his face. "Why didn't I see it sooner?"

"What? What is it?" Miriam asked.

"Priya, bring the first verse of Ezekiel chapter 44 on monitor eight, please," Nagi commanded. He slid his fingers over his desk. Images moved from one screen to the next as he explained. "Although the Book of Daniel is not found with the Prophets—the Nevi'im—of the Hebrew Bible, because it is in the Writings—the Ketuvim—it *is* grouped with the Major Prophets of Christian Bibles."

"Image is on-screen," Priya spoke. "Would you like for me to read it aloud?"

"That would be most appreciated," Nagi replied.

"Then He brought me back to the east gateway in the outer wall of the Temple area, and it was shut," Priya's voice echoed over the speakers.

"The Golden Gate has been sealed off for centuries," Miriam said.

"Indeed it has," Nagi said. "And according to scripture this is because the God of Israel has entered through it."

"Isn't that the gate Jesus used to enter into Jerusalem?" Angelo asked.

"Yes, but the reference here links the Golden Gate to its eschatological role particularly in Judaism and Islam," Nagi said. "Although Islam recognizes that Jesus passed through it as a prophet, the importance of the gate in early Islamic traditions associate it with the end of time."

"In Judaism, however, the Divine Presence used to appear through the eastern Gate, and will appear again when the Messiah arrives, but only *he* will be permitted to do so in the presence of the Lord," Miriam added.

"What does this have to do with the Book of Daniel references?" Angelo wondered.

"If we look closely at the Daniel verses that have been presented to us in chapters eight and nine, and combine that with the Ezekiel reference found on the second victim, I'd say there is an allusion to Biblical prophecy here," Nagi said.

"People have been announcing the end of times for centuries," Angelo dismissed the notion.

"True," Nagi said, "but given what has transpired in Palestine over the past seven decades there is a clear connection here that we need to think about. And I'm willing to bet that the corpse left at the Golden Gate was a symbolic gesture made by whoever is behind these murders."

THE SECRET OF SCRIPTURE

"What do you mean?" Angelo asked.

"First consider the significance of the number seven in the Bible. Whether it's the Seven-Day Theory in the Old Testament, or the four corners of the earth being linked with the Holy Trinity in the New Testament, or the fact that both the Old and New Testaments combined were originally divided into seven major divisions, and the total number of divinely inspired books was forty-nine. Seven multiplied by seven demonstrated the absolute perfection of the Word of God," Nagi said. "Now take into account the phrase 'three-score and ten,' since three-score means sixty and ten adds up to seventy, that takes us back seventy years—seven decades—to when Israel declared itself as an independent nation in 1948."

"That could merely be coincidence," Angelo said.

"Perhaps, but is it any coincidence that since that time we have seen a number of prophecies come to fruition?"

"What prophecies?" Angelo's brow furrowed.

"The Ezekiel reference left on the second victim is clearly aimed at the Vision of the Valley of Dry Bones. A revelation made to the prophet Ezekiel when he stood in a valley of human bones to see God gradually gather, and connect the bones to form a skeletal body. The skeletons eventually were bonded with tendons and muscle tissue before being covered with skin."

"That's a bit macabre," Angelo said.

"I think you're onto something, Nagi," Miriam said, "with the symbolism, I mean, because God then revealed to Ezekiel that the bones represented the People of Israel in exile."

"They were scattered, first by the Babylonians," Nagi said.

"Then the Assyrians exiled the Ten Lost Tribes of Israel before the Diaspora at the hands of Alexander the Great," Miriam added.

"And then again more completely after the Roman destruction of the Second Temple in 70 A.D.," Nagi said.

"They suffered persecution in every nation they lived, before being regathered seventy years ago," Miriam added.

"Anti-Semetic atrocities occurred in the Middle Ages when over one-million Jews were killed in Europe," Nagi continued.

"And then there's the statement made by the head of Hezbollah, 'If all the Jews gather in Israel it will save us the trouble of hunting them down worldwide,'" Miriam quoted.

"So, the regathering has occurred, then?" Angelo said. He looked at Prescott, who sat silently and listened.

"That's just the beginning," Nagi said. "Zephaniah 3:9 talks of God's promise to restore the language of Israel. Keep in mind that even in the days of Christ, most Jews did not know how to speak or read Biblical Hebrew, because Greek was the common tongue due to the Hellenstic era much like English is used today."

"The Book of Ezekiel makes numerous references to the land of Israel being returned accordingly to the Twelve Tribes of Israel, the return of the shekel as a form of currency, and even prophetic words about restoring waters of life in the desert," Miriam said.

"Not only has the Negev Desert shown signs of life with pools of water and vegetation, but even the Dead Sea has defied the laws of nature with an abundance of fish, microorganisms and special minerals feeding sea vegetation."

"Are you saying these miracles are all part of the prophecies?" Angelo asked.

If all of this is true, then it explains why Omar sent me here to find the missing scrolls, Prescott thought to himself as he listened.

"It was prophecied in Isaiah 27:6, 'Israel will bud and blossom and fill the whole earth with fruit,'" Miriam added. "Along with Joel 3:18 echoing those words, one can't help but notice that Israel exports pomegranate, olives, peppers, avocado, and wine."

"You ask if it is a miracle of prophecy," Nagi looked at Prescott before he turned his gaze back to Angelo. "It all depends on who you ask."

"What do you mean?" Angelo said.

"The reality is that any country in the region could achieve these same results with the right financial resources. Am I right?" Nagi swiveled his chair to look at Miriam on the monitor, and she shrugged.

"You're saying the state of Israel had help?" Angelo asked.

"Yes sir," Nagi nodded.

"Help from who?"

"The good ole U.S. of A," Nagi tapped on his desk. A spreadsheet appeared on one of the monitors with columns that detailed allocation of funds for various usages: economic, military, immigration, interest, and all other miscellaneous spending. "To the tune of over $130-billion dollars, and that's just a conservative estimate because accounting for an exact amount is impossible, since portions of U.S. aid are buried in the budgets of various U.S. agencies."

"How is that even possible?" Angelo said incredulously.

"A large portion of these funds go to Israel's military, and then economic spending," Nagi said.

"Imagine how useful those funds would be here in America to provide medical coverage and educational benefits to its citizens," Miriam said.

"But you know how it is in this country," Nagi interjected. "Keep the masses distracted with bickering over undocumented immigrants and they'll remain ignorant to the truth of how their tax-dollars are being spent while they keep voting for politicians who spout fear-mongering about Arabs and Muslims to justify our support of Israel."

"That's just insane," Angelo turned away shaking his head.

"This is perpetuated by countless Christians who believe that the return of Jews to Israel is a prerequisite for the Second Coming of Christ," Miriam said. "American politians exploit that for the sake of those votes."

Prescott looked on, but otherwise remained silent.

"The current conflict, though, goes back to the Balfour Declaration made by the British government during the First World War," Nagi said. "Although Theodor Herzl is considered the founder of the Modern Zionist movement, it was Chaim Weizmann who spearheaded the move for a Jewish State. Once Britain was onboard, he sought wording in the declaration for 'The reconstitution of Palestine as a Jewish national home,' but instead received wording that declared, 'A Jewish national home in Palestine.'"

"The rearrangement of words made that much of a difference?" Angelo asked.

"Yes, it did," Miriam interjected, "and that was a cowardly move on behalf of the Brits, because they sought to appease both the Arabs and the Jews, but struggled to manage the situation."

"Weizmann is known to have persuaded many Jews not to wait for official decrees and encouraged his kin to build and invest in Palestine in order to pre-emptively establish the Jewish State," Nagi added.

"As a consequence of these actions, Arabs viewed Jews as usurpers of their land and attacked Jewish homes and businesses," Miriam said.

"When the Jews retaliated, the Brits dealt with the Arabs harshly, while they merely limited Jewish immigration into Palestine."

"This is about the time Jews in Nazi Europe were condemned to death," Miriam said.

THE SECRET OF SCRIPTURE

"The U.N. was given oversight of the region of Palestine, and in November of 1947 the U.N. recommended a partition, which the both sides promptly rejected."

"Six months later, Israel declared itself an independent State despite the U.N.'s opposition, and that's when Egypt, Jordan, Syria, Lebanon, and Iraq attacked the following day," Miriam said.

Bloody hell, no wonder the region has so much conflict, Prescott thought.

"Roughly 700,000 Palestinian Arabs either fled or were expelled from their homes, and though promises were made that they might someday be able to return, the truth is that none of them have been permitted to set foot in their homes again," Nagi said. "This is what they refer to as 'the catastrophe.'"

"The shame of it is that it is forbidden for Jews—themselves—to forcibly remove innocent people out of their homeland," Miriam said.

"Why won't they let them return?" Angelo asked.

"There's a plethora of reasons, but I think one of the most important reason lies in scripture," Nagi said. "As part of the prophecies."

"You've got to be kidding me," Angelo said. "There's more?"

"Whether it was the initial strike in 1948 by the aforementioned nations, the Six-Day War of 1967, and the 1973 attack on the holiest day of the Jewish calendar—Yom Kippur—the result was always the same," Nagi said. "Israel emerged victorious."

"There are Jews who believe these victories were prophecied in Zechariah 12:3, 'on that day I will make Jerusalem an immovable rock. All the nations will gather against her, but they will only hurt themselves,'" Miriam said.

"So, it stands to reason that if they don't feel inclined to surrender to their enemies it's because it has been foretold," Nagi said. "And if they believe this, then it's no surprise that whoever is carving Biblical references onto these bodies is equally convinced of a divine mandate about the fate of Israel."

"Which begs the question of where the terrorist will attack next?" Miriam said.

"You mean he's not done?" Angelo asked.

"Aiden said the clues hinted at an attack on Christianity and believed that the next target might be a Christian holy site," Miriam said.

"Hmm, I don't know," Nagi pursed his lips. "That might be a misdirection to lead the authorities away from their intended target."

"You think so?" Miriam said.

"From what I'm looking at here, I can't help but wonder if this isn't a ploy to regain full control of Jerusalem in order to fulfill one of the most important prophecies to bring about the Messianic age," Nagi speculated.

"Oh no," Miriam realized what Nagi alluded to.

"You're killing me with anticipation here," Angelo threw his arms up. "What's the true motive, then?"

Prescott's eyes darted from Angelo to Nagi, and then to Miriam on the monitor, yet he remained silent.

"Taking control of the Al-Aqsa compound in order to destroy the Al-Aqsa Mosque and the Dome of the Rock, and then build the Third Temple in Jerusalem," Nagi said.

25
LION'S GATE OLD CITY
Jerusalem, Israel
10:05 a.m.

Yisrael felt his smartphone vibrate in his pocket as Matti navigated northbound along the 417 past the Tomb of the Unknown Soldier.

"Everything all right, Dr. Avrohom?" Matti glanced over at him after the vehicle came to a halt at the stop light.

"Yes, it's just my assistant asking when I'll be returning to the office," Yisrael lied as he read the text message he received from Batya. *Did they find the body*, she asked.

Yes they did, well done! Are you in position? He messaged back.

Almost. I'm looking for Farhad, but I haven't seen him.

He should be inside. Look for him in the lower level. I'll be in touch.

"She must have been really worried about you," Matti said as he proceeded through the intersection and turned westbound onto Sultan Suleiman Street.

"I'm simply instructing her to gather the contact information I will need when I arrive," Yisrael said.

"That's a good idea. Saves time," Matti looked ahead at the traffic jam. "I wonder what's going on up there?"

"Who knows," Yisrael shrugged without looking up. He knew they were headed toward the Damascus Gate. He knew what had been the cause for the traffic jam. He initiated another text message to someone else.

Everything is in place. Farhad has been eliminated, and Batya will be next. Proceed to phase three.

26
UNDISCLOSED LOCATION
Israel
10:10 a.m.

Arwan Ansari read the text message from Yisrael Avrohom and slid the smartphone into his jacket pocket. He stood momentarily with his back to his comrades and contemplated the consequences of their next move. *We have been at odds with the People of the Book for centuries. The Preceptor was right. The time for change is now.*

"Was that the Preceptor?" Ali Azharuddin approached from behind.

Arwan nodded, but did not turn to face him.

"What did he say?" Ali waited for a response.

Once we commit to this endeavor there is no turning back. Arwan recalled what the Preceptor had said. *There is no turning back.* Arwan cleared his throat before he spoke. "We are to proceed as planned."

"We are doing God's work," Ali placed a hand on Arwan's shoulder. "Allah planned this in the beginning, and chose us to carry it out in the end."

Arwan nodded again without saying a word.

Ali turned away and shouted orders to the others. Four men scrambled to make the necessary preparations. One ran behind a camera and waited for another to activate the lighting. The third and fourth men disappeared into an adjacent room. Muffled cries and a brief scuffle could be heard coming from the darkness before they emerged with a man who had been bound, gagged, and blindfolded.

He struggled against them with his hands tied behind his back before one of the men elbowed him in the stomach. The prisoner fell to his knees. The other man struck him in the back of his head with the butt of his M-16 rifle.

"Enough!" Arwan approached. He squatted before the prisoner and pulled him close enough to whisper in his ear.

THE SECRET OF SCRIPTURE

"To be injured is better than to be dead. Your wounds can heal. Death is final. Do you understand me?"

The prisoner sobbed helplessly.

"Nod if you understand me," Arwan hissed.

The prisoner nodded.

"Then do as these men say, and you may yet live. Fight them, and they will be left with no choice but to make an example of you for the others. Do you want that?"

The prisoner shook his head.

Arwan stood and instructed his men to line the prisoners up along the wall facing the camera. He strode past them and stood in the doorway of the adjacent room.

"Do as these men instruct, and you will remain unharmed. Fight them, and they *will* kill you!" Arwan shouted into the dark room where the other prisoners sat huddled in a corner.

"When do you want me to activate the feed?" Ali asked.

Arwan checked his wristwatch. He raised five fingers before he stepped out of the room. The wooden door closed behind him as he walked through a darkened tunnel with only the sunlight at the opposite end to guide him. He climbed a short flight of stone steps and emerged beneath a clear blue sky. Car horns and groaning engines could be heard in the distance. He glanced over his shoulder before he retrieved his smartphone from his jacket pocket and initiated a text message.

27
TOWER OF DAVID MUSEUM OLD CITY
Jerusalem, Israel
10:10 a.m.

Batya glanced at her phone once again, but still no response from Farhad. The signal strength indicator on her phone showed all four bars. She turned her gaze toward the walls, the windows, and the ceiling of the ancient structure. The natural and artificial lighting against the stones cast a golden glow.

Signage directed visitors to the various exhibits of the museum. Including an impressive lightshow intended to impress pilgrims with a visual story of the Biblical king who shared the museum's namesake.

He lived a thousand years before the citadel was built; yet believers come to the Old City and this museum to somehow feel connected to the boy shepherd that defeated Goliath and later became king, Batya reflected as she weaved through the crowds.

"It's not like Farhad to ignore my text messages," Batya muttered to herself. She lifted her smartphone above her head to obtain a better signal. Perhaps I should go outside.

Her phone vibrated in her hand. She looked at the screen and swiped at it to read the incoming message from Arwan.

Exit the museum, immediately! Batya's brow furrowed when she read the text. She replied with a question mark.

There is no time to explain! I'll be in touch. Just get out now!!!

Batya turned and made a beeline for the nearest exit.

She heard a woman laugh. She heard a child cry. Just as she crossed the threshold, she heard an explosion from behind and all went dark.

28

CHURCH OF THE HOLY SEPULCHRE OLD CITY
Jerusalem, Israel
10:10 a.m.

Aiden and Yeshua arrived at the main entrance of what Christians believe is the site of the most important event in human history. The ancient structure housed the traditional sites of Jesus' crucifixion, burial, and resurrection. It towered over the courtyard where Believers congregated and entered in groups and in pairs. Aiden scanned the dun-colored façade, a Romanesque basilica with grey domes built with stones steeped in prayer, hymns and liturgies.

Each stone placed must be destroyed to conceal the truth within a god's tower, Aiden reflected on the lines of the poem.

"Well, we are here, now what?" Yeshua looked over his shoulder at the throng of noisy pilgrims.

"I'm trying to figure out how the lines in the poem are connected to the Ezekiel 44 reference that was left on the body," Aiden turned to the chief inspector.

"Is there anything in Ezekiel that could be considered a reference to the Jew as the Messiah?" Yeshua asked.

Aiden rubbed his chin momentarily. *We were directed here from the Golden Gate.* He closed his eyes and went over the chapter in his head.

"It would have to be verse three," Aiden finally said. "It is for the prince; the prince, he shall sit in it to eat bread before the Lord; he shall enter by the way of *that* gate, and shall go out by the way of the same."

"You said Christians believe he fulfilled the prophecy by entering through that gate, correct?"

"Yes," Aiden nodded, "and if we connect that to the Golden Gate's association with the Immaculate Conception then we need to check anything within the shrine that's connected to Mary."

"Where do we begin?"

"The Chapel of the Three Mary's," Aiden said.

"Lead the way, professor," Yeshua motioned at the entrance.

An explosion echoed through the air, and the ground shook.

"What the hell was that?" Yeshua glanced over his shoulder toward the Jaffa Gate.

"Do you think a bomb went off?" Aiden asked.

"I don't know," Yeshua scanned the area.

Many of the pilgrims fell silent. Some exchanged curious glances, and others looked to the sky.

"We need to hurry," Yeshua said. "I'm sure I'll receive a call from headquarters if I'm needed elsewhere."

Immediately upon entering the church they stood before the Stone of Annointing. A two-meter slab of reddish stone on the ground marked the spot where the body of Jesus was laid down after having been taken down from the cross. Candlesticks with a row of eight elaborately decorated lanterns hanging over it flanked the stone slab. An elderly woman and a middle-aged man knelt before it. They offered a silent prayer and kissed the stone before pulling away.

Aiden observed the confused look in the chief inspector's eyes.

"You've never been here before, have you?" Aiden asked.

The chief inspector shook his head as his gaze swept across the stonework and a Greek mosaic on a wall directly across from them. It depicted the scene of Christ being taken down from the cross, his body being prepared for burial, and then being taken to the tomb.

"This is the spot where tradition holds that Jesus' body was placed in preparation for his burial according to Jewish custom," Aiden nodded at the stone.

"Interesting," Yeshua said.

"The Chapel of the Three Marys is this way," Aiden turned left and led the chief inspector away from the stone.

THE SECRET OF SCRIPTURE

"The Three Marys?" Yeshua followed alongside the professor.

"Mary the Mother of Jesus, Mary the wife of Clopas—who is believed to be her sister, and of course Mary Magdelene," Aiden said. "This area here marks the location from where the Three Marys stood to watch the crucifixion, and then the burial of Jesus."

They arrived at a small circular slab with four pillars surmounted by a marble canopy.

"This is the Station of the Holy Women," Aiden pointed at the Armenian shrine.

Yeshua admired the elaborate carving of the stonework before he focused his attention on the large mosaic that recalled the scene.

"If we stand behind this chapel and look toward the Golgotha—believed to be the exact location where Jesus was crucified—we will have the same view the Three Marys had on that day," Aiden led Yeshua around the shrine.

"What are we looking for?" Yeshua glanced around.

Aiden pursed his lips. *What are we looking for, indeed?* He scanned the area for a clue that linked the Virgin with the Christ, the prophecy, and the poem. "Golgotha," Aiden said softly.

"What is its significance?" Yeshua looked on.

"This church was built here at the site of Golgotha, because Emperor Constantine's mother identified it as the place where Christ was crucified and buried," Aiden said. "Scholars questioned this claim in the 19th century, because the church was inside the city walls of the present-day Old City."

"Which would have been inconsistent with Jewish burial customes, since the dead were always buried outside the city walls," Yeshua said.

"Archaeologists later confirmed that the current city walls did not encompass this site in the time of Jesus when they discovered a burial site that contained the tomb of Joseph of Arimathea," Aiden said.

"Who was he?" Yeshua asked.

"Some refer to him as a secret disciple of Jesus, who buried the Christ in his own tomb. He was a wealthy man and used his clout to secure the body of Jesus for a honourable burial before sunset," Aiden said. "That is an important detail often overlooked by modern Christians."

"Biblical days, even Jewish holidays, begin at sunset," Yeshua said.

"The Jewish holiday that most closely correlates with the death of the Christ is Passover," Aiden said.

"A Jewish holiday that commemorates the Exodus from Egypt," Yeshua said.

"Note the symbolism," Aiden crossed his arms and rubbed his chin. "Just as the Jews painted the blood of the lamb on wooden beams above their doors, Jesus became the Lamb of God, and his blood stained the wooden beams upon which he was crucified."

"How is this connected with the mother of Christ?"

"Perhaps it isn't connected to her directly, and the terrorist provided us with just enough clues to think outside the box." Aiden paced back and forth momentarily.

"So, we have the Golden Gate through which a prince must pass. The gate symbolized the Virgin as the mother of the Christian Messiah. The Virgin is associated with this chapel, and mosaics along the chapel walls depict the crucifixion and burial of the Messiah." Yeshua glanced around before he turned his attention back to Aiden. "Am I right, so far?"

"Yes," Aiden answered. "And though the cross is no longer here, it is through the mother's blood that God became man."

"According to Christianity," Yeshua added.

"That goes without saying," Aiden said.

"So, what is the connection with the mother?" Yeshua checked his wristwatch. He felt they were running out of time.

"That's it!" Aiden turned around. "The mother and the symbolism. It was through Mary, the mother of Jesus, that God became man. Centuries later, it was through the mother of the emperor that man became God."

"What?" Yeshua's brow furrowed.

"Follow me, I'll tell you on the way," Aiden strode past the Tomb of Christ. Light cascaded in through the hole in the elaborately decorated Anastasia Rotunda high above.

Yeshua felt his phone vibrate against his chest. Several cell phones began to ring around them simultaneously. As Aiden and Yeshua walked past the Altar of Mary Magdalene, and then beneath the Arches of the Virgin Mary several visitors answered their phones and looked at their screens.

"Wait a minute," Yeshua stopped dead in his tracks.

"What is it?" Aiden looked over his shoulder.

The chief inspector read the message on his phone. "I need to call headquarters," he approached and lowered his voice as he spoke in a conspiratorial tone. "A bomb just went off at the Tower of David Museum near the Jaffa Gate."

29
BREAKING NEWS i-24NEWS
Israel
10:15 a.m.

People gathered around televisions in the region and around the world. News anchors announced the explosion that occurred only minutes ago.

"Authorities confirmed they received an anonymous tip moments before the blast, but the caller has yet to be identified as the tally of dead and injured remains unknown."

A looping news ticker read: EXPLOSION AT OLD CITY IN JERUSALEM ROCKS THE HOLY LAND...NO ONE HAS CLAIMED RESPONSIBILITY FOR THE ATTACK.

Reporters and analysts reviewed the long and violent history of clashes between Palestinians and Israelis as scenes of the destruction flashed across the screens.

"Since its inception, the State of Israel has been a point of contention on both sides," one reporter said.

"The escalating conflict has been on-going for over seven decades. Has it finally reached a tipping point?" said another.

A news anchor interrupted the discussion panel with an update. "It appears we have a reporter, Maya Levy on-scene and are going live with her right now. Maya, this is Binyamin at the news desk, can you tell us what's going on down there?"

"It's pure chaos at the moment. We were in the area after wrapping up our segment on the confrontation at the Dung Gate when we heard two explosions within minutes of each other."

"I'm sorry to interrupt, Maya, but did you say there were *two* explosions?" Binyamin asked.

"Yes. We did hear two explosions. One was more faint than the other and we just happened to be driving in the direction of the more powerful explosion here at the Tower of David Museum. Casualties are piling up as you can see people working together to sift through the rubble and rescue any survivors," Maya said.

"Thank you for the update Maya. We'll come back to you shortly for more," Binyamin said. Maya nodded before the screen-in-screen image on which she appeared was gone. "Our condolences to the families of those who have been affected by this cowardly act. We'll be back with more after this."

30
UNDISCLOSED LOCATION
Israel
10:15 a.m.

"Are we ready?" Arwan turned to Ali.

Ali stood over a man seated before a laptop and leaned in over the man's shoulder to confirm their readiness. The man pointed at the laptop screen and nodded. Ali lifted his gaze and met Arwan's intense stare. He signaled a thumb up. Arwan nodded before he pulled a black ski mask over his face and gave the command.

The room went dark momentarily before three overhead lights came to life. Another man stood behind the camera and signaled that the feed went live.

"Today, you have been given a sample of what we are capable of achieving under your very nose," Arwan spoke into the camera. "In a world of half-measures and prejudice against non-Christians, we are prepared to do whatever it takes to put an end to the conflict that divides the People of the Book."

The camera zoomed out to reveal a line of prisoners who knelt before Arwan and faced the camera. Their hands were tied behind their backs. Their muffled sobs could be heard from beneath white hoods.

"The enemies of Israel will collapse under the weight of their own hatred. Their defiance of the will of God shall lead to their destruction. It begins today," Arwan stepped directly behind one of the prisoners and brandished a machete. "We have ten prisoners. Each is a progeny of world leaders from the nations that are enemies of Israel. These youths attend universities in the region. We will publically execute each one at the top of the hour unless the Palestinians are exiled from Jerusalem and authority over the Temple Mount is turned over to Israel."

The prisoners continued to sob and quiver on their knees.

THE SECRET OF SCRIPTURE

"We are the Sons of Light and act on behalf of the Preceptor of Righteousness, for we are not among those who seek smooth things," Arwan concluded. When the screen went dark, a woman could be heard screaming before the feed disconnected.

31
CHURCH OF THE HOLY SEPULCHRE OLD CITY
Jerusalem, Israel
10:20 a.m.

Yeshua ended his call with police headquarters and turned to Aiden as he scanned their surroundings. Many of the pilgrims turned to one another and shared the information that appeared on their social media feeds and breaking news alerts. They urged each other to head toward the exit, moving along hurriedly in an orderly fashion and shared the news with others along the way.

"What did your headquarters say?" Aiden noticed the crowds following each other.

"I'm to report to a staging area just beyond the city walls and prepare to evacuate the Old City immediately."

"Did you tell them where we are?"

"I told them where *I* am, yes, but evacuating this chapel by myself—"

"Is going to be next to impossible," Aiden cut him off. "Especially since there's only one entry-exit point!"

"I thought they were building a fire escape?"

"It has yet to be completed due to the constant infighting among the six Christian sects," Aiden said. "Even after the tragedy of 1834 when several hundred people were crushed in a stampede during the Holy Fire ceremony, the clergymen have yet to find a way to come to an agreement regarding renovations that are needed for the greater good."

Yeshua shook his head pensively. Though he had never been needed to respond to the frequent fistfights that broke out among the Greek and Armenian priests over the way certain ceremonies are conducted, or the long-running fued between the Ethiopians and Copts over possession of a rooftop monastery, he was well-aware that the Status Quo between the Greek Orthodox, Roman Catholic and Armenian clergy had to be treated with caution.

THE SECRET OF SCRIPTURE

"What a great way to lead by example," Yeshua shook his head.

"It's the reason why responsibility of the key and the door to Christianity's holiest sites has been entrusted to two Muslim families for centuries," Aiden said.

"I didn't know that," Yeshua cast him a confused look.

"The Joudeh family has protected the 500 year old cast-iron key to maintain a neutral guardianship of the Church of the Holy Sepulchre. The designation goes back to the time of the caliph, Umar ibn Khattab," Aiden said. "The family shares the responsibility of allowing pilgrims entry into the Church with the Nuseibeh family. Their representative is handed the key and he climbs a small wooden ladder to unlock both the top and bottom locks."

"I'll be damned," Yeshua looked around with his hands on his hips.

"Define irony when many Christians believe Muslims are intolerant, yet these two Muslim families are a model of interfaith cooperation that Church leaders here have yet to epitomize," Aiden said.

Yeshua sighed.

"What are you going to do?" Aiden looked at the chief inspector. "It looks like these people are showing themselves out, and for the time being no one seems to be in a panic."

"You were onto something before I got the call," Yeshua said. "You mentioned something about 'through the mother, God became man, and through the mother, man became God.' What does that mean?"

"Given the clues we have been given that led us here, it was through the Virgin Mary that God was made flesh, right?" Aiden said. "Well, fast forward three centuries later to the ecumenical council convened by the Roman Emperor Constantine. Even though he was a lifelong pagan and didn't convert to Christianity until he was on his deathbed, he played a pivotal role in the proclomation of the Edict of Milan in 313 A.D. to declare religious tolerance for Christianity in the

Roman Empire. Furthermore, it was on his orders that the Church of the Holy Sepulchre was built after his mother—who had already converted to Christianity—had journeyed to the Holy Land and claimed to have found the True Cross upon which Jesus had been crucified."

"And it was at this council where Jesus the man was equated with God," Yeshua recalled what Aiden and Yisrael had explained earlier.

"Precisely!" Aiden nodded. "Anyone who refused to sign the Nicene Creed was banished to Illyria."

"So, we're looking for something to do with Constantine, or his mother?" Yeshua looked around the chapel.

"His mother, Helena, to be exact," Aiden continued to walk through the dark corridor of the Arches of the Virgin Mary.

The patchwork of stones along the floor diverged in style and cut from the walls that rose out of the stone floor to lofty heights down the hallway. A row of columns down the center of the hall split it into two sections. The different building styles between the smaller rough columns and the larger smooth columns allowed visitors to see evidence of how much had changed from the time of Constantine to the Crusader era.

"Although the Arches of the Virgin memorialize Mary's presence during the crucifixion and the resurrection of Jesus," Aiden said he as led the chief inspector through the area of chapels built to mark the final journey of Jesus. "We are looking for the Chapel of St. Helena, which is just down this stairway here."

Yeshua followed Aiden to the Lower Level of the Church of the Holy Sepulchre. Hanging lamps illuminated their path as several pilgrims urgently climbed the steps. The long staircase widened at the base, and they arrived beneath a golden chandelier and more hanging lamps that illuminated an elaborately decorated clearing. Marble benches sat along the walls, and red velvet ropes cordoned off a large decorative mosaic that adorned the center of the clearing. The mosaic contained images of Noah's Arch on Mount Ararat as well as several Armenian churches. The bottom of the 20th century artistic masterpiece contained a passage entirely in Armenian script.

An iron fence separated the main altar from the clearing, and several pilgrims stood in line along the western wall to take pictures of the altar despite the news of the explosion nearby. Gradually, some of the visitors made their way down another staircase. Others turned their camera phones up to the religious artwork along the dome's interior and the paintings on the walls, while they waited to approach the altar, and then the stairwell.

"What is all this?" Yeshua gazed in awe at the artistry.

"These are paintings depicting significant events relating to Christianity and the chapel," Aiden followed the chief inspector's gaze. "Armenians feel a unique bond to Christianity, because the Kingdom of Armenia became the first nation to adopt Christianity as a state religion. Hence, the importance of that painting that depicts the return of the True Cross to Jerusalem through Armenia."

"Is that Mount Ararat in the background of that image?" Yeshua pointed.

"Indeed it is, which according to Christian tradition is the resting place of Noah's Ark," Aided added.

"What's in there?" Yeshua pointed at a locked gate door that had also been cordoned off.

"That leads to St. Vartan Chapel," Aiden said. "It's only opened for special occasions. There's a 4th century drawing on a stone made by a pilgrim who arrived to the Holy Land by boat. It depicts an image of a man on a boat with the phrase 'Domine Ivimus,' which translated means 'We go to the Lord.'"

"Interesting," Yeshua nodded pensively.

"That one there," Aiden pointed at the large painting on the south wall, "that depicts the discovery of the True Cross by Helena."

"Is this what the terrorist intended for us to find?" Yeshua turned to Aiden.

"I'm not sure," Aiden studied the painting and the area immediately surrounding it.

"Is anything else here related to the True Cross?"

"We can go down to the Cistern where Helena supposedly found the True Cross," Aiden pointed at the stairwell to the right of the main altar. A large portrait of Helena standing beside a cross hung over the opening to where the staircase descended.

"Follow me," Yeshua led the way. He brandished his badge as he shouldered his way through the crowd. Though they grumbled their dissatisfaction no one dared voice their complaints.

A Greek Orthodox priest wearing a blue sticharion with a blue and gold stitched epitrachelion—often called a stole—stood beneath a low-hanging stone ceiling as he swung a thurible over a collection of lit candles in the far corner where it is believed St. Helena found the cross.

"The right side of the room where that priest is standing is maintained by the Greek Orthodox Church," Aiden spoke softly to the chief inspector. "The left side of the room over here is maintained by the Roman Catholic Church."

Yeshua observed the priest momentarily before he turned away.

Lighting situated behind glass walls along the perimeter illuminated the cave-like section of the chapel where remnants of 12-century frescoes linger like fading memories of a forgotten time. The high ceiling of the other half of the chamber disappeared into shadows due to the overhead lighting having already been turned off.

Pilgrims snapped photos of the priest, and then turned their attention immediately to the stone altar with a marble top.

THE SECRET OF SCRIPTURE

A stone column stood as part of the wall behind the altar with an obscure sculpture that loomed like a sentinel in the shadows at its crown.

"So, this was a cistern, huh?" Yeshua scanned the chamber with his hands on his hips.

"You see those square-shaped openings in the ceiling?" Aiden pointed.

"Yes," the chief inspector answered without looking at the professor.

"Buckets were lowered through there to retrieve water from down here," Aiden said.

"Unbelievable," Yeshua shook his head. "And it was down here where she found the True Cross?"

"According to legend, three crosses were found as well as a titulus inscribed with the phrase: Iesus Nazaranus Rex Iudaeorum, which was Latin for Jesus, King of the Jews," Aiden said.

"How did they know which was the True Cross?"

"A woman dying from a terminal illness had been brought to the three crosses. She touched each one in succession, and after she touched the third cross, she was cured," Aiden said. "After which Helena ordered the erection of the church to mark the location where Jesus was crucified and resurrected. Hence, the Chapel of the Finding of the Cross."

"Here," Yeshua guessed.

"The True Cross was preserved until sometime around 614 A.D."

"Yes, you mentioned that earlier," Yeshua recalled the history lessoned that Aiden and Yisrael gave him. "Now what?"

"There," Aiden pointed at the black stone statue situated well above eye level atop the column behind the altar. "That is a statue of St. Helena holding the Cross of Christ."

"Why is it hidden in darkness? Isn't the point of this chapel—"

"To marvel at the beautiful statue commemorating the find?" Aiden cut him off. "Yes, it is, but I'm guessing someone had the overhead lights shut off for a reason."

Both he and the chief inspector neared the altar and inched past it on opposite sides.

"Is that a book?" Aiden mouthed to the chief inspector.

"I think so," Yeshua replied in a low voice.

Aiden glanced at the group of visitors behind them. Yeshua nodded and instructed the professor to stand by as he turned to the crowd.

"Forgive the interruption laides and gentleman, but I'm afraid this chapel must be closed immediately due to safety concerns," Yeshua held up his badge.

"What safety concerns?" said one of the visitors.

"I'm not at liberty to say, but if you would please make your way back up the steps and to the exit of the Church in an orderly fashion your cooperation will be greatly appreciated."

"I'm not going until you tell us what the hell is going on?" A heavyset man wearing a cowboy hat with a pinched, teardrop crown and shapeable rodeo brim spoke out.

"Tell them it's a matter of national security," Aiden said just loud enough for only the chief inspector to hear.

"National what?" Yeshua said over his shoulder.

"That's what they say back in the United States."

"Well, this isn't the United States," Yeshua hissed back.

"True, but many of these visitors are American. They'll get it and the rest will follow."

"Ahem, yes, well without divulging too much all I can say is that it is a matter of national security," Yeshua finally said.

"National security?" the man scowled.

"Yes sir, so please move along to the main exit."

"I don't buy it," the man snapped.

THE SECRET OF SCRIPTURE

"Oh, come on Jim," an elderly woman slapped him on the arm. "Why do you always have to be so difficult?"

The priest approached after most of the visitors had begun to climb the steps.

"What is this matter that you are speaking of?" he asked in a low voice. "And what authority do you have here?"

"My name is Pakad Yeshua Schwartz, chief inspector of the Israel Police force. Though I'm afraid I cannot go into further detail about my investigation, I do ask that you ensure these people exit the building safely."

The priest eyed him suspiciously before he nodded at Aiden. "And who is he?"

"He is a professor of biblical studies from America who is assisting us with our investigation," Yeshua replied.

"What need is there in the Holy Land for a professor of biblical studies from America?" The priest said with an incredulous look on his face.

"He's a world-leading expert on matters pertaining to our investigation, and I just happened to be near the hotel where he is staying when I decided to request his assistance," Yeshua said.

"I recognize you now," the priest said. "You're the one who's always giving interviews on the television. What does a man without faith know about faith to speak on such things?"

"I don't mean to—" Aiden began to say before Yeshua cut him off.

"Now is not the time for this discussion. If you would please ensure everyone exists the church safely, my colleagues will elaborate on the situation."

The priest reluctantly relented his position, but promised to take the matter up with his superiors. He turned and strode toward the staircase, occasionally glancing over his shoulder as he ascended the steps.

Aiden waited until the priest disappeared from view before he rushed behind the altar and reached for the book behind the statue.

"Wait, this isn't a book," Aiden said as he placed it on the altar. "This is a bible-design laptop cover."

"Perhaps I should get this back to headquarters and have—"

"There isn't any time," Aiden cut him off. He unzipped the cover and slowly pulled the laptop open. The screen glowed to life with a prompt for a passcode via fingerprint scan. "Whose fingerprint do you suppose is required?"

"I don't know," Yeshua shrugged. "Let me try mine."

Incorrect passcode, flashed across the screen before a second sentence appeared. *Please try again, professor.*

Aiden and Yeshua exchanged confused glances.

"Well, here goes the old college try," Aiden placed his thumb on the fingerprint scanner.

The screen went blank momentarily before the face of a woman appeared and she began to speak. Her olive skin, hazel eyes and dark brown hair complimented the elgance of her high cheekbones and slender neck.

"Greetings Professor Aiden Leonardo, I am Sarai. Though you may recognize my name from biblical lore, the acronym of my name is Science And Religion Artificial Intelligence," said the image of a woman on the screen with S.A.R.A.I. swirling around her.

"Biblical lore?" Yeshua turned to Aiden.

"Like Abraham, who—as I'm sure you know—was originally named Abram, meaning exalted father, and later renamed Abraham the father of many," Aiden began to say. "Sarai was the birth name of Abraham's wife, later renamed Sarah by divine command."

"Beautifully articulated, professor," Sarai said.

THE SECRET OF SCRIPTURE

Aiden and Yeshua looked at her image on the screen before they exchanged a furtive glance and focused their attention on her again.

"How did you know I'd be here?" Aiden finally asked.

"The Preceptor said you would come," Sarai said.

"Who is the Preceptor?" Aiden asked.

"Preceptor?" Yeshua's brow furrowed.

"It's a synonym for teacher," Aiden answered him and turned back to the screen.

"The Preceptor will reveal his true identity at the appropriate time, professor," Sarai said. "In the interim, you are charged with a task."

"A task? What task?" Aiden said.

"Answer my riddle correctly and you will disable the explosive device built into the hard drive of this computer. Failure to do so will result in a catastrophic event," Sarai said.

"Catastrophic event? What catastrophic event?" Yeshua demanded.

"The other explosives will be detonated at sunset to mark the end of the day and the end of an age," Sarai replied. "However, if you answer my riddles correctly, not only will you disable the explosive within this device, but you will have a clue to where the next device is hidden. You will also receive an image after each riddle that you must decipher in order to reveal the secret of scripture. Disable each in a specific order, and you may yet prevent this catastrophic event from happening."

"You have got to be kidding me?" Yeshua turned away.

"Please note, professor, that you—and only you—can open the laptops and disable the bombs. Any attempt to deceive me will result in automatic detonation of the other explosives hidden in the Old City."

"Deceive you?" Aiden asked.

"Yes," Sarai said. "Although you see me on your screen, I am communicating to you from a cloud. So, we will see each other again at each site to where you are directed. Are you ready to begin?"

"Wait. How many attempts do I get to answer correctly?"

"You have unlimited attempts, professor, but note that time is of the essence," Sarai said.

"Yeshua checked his wrist watch," and shrugged.

"Are you ready, professor?" Sarai asked.

Aiden sighed before he nodded. "God help us," he muttered.

"Funny you should say that professor," Sarai replied. "Let us begin."

32
EL-AMIN RESIDENCE
West Chicago, IL.
3:35 a.m.

"Wait, I'm confused. The Third Temple?" Angelo turned to Nagi before he looked up at Miriam on the screen.

"Have the people of Israel build me a holy sanctuary so I can live among them," Nagi said.

"You're talking about Exodus 25:8," Angelo said.

"Ah, so you *do* know your scripture, huh, detective," Nagi nodded.

"To be honest, I've spent the past three years doing a little soul searching, so I haven't read the Bible as frequently as I once did, and only remember some passages," Angelo confessed.

"Yes, well, there are those who remain faithful to the commandments of God, such as the Temple Mount Faithful Movement in Jerusalem, whose goal is to rebuild the Third Jewish Temple on the Temple Mount in the Old City of Jerusalem," Nagi said.

"The conundrum, however, is that it is currently the site of the Dome of the Rock and the Al-Aqsa Mosque," Miriam said. "Although the Dome is not a place for public worship, it is the first monumental building in Islamic architecture and stands as a Muslim shrine."

"And the Jews permit this?" Angelo asked. He turned to Prescott when he saw him shift in his seat.

"Yes and no," Nagi sat up in his seat and slid his fingers over his desk. A series of images appeared on all the monitors except the one with Miriam's FaceTime call. "Although it was built by the ninth Islamic Caliph, Abd al-Malik, to commemorate his conquest of Judaism's capital and the former site of the Jewish Temple—also known as the Holiest of All—it also served as a flag of victory for whoever conquered Jerusalem."

"The Crusaders turned it into a Catholic church in 1099 before Saladin recaptured the city and turned it back into a Muslim shrine," Miriam added.

"When the Israeli army emerged victorious from the Six Day War, two Israeli paratroopers climbed the Dome of the Rock and hung the Israeli flag from its crown," Nagi continued.

"That is until the Israeli Defense Minister, Moshe Dayan, ordered it to be taken down," Miriam said.

"It is said that he asked the soldiers if they wanted to see the Middle East burn," Nagi said.

"Wow," Angelo mouthed.

"In order to keep the peace, the Israeli government declared sovereignty over the Temple Mount and handed its management over to an Islamic religious trust, the Jerusalem Islamic Waqf for management and control of the Islamic edifices of the Temple Mount," Nagi said.

"Orthodox Jews initially supported Dayan's decision, since the exact location of the Holiest of All was unknown, and they feared inadvertently setting foot on sacred ground, but the recent movement for the building of the Third Temple has led to increased tensions on both sides, which only exacerbates the problem that has intensified over the past seventy years," Miriam said.

"Part of the conflict in Israel has to do with the expulsion of Palestinians from their land," Nagi said. "From 1948 through 1966, Palestinians in Israel were under the rule of a military government, and then in 1967 the populace was transferred over to the West Bank and Gaza and East Jerusalem."

"When people talk about racial profiling in America, it pales in comparison to the human rights violations occurring in Israel with regard to how the Palestinians are being treated," Miriam shook her head. "They are required to carry specific identification that segregates the population of Jews from Palestinians. They are subjected to vehicle inspections and individual patdowns at various checkpoints while on their way to work, or home, and have even been forced to perform menial labor tasks when the situation arises."

"Sometimes at gunpoint," Nagi said. "But you won't see any of it on the news."

"Close to three-quarters of a million human beings who were displaced and left in need of charity and assistance have been caught in the crossfire of a conflict deeply rooted in ideological disputes," Miriam said. "Take a guess at how many good Christians have offered to help these people who have endured a great injustice committed by Israel in order to create itself."

Angelo sighed, and Prescott lowered his head.

"Those who remained in Israel became citizens of the new state, but were denied the rights of Jewish Nationality," Miriam continued. "These circumstances remind us of the words of Albert Einstein: 'The attitude we adopt toward the Arab minority will provide the real test of our moral standards as a people.'"

"Yet, Western media finds a way to group all Muslims—even the innocents—into the same category as Islamist extremists who fight back without providing a more accurate picture of why things are the way they are," Nagi said.

"Fight back?" Angelo turned to Nagi and eyed Prescott with a sidelong glance.

"What you have to bear in mind is that many of the men who have become embroiled in the conflict were just boys when they saw their fathers brutally beaten and mistreated by Israeli police officers," Nagi said. "It was an environment that breeded resentment."

"Which made them more susceptible to the rhetoric preached by men who sought to meet violence with violence," Miriam added. "Recruiting them into the various terrorist groups that have emerged over the following decades."

"A call to arms in the fight for their land," Nagi said.

"Well, they believe it's their land, because according to history the name 'Palestine' originates from the word 'Philistia,' referring to the Philistines who occupied part of the region circa the 12th century B.C.E.," Miriam interjected. "Many kingdoms ruled the region throughout history including the Assyrians, Babylonians, Persions, Greeks, Romans, Arabs, and lastly the Ottoman Empire for roughly 400 years until the end of World War 1."

"Although the Torah contains an account between Abraham—and later his son, Isaac—as agreeing to a covenant of kindness with the Philistine king and his descendants, the dispute over land rights has pushed that agreement into the shadows of memory," Nagi added.

"On the one hand, they have remained constant occupants of the region throughout the Jewish Diaspora that has spanned close to twenty centuries." Miriam said. "On the other hand, archaeological discoveries hinted at the possibility that the Philistines could have had Aegean origins."

"What does that mean?" Angelo shook his head.

"It meant that they were believed to be seafarers who settled in the region after making landfall and invading the surrounding communities," Nagi said.

"The latest research, however, indicates that they weren't Aegean pirates, but instead may have been a native Middle Eastern population from the region of modern day Syria who migrated south into Canaan," Miriam said.

"In any case, the modern conflict is that if they *have* been there since ancient times—including during the Diaspora—then they believe it is their homeland, which directly contraditions what Jews believe about the region being *their* homeland as promised by God, and that brings us back to the subject of the Third Temple."

"Building of the Third Temple is sacred in Judaism. The thrice daily Amidah prayer is a formal prayer for the Temple," Miriam continued, "because its construction must be completed prior to the arrival of the Messiah."

THE SECRET OF SCRIPTURE

"You mean, Jesus," Angelo said.

"Negative," Nagi shook his head. "Jesus is believed to be the Messiah to Christians, but the Jewish tradition doesn't recognize Jesus as the Messiah, because their understanding adheres to the belief that the Messiah's arrival will be marked by peace, untiy, and a world without evil."

"None of which occurred when Jesus lived and died," Miriam said.

"But it could have," Angelo said. "If people had adhered to his teachings."

"Perhaps, but the fact remains that it didn't happen," Nagi said. "And there's nothing in scripture that accounts for exceptions to the rule. As law, the Word of God is definitive. Think of the Ten Commandments. There aren't any amendments to the laws of God. There are strict rules for how people should carry on with their daily lives, strict dietary and hygiene standards that they must be adhere to, otherwise one is living in defiance of God's laws."

"So, when we talk about the Messiah from the perspective of the Torah, we need only look at Isaiah 2:4 'The Lord will mediate between nations and will settle international disputes. They will hammer their swords into plowshares and their spears into pruning hooks. Nation will no longer fight against nation, nor train for war anymore," Miriam recited the passage.

"Again, that didn't happen when Jesus lived and died, which is the reason why the Jewish and Islamic traditions don't view him as the Messiah," Nagi said.

"Yet, the believers of these two faiths remain at odds over the sacred site upon which the Dome of the Rock now stands," Miriam added. "In some circles, building the Third Temple would require destruction of the Dome of the Rock and the Al-Aqsa Mosque, which would lead to severe international conflicts."

"Others contend that it must be built on the same exact location as the two previous temples, but uncertainty over where the Holy of Holies existed in ancient times deems that a near impossibility now," Nagi said.

"And then there's the conundrum of the conflicting views within the Jewish community," Miriam said. "Many Jewish-Orthodox scholars don't agree with attempting to build the Third Temple prior to the arrival of the Messiah, while others contend that Jews should endeavor to rebuild the temple as soon as possible."

"And you think that whoever is behind these murders is attempting to remove all obstacles to that end by targeting Christian sites within the Old City," Angelo concluded.

"Bingo!" Nagi snapped his fingers.

"Pardon the interruption," Priya's voiced echoed over the speakers, "but there are reports from Israel about an explosion in the Old City of Jerusalem."

"What?" Miriam shouted.

"Bring it on-screen, Priya," Nagi said.

Angelo watched Miriam turn away from their FaceTime call to turn on the television in her hotel room.

"With two dozen confirmed deaths from the explosion and dozens more injured, many are asking if the authorities will concede to the demands of the terrorists," the reporter spoke into the camera. "At the moment, the Sons of Light—as they have referred to themselves—have not been identified as being aligned with any of the well-known terrorist organizations in the world, and experts are left guessing about who is the Preceptor of Righteousness they mentioned as their leader."

"Maya, have authorities on-scene initiated an evacuation and been able to determine if there are additional explosives in the Old City?" Binyamin asked from the news desk as he appeared on a split screen.

"Not that we have been made privy of," Maya Levy said. "As you can see behind me, many people are focused on rescue efforts at this time, while others gather in defiance of the attacks, but I imagine authorities are working diligently behind the scenes to assess the gravity of the threat to this ancient city and center point of conflict among the three great religions of the world."

"Holy—" Nagi began to say.

"Nagi, I've got to get ahold of Aiden," Miriam cut him off.

"Stand by your man, girl, we've got this on our end," Nagi tapped his desk to end the call, and then tapped another to mute the news report.

"What did they mean by Preceptor of Righteousness?" Angelo asked.

"If it means what I think it means, then it's a reference to one of the lost sects in Judaism from the time of Jesus," Nagi said pensively as he turned his attention to Prescott. "What we need to figure out is how you're involved in all this."

33
CROWNE PLAZA TEL AVIV CITY CENTER
Tel Aviv, Israel
10:45 a.m.

Miriam held the phone to her ear as it rang. "Come on, pick up, pick up damn it!"

Her smartphone chimed again with another incoming message from Susan.

"Crap! I keep forgetting to get back to her."

She considered staying on the line in hopes that Aiden would answer, but after several rings she decided to click over and take her call.

"Hello, Susan?"

"There you are, stranger," Susan said. "I was beginning to wonder if you were ignoring me."

"No, I'm sorry," Miriam cleared her throat. "We've had a lot going on here. Actually, I'm glad you called. I need your help."

"Sure, what's going on?"

"I need to sneak into the Old City."

"You sure have a death wish, don't you?"

"So, you've heard?" Miriam paced the length of the hotel room.

"It's all over the news," Susan said. "The terrorists have made demands, people are going to be evacuated from the Old City due to threats of explosives, and they're planning on closing all the gates."

"I just saw that," Miriam said.

"What's going on, exactly?" Susan asked.

"Aiden is in trouble," Miriam said.

"Seems to be a pattern with him," Susan said.

"The police came to our hotel to question him about a murder. He left with the chief inspector to assist with their investigation, but the last I heard from him was nearly an hour ago. Now he's not answering his phone, and I'm losing my mind over here thinking the worst!"

THE SECRET OF SCRIPTURE

"I get it. I've been there, remember?" Susan said.

Miriam did remember. It was only a few years ago that Susan's fiancé, Lorenzo de Medici had convinced Miriam to spring Aiden from the hospital before the authorities could question him about the murder of Lorenzo and Aiden's father, Lazzaro.

Though Lorenzo didn't doubt Aiden's innocence, he was more concerned with the ancient artifact worth millions than he was with Aiden's involvement, or Lazzaro's demise. In the end, it cost him his life and left Susan to grieve alone.

No one had heard from her for the better part of the past three years until she reached out to Miriam the week before her and Aiden's trip to Israel. She'd learned of their planned attendance at the summit and asked Miriam if she'd be willing to meet for lunch. Their lunch date, however, would have to be postponed.

"I can get you into the Old City, but if it's rigged with explosives—"

"You don't have to stay," Miriam cut her off. "Just help me get within the city walls and I'll find Aiden on my own."

"All right, if that's what you want?"

"He's my husband," Miriam said. "I can't *not* try to get him out of there."

"I understand," Susan said softly.

"I'm sorry Susan. I didn't mean…" Miriam's words trailed off.

"Don't worry about it," Susan replied. "I'll meet you in the lobby lounge of your hotel in ten minutes."

"Thank you," Miriam sighed.

"Don't thank me yet," Susan chuckled. "But when this is over, you'll owe me."

34

CHURCH OF THE HOLY SEPULCHRE OLD CITY
Jerusalem, Israel
10:50 a.m.

Aiden and Yeshua stared at the laptop screen as Sarai's image vanished and a series of lines appeared on the screen. Sarai recited the poem for them, and then she instructed Aiden to explain each line of the poem.

"May I take a moment to review the riddle, or poem, or whatever this is?" Aiden asked.

"Take as long as you'd like," Sarai said. "Though I must reiterate that time is of the essence."

"I understand," Aiden nodded, and he reread the poem in a low voice.

> There were seven among seven among the Heavenly Host
> His was the Holy Spirit, but not the Holy Ghost
> To them all the mysteries of heaven were not yet revealed,
> To him was given the title of a man filled with zeal
> In the ages of empires faith turned imperialistic,
> This one is the faith that is not monotheistic.

"Do you know what it means?" Yeshua cast Aiden a perplexed glance before he turned back to the computer screen.

Aiden paced back and forth in silence with his arms crossed and a hand on his chin.

Yeshua checked his wristwatch and sighed.

"There were seven among seven among the Heavenly Host," Aiden repeated. "God and the Gods!"

"What?" Yeshua said startled.

"The seven among seven refers to the seven names of God: Yahweh, El, Elohim, Adonai, Allah, Shaddai, and then Lord. The last one being used most frequently due to the

THE SECRET OF SCRIPTURE

Jewish tradition believing that God's divine name is too sacred to be spoken," Aiden said.

"What does the other seven stand for?" Yeshua asked.

"The gods," Aiden met his gaze.

"The gods? I'm not sure I follow," Yeshua said.

"In Genesis, God refers to Himself in the plural when he says in chapter 1 verse 26: 'Let us make man in our image,' which then elaborates on the creation of man and woman."

"Wow!" Yeshua blinked and stared ahead absently. "But who are, or were the other seven gods?"

"Well, believe it or not, in the great traditions of the world seven represents the number of the great gods of the solar system. The names of the seven gods are where the seven planets got their names. The seven among the seven names of God and the Heavenly Host; the Heavenly Host, of course, refers to the army of angels," Aiden turned to Sarai. "Am I correct?"

"Indeed you are, professor," Sarai said. "Please continue."

"His was the Holy Spirit, but not the Holy Ghost," Aiden read the line aloud.

"The Holy Spirit clearly refers to God," Yeshua said.

"Yes, and I'm willing to bet that this refers to the schism between Judaism and the early Jewish Disciples of Christ," Aiden said.

"Please elaborate, professor," Sarai reappeared on the screen as the poem shifted beside her.

"It refers to the common misunderstanding of God's nature, which complicates the nature of Christ after the resurrection, because people often use the terms spirit and ghost interchangeably, which is an incorrect practice with regard to scripture and how the word 'spirit' is used in the Hebrew Bible," Aiden said.

"You are correct, so far, professor," Sarai nodded. "Please continue."

"Although religious leaders have incorrectly taught their congregations that the Holy Spirit is a person, the Bible actually reveals that the Holy Spirit is the divine force of God," Aiden turned away and rubbed his forehead. He turned back to Yeshua and Sarai, and recited the first verse that popped into his head. "And the Spirit of God came mightily upon David from that day forward."

"The line reads: His was the Holy Spirit, but not the Holy Ghost," Yeshua looked at the screen once more.

"That's because a ghost is often referred to as the essence of someone who has passed but became a spirit, however there is no reference to that concept in the Bible," Aiden said. "Once a person dies he or she does not become a spirit. That person merely ceases to exist until the appointed time when God will resurrect their souls on the Day of Judgment."

"So, you are saying that when the Disciples of Jesus claimed to see his ghost after the crucifixion, they equated him with the spirit of God," Yeshua concluded.

"Yes," Aiden nodded.

"Next line," Yeshua said as he turned to the laptop. "To them all the mysteries of heaven were not yet revealed."

"To them, to them, to them," Aiden paced the length of the chamber.

"The Believers, the priests, the Disciples, the prophets?" Yeshua guessed.

"Hmm, I don't know," Aiden shook his head. "It could be one of them, but if we focus on the preceeding lines in the poem none of those are listed."

"Given that it's a plural reference, the answer could either be the seven gods, or the angels," Yeshua guessed.

"Bingo!" Aiden pointed at the chief inspector. "The angels."

"Anyone in particular?"

"Well, as the angels are described in Biblical lore, there's a hierarchy among their ranks. This stems from the influence of Mesopotamian and Canaanite traditions that pre-date Judaism," Aiden said.

"How do you mean?"

"Prior to the advent of monotheism, the world believed in many gods, hence the seven of seven reference made earlier in the poem, which made up the Divine Council. They were the lesser gods who presided over other celestial beings. In order to distance itself from other religions of the time, the God of Israel's superiority had to be firmly established by downgrading the lesser gods into angels," Aiden said. "The seven gods became the seven archangels who presided over the various orders of angels: Highest, Middle, and Lowest order, but the ones I'm thinking about are the ones associated with the fall."

"The Fallen Angels then," Yeshua guessed.

"No. I'm referring to the fall of the Watchers, a group of angels who—according to tradition—rebelled by foregoing their celestial existence to mate with human women," Aiden said. "Though there is a brief mention of them in Genesis 6, it is in the Books of Enoch and Daniel that their activities are elaborated upon."

"How is this connected to the poem?" Yeshua wondered.

"It's in the Book of Enoch where God says to them: 'You have been in heaven, but all the mysteries had not yet been revealed to you.'"

"Is he correct?" Yeshua turned to the laptop.

"Yes, he is," Sarai said.

"All right, next line: To him was given the title of a man filled with zeal," Yeshua read the sentence to Aiden. "Sounds to me like a reference to Jesus."

"You're correct," Aiden nodded. "In fact, I believe the final three lines are a direct reference to Jesus."

"Jesus was regarded as a zealot," Yeshua said. "How are the other two lines connected?"

"In the ages of empires faith turned imperialistic," Aiden read the next line. "Although empires have long existed since ancient times, the Roman Empire reached its greatest territorial expanse and had a period of unprecedented stability during the Pax Romana. Two centuries later, Christians rose to power following the Edict of Milan."

"That's when Constantine held the councils that you and Dr. Avrahom mentioned earlier," Yeshua remembered.

"It was during the reign of Theodosius the Great that the Catholic Church became the state church of the Roman Empire," Aiden added. "Though, even after the fall of the Western Roman Empire, and then long after the Middle Ages, European powers expanded into the New World with imperialistic agendas. Through which indigenous people were forcibly converted to Christianity."

"Last line of the poem: This one is the faith that is not monotheistic," Yeshua read the sentence, and then turned to Aiden.

"Although Christianity is referred to as one of the three monotheistic faiths, it is the only one of the three that truly can't be considered monotheistic, because monotheism—by definition—is the belief in one god," Aiden said. "Christians argue that the Trinity of the Father, the Son, and the Holy Spirit are not three deities, but three separate entities who exist as one substance, yet they don't realize the fallacy in that argument that merely serves to justify their faith."

"Otherwise, why pray to Jesus, or refer to Jesus as God," Yeshua surmised.

"Hence, the belief that the archangel Gabriel descended upon the earth, because men had corrupted the Word of God, and charged Mohammad with the task of reminding the world that there is no god, but God," Aiden said.

"Well done, professor," Sarai said before her face disappeared from the screen. Another image appeared on the laptop's monitor. "Take this image with you. You will need it to reveal the secret of scripture. I'll see you at our next rendezvous."

35
CROWNE PLAZA TEL AVIV CITY CENTER
Tel Aviv, Israel
10:55 a.m.

Miriam exited the elevator to the main lobby of the hotel. It bustled with activity as guests walked to and fro. Couples walked hand-in-hand, business men and women checked in and out at the front desk, while tourists confirmed they had everything they'd need in their satchels and purses. Sunlight cascaded through the floor-to-ceiling plain glass windows. The sky was clear and boundless beyond the glass.

Miriam made her way through the air-conditioned lobby and arrived at the lounge with chic décor reminiscent of cosmopolitan cities in the West and did not feel out of place in the Middle East. She sat on a red leather sofa, anxious about Susan's arrival. *God, I hope she isn't delayed*, she thought to herself as she slid her palms against the grey fabric of her dress slacks. Her red, turtleneck design top was a conservative choice given the restrictions of her destination, yet it consisted of thin cotton fabric to let her skin breathe in the pressing heat of the region.

In only a matter of minutes she saw Susan enter through the front doors of the lobby. She too wore modest attire. Her Ann Taylor ¾ sleeve wrap top with soft jersey fabric was ideal for the climate. The crossover, high v-neck design appropriate for the conservative values of the region even with its flattering fit as she made her way toward Miriam. It wasn't until she neared that Miriam noticed just how much her top accentuated her green eyes.

"Susan, hi, thank you for coming," Miriam stood to greet her.

"Miriam, it's so good to see you," she embraced her.

"It's been what, three years?" Miriam pulled away.

"I know, I'm sorry, it's just after Lorenzo…" she lowered her gaze.

THE SECRET OF SCRIPTURE

"I understand, and I'm sorry things turned out the way they did," Miriam took hold of Susan's hands.

No, you don't understand, Susan thought to herself. *I hate it when people say they understand; yet they've never grieved the loss of a loved one.*

"I tried reaching out to you after—"

"I know, but I just needed to be alone for a while to reassess my life. Lorenzo and I had been together for five years that to lose him so suddenly, and then to discover he had been lying to me about so many things," Susan sighed.

"I can't even begin to imagine what that must have felt like for you," Miriam squeezed Susan's hands.

"It's in the past," Susan shook her head. "We're here now, and Aiden needs our help."

"I'm still in shock about the terrorist attack on the Old City?" Miriam met her gaze.

"It's unbelievable! Have they figured out who's behind the attack?"

"Not that I'd heard on the television before I came down," Miriam shook her head. "Apparently, the authorities are expected to evacuate the Old City, but the inhabitants and the faithful are gathering, which may make it difficult. Do you still think you'll be able to help me sneak into the Old City?"

"Most definitely," Susan said. "I specialize in gaining access to places where no one is allowed to enter."

"Do you want to drive, or should I drive?" Miriam asked. "It'll probably take us over an hour to get there with all the traffic."

"I'll do you one better," Susan smiled mischeviously. "I have a helicopter on standby less than a mile from here. He's a friend who owes me a favor, and will get us there in half-an-hour."

"Oh my God, Susan, that's great!" Miriam said with a sigh of relief. "Thank you so much."

"Like I said before, don't thank me just yet," Susan winked. "We still have to get you there, and you'll owe me when this is over."

36
EL-AMIN RESIDENCE
West Chicago, IL.
3:55 a.m.

Priya continued to ask Prescott questions that Nagi instructed her to translate, but Prescott merely answered by shaking his head. Nagi leaned back in his chair and exhaled as he stared up at the ceiling.

"I don't know what to make of this," Nagi finally said. "He's not from Israel. He has never been to Israel. He's not associated with anyone who lives in Israel, and he has no knowledge of who's behind the attacks in Israel."

"Screw this," Angelo snapped as he brandished his weapon, rocked back the slide, and aimed it directly at Prescott. "He's not worth anything to us alive, so I'm ending this charade and dumping the body."

"No-no-no-no-no!" Nagi protested. "You promised you wouldn't shoot him."

"That was before he proved to be more trouble than he's worth." Angelo stepped forward and pressed the barrel of his gun against Prescott's forehead.

"Wait-wait-wait-wait-wait!" Prescott turned away with his arms up.

"Hold the fuckin' phone," Nagi cast Prescott an incredulous glance. "You speak English?"

"I knew this asshole was up to something," Angelo snapped.

"Fuck it, man, shoot him," Nagi threw his arms up and turned away in his swivel chair.

"No, no, please, listen I have information," Prescott pled.

"Do we look like we're interested in cutting a deal?" Angelo leaned in, "I put my career on the line over your bullshit."

"The information I have could potentially salvage your career," Prescott contested.

"You don't have much of a career anyway, dude, so just shoot the bastard for putting us through this shit," Nagi shrugged.

"This information is worth hundreds of millions of dollars," Prescott said.

"Hundreds of millions?" Nagi swiveled back around, and then he glanced up at Angelo. "Couldn't hurt to listen."

Angelo shrugged.

"All right, start talking," Nagi said.

37
BREAKING NEWS i-24NEWS
Israel
11:00 a.m.

In the wake of the bombing at the Tower of David Museum, thousands converged on the gates to the Old City. Media vans weaved through the crowds at a snail's pace as each outlet jockeyed for position to provide exclusive coverage to their audiences. Every television channel and online news outlet centered its attention on Jerusalem.

"Binyamin Shalev here of i24 News bringing you live coverage from around the world," the news anchor appeared on screens all over the globe. "For those of you who are just joining us, we are back with more on the devasting tragedy that occurred less than an hour ago in the Old City of Jerusalem. A terrorist group calling itself the Sons of Light claimed responsibility for the attack and is calling for the expulsion of Palestinians from Israel, or else they will execute relatives of world leaders from nations deemed enemies of Israel if their demands are not met."

"It's all a bit confusing," a political analyst began to speak. "These terrorists want full control over the Al-Aqsa compound to be turned over to authorities in Israel, yet they destroyed an important site in Jewish history."

"The citadel as it stood until today dates back to the 13th century, it was built over a series of earlier fortifications spanning back to the era of the Hasmonean kings," Binyamin said. "The question that remains now is: What will the nations of the world do as I imagine many of them are reaching out to their families to ensure their children are safe and not being held captive by the terrorists?"

"Yes, those personal measures are being taken behind the scenes. On the world stage, the U.N. has called for a special session as dictated under the resolution of 377A(V) in November of 1950," the political analyst said.

"Can you tell us more about the resolution?" Binyamin said.

"Basically, when the General Assembly is not in session and there is a breach of peace or act of aggression, an emergency special session is called to discuss the possibility of utilizing armed force to maintain or restore international peace."

"This is imperative, now more than ever," Binyamin said.

"Indeed, it is," the analyst added. "World nations have been at odds over the situation in Israel for seventy years. The United States allegiance to Israel has been a point of contention for many Arab states, but in the beginning when the U.S. supported the Balfour Declaration of 1917, then-President Franklin D. Roosevelt had assured Palestinian Arabs in 1945 that America would not intervene without consulting both the Jews and the Arabs in that region."

"Will you elaborate on the fallout that occurred?" Binyamin asked.

"After President Truman took office, he established a special cabinet in the summer of 1946 to study the issue in Palestine. In the aftermath of World War II, it was decided that displaced Jews be allowed to migrate to Palestine, but in controlled numbers," the analyst continued. "U.N. Resolution 181 recommended the Partition of Palestine into a Jewish and Arab state, and under the resolution, the area of religious significance in Jerusalem was to remain a corpus separatum."

"Corpus separatum, which comes from Latin to mean: separate entity," Binyamin said.

"Yes, and as a separate entity it would have remained under international control administered by the United Nations," the analyst said.

"A matter of great significance given the tragedy that occurred nearly an hour ago," Binyamin said somberly.

"In light of these events, I wouldn't be surprised if we hear of militaries mobilizing within the hour," the analyst said.

THE SECRET OF SCRIPTURE

"Pardon the interruption, but it appears we are receiving another transmission from the Sons of Light," Binyamin said. "Stay with us as we go live with their feed."

"The first hour has passed and you have chosen not to heed our warning," Anwar said from beneath a black hood. He stood over an unidentified hostage who had a white hood over their head. "Politicians send the sons and daughters of the poor into war zones to fight their battles. Now they will suffer the anguish other parents have endured in the name of their war on terror."

The cries and pleas of the other hostages could be heard though they did not appear on screen. Anwar brandished a bloodstained machete and brought it to his hostage's neck. "One by one, until sunset, we will mark the hours with blood. 'And give these rebels, the people of Israel, this message from the Lord: O house of Israel, I will no longer tolerate your detestable practices!'"

Anwar raised the machete over his right shoulder. He swung down hard and fast. The screen went blank just before the blade made contact. The group of hostages' off-camera screamed in terror. A thud could be heard just before the transmission terminated.

38
NORTHWESTERN UNIVERSITY
Evanston, IL.
4:00 a.m.

The traffic cameras in DuPage County provided a visual of the vehicle they believed Marquez was driving in: a late model sedan with three occupants and a license plate that registered to the village of Skokie. Knowing it was not Angelo's luxury SUV, he concluded that Angelo may have been attempting to elude authorities by using someone else's vehicle, and proceeded to track Angelo's position based on his cell phone's GPS tracker signal.

"There it is," Cruz pointed ahead as the sedan passed eastbound on Clark Street in front of the Administrative Offices of Northwestern University."

"I saw it," Solinski said as the squad approached the end of Orington Ave—a one-way street that t-boned at Clark—and slowed down enough to ensure no pedestrians approached the corners.

After he turned the corner, he sped up and instructed Cruz to initiate traffic stop procedures with their dispatch center.

"Base, copy a traffic stop," Cruz spoke into the radio mic on his shoulder.

Solinski caught up to the vehicle. He turned on his squad's emergency lights, and sounded off the siren in short bursts of rapid succession. The vehicle slowed as it pulled over curbside.

"Vehicle twenty-eight is L-lincoln, A-Adam, W-William, S-Sam, T-Tom, D-David, T-Tom," he paused briefly before he asked, "need a repeat?"

"Negative, I copied the twenty-eight," the dispatcher said over the radio. She repeated the license plate and provided a description of the vehicle as registered with the Illinois Secretary of State along with the driver's name and home address, and added that the registered owner's drivers license was valid with no outstanding warrants, or restrictions.

"Ten-four," Cruz said.

He, Solinski, and the two officers in the back seat proceeded to exit the squad and approached the vehicle on both sides. Solinski stopped just shy of being directly beside the driver side window, which forced the driver to look over his shoulder. Cruz did the same at the front passenger side of the vehicle, while the two other officers flashed their flashlights into the rear windows.

"Is there a problem officer?" the twenty-something year old driver asked.

Solinski peered into the vehicle to get a better view of the passengers inside. *Marquez isn't in this vehicle.* "Where are you coming from at this hour?" he asked.

"We were visiting some friends, why?"

"And who were these friends?"

"I don't see how that is pertinent to you stopping me on my way home."

"You live in Skokie," Solinski said. "Aren't you a bit past your destination?"

"I believe I'm at liberty to take whichever route I choose," the young man said.

"True, but did you have another passenger this evening?"

"I still don't see how that is pertinent to the reason for this traffic stop."

"You sure seem to ask a lot of questions for someone who is on his way home," Solinski said.

"I study pre-law here at Northwestern University, so—"

"Yes, well, studying the law and enforcing the law are two different things," Solinski cut him off.

"And what law are you enforcing today, officer?"

"It's Sergeant," Solinski snapped.

"My apologies, Sergeant," the young man replied. "Though I must also ask why the Chicago police is enforcing the law in Evanston. Isn't this a bit out of your jurisdiction?"

"I have reason to believe that a device used in the commission of a crime is inside this vehicle?" Solinski said.

"Interesting," the young man feigned being convinced. "What was the crime?"

"I am not at liberty to say," Solinski said.

"Where did this crime occur?"

"I cannot divulge that information at this time," Solinski said.

"You can't, or you won't?"

Solinski straightened his back and sighed. *This damn kid*, he thought to himself. He glanced up at Cruz and the two veteran officers, who had scanned the vehicle through the glass, but saw no sign of Marquez, or his cellphone in plain sight.

"Let me make this easy for you, Sergeant," the young man said. "I'm well within my rights to inquire about the reason behind your decision to initiate this traffic stop. You say you're investigating a crime, however, you have no proof that I have committed a crime. Furthermore, unless the crime you're investigating occurred in your primary jurisdiction—Chicago—you aren't authorized to make an arrest in another police department's jurisdiction."

"Do you want me to arrest you for obstruction of justice?" Solinski snapped.

"On what grounds? What exactly am I obstructing?"

"James, quit antagonizing the officer. He's just doing his job," the woman in the front passenger seat said.

"I'm not antagonizing him. I'm merely exercising my rights."

"You should listen to your lady-friend, she's talking with some sense," Solinski said.

"Well, she's not pre-law, so she doesn't know which questions to ask under these circumstances," James said.

THE SECRET OF SCRIPTURE

"Right," Solinski said. "Sir, may I see your driver's license, registration and proof of insurance?"

"I can't believe it took you this long to ask," James said.

"Since you know the law so well, then you know you are required to provide me with both upon request," Solinski said.

"Perhaps, yet you have not provided me with a clear and concise explanation about any charge or citation, despite my respectful requests." James shifted in his seat. "You and I both know that the 4th Amendment prohibits you from conducting unreasonable searches and seizures. A traffic stop qualifies as a 'seizure' within the context of the 4th Amendment, so unless you are able to provide specific articulable facts that justify a reasonable suspicion of criminal activity, then this traffic stop is a violation of my 4th Amendment rights."

"Your license, registration and proof of insurance, sir," Solinski said.

"James, please," the woman beside him pled.

James knew that by law he was required to provide the officer with the information he requested, but did not have to answer any other questions the officer asked. He told Solinski that he had to reach into his back pocket to retrieve his wallet, which contained his driver's license, and then he had to retrieve his registration and proof of insurance from the glove compartment.

"Just don't make any sudden movements," Solinski said.

Cruz and the two vets each placed a hand on their sidearms, but did not brandish their weapons. James handed Solinski the information he requested, and remained silent when Solinski told him he'd be right back. Solinski walked back to his squad and climbed into the driver's seat to enter the name, date of birth and driver's license number into the computer.

A moment later, a response confirmed the information that Dispatch provided when he initiated the traffic stop. He contemplated his next move. He knew that James would not consent to a search of his vehicle, and without conducting that search there was no way for Solinski to find Marquez's cellphone.

He reached across the dash and took hold of the tablet Cruz had used to monitor Marquez's movements. The red dot blinked at their current location. "If you're not here now, then when did you get out of the vehicle?"

Cruz approached the squad and climbed into the front passenger seat. "What's the next move, Sarge?"

"The tracking signal indicates that Marquez's cellphone is in that car," Solinski stared ahead.

"Yeah, well, Matlock-in-the-making over there isn't likely to cooperate further," Cruz said.

"Aren't you a little young to know about Matlock?"

"It was my grandmother's favorite show. She used to make me watch it with her while my mom was at work," Cruz shrugged.

"And your dad?" Solinski asked.

"Never knew him," Cruz shook his head.

"I see, well," Solinski began to say, but his words trailed off when another vehicle approached from the opposite direction of travel. He shielded his eyes from the headlights shinning through his windshield. "Fucking great."

"Evanston PD," Cruz read the decal on the side of the squad as it pulled to a stop.

"Here's hoping they don't whine about us stepping on their toes," Solinski opened his squad door and exited the vehicle.

39
EL-AMIN RESIDENCE
West Chicago, IL.
4:10 a.m.

Angelo and Nagi listened as Prescott recounted the events that led them to the moment their fates intertwined. A tale that seemed improbable, a destiny two thousand years in the making, and somehow it all connected to the events Aiden and Miriam were contending with in the Old City of Jerusalem.

"So, let me get this straight," Angelo finally said. "You know nothing about this Identity Theft ring I have been investigating?"

"It's as I said before," Prescott shrugged. "My employer sends me an envelope containing three forms of identification, which includes a passport, credit cards, and cash for the country I am traveling to, and a briefing on the item, or items I must retrieve. The passports, credit cards and identification are provided by an entity unknown to us. Perhaps their anonymity protects them in the event one of us is taken into custody."

"That's pretty smart, actually," Nagi said.

"What about your employer, Omar, how does he communicate with these people?" Angelo asked.

"Honestly, I don't know. I only meet with him to discuss the items I am hired to retrieve, and then again to hand him the items directly."

"And he is in the Middle East?"

"A lion seldom leaves his territory," Prescott said.

"The scrolls you were hired to retrieve," Nagi interjected. "Were you able to obtain them?"

"No," Prescott shook his head. "I had arranged a meeting for the exchange with a rabbi, but when he arrived at the motel room without the scrolls I knew the deal had gone south."

"A rabbi?" Angelo looked at him askance.

"Would you go to a banker in order to obtain a recipe for baking cookies?" Prescott said.

"He's got a point," Nagi said.

"What about the money you were supposed to use to purchase the scrolls?" Angelo asked, as he made a mental note of the rabbi at the hospital.

"I kept it in the safe of the hotel room that I originally checked in to when I first arrived in Chicago. I knew better than to bring it with me to the motel where we scheduled our first meeting, because I've learned to follow my instincts in these matters."

"What's so special about these scrolls?" Angelo's gaze shifted from Prescott to Nagi, and then back to Prescott.

"Oh brother, if you only knew," Nagi swiveled his chair around and ran his fingers over his desk. "To better understand the importance of the two scrolls that Black Jesus here is trying to acquire, we need to look at the bigger picture."

Images of the Dead Sea Scrolls appeared on the monitors.

"Considered the greatest archaeological find in history, the Dead Sea Scrolls remained hidden in the caves of Qumran near the Dead Sea for roughly 2,000 years. It serves to note that their discovery in 1947 occurred the year before the State of Israel was established in the modern era," Nagi said.

"I thought all of the scrolls were kept in Israel?" Angelo said.

"At the Shrine of the Book at the Israel Museum," Prescott added.

"Most of the ones that were found, yes," Nagi said. "However, political turmoil and human greed has led to some unscrupulous activity since their discovery."

"What do you mean?" Angelo said.

"Although the majority of the Dead Sea Scrolls were written in Ancient Hebrew—or Biblical Hebrew—and Aramaic, there are other scrolls that were written in Old Hebrew, also referred to as ancient paleo-Hebrew, which fell out of use during the fifth century B.C.E." Nagi replied. "Translating the scrolls was a painstaking process that took decades. Part of the controversy that arose over the years revolved around the fact that Jewish scholars were excluded from the original team charged with studying and translating the scrolls."

"They were all Christian, correct?" Prescott said.

"Yes, which led people to speculate that the scrolls contained a hidden truth about Jesus that the Vatican feared would undermine its authority," Nagi said.

"Did they contain anything of the sort?" Angelo asked.

"Nothing in the scrolls is directly connected to Jesus, however they do provide modern minds with a better understanding of Jesus' broader Jewish context," Nagi said. "All of the translated and untranslated texts were made available to scholars worldwide in 1991. The Biblical Archaeological Society published a computerized version, while the Israel Antiquities Authority authorized a microfiche edition."

"Omar did tell me that historians, theologians, archaeologists and linguists all have access to digital copies of the texts," Prescott said, "but that it has been confirmed that there are two missing scrolls."

"Two scrolls that were stolen and sold onto the Black Market," Nagi said. "I heard about it a few years ago."

"What's so important about these two scrolls?" Angelo asked.

"That is the question of the hour, indeed," Nagi turned to Angelo and Prescott. "The thing about Ancient Hebrew writing, which is vastly different from the Hebrew letters used in modern times is that it was a pictoral language that also represented sound. In essence, it was through Ancient Hebrew that God is believed to have revealed truths about Himself."

"You mean, like a code?" Angelo's brow furrowed.

"Yep," Nagi nodded.

"What code?" Angelo asked.

"As long as the scrolls remain hidden, that remains a mystery," Nagi said. "All we have to work with is in what is known as the Bible Code using Modern Hebrew, but I venture to guess that would lead to an incomplete message."

"How do you even know that these missing scrolls will contain a message?" Angelo placed his hands on his hips.

"We know this because of the scrolls that were found at Qumran," Nagi turned back to the monitors. "The Dead Sea Scrolls not only contained all the books of the Old Testament—aka the Torah—sans the book of Esther, but they revealed that the text virtually remained unchanged despite the many translations since 200 B.C.E. Making them the oldest surviving text of the Hebrew Bible ever found."

"How did they survive for so long?" Angelo studied the images on the monitors.

"That's because of the Essenes," Prescott said.

"Look who knows his history," Nagi glanced over his shoulder.

"I heard it's just a theory," Prescott added.

"The most logical theory at the moment," Nagi said.

"I don't understand," Angelo turned to Prescott, and then Nagi. "Why is it just a theory?"

"According to the historian Josephus, the Essenes were a Jewish sect that broke away from the Temple after a disagreement with the Sadducees over adherence to Jewish law," Nagi said. "They devoted themselves to a communal life of poverty, ritual purity, and asceticism."

"I've heard of the Pharisees, but I only know of the Sadducees from what is in the New Testament," Angelo confessed.

"That's because they left no written works of their own," Nagi said. "In short, they originated from the Zadokites, were the conservative wealthy elite in Jerusalem who maintained political and social stability to preserve their economic interests by accommodating foreign rulers, which is one of the reasons they were despised by their contemporaries."

"I suppose some things never change when you think of wealthy conservatives being hated for preserving their financial interests," Angelo scoffed.

"It's the way of the world, my friend," Nagi shrugged. "In any case, the Sadducees only adhered to written scriptures, which meant that they rejected oral interpretations of Biblical law. They also rejected the Pharisaic doctrine of individual resurrection, because there is no such doctrine explicity mentioned in the Hebrew Bible. And just as the Sadducees perceived the Pharisees as being lax in observance of the laws of God, so too did the Essenes view the Pharisees and Sadducees in the same manner. So much so, that they referred to the other two sects as 'seekers of smooth things.'"

"That's when history records that they left Jerusalem for Qumran," Prescott said.

"Taking with them scrolls that they later copied and stored in clay jars that were left untouched for two millennia," Nagi said.

"How is this just a theory, then?" Angelo asked.

"When the Romans destroyed the Second Temple, they set out to annihalate any remaining factions that would dare to rebel against the power of Rome."

"If this was just a group of poor priests, why would Rome consider them a threat?"

"Leading up to the arrival of Jesus, the Roman authorities were fed up with having already crushed two-dozen or so movements and their would-be messiahs," Nagi said. "Given that the Essenes believed they were living in the end of days and referred to their leader as The Teacher of Righteousness, the Romans simply couldn't risk another uprising."

"So they attacked a group of defenseless priests?" Angelo shook his head.

"According to Jospehus, as soon as the Essenes learned of the approaching Roman legions they scrambled to preserve their writings and teachings in clay jars, which they stored in a series of caves near the Dead Sea." Nagi tapped on his desk. A map of the area near the Dead Sea appeared on one of the monitors with site markers for Jerusalem and Qumran."

"They remained there for 2,000 years?" Angelo asked.

"Yep," Nagi nodded.

"It's a theory in some circles, because there are scholars who claim there is no evidence to definitively connect the scrolls to the Essenes," Prescott said.

"The only thing we have to go on is the basic logic of human behavior with regard to the promiximity of the site where they lived in Qumran and the caves," Nagi said.

"I don't understand," Angelo shook his head. "What do you mean?"

"If they hid the scrolls in the caves when they learned of an impending doom, why didn't they return for the scrolls after the danger had passed?" Nagi said.

"Unless there were no survivors," Angelo concluded.

"Exactly," Nagi said, "because human nature dictates that even after some calamity—say a hurricane, earthquake, or fire—people return home to salvage whatever they can find amid the ruins."

"Fast-forward two thousand years to when the scrolls are discovered, and we have a collection of priceless artifacts," Prescott said.

"Two of which you are tasked with obtaining for your employer," Angelo turned to Prescott.

Prescott nodded.

"How do I even know if you're telling the truth?" Angelo squared his shoulders. "You pretended not to speak English until twenty minutes ago."

"To be honest, it's just that I didn't remember how to speak it," Prescott clarified. "I knew what I wanted to say, but for some reason—"

THE SECRET OF SCRIPTURE

"You only knew how to verbalize it in Ancient Hebrew," Nagi cut him off. "Temporary amnesia caused by blunt force trauma to the head."

"The rabbi at the hospital said you couldn't know Ancient Hebrew without a formal education in that idiom," Angelo said.

"There was a rabbi at the hospital?" Prescott asked.

"It's not unheard of," Nagi shrugged. "Death doesn't discriminate, so it stands to reason that people find comfort in the presence of a clergyman when they're in the hospital. He could have been there for someone else."

"In any case, how do you explain your knowledge of this ancient language?" Angelo pressed.

"The story behind it actually goes back to how I met Omar after a man attempted to steal a relic from the home where I was living," Prescott said.

40

CHURCH OF THE HOLY SEPULCHRE OLD CITY
Jerusalem, Israel
11:15 a.m.

Aiden and Yeshua stared at the image on the screen. It appeared to be an incomplete drawing in black ink.

"What do you suppose it means?" Yeshua tilted his head.

"I don't know, but it appears to be part a bigger picture," Aiden studied it momentarily.

"What did she mean by take it with you? Are we supposed to take this laptop with us?" Yeshua said.

"That *is* one option," Aiden shrugged.

"But it has a bomb built into it!"

"We deactivated it, remember?"

"Just because she claims we have deactivated it doesn't make it so," Yeshua said.

"True, but do you really want to leave it here?"

Yeshua contemplated their predicament. "You're right, we can't leave it here, but if we take it with us, we could be walking into a trap."

"What do you mean?" Aiden looked at him perplexed.

"What if the plan is to get us to gather all of the explosive devices to one central location where they can be detonated simultaneously?"

"You're right," Aiden said. "I hadn't thought of that, but if they left it here then it stands to reason they could have simply left it at this unknown location where you think we are headed."

"Good point. I can get this to our bomb squad to ensure it is deactivated, or at best have it detonated in a controlled environment to avoid mass casualties," Yeshua said.

"That's probably the best course of action," Aiden agreed. "But how do we link the image to the others that she alluded to?"

THE SECRET OF SCRIPTURE

"I don't know," Yeshua pursed his lips. After a brief moment of silence he suggested they take pictures of the image with their cellphones to utilize later in the event they are unable to retrieve the image on the computer screen again.

They closed the laptop and zipped the case closed. Yeshua tucked it under his arm and motioned for Aiden to lead the way to the location of the next bomb. As they ascended the steps of the now mostly empty church they heard the familiar voice of the priest who questioned them earlier.

"Right this way officers," his voice echoed off the stones. "I last left them in the Chapel of the Finding of the Cross, and I did not see them among the crowd of visitors who stood in the courtyard near the entrance."

Yeshua grabbed Aiden's arm and pulled him back. They froze and listened as the voices and footsteps drew near. Yeshua motioned for Aiden to follow him. Together they darted past the chapel's entrance at the top of the staircase and raced toward a secluded corner behind the main altar of the Chapel of St. Helena.

"You're going to have to continue on without me, professor," Yeshua said in a low voice.

"What do you mean?" Aiden cast him a perplexed glance.

"Given the circumstances, there is no way my superiors will allow you to remain in harm's way. They'll insist that you go back to headquarters for questioning in lieu of letting you assist with finding these bombs."

"Can't you just explain to them—"

"Politics, professor," Yeshua cut him off. "Politics play a major role in world events. Make no mistake; this situation has already escalated to the world stage. An American in danger on Middle Eastern soil will only serve to undermine our goal of preventing this catastrophe. My colleagues and I are good at our jobs, but I fear no one else is as qualified as you are to thwart this catastrophe. Wait until I lead these officers away from here before you continue on ahead. I will find you later."

Aiden stared at Yeshua as he processed the chief inspector's instructions.

"Are you sure?" Aiden finally asked.

"You said you wanted to find this bastard who killed your friend, so find him," Yeshua said firmly.

The voices were only meters away.

"Wait until I've lead them away," Yeshua reminded him.

Aiden nodded and sunk back into the shadows as Yeshua turned and stepped away.

"There!" The priest pointed from the top of another staircase. "He's down there!"

"Pakad Yeshua Schwartz," an officer called out to him as he descended the steps to meet the chief inspector halfway. "Why have you not been answering your phone?"

"Bad signal, I suppose," Yeshua retrieved his phone from his pocket.

"You are to come with us," the officer said. "Commander Shalom insists we escort you back to headquarters."

"To headquarters?" Yeshua's brow furrowed. "What about the staging area for the evacuations?"

"The task has been given to someone else. You are to come with us to headquarters, immediately."

"That doesn't make any sense," Yeshua protested. "We need all hands on deck here."

"You may discuss the matter with the commander," the officer said before he turned to the two officers standing behind him. "Take him into custody."

"Why am I being arrested?"

"For failure to obey a direct order," the officer took possession of the laptop.

"Where is the other man?" The priest questioned Yeshua. "The professor that is always on the television."

THE SECRET OF SCRIPTURE

"Is that the man who the rookie, Shoter Moshe, said was with you?" The officer turned to Yeshua as he was being handcuffed with his hands behind his back.

"Yes, but I sent him ahead when I realized the danger," Yeshua lied.

"What danger?"

"That case you're holding contains a bomb," Yeshua nodded at the laptop.

"Are you mad?" the officer shouted.

"Don't worry," Yeshua said. "It's deactivated. I was on my way to take it to the bomb squad when you arrived."

"Let's get him and this bomb out of here before we have a war on our hands," the officer said.

"I didn't see the professor outside," the priest said.

"Well, in my experience, people like you only see what you want to see," Yeshua scoffed as the officers led him away.

Aiden watched silently from the shadows. He waited until they disappeared from view before he stepped forward. He stood alone near the main altar of one of the holiest shrines in Christendom. Sarai's words reminded him of Lazzaro's last words, and they echoed in his mind as he studied the image on his smartphone, *reveal the secret of scripture*.

41
TEL AVIV UNIVERSITY
Tel Aviv, Israel
11:20 a.m.

Matti pulled his squad up to the curb in front of the Vladimir Schreiber Institute of Mathematics at Tel Aviv University. He observed officers patrolling the perimeter and another standing guard at the front door.

"Is this the place?" he asked.

"Yes," Yisrael said as he unbuckled his seat belt. "Would you accompany me inside?"

Matti agreed, and together the two men exited the vehicle and made their way toward the front door.

"Hello again, Samal Sheni Badani," Yisrael greeted the sergeant when they stood before him. "I just need to gather some things and to make a few phone calls upstairs."

The sergeant nodded and opened the door to let them pass.

Matti eyed the higher-ranking officer and felt a strange knot in his stomach.

"The items you requested earlier have been left as you instructed," Badani said.

"Thank you, sergeant," Yisrael said over his shoulder.

Matti followed along in silence. He assumed the sergeant referred to the contact information that Dr. Avrohom had contacted his secretary about via text messages when they left the Old City.

"We'll have to take the stairs," Yisrael pushed through the heavy door that led into the stairwell. "The elevators have been out all morning."

Matti followed him and they ascended the steps two at a time. Yisrael maintained his pace as they passed the third floor, but Matti slowed and eventually stopped to lean against a railing.

"Are you okay, shoter?" Yisrael asked from above.

"I just need a minute," Matti said with labored breaths.

THE SECRET OF SCRIPTURE

"Let me guess, you're a smoker," Yisrael said.

Matti nodded as he struggled to steady his breathing.

"If you're not careful those poisonous chemicals will kill you."

Matti straightened up and proceeded to climb the steps again.

"You okay?" Yisrael waited for him to catch up.

"I'll be fine," Matti inhaled deeply. "Lead the way."

"Just two more flights," Yisrael proceeded ahead.

"I'm right behind you," Matti grasped the railing.

They arrived at the desired floor and stepped into the vacant corridor. Yisrael led Matti to Emmett's office and held the door open for the officer.

"Professor Emmett Ben Yaakov," Matti read the nameplate. "Isn't he the one who was murdered?"

"Yes, a tragedy," Yisrael pushed the door closed behind him.

"This is your office?" Matti turned to Yisrael.

"Not exactly," Yisrael shook his head. "He was letting me use it during my time here for the technological summit."

"I see," Matti nodded. An uneasy feeling tugged at his core.

"There should be a call list on the desk there, if you wouldn't mind grabbing it," Yisrael said as he turned away. "I've got to retrieve some files from this cabinet, and then we'll be on our way."

"I'm not sure we should touch anything given that this is a crime scene," Matti scanned the room and saw the blood on the floor.

"It's all right. I was here earlier with Pakad Schwartz and Professor Leonardo before we went to the Old City," Yisrael pulled the top drawer of the filing cabinet open. "Just grab the call list from the pile of papers."

Matti looked at the scattered sheets of paper without touching anything, but he didn't see anything that resembled a call list. "Are you sure it's here?"

"Yes," Yisrael glanced over his shoulder as he took hold of a needle that lay beside a gray plastic cylinder labeled: Lab Grade Chloroform. "It probably got shuffled with all the other papers there."

Matti reached into his uniform for a pen. He'd use that to move the papers around without contaminating evidence. He heard movement behind him, and then he felt a slight pinch in his neck. *What the*—" All went dark.

"Apologies, young man, but an injection directly into the bloodstream was necessary, because inhaling chloroform from a cloth would have taken a few minutes to render you unconscious, and well time is of the essence," Yisrael pressed the entire dosage into Matti's carotid artery and carefully laid him on the ground.

He proceeded to remove Matti's uniform from his body and laid the items aside when he was done. His cellphone chimed with an incoming message. He read the electronic missive and replied quickly. It took him only a few minutes to change clothes, and then he placed a call when he was done.

"One of the devices has been deactivated," Arwan said.

"Just as I anticipated," Yisrael tucked the uniform shirt into his pants.

"News reports indicate that the nations of the world are preparing for war," Arwan added.

"People are so predictable," Yisrael sighed. *My experiment is going according to plan.* "And the hostages?"

"They are cooperating," Arwan said.

"The prospect of death will do that to people," Yisrael scoffed.

"When should we be expecting you to arrive?"

"I should be there within the hour," Yisrael said.

"How do you want us to handle the professor?"

"Leave him to me," Yisrael said. "I want to see the expression on his face when he learns the truth before he dies."

42
SCHMIDT'S GIRLS COLLEGE
Jerusalem, Israel
11:25 a.m.

The MH-6 Little Bird helicopter hovered over a citadel-like structure east of the Damascus Gate across Sultan Suleiman Street. From their vantage point, Miriam and Susan saw first responders gathered near the Damascus Gate and in a parking lot just southeast of it. A torched vehicle was being towed away on a flatbed; an ambulance and fire engines were parked haphardly among a series of police squads. Traffic was at a standstill as police guided civilians away from the scene where Farhad's car had exploded.

"We're going to have to exit the helicopter here," Susan shouted over the thrumming of the helicopter's propelers. "This is as close as he can get us considering what's happening in the Old City!"

Miriam nodded and gave Susan two thumbs up. Despite the noise cancellation headsets they wore with built-in microphones, it was near impossible to hear her clearly, but she made out what Susan said and prepared to dismount from the helicopter.

Susan handed Miriam a backpack. She grabbed another one for herself, and then thanked the pilot before they removed the headsets and opened the hatch door. They leapt out, and then Susan pushed the hatch door shut before she led Miriam toward a battlement-like wall several meters away. The helicopter floated away as they arrived at the low wall.

The rooftop terrace offered a magnificent view over the Old City that spanned from the Mount of Olives to Al-Aqsa Compound and the Church of the Holy Sepulchre. The Paulus Haus had the air of a crowning achievement in modern architecture with an ancient spell.

"Quick, over here," Susan led her along the wall of the rooftop terrace.

"What's wrong?" Miriam asked when she crouched beside her.

"Nothing, yet, hopefully," Susan peered over an opening. "There are armed guards atop the Damascus Gates. Though I'm sure the helicopter got their attention, I didn't want them to see us."

"Shit!" Miriam hissed. "You think they'll come looking for us?"

"They'll definitely have officers check the grounds, but as long as they haven't seen us, they won't know who to look for," Susan said.

"What's with the backpacks?" Miriam asked.

"They're equipped with things we'll need in the tunnels like flashlights, gloves and water, but I also had my friend pack us rappelling gear in the event we can't gain access through a door to a stairwell."

"Here's hoping," Miriam crossed her fingers.

"Let's move, there's a door right over there, but stay low," Susan maneuvered swiftly, shifting sideways in a squatted position to ensure she wouldn't be spotted by the guards using the scopes on their rifles.

Miriam followed, trying to keep up and to keep her balance as she kept falling forward with each step. *Clearly she must do squats on a regular basis*, she thought to herself as she tried to mimic Susan's movements.

Susan pulled the door handle when they arrived at the rooftop entrance. "Shit, it's locked," she hissed.

"Now what?" Miriam asked. "Do we rappel?"

"Not yet," Susan shook her head. She shook off her backpack. "I want to try something first."

"Works for me," Miriam said.

"Keep an eye out," Susan said as she unzipped her backpack and searched for her lock-picking tool set. She quickly glanced up at Miriam when her handgun moved into view, but Miriam's attention was focused in the direction of the Damascus Gate. "Got it!"

THE SECRET OF SCRIPTURE

Miriam turned back to Susan.

Susan resealed her backpack and threw it over her shoulder. She shifted to squat directly in front of the lock and moved skillfully to unlock the door. Miriam kept glancing over her shoulder. Sweat beaded on her forehead as the sun beat down on them. The faint breeze barely provided comfort. The locking mechanism clicked.

"There we go," Susan pressed the lever lock on the door handle and she felt the latch bolt giveway. "Come on," she motioned for Miriam to follow her as she pulled the wooden door open.

Bullets struck the wood and the concrete wall and frame.

"I knew it!" Susan hissed as more bullets rang.

They slithered inside and pulled the door shut.

"Why are they shooting at us?" Miriam asked.

"Arriving by helicopter amid all the commotion in the Old City probably wasn't the best idea," Susan admitted.

"You think?" Miriam snapped.

"Hey, I warned you this would be dangerous," Susan glared at her.

"You're right, I apologize," Miriam said.

"Don't worry about it. We simply need to keep our heads, or we'll either end up in jail, or dead."

"What's behind door number three?" Miriam asked.

"Let's find out," Susan led the way down a shadowed corridor.

Sunlight fell through the glassless squarefoot-sized windows typical of ancient stone structures that were spaced evenly apart and provided enough light for them to see where they were headed.

"What if someone in the building sees us?" Miriam said in a low voice.

"It's not likely, given that school doesn't resume for another week and a half," Susan said. "We'll probably see a few staff members, but definitely no students."

FELIX ALEXANDER

They arrived at another wooden door and stood silently for a brief moment to listen for movement on the other side. Susan pulled the door open just enough to peer into the chamber.

"Coast is clear," she said and she led Miriam out of the corridor.

Sunlight fell through the large open windows. The limestone floors and walls appeared to make the room glow.

"I'd always wished I had attended school here," Miriam scanned the room in awe. Although the original college was established in the late 1800's during the Ottoman Empire and was frequently closed during times of war, this grandois structure entrusted to the Sisters of the Congregation of Jesus had become a prestigious institution that continues to follow its German traditions in a predominantly Muslim region.

"Not only has the original layout of this building been preserved, but to this day it contains the furniture that was donated at the time of Kaiser Wilhelm the Second," Susan ran her fingers over an elegant desk.

"Isn't it a tragedy to think of what is lost during times of conflict?" Miriam continued to follow her.

"And the people lost, too," Susan replied silently.

"I'm sorry, Susan, truly," Miriam placed a hand on her shoulder.

Susan froze.

Sirens wailed and car horns honked in the distance. Miriam and Susan stood silently in the vacant room. The memory of Lorenzo being shot haunted her dreams. For a while, she blamed herself. She thought that if only she had never agreed to the job Lazzaro had contracted her to do—acquire the lost bible—then Lorenzo would still be alive.

She no longer blamed herself. She knew better, now. It was Aiden's fault. Had he followed in his father's footsteps and went into the world of finance, just as Lorenzo had done, then he never would have been in a position to search for the lost bible.

Over the centuries, that damn book had caused more trouble than it was worth, she reflected. Lazzaro had entrusted it to Aiden, and when the magistrate realized Lorenzo had been excluded from its whereabouts he murdered him. Her life, her partner was taken from her over an ancient artifact that has once again disappeared.

Miriam, however, still had Aiden. And Aiden had enjoyed a prosperous career as a renowned professor of biblical studies. He gave interviews on national television and engaged audiences at international speaking events. He had joined the world's elite as a respected member of scholarly circles and the foremost expert on religious history.

They enjoyed a life together, whereas Susan grieved alone. That would change after today. The Preceptor had promised her it would, as long as she did her part to bring Miriam to the designated location before sunset.

Now, as Susan's thought returned to the present, she gave Miriam an appreciate smile over her shoulder.

"If you need anything," Miriam began to say.

"Right now, I need to get you into the Old City," Susan proceeded ahead.

Miriam followed. They approached the main door. Susan held it ajar as she peered through the opening. Voices echoed off the walls and high ceiling. They came from a lower level. Susan led Miriam out of the room. They glanced over the railing without being seen. Two staff members discussed agenda items for the final meeting they'd have before the school year commenced.

Pounding on the front doors thundered throughout the building.

Susan cursed under her breath and she hurriedly led Miriam toward a flight of stairs leading down to the next floor. An elderly nun opened the main door to a group of officers demanding entry into the building. The nun turned to a priest who approached her from behind.

"This way," Susan whispered as she and Miriam darted past an oakwood grandfather clock with a cross at its crown.

They fled down another flight of stairs and raced through a vacant corridor.

"What is the meaning of this?" The priest shouted behind them.

"You have intruders who gained access from the roof by way of helicopter!"

"What?"

Miriam and Susan glanced over their shoulders. No one was behind them, but they failed to see the woman who approached from another corridor as she turned the corner. The collison drew everyone's attention.

The officers shouldered past the priest and the nun and scattered.

"Sorry!" Miriam said. "Are you okay?"

"Who are you and what are you doing here?" the woman replied as she recovered from the fall.

"She's fine, come on," Susan urged.

"There they are!" An officer shouted to the others. He gave chase, and his comrades followed.

Susan and Miriam turned another corner and arrived at a set of glass doors leading into a courtyard. They pushed through the double doors and leapt over a short flight of steps. Susan shifted her backpack and reached inside as they sprinted across the vacant opening.

"Where are you doing?" Miriam asked.

"You'll see," Susan stopped at the opposite corner of the courtyard and waited for the officers to see them. "On my signal, run that way," she motioned with her head.

The group of policemen bolted through the door and spotted the women across the courtyard.

THE SECRET OF SCRIPTURE

"Now!" Susan shouted. Miriam took off past her. Susan waited until the officers were at a full sprint before she smashed two jars full of marbles at their feet. She turned and chased after Miriam. She laughed at the sound of the commotion behind her.

"Where to next?" Miriam said when they arrived at a secluded corner surrounded by tall pine trees.

"This way," Susan led her into one of three doors that each led into separate buildings. Sunlight pushed back the darkness when they entered, but the darkness swallowed them when she pulled the door shut. "Quick, your flashlight."

Miriam rummaged through her backpack and retrieved it. She turned it on and scanned the darkness.

"Shine it this way," Susan insisted, she felt around for a wooden bar. *Found it!* She lifted it from the corner and slid it into the securing mechanism attached to the doorframe and door. "That takes care of that," she dusted the dirt off her hands.

"Where are we?" Miriam scanned the room with her flashlight.

"This stairwell leads into the basement that was converted into a museum by the German Association of the Holy Land," Susan retrieved her flashlight and walked past Miriam.

"Isn't that where they keep models of Jerusalem from various time periods, which includes a model of Solomon's Temple?"

"The very same," Susan grabbed the handrail as she descended the steps.

"Won't we be seen?" Miriam followed. "The museum is open today."

"We'll blend in as we cut through the museum, though it generally isn't as busy as other tourist attractions, so just act natural."

"I can do natural, but what's the plan?"

"There's a door on the eastern most side of the museum that hasn't been used since the Six-Day War. There's a tunnel that originally led to the adjacent building built in 1965, but was secretly extended to connect to Zedekiah's Cave."

"How do you know this?"

"It's my job to know what no one else knows," Susan shrugged. "It's how I managed to successfully evade the authorities over the years."

"Do you still—"

"No, not since Lorenzo died," Susan cut her off. "And if you apologize one more time, Miriam, I swear..." her words trailed off.

"Just lead the way," Miriam said.

They arrived at the bottom of the darkened staircase.

"You ready?" Susan grabbed the door handle.

"Yes," Miriam said.

"Stay close. We'll be at the cave in no time."

43
NATIONAL HEADQUARTERS OF THE ISRAEL POLICE
Kiryat Menachem Begin
Jerusalem, Israel
11:30 a.m.

Upon entering police headquarters in handcuffs, Yeshua met the inquisitive looks from his co-workers and lowered his head in shame. The officers that took him into custody led him through the lobby that bustled with activity to an open elevator. Once inside, the lead officer selected the appropriate floor before he pressed the button to close the doors.

"Hold the elevator, please," a young female officer approached. "I have something for the pakad."

The lead officer shook his head as the doors closed.

"Why didn't you let her in?" Yeshua said. "She had something for me."

"Our instructions were clear," the lead officer turned to the chief inspector. "We are to escort you to your office, and you are to have no contact with anyone else."

"My office?"

"That is where the commander is waiting for you," the lead officer turned away.

The elevator dinged to indicate its arrival on the designated floor and the doors slid open. A robust man with a thick grey mustache and short-cropped hair approached as they crossed the threshold.

"What is the meaning of this?" the man demanded.

The lead officer recognized the man's offical looking uniform and noted the rank insignia on his shoulders.

"I appreciate your conerns, Sgan Nitzav Hefetz, but as Chief Superintendent, I'm sure you know to direct your queries to my commander," the lead officer said as he led Yeshua and his two officers around him.

"You're damn right, I will," Hefetz followed them to Yeshua's office.

FELIX ALEXANDER

When they arrived, they opened the door to find a tall, slender man on his cellphone and standing behind Yeshua's desk.

"Yes sir, I'll be in touch," he said before he terminated the call and placed his cellphone on the desk.

The officers led Yeshua into his office, and the chief superintendent followed.

"You only said you were bringing him in," Hefetz shouted.

"And that is precisely what I did," Commander Shalom stated calmly.

"You never said anything about dragging him in wearing handcuffs like some common thug!"

"I needed to send a message," Commander Shalom said.

"What message?" Hefetz said incredulously. "That a highly respected and decorated officer will not be afforded professional courtesy."

"The message that no one is above the law," Commander Shalom moved around the desk. "Have you forgotten that the Lahav 433 was established to investigate national crimes and corruption? My actions are consistent with our initiative. Now, if you'll please excuse us, I have some important matters to discuss with the pakad regarding why he chose to disobey a direct order."

"I demand to be present during this interrogation!" Hefetz insisted.

"This is not an interrogation, Sgan Nitzav," Commander Shalom said. "I assure you that you will be apprised of the details of our discussion in due time."

"If it is not an interrogation, then remove the handcuffs," Hefetz demanded.

Commander Shalom sighed and motioned for his officers to acquiesce the request.

"Thank you," Yeshua said as he rubbed his wrists.

"This will not be the end of it," Hefetz promised, and he turned to exit the office.

"He was carrying this when we found him," the lead officer handed the commander the laptop. "He says it's a bomb he disabled moments before we arrived."

The commander met Yeshua's gaze.

Yeshua nodded.

"What did you intend to do with this explosive after you disabled it?" Commander Shalom asked Yeshua.

"I had planned to turn it over to the bomb squad to ensure it was no longer active, and then have the evidence techs process it for any additional clues about the terrorists."

"Take this to the bomb squad," Commander Shalom handed it back to the lead officer. "Once they are certain it is no longer of any danger, have the evidence team process it accordingly."

"Yes, commander."

"You may leave us," Commander Shalom instructed his officers.

They exited the office. The chief superintendent continued his tirade as he returned to his own office. The last officer pulled the door closed behind him. The commander motioned for Yeshua to have a seat on one of the chairs in front of his desk.

"Pakad Yeshua Schwartz," Commander Shalom walked around to the front of the desk and leaned against it. He stood with arms crossed and a hand on his chin. "You've had an illustrious career up to this point, which leads me to wonder why you would jeopardize everything you have achieved amid the gravity of today's events."

"I had to follow up on a lead," Yeshua said. "You know as well as I do that ninety percent of good police work is cops following their hunches."

"What did you discover upon following this lead?"

"The bomb you just sent downstairs."

"And what led you to this bomb?"

"Evidence found at the Golden Gate."

"Interesting," Commander Shalom nodded. "What evidence was that, exactly?"

"The reference to Ezekiel that was left on the body we found inside the chamber of the modern entryway."

"The body that was left without skin and nearly picked clean by crows?"

"There was a small patch of skin left on the chest—"

"Yes, I'm aware of that," Commander Shalom cut him off. He turned and lifted a large envelope off the desk. "These were processed as a priority per your instructions."

He handed the envelope to Yeshua and stood to walk around to sit in the chair behind the desk as the chief inspector pulled the photos out of the envelope. The first few images were of the mutilation on the chest and the skeletal remains.

"The evidence technicians promptly arrived after you left. They processed the scene and the body just as they have been trained to do. They noted the incision in the skull that you relayed over the phone when you called them to the scene, but there's something that you missed."

Yeshua lifted his gaze from the photographs.

"One of the fingers was wrapped in plastic. Perhaps you didn't notice it given the darkness of the chamber, but it was the ring finger of the left hand. Someone intended for us to find it and use it to identify the victim."

"Who was it?"

"He has been identified as Adam Goertzel, the Chief Scientist of Hanson Robotics who was in charge of the Artificial Intelligence Humanoid Robots that were scheduled to be presented at the tech summit later today."

Yeshua lowered his gaze to the photographs as he shook his head. "Who would be capable of such an atrocity?"

"We're still working to figure that out, but what we do know is that he wasn't working alone," Commander Shalom said.

Yeshua met the commander's dark beady eyes.

THE SECRET OF SCRIPTURE

"You've identified an accomplice?"

"Her name is Susan Rosario," Commander Shalom pointed at the photographs in Yeshua's hands. "You'll see images of her having drinks with Adam in a hotel bar in Tel Aviv."

Yeshua flipped through the photos while the commander continued to speak.

"One of the images shows her slipping something in his drink when he turned to summon the bartender. They left the bar together, but Adam is never seen alive again." Commander Shalom sat up in his seat. "The toxicology report revealed that he was drugged with Rohypnol, better known by its street name, Roofie. Trace evidence of it was found in what remained of his brain."

"In other words, he witnessed his own mutilation?" Yeshua asked incredulously.

"Unless they killed him first," Commander Shalom said.

"What do you know about this woman?" Yeshua asked as he studied the photographs.

"What I know is as important as what you don't know," Commander Shalom said.

"What's that supposed to mean?" Yeshua met the commander's glare.

"You never did elaborate on how you made the connection between the Ezekeil reference and the location where you found the bomb."

Yeshua sighed and shifted in his seat. He did not want to reveal Aiden's assistance with the investigation lest the commander initiate a search to extract the professor from the Old City. *It is the Preceptor's wish that Aiden be the one to disable the bombs.*

"We'll come back to that," Commander Shalom broke the silence. "Why don't you explain to me why a chief inspector of the Jerusalem District was investigating a murder that occurred in the Tel Aviv District?"

"I needed to find the connection," Yeshua answered promptly.

"Why not have the authorities in Tel Aviv investigate the murder and apprise you of their findings?"

"There was no time to deal with all the red tape that would come with interjurisdictional procedure."

"Yet there was time enough for you to drive an hour out of your way, and then drive an hour back with a threat looming over the Old City."

"I was not aware of the threat to the Old City until after I had returned."

"That's when you returned with the professor," Commander Shalom said.

Yeshua pursed his lips. "I went to question him, because he was the last person to see Ben Yaakov alive. After his alibi checked out, I brought him on as a consultant, since I knew of his expertise in the field of Biblical Studies, and it's because of *him* that we located the second body."

"I'm aware of his involvement in this investigation," Commander Shalom said. "I wonder if you understand the full scope of his role in this scheme?"

"I'm afraid I don't understand what you are aiming at," Yeshua responded.

"The woman in the photographs that poisoned Adam Goertzel was once engaged to a man named Lorenzo de Medici," Commander Shalom said.

"That name means nothing to me," Yeshua shook his head.

"It should," Commander Shalom said. "He was the half-brother of Professor Aiden Leonardo."

Yeshua flinched.

"Lorenzo was being investigated by the F.B.I. a few years ago in connection to a Lost Bible the Turkish government claims their father, Lazzaro de Medici had stolen from right under their noses. Rumors persist that Lazzaro hired Susan to acquire the ancient artifact, but no one has been able to gather the evidence needed to prove it. Both Lazzaro and Lorenzo ended up dead, and according to Interpol Susan Rosario vanished three years ago, until she was spotted in these photographs."

Yeshua looked down at the images in his hands. He knew of Aiden's cooperation with the investigation that exposed government corruption, but he had no idea of an ancient relic having been at the center of the controversy.

"Oddly enough, it was shortly after these circumstances that the professor emerged as the preeminent scholar of Biblical studies, which leads one to wonder if *he* is in possession of the Lost Bible," Commander Shalom leaned back in his seat. "Doesn't it strike you as odd that he made the connections between the clues every step of the way?"

"But I don't understand," Yeshua began to say before his words trailed off.

"He played you, chief inspector, and now he's in the Old City playing God by igniting a war that threatens to destroy our holiest capital."

Yeshua reflected on the way Aiden spoke of Christianity and religion. Almost as if it was with veiled animosity that he recounted history. *Perhaps that is where the clerics and I diverge*, Yeshua remembered the professor's words.

"What are we going to do?" Yeshua met Commander Shalom's intense gaze.

"*You* are not going to do anything," Commander Shalom said. "You're off the case, and you are to remain here until this matter is resolved."

"You can't take me off this case!" Yeshua protested.

"I just did!" Commander Shalom snapped.

"What about the professor?"

"I'm sending in a team to take him into custody."

"But he's the only one who can deactivate the bombs!"

"How would you know that, chief inspector?" Commander Shalom cast him a curious glance.

Yeshua turned away in silence.

"I will not take you into custody out of respect for everything you have accomplished, but mark my words if I find evidence of your involvement in this catastrophe—" Commander Shalom stopped short of completing his threat.

After a brief silence, the commander stormed out of the room and slammed the door shut behind him. Yeshua heard the commander shout from the otherside of the door.

"Where are we on decrypting the feed to locate the hostages?"

A moment later, there was a soft knock at the door. Yeshua sighed and contemplated his next move. The knock came again.

"Come in," Yeshua cleared his throat.

"I'm sorry to interrupt, chief inspector," the young female officer who was at the elevator downstairs peered into his office. She moved strands of her bangs away from her face as she stepped inside. "I have something that the evidence techs insisted be brought directly to you."

Yeshua motioned for her to enter. She carefully pushed the door closed behind her, and then turned clutching the folder close to her chest.

"Give it here," he motioned. "What is your name?"

"My name is Abigail Epshteyn," she approached his desk. Her light brown eyes blinked rapidly as she handed him the file. He flipped through the pages, scanning each one quickly. She stood silently beside him, fidgeting.

"A partial fingerpring was found on the skull?" Yeshua turned his gaze to Abigail.

She nodded with a smile and directed him to turn the page.

"Partial fingerprint scan run through international database found a match to subject named," Yeshua read the statement in a low voice. "Dr. Yisrael Avrohom."

THE SECRET OF SCRIPTURE

44
EL-AMIN RESIDENCE
West Chicago, IL.
4:30 a.m.

Prescott had revealed that he grew up in an orphanage in London and ran with a group of boys—also orphans—who had formed a gang of theives that lived like brothers. In their youth, they had started off picking pockets and stealing fruit from the markets before they escalated their crimes to stealing motorcycles and cars. By their early 20's most of them ended up in jail, leaving Prescott to fend for himself. He, too, seemed on a direct path to prison when he was caught breaking into the home of a Jewish scholar who took pity on the young man and gave him a chance at redemption.

"What were you trying to steal from him?" Nagi asked. "I mean, what does a common thief know about the value of ancient Jewish literature? No offense."

"Honestly, I didn't know the value of what I had attempted to steal," Prescott said. "A man approached me one day, said he knew a few of my brothers, and offered to pay me five hundred pounds for a large scroll known as a Sefer Torah."

"Five hundred?" Nagi said. "Those are worth tens of thousands!"

"I know that now," Prescott shrugged.

"So, what happened when he caught you?" Angelo asked.

"He questioned me about why I was after the scroll," Prescott said. "After I told him I needed the money, because I was homeless, he offered me another path."

"What path was that?" Angelo said.

"He offered to let me live with him in exchange for doing things around the house."

"What things?"

"Fixing pipes, painting walls, building fences, tending to his garden, and cleaning."

THE SECRET OF SCRIPTURE

"What about the guy who originally approached you about stealing the scroll?" Angelo wondered.

"I never saw him again," Prescott shrugged. "I imagine that Peter—that was the name of the man who took me in—knew him, because he didn't seem surprised when I described the man who hired me."

"That's not unheard of when you consider the value of something like that," Nagi said.

"Then what happened?" Angelo pressed.

"One day while I was cleaning the library, Peter found me admiring the Sefer Torah. I realized in that moment that I had never seen anything so beautiful."

"Well, yeah, it's a Torah Scroll!" Nagi said.

"I don't understand, what's the big deal?" Angelo looked at Nagi.

"It's a handwritten copy of the Torah that is mainly used in the ritual of Torah reading during Jewish prayers," Prescott said. "Generally, it is kept in the holiest place within a synagogue. According to the collective body of Jewish religious laws known as halakha, it must be handwritten on gevil—forms of parchment—with a quill dipped in ink, and then sown together. Everything used to create one must come from ritually clean—kosher—animals."

"It's a long and arduous process," Nagi added. "It can take up to a year and a half to create one."

"Did he teach you how to make one?" Angelo said.

"He described the process, but no we never created one of our own," Prescott said. "Instead, he taught me how to read and write Ancient Hebrew, because he felt it would give me a better appreciation for the history behind the sacred text."

"How long did you live with him?" Angelo wondered.

"Close to fifteen years, until he passed away," Prescott lowered his gaze. Sadness washed over his eyes as he looked to the floor.

"How did he die?" Nagi asked.

"There was a break-in," Prescott lifted his gaze. "I arrived home one night to a commotion in the library. He had apparently caught another thief trying to steal the scroll. There was a struggle. The thief had overpowered him and fled the scene. I gave chase and caught him a few blocks away."

"Then what happened?" Angelo asked.

"I gave him a proper thrashing."

"Did you call the police?" Angelo said.

"I couldn't, because my phone broke during the confrontation."

"What happened then?" Nagi asked.

"I raced home with the scroll only to find Peter unconscious. I called the police and the paramedics, but by the time they had arrived he was already dead," Prescott said solemnly. "They said he had died from cardiac arrest."

"Did they ever catch the guy?" Angelo asked.

"Police said they couldn't find bloke. I didn't know anything about him until a few days later when Omar arrived at my door."

"I thought you said the lion never leaves his territory?" Angelo said.

"I said he seldom leaves, not never," Prescott corrected him.

"Why did Omar go to your house?" Nagi wondered.

"He said he had heard about Peter's passing, and after I had caught one of his best operatives he offered me a job as a way to make things right."

"You're kidding," Angelo scoffed.

"I'm serious," Prescott said.

"And you accepted?" Angelo looked at him quizzically.

"I needed the work," Prescott said. "After Peter passed, I was soon to be out on the street again."

"And that's how you met Susan," Angelo concluded.

"Does she still work for Omar?" Nagi asked.

"She left the team after Lorenzo died," Prescott answered.

"The magistrate shot him right in front of her," Angelo said.

"I remember," Nagi added. "That was some cold-blooded shit."

"She was in a dark place after that," Prescott recalled. "A few months later she informed Omar that she was walking away from the job."

"Damn," Nagi whispered.

The doorbell chimed and Priya announced that an unknown subject stood at the front door.

"Bring it on-screen," Nagi instructed her.

"What the—" Angelo said.

"You know him?" Nagi turned to Angelo.

"He's the rabbi I spoke with at the hospital," Angelo pointed at the monitor.

"That man was at the hospital?" Prescott cast Angelo an incredulous glance.

"Do you know him?" Nagi asked Prescott.

"He was one of the blokes who attacked me in the motel room," Prescott replied. "Him and three other men attacked me when I told them I didn't have the money."

"There doesn't appear to be anyone here," the rabbi could be heard speaking on the doorbell's microphone as he pressed it again.

"Priya, run a facial recognition scan while I try and stall him," Nagi commanded.

"She can do that?" Angelo asked.

"I told you, she's Priya, she can do anything," Nagi slid his fingers across his desk. "Keep quiet, I'm going to speak with him."

Angelo and Prescott exchanged a quick glance before they turned their attention back to the monitor.

"Uh, hello," Nagi feigned sleepiness before he yawned. "May I help you?"

"Yes, good evening, I'm looking for a couple of friends," the rabbi spoke into the mic.

"A couple of friends?" Nagi mouthed to Angelo and Prescott.

"Tell him you're home alone?" Angelo urged.

"I see one of their cars is in your driveway," the rabbi turned to Angelo's SUV.

"So much for that idea," Nagi muttered.

"Hello?" the rabbi turned back to the microphone.

"Facial recognition complete," Priya said. "Information is on-screen."

The man's full name, date of birth, height, weight, hair and eye color, as well as his rank and position appeared on the screen beside an image of his face without the rabbi disguise.

"Hello?" the rabbi spoke into the mic again.

"Umm, yeah, sorry," Nagi began to reply. "You caught me at a bad time. Please give me a moment. I was just actually on my way to the bathroom. I have a weak bladder."

"I can't believe you just said that," Angelo hissed.

Nagi shrugged before he turned back to face the monitor and told the rabbi to hold on another moment.

"Okay," the rabbi shook his head.

"He's C.I.A.!" Nagi turned to Prescott. "Dude, what the fuck are you into?"

"I didn't know he was C.I.A." Prescott said.

"Well, he knows who you are, I guarantee you that shit!" Nagi said.

"What do you propose we do?" Prescott's gaze shifted from Nagi to Angelo.

"There's no way the C.I.A. is coming into this house," Nagi said. "That's for damn sure."

"They don't have jurisdiction on U.S. soil anyway," Angelo said.

"I don't think rabbi what-the-fuck gives a shit about jurisdiction," Nagi snapped.

THE SECRET OF SCRIPTURE

"We need to lead him away from here," Angelo said as he studied the man on the monitor, and then read the short list of details from his file. *Robert J. Bauer, born in 1967, 5'11" 215 pounds, former Navy Seal, current assignment: Covert Ops.*

"I'll lure him out back, so we can make a break for it," Nagi said.

"How do you propose we do that?" Prescott's brow furrowed. "Given that Detective Marquez here is an officer of the law, chances are that every police agency in the state will have a beat on his license plate and vehicle description."

"You two go into the garage, I'll meet you there in a minute," Nagi directed them before he tapped a few digital keys on his desk. "Priya, my love, we're going mobile."

"Going mobile, copy," Priya responded.

"Hello, sir," Nagi spoke to Rabbi Agent Bauer.

"Yes?" Bauer leaned into the mic. "It's a bit chilly out here."

"My apologies, sir, I'm unable to go to the front door at the moment. I'm bound to a wheelchair," Nagi lied. "But if you could walk around to the rear there's a door that leads directly into the walk-in basement."

"Uh, okay," Bauer said, and he proceeded to descend the short flight of steps at the front door.

Nagi noted how the agent feigned having difficulty with each step.

"Man, he's really into maintaining character," Nagi reflected. "Dude should get an Oscar with his fake-ass."

Nagi ran into the basement where Angelo and Prescott waited for him beside his smart car.

"What are you waiting for, get in the car," Nagi pressed a few buttons on the keypad beside the door that led into the house.

"You expect us to get away in *this*?" Angelo said. "It's the size of a can of tuna!"

"Hey, don't knock the Phat Mobile," Nagi approached.

"The Fat Mobile," Prescott said. "It looks pretty small."

"That's what she said," Nagi pulled the door open and climbed inside. "It's the Phat Mobile, P-H-A-T, as in Pretty Hot and Technological. Now get inside, there's plenty of room."

Angelo and Prescott climbed in after him. They slid into the rear seat, while Nagi sat in the driver's seat that resembled a cockpit without a steering wheel.

"Oh wow, this *is* rather spacious," Prescott said. "Where's the front passenger seat?"

"It folds into the floor. I made a few modifications, which allows for plenty of leg room, among other things," Nagi pulled out a glasstop tray. He slid his fingers across the tray, and a series of buttons glowed to life. "All right Priya, what's the battlefield look like?"

"A dozen vehicles are on this block, all except one belong to residents and are unoccupied," Priya said.

"Where's the enemy?" Nagi looked up at the windshield, which instantly turned into a widescreen monitor.

A van appeared on-screen with two occupants visible through its windshield.

"Their mode of transport is parked five hundred meters south of our location," Priya zoomed in on the van.

"How are we able to see them?" Angelo asked.

"I'm using the security cameras on my house," Nagi said without turning away from the monitor.

"Brilliant," Prescott said.

"Yeah, Xfinity Home ain't got shit on me," Nagi bragged. "Okay, now to see where Father Time is at."

Nagi tapped the luminous buttons of his glass tray. The monitor turned into a split screen. One side kept the visual on the van, and the other scrolled through the camera feeds surrounding the house.

"There you are you filthy animal?" Nagi observed the agent arrive at the back door. The rabbi proceeded to knock.

THE SECRET OF SCRIPTURE

Nagi began to sing in his best Cheech Marin impression, "Keep on knocking, but'chu can't come in!"

Angelo shook his head.

"Priya, now!" Nagi shouted.

"Initiating alarm activation signal," Priya responded.

The garage door began to open and the car alarms of every vehicle on the street simultaneously blared to life. The agents in the van jumped in their seats and immediately searched their surroundings.

Once the garage door fully opened, the smart car zoomed past Angelo's SUV and turned northbound onto the street. They saw the rabbi scramble to return to the front of the house. The garage door closed behind them. The van, which had been running idle turned on its headlights and sped to the front of Nagi's home. One of the doors slid open and the agent leapt inside.

"And for our second act," Nagi rapidly tapped the glowing keys. "Watch this shit."

Angelo and Prescott looked over their shoulders. Though they didn't see the lower rear compartment of the smart car open, they observed several pieces of metal glint under the streetlamps as the van approached. The van drove over the pieces of metal and a moment later screeched to a halt.

"Say hello to my little friends!" Nagi shouted into the rear view mirror before he turned east bound on Route 64. "All right, we've lost them for now."

"What was that?" Angelo turned back to Nagi.

"You ever played Jacks?" Nagi said.

"Who hasn't?" Angelo said.

"Well, I just unloaded about five hundred pieces of metal. Each designed like Jacks to puncture the tires of that van," Nagi said.

"What about your neighbors?" Angelo asked.

"Casualties of war, my friend. Besides, I don't like 'em anyway," Nagi shrugged. "They're constantly calling the cops on me and talking shit about how they think I'm a terrorist."

"You've got issues," Angelo shook his head.

"That's my problem, but at the moment we need to focus on your problem," Nagi replied.

"What is the plan, exactly?" Prescott leaned forward in his seat.

"Well, we're not going to be able to dodge the C.I.A. for long," Nagi said. "Not to mention that your friends at the Chicago PD are going to be onto us sooner than later. So, I don't know how long I'll be able to keep us under the radar."

"You're not going to have to keep us under the radar for long," Angelo said.

"What do you mean?" Nagi looked at him over his shoulder.

"I know a guy," Angelo smiled mischievously. He retrieved his cellphone from his pocket and swiped at the screen to bring up his contacts. A moment later he brought his phone up to his ear.

"Dude, who are you calling?" Nagi said as his seat swivled around to face the rear of the car.

"Whoa, don't you need to keep your attention focused on the road?" Prescott said.

"Priya is driving," Nagi said.

"How is that even bloody possible?" Prescott looked at the monitor that displayed the road ahead.

"She's using satallites to pinpoint the location of other cars on the road through their GPS systems," Nagi shrugged.

"Not all cars have GPS," Prescott noted.

"True, but all cellphones do, which is how Uber and Lyft drivers get around, so she's accounting for any smartphone that's in a vehicle that doesn't have its own GPS."

"What if someone is in a car without a smartphone *and* without GPS?" Prescott asked.

"The probability of that happening is miniscule, at best," Nagi shrugged. "And at this hour, a damn near improbability. In any case, she's also using traffic cams and all security cameras of businesses and residents to account for vehicles on the road. So, even if she can't account for them via satallite, she'll still be able to see them coming and calculate time, distance, and rate of speed to avoid a collision."

"Wow!" Prescott said.

"Yeah, I'm a genius," Nagi said. "Besides, this is part of how self-driving vehicles will function in the next decade, or so."

"Hey, Condlin, it's me, Angelo," Marquez spoke into his cellphone.

"Marky-Marquez, what's up my brotha-from-anotha-motha?" Condlin could be heard over the phone's receiver.

"Have you been drinking?" Marquez asked.

"It's called retirement, buddy. Have to stay busy somehow," Condlin said. "What are you doing tonight? Wanna come out and get a lap dance?"

"I'm in a bit of a jam, you still have that safehouse on the Westside?" Angelo said.

"It belongs to my former employer, but one of the guys from my old team still uses it. Why? What do ya need?"

"How'd you like to come out of retirement?"

"I might be a little rusty like MJ wearing number forty-five, but I've still got it," Condlin said. "What do ya have in mind?"

"Get your old team together. We're about to go seventy-two and ten."

45
NORTHWESTERN UNIVERSITY
Evanston, IL.
4:40 a.m.

The group of police officers retreated to Solinksi's squad as James drove his vehicle away. They watched as it turned into a ChargePoint Charging Station and public parking lot half a block down the road.

"I'm sorry again that you had to come out here for this," Solinski said to the Evanston PD Watch Commander.

"No worries," the Watch Commander waived it off. "I needed to get out on the road for a few anyway. You know how it is, one can get a little stir crazy sitting in the office all night."

"It's a shame he didn't let us get a look inside his vehicle," Cruz said.

"You're sure your officer's cellphone is in that car?" The Watch Commander looked over his shoulder at the charging station.

"The GPS tracker on his phone indicated as much," Solinski said. "The thing is, the people in that vehicle didn't seem the type to be a part of Marquez's inner circle."

"Well, good luck finding him," the Watch Commander said as he returned to his vehicle.

"Thanks again for understanding," Solinski turned to climb into his squad.

Cruz lifted the tablet off the dash and watched as the red dot blinked down the road.

Solinski dialed Marquez's phone number again. It rang on his end just as it did when he called the cellphone while standing beside James' vehicle when the windows were down. It did not emit a sound from James' car, and no one answered the phone.

"Damn it," Solinski cursed. "Where the hell is he?"

THE SECRET OF SCRIPTURE

"Want me to have DuPage County Deputies check the address where he was at before the GPS showed he was on the move?" Cruz turned to Solinski.

"Yeah, might as well have them try to make contact with the residents to see how they know Marquez, or the subject in his custody," Solinski stared straight ahead at James' vehicle.

James stepped out of his car after he turned off the engine and he moved to connect it to a charger.

"What the—" Cruz's brow furrowed as he looked at the tablet.

"What is it?" Solinski turned his attention to Cruz.

"The red dot stopped blinking," Cruz looked at Solinski before they both turned their attention to James and his vehicle.

The tablet chimed again. They turned to the tablet as the map on the screen shifted to another location.

"He's on the move again?" Cruz watched as the red dot moved eastbound on Route 64 through the western suburbs of Chicago.

"That mother fucker!" Solinski shifted the vehicle into drive as he fastened his seatbelt. "Where does it show him at now?"

"He appears to be approaching I-355," Cruz said.

"Son of a bitch!" Solinski pounded his steering wheel. "Have DuPage County check that address anyway. Just in case we're chasing shadows."

"Got it," Cruz retrieved his cellphone from his outer vest pocket.

"Keep an eye on his movement," Solinski demanded. "I swear to God, when I get a hold of Marquez…"

You're not the only one who wants to get ahold of him, Cruz cast Solinski a sidelong glance. The man who had called him was clear about the objective. "Wherever he goes, whatever he does, we need eyes on him at all times."

"What is this all about?" Cruz had ventured to ask.

"All you need to know at this time, Officer Cruz, is that it is a matter of national security. Do you part and your daughter will be fine. Failure to achieve the stated objective will result in you being listed as an enemy of the State."

"DuPage County Dispatch, this is Laureen," the voice echoed over his receiver and brought him back into the present. "What is the address of your emergency?"

"Hello Laureen," Cruz spoke into his phone. "This is Officer Eli Cruz of the Chicago PD. Wondering if you can have one of your deputies check an address for us regarding that incident at CDH earlier this evening."

"Sure, what's the address?" Laureen asked.

Eli tapped the tablet screen to shift from one window to the next and read the address to her before he returned to the GPS map-tracking application.

"That's odd," she said.

"What's odd?" Cruz asked. He and Solinski turned to each other briefly as Cruz put the phone on speaker.

"I already have three units headed into the area of that address," Laureen said. "We received numerous reports of multiple car alarms on that street going off simultaneously. The address you're inquiring about has a special note attached to it in our system."

"What's the note about that address say?" Cruz asked.

"Suspicious ties to terrorism," Laureen said.

"What the hell did you get yourself into Angelo?" Solinski muttered. He turned on his lights and sirens as he put the pedal to the metal.

"Thanks Laureen," Cruz said. "Call me back with whatever your deputies find."

46
JAFFA GATE OLD CITY
Jerusalem, Israel
11:45 a.m.

The crowds beyond the Jaffa Gate swelled after the televised beheading aired at the top of the previous hour. Believers gathered in multitudes beyond what anyone had anticipated as they doubled their efforts to rescue any survivors that remained amid the wreckage at the Tower of David Museum. News vans continued to snake their way through the crowds. Inching ever closer to the location where i24News anchor Maya Levy remained the only correspondent on-scene.

"What can you tell us about the atmosphere on the ground?" Binyamin asked her from the studio.

"The people here are divided," Maya stood before the camera, surrounded by a throng of protestors. "In the distance, you will see people regardless of their faith helping one another to save lives. Just behind me, however you'll see a group who believe the Israeli government staged this attack to force the Jerusalem Islamic Waqf to relinquish control of the Temple Mount. The Islamic religious trust, as you know, was permitted to retain authority over the area of the Al-Aqsa compound after the Six-Day War in an effort to keep the peace. Peace now teeters on the edge of a knife after this morning's events."

Men could be heard on megaphones chanting phrases of protest in various languages. Helicopters flew overhead. Their cameras televised for the world a chaotic scene of believers divided into groups that were separated by police officers and arriving soldiers.

"Thank you, Maya, keep us posted on how things progress, and be safe," Binyamin said.

The televised events remained in a split screen between the overhead view of the helicopters and anchors in the news studio. A ticker ran along the bottom of the screen recounting the sequence of events that had occurred throughout the morning with statements from various government officials denouncing the violence in the Old City of Jerusalem.

"Once again, our thoughts and prayers are with the victims of this horrific attack as world leaders gather to find resolution amid rising tensions in the Middle East," Binyamin continued. "Meanwhile, at the Damascus Gate, crowds gather near the site of a car bomb that exploded moments before the attack at the Tower of David Museum. Officials have yet to determine if these events are related, but one would find it difficult to imagine that they are separate and random acts occurring on the same day."

Another helicopter flew overhead with images of police squads and fire engines gathered in a parking lot near the gate.

"Officials confirm one dead and two others injured, but the investigation is on-going," Binyamin continued as the helicopter view circled over the crowds. "Decades of conflict in a region steeped in culture and religion, today we are witnessing what many had feared, but hoped would never happen."

"We'll be back with more after this," he said, as the screen went blank.

47
NATIONAL HEADQUARTERS OF THE ISRAEL
POLICE
Kiryat Menachem Begin
Jerusalem, Israel
11:45 a.m.

Yeshua sat the phone on its receiver after he thanked the person on the other end of the line for his time. He sighed as he rubbed his eyes and leaned back in his chair.

"What are you going to do now?" Abigail asked.

"I have to speak with Commander Shalom," Yeshua rubbed his temples. *This is not a conversation I am looking forward to having.* "By the way, has anyone heard from Batya?"

"Not that I am aware of," she said.

"Do me a favor," Yeshua straightened in his seat. "Run a search for her phone's exact location. Get ahold of me as soon as you find out where she is."

She nodded and headed for the door.

"Oh, and Abigail, thanks," Yeshua said when she turned back to him.

She smiled and nodded before she left the office. It was only her second year on the job, and she hoped to be a productive contributor in a field where women were often overlooked. Except when certain superiors took notice of women for the purposes of harassment, which was one of the stains the Israel Police Force had to contend with in recent years.

Yeshua stood and lifted the file off of his desk. He walked out of his office and stopped momentarily when all eyes focused on him. The embarrassment of being escorted into his own office in handcuffs bubbled to the surface of his consciousness.

One of his colleagues started to clap. Others followed suit. Before he knew it, everyone gave him a standing ovation. He suppressed a smile, nodded and waved at everyone with the file in his hand as he made his way to Chief Superintendent Hefetz's office. The eyes and applause followed him until he arrived at the door and knocked.

"Come in," Hefetz said.

Yeshua turned the knob and pushed the door open. Commander Shalom was in there with Hefetz, and their conversation fell silent.

"What do you need," Hefetz waved him in.

"I have some information the commander may find useful," Yeshua closed the door behind him.

"I thought I already told you that you're off the case," Commander Shalom said.

"Yes, well, this was brought to my attention by my evidence techs," Yeshua handed him the file.

"I was just telling the commander here that I'm going to fight any and every attempt to charge you with conduct unbecoming of an officer of the law," Hefetz said. "We shouldn't be turning on our own. Especially when we clearly have an enemy we need to focus on in order to save lives."

Yeshua handed him the file and waited silently as the commander examined each page.

Commander Shalom lifted his gaze momentarily before he focused his attention back to the file in his hand. "Do we know who this Dr. Yisrael Avrohom is, and where to find him?"

"I spoke with his colleagues at Oxford where he once worked as a Research Fellow of Social and Cultural Anthropology," Yeshua said.

"He is no longer under their employ?" Commander Shalom asked.

"They terminated his employment six months ago after he initiated an experiment where a village's water supply was poisoned without their knowledge, while making the situation known to surrounding communities in an effort to study their reaction," Yeshua said.

"He sounds like a man of extremes," Hefetz said.

THE SECRET OF SCRIPTURE

"The university didn't wait for public outrage to make a decision to release him, but by the time officials went to apprehend him, he had already fled to Iran," Yeshua said.

"Why did he flee to Iran?" Hefetz asked.

"Britain currently doesn't have an extradition agreement with Iran," Commander Shalom said.

"That must be where he formulated his plan to attack Jerusalem," Yeshua speculated.

"And he used whatever ties he made in Iran to sneak into Israel with the aid of Palestinian terrorists," Commander Shalom said.

"I confirmed with the university in Tel Aviv that he had no association with the technological summit scheduled for today," Yeshua said. "His stated involvement was simply a ploy to insert himself into our investigation."

"Where is he now?" Commander Shalom asked.

"He should be in Tel Aviv," Yeshua said.

"He should be?" Commander Shalom closed the file.

"He was with us in the Old City when I had Rav Shoter Matti Davidi escort him back to his office this morning," Yeshua admitted.

"You mean to tell me that he was in your custody and you let him get away?" Commander Shalom slammed the file on Hefetz's desk.

"I admit I had my suspicions, but I had no proof he was involved at the time," Yeshua said. "Professor Leonardo had vouched for him as an expert in evolutionary game theory."

"Evolutionary game what?" Commander Shalom cast him an incredulous glance.

"It has to do with the study of mathematical models to determine the strategic interaction between rational decision-makers by focusing on the dynamics of a change in strategy within a population," Yeshua said. "I didn't have reason to believe his work was connected to the events taking place in the Old City, and since his knowledge of religious history proved helpful I felt it was most prudent to keep him close."

"Close enough that you sent him an hour away," Commander Shalom stood and cursed under his breath.

"That was in an effort to get him to liase with participants of the technological summit for everyone's safety," Yeshua clarified.

"Which he used as a cover to evade capture, since he had to know we were going to identify the body found at the Golden Gates," Commander Shalom said.

"You think he knew we were going to connect him to the murder?" Hefetz lifted the file off his desk.

"Consider everything that has transpired today," Commander Shalom said. "Each aspect of these events appears to have gone off like clockwork. Someone who executes a plan with such precision doesn't *accidentally* leave a partial fingerprint as evidence."

"He wants us to know he's behind it," Yeshua said.

"He's toying with us!" Commander Shalom shouted. "Perhaps he left us the clue as a distraction."

"A distraction from what, though?" Hefetz wondered.

"A distraction from the role of the professor of Biblical studies that Yeshua here left in the Old City," Commander Shalom pointed at Yeshua.

"I still have trouble believing that Professor Leonardo is somehow involved in these attacks," Yeshua protested.

"Forgive me if I don't trust your judgement, chief inspector," Shalom headed toward the door. "If you'll excuse me, I have to relay this information to my teams in the field." The commander turned to Hefetz. "Have the Tel Aviv District office deploy a team to apprehend Dr. Avrohom, if he's still in the area."

"What about Professor Leonardo?" Yeshua asked.

"I'll have my men find him and take him into custody until I can determine his innocence, or guilt."

"We need him to disable those bombs," Yeshua said.

THE SECRET OF SCRIPTURE

"I'm trying to prevent a war here!" Commander Shalom snapped. "We need to decrypt the feed the terrorists are using in order to find where they are holding the hostages."

"You focus on that, then, and let me take a team into the Old City to find the professor," Yeshua suggested.

"I already told you that you're off the case," Commander Shalom said. "You aren't permitted anywhere near the Old City while you're under investigation. Now stay out of my way, chief inspector, or I'll make sure you regret it for the rest of your life!"

Commander Shalom stormed out of the office and slammed the door shut behind him.

"He sure enjoys making a dramatic exit," Yeshua turned to Hefetz.

"You're convinced of Professor Leonardo's innocence?" Hefetz asked.

"Well, I'm not convinced of his guilt, but I do need to find him in order to prove his innocence."

"You know," Hefetz shifted in his seat. "Commander Shalom is technically unable to initiate any investigation into your actions until *after* the crisis has passed."

Yeshua cast the chief superintendent a curious glance.

"Everyone here respects you, Yeshua, regardless of how the Lahav brought you in," Hefetz said. "I'll cover for you as long as I can, but you won't have a lot of time."

"Perhaps God will grant me all the time I need," Yeshua made for the door.

"Here's praying He will grant us more than that," Hefetz said.

48
CHURCH OF THE HOLY SEPULCHRE OLD CITY
Jerusalem, Israel
11:50 a.m.

Aiden emerged from the Church of the Holy Sepulchre and stepped into the empty courtyard at its entrance. The sun had reached its highest point in the sky, and the heat of the day had intensified. He retrieved his smartphone from his pocket, but the screen indicated that there was no signal.

"So much for calling Miriam back," Aiden muttered to himself.

A crow flew high above and disappeared behind the church's crown. *I wonder if they identified the body found at the Golden Gate?* He sighed and listened for voices, or footsteps, but there remained no sign of another soul in the area.

"I better get moving to the next location," he said to himself. "What is that next location, though?"

Aiden reflected on the riddle he had just solved. Though it touched on the topic of God, the gods of other religions, and the angels, it had focused on Jesus and his place in the celestial realm and the world of men.

"The next location must have something to do with how the historical Jesus became a deity," Aiden speculated. "The Golden Gate represented where Jesus entered the Old City. The Tower of David Museum is where Pontius Pilate's judgment of Jesus occurred in Herod's palace. The Church of the Holy Sepulchre marked the sites of Jesus' birth, crucifixion, and resurrection. The Chapels of St. Helena and the Finding of the Cross commemorated the symbol that represented the divinity of Christ. What am I missing?"

Aiden took a few steps in hopes of spotting something that would provide a hint. *Come on; give me something here, a structure, a statue, anything that might help.*

"You two go that way. We'll check down here," a man's voice broke Aiden's train of thought.

THE SECRET OF SCRIPTURE

Aiden fled in the opposite direction. He raced past St. Abraham Monastery and disappeared around the corner. He found himself in an alleyway of a now vacant and closed series of shops. The voices and footsteps seemed to be closing in on him. He turned left after passing an Orthodox Church. The street sign read: Beit HaBad Street. He continued northbound beneath a series of stone archways until the street ended at a three-way intersection.

"Left or right?" He asked himself. "Left leads back towards the Church of the Holy Sepulchre. Right leads to…" he paused momentarily and reflected on the poem again. "Yes! The Via Dolorosa, that's it. The next site is down that way."

Aiden dashed around the corner and took each of the long wide steps carefully as he followed the path. The Via Dolorosa is widely believed to be the processional route in the Old City that Jesus walked on the way to his crucifixion.

Aiden slowed when the voices and footsteps of his pursuers faded. He leaned against a wall, beneath another stone archway to catch his breath. *Miriam's right, I really need to exercise more*, he reflected.

He looked around at the ancient structures that loomed over him. Although the current route of Christian pilgrimage had been established in the 18th century, the buildings themselves had stood for much longer. The fourteen Stations of the Cross depicted in a series of images to commemorate one of the most important events in human history marked each location in numerical order.

"The next location has to be along this path," Aiden continued ahead. *Not all of them are accurate, so I have to be meticulous in deciphering fact from fiction.*

He neared the Synagogue Hzon Yehezkel, which stood ahead on his right. The ancient architecture and elaborate stonework of the buildings fascinated him. Double and triple arched windows were protected with iron screens; some even had signs of the cross at their center. Roman and Armanian script were etched in stone over doorways and windows, as were images of the Jerusalem cross—also known as the Five-fold Cross—that symbolized the Five Wounds of Christ.

Aiden turned left on Al-Wad Street where the Via Dolorosa ended. He proceeded north along another alley of closed shops to where the Via Dolorosa resumed eastward. The Church of St. Mary of Agony towered over him to his right, and he continued past it. He noticed that the Austrian Hospice and Armenian Guesthouse hotels were vacant and closed.

He approached the Greek Orthodox Monastery; its whitewashed and cream-colored stones seemed to glow in the sunlight. An inscription in Greek decorated the façade above the arched entrance. A sign in English and in Greek beside the door indicated that it had once been the Prison of Christ.

"Hmm," he paused momentarily to think. "Could this be the place?"

He neared the open door and peered inside.

"No, not the prison," he said to himself. "That doesn't represent anything of symbolic importance with regard to Christ's divinity."

Aiden stepped back and continued eastbound. He stopped at the Convent of the Sisters of Zion. The Roman Catholic convent stood at the heart of the Old City near the eastern end of the Via Dolorosa. Also known as the Basilica of Ecce Homo, because it's traditionally believed to be the place where Pontius Pilate presented a scouraged Jesus—bound and wearing his crown of thorns—with the words, "Ecce homo, Behold the man."

"Behold the man," Aiden repeated. A mock gesture made before a hostile crowd for the King of the Jews, which has been depicted in Christian art for centuries.

Aiden gazed at the stone structure with its elaborately carved arched entrance and the numerous gated-windows that completed its façade.

THE SECRET OF SCRIPTURE

"Behold the man," Aiden pinched his nose. *Think! Think!* "What symbol possesses the most important historical significance for the Son of Man to become God?"

"How about the cross?"

Aiden turned to see Miriam emerge from around the corner. Susan followed close behind.

"Miriam!" Aiden rushed to embrace her. "What are you doing here?"

"I'm here to get you out of the Old City," Miriam sighed with relief. "I've been worried sick about you."

"I tried to call you, but there's no cell service," Aiden said.

"Where's the chief inspector?" Miriam looked around.

"The Lahav 433 took him into custody," he said.

"They what? Why?" Miriam cast him an incredulous glance.

"Long story, but he made sure they didn't come looking for me," Aiden said.

"Well, *I* came looking for you," she replied.

"How did you get in here?" Aiden asked.

"Susan helped me," she turned to glance over her shoulder.

"Hello, professor," Susan leaned against a wall with arms crossed, and waved.

"But how?" His eyes darted back and forth between Miriam and Susan.

"Long story," Miriam said. "Are you ready to get out of here?"

"I can't," Aiden shook his head.

"What do you mean, you can't," Miriam shot him a cold look.

"There's two more bombs hidden in the Old City," Aiden said. "Whoever planted these devices made sure that I would be the only one to deactivate them."

"What? Oh no, we're not playing along with some psycho's game plan," Miriam protested.

"It's the only way to preserve the history and the—"

"Aiden, baby, you know I appreciate the preservation of history and all, but this is *not* one of those moments when the preservation of important sites takes precedence over the preservation of life. Especially when the life in question is my husband."

"This is bigger than me," Aiden placed his hands on his hips.

Miriam crossed her arms before she spoke. "Aiden, my love, I swear to God that I'm about to knock you over the head with one of these stones and drag you out of here."

"How do you know there's only two?" Susan interrupted their conversation.

"Sarai, the A.I. that is linked to each of the bombs informed me when she provided me with explicit instructions on how to go about deactivating the bombs and finding the next," Aiden said. "That's why the chief inspector made sure the Lahav agents did know where to find me."

"Well, it's not *his* spouse's life that's on the line here," Miriam protested.

"How close are you to finding the second bomb?"

"Susan, you're not helping," Miriam turned to her.

"Let's assess the situation," Susan approached. "We're already here, and nearly at the center of the Old City."

"I think you were onto something," Aiden turned to Miriam. "The cross is of symbolic significance, because even though crucifixion was a common form of execution by the Romans it became the most important symbol by which Jesus would be revered."

"What's your point?" she said with her arms still crossed.

"The site where Jesus first accepted the cross is just over there along the road that currently runs between the El-Omariya Muslim College and the Franciscan compound that contains the Church of the Condemnation and the Imposition of the Cross, and the Church of the Flagellation," Aiden pointed down the road.

"I don't see anything there, except for those two video cameras overhead that face north and south from the intersection," Susan said over her shoulder.

"Chances are that it's hidden beneath us in the tunnel system that was in use during the Roman Period," Aiden said.

"How do we get down there?" Miriam said impatiently.

"We could find an entrance in the lower levels of one of these churches," Susan suggested.

"What are we waiting for," Aiden said. "Let's get moving!"

49
BREAKING NEWS i-24NEWS
Israel
12:00 p.m.

"Welcome back to i24 Breaking News in Israel. Binyamin Shalev here with an update on the reactions from around the world after this morning's tragic events in the Old City of Jerusalem."

The screen split to show world leaders arriving at airports in their respective countries, while those whose trip did not take as long disembarked their private jets to attend the emergency session.

"Despite the show of solidarity around the globe denouncing the attacks of terrorists," Binyamin said. "Satallite images have leaked that show numerous militaries have mobilized."

The images of several countries appeared on the screen.

"Our political analyst and politics professor at Hebrew University of Jerusalem, Daniel Hazan joins us with more," Binyamin turned to his guest as the images around the world continued to flash on a large monitor behind them. "Daniel, first of all, thank you for being here."

"Thank you for having me, Binyamin, it's a pleasure to be here, given these circumstances."

"What can you tell us about the political ramifications this tragedy has on the global stage?" Binyamin asked. "It seems everyone has gone on record to denounce this cowardly act, yet support appears to be divided and lines are being drawn in the sand."

"The consequences of divergent alliances will certainly have a profound effect on everyone," Daniel said. "So much so, that the domino effect will rival the fallout that led to the First and Second World Wars."

"You make an interesting point, Daniel, since we have received word that North Korea has broken its treaty with

THE SECRET OF SCRIPTURE

South Korea, while Pakistan and India have mobilized their militaries at their borders in what appears to be preparations for a face off," Binyamin said.

"If an attack is made on Israel, or if Israel attacks one of its neighbors," Daniel said. "Let's say Iran, given the history between them. We're looking at a war that will land on the doorstep of every country. This will no longer be a problem in the Middle East, but instead it will ripple around the world and affect everyone's daily life."

"You're saying an attack on Israel, or by Israel could trigger a series of orchestrated events around the world through Iran's proxies," Binyamin said.

"Clearly, I'm using that as one example, but yes," Daniel nodded. "But we're not simply talking about governments declaring war on each other."

"Please continue, Daniel, " Binyamin said.

"Islamic radicals may decide to launch attacks in every country where sleeper cells lie in wait for an occasion such as this," Daniel said. "Yet, there are also radical Christian sects and Neo Nazi's who are willing and ready to strike back."

"How do you think this affects Israel's relationship with its allies in the region and around the world?" Binyamin clasped his hands on the news desk.

"Israel has been under constant criticism for the staggering civil-liberties abuses and institutional oppression against its Palestinian citizens. Even Israel's allies will no longer be able to turn a blind eye on the violation of countless U.N. resolutions," Daniel said. "This incident has essentially put the spotlight squarely on the military occupation of land legally possessed by Arabs. As Israel systematically colonizes Palestinian territory by linking illegal Israeli settlements through military constructed roads deemed 'Jewish only' in the West Bank, the world will have to take notice and wonder about what ignited this morning's attacks."

"Do you believe that even Israel's allies will be unable to come to its aid if a public condemnation of these atrocities comes to the fore?"

"It could be something to consider, but Egypt and Saudi Arabia are also guilty of human rights violations that to turn their back on Israel would be viewed as hypocritical, which would put the onus on America to step in," Daniel said.

"Is it possible the United States still has enough sway in the Middle East to quell the fires?"

"That would be difficult to say with any certainty, given that U.S. allies in the Middle East have distanced themselves since the disengagement of the Obama administration," Daniel said.

"Will you elaborate on that for us?"

"Although Russia has maintained a cautionary distance from the Arab-Israel peace process, it has recently engaged in talks with U.S. allies like Turkey and Saudi Arabia, whose monarch chose to visit Russia over the U.S."

"Word is that Russia has welcomed more visits from leaders in the Middle East, who have opted to meet with the Russian president over the U.S. president in recent years. Is this a cause for concern?" Binyamin asked.

"Indeed it is," Daniel nodded. "These meetings offer the Russian president new opportunities of influence in the region as the United States shifts focus to counter Russian and Chinese expansion in other areas of the world."

"Where do the Chinese stand in all this?" Binyamin asked.

"Well, America released a statement just this past hour that it will not permit the Old City to fall to terrorists, and China has threatened U.S. interests if it strikes at any country in the Middle East. So, it appears we are at a bit of a standoff," Daniel said. "Let's keep in mind, however, that Russia is using its recently established channels of communication to negotiate peace."

THE SECRET OF SCRIPTURE

"It seems like an improbable outcome at this moment, but we will pray that the U.N. will arrive at a consensus to resolve the matter quickly and peacefully," Binyamin said as the camera focused on him. "This just in, it appears we have another transmission coming from the terrorists. We are going live with it now."

50
UNDISCLOSED LOCATION
Israel
12:00 p.m.

Arwan appeared on screens worldwide wearing a black hood and standing over the row of remaining hostages. Most of the hostages fidgeted and sobbed as they knelt before him with their hands tied behind their backs wearing white hoods and faced the camera. The one directly in front of Arwan remained motionless and silent as Arwan held the machete near the neck.

"You have witnessed our resolve, yet our demands have not been met. Perhaps you wish to test us further. I assure you it is something you will soon regret." The camera zoomed in on him and the hostage before him.

"Please, somebody stop these monsters!" One of the hostages shouted.

"Silence!" Ali struck the hostage in the back of the head with the butt of his rifle.

The man cried out in pain as he collapsed face first on the ground. Ali grabbed the man's collar and pulled him back on his knees.

"Say another word, and I *will* kill you," Ali hissed into the man's ear.

"Everyone talks of peace, but no one is willing to take drastic measures to achieve drastic change," Arwan said. "We will do whatever is necessary to do God's will."

"You don't know God's will!" A female hostage shouted.

"I said silence!" Ali punched the woman on the side of the head.

She shrieked and collapsed. Ali reached for her collar and she tried to roll away from him, but he kicked her in the stomach, and then punched her in the face. The commotion could be heard from off-camera, but it proved enough of a distraction to force Arwan to step out of view.

THE SECRET OF SCRIPTURE

He crouched over the woman and said in a low voice. "Do not test my patience, woman, or I will end you."

She froze. Blood stained her hood from within.

"Nod if you understand," Arwan said.

She nodded and whimpered.

He and Ali pulled her up on her knees before Arwan resumed his place in front of the camera and behind his silent hostage.

"Your nations gather as if they have a choice in how to resolve this matter," Arwan said. "This is not a matter to be decided by men, for it is a matter that will be decided by God. If any nation dares attack Israel, it will find such an endeavor to be futile. Scripture has already prophesied, 'On that day I will set out to destroy all the nations that attack Jerusalem.' So stand down your armies and surrender the Temple Mount."

"Please do as they ask," another hostage pled.

Arwan raised his machete over his shoulder and swung at the neck of his silent hostage. The screen went dark just before the strike, and once again a woman screamed and a soft thud could be heard on the ground before the feed went dead.

51
CHURCH OF THE FLAGELLATION
Jerusalem, Israel
12:05 p.m.

Aiden and Miriam followed Susan through the mostly vacant church as they descended another flight of steps that led deep into the bowels of the Old City. Though they heard the voices of priests upon entering the Roman Catholic Church located within the Franciscan compound, they had not crossed paths with anyone on their way to the lower levels.

Unlike the impressive architecture of the main chapel built in 1904 by the Franciscan Brother Wendelin of Menden with its high-arched celing, smooth stone finish, marble pillars, and beautiful art depicting scenes from the Stations of the Cross, the lower levels consisted of rough stone steps and walls. The dim lighting offered scant views of the remnants of the ruins of the 13th century chapel upon which the current structure had been built.

"This way," Susan led them down a long, dark corridor.

"It's cold down here," Miriam rubbed her arms.

"A relief from the heat, though," Aiden remarked.

Miriam glared at him momentarily before she continued ahead in silence.

"I can't help but to think of the irony of this place," Aiden said.

"How do you mean?" Susan glanced over her shoulder as she continued ahead.

"Tradition holds that this is the site where Jesus took up his cross after being sentenced to death. Instead, he achieved immortality and became forever linked with that same cross."

"Here we are," Susan turned another corner and stopped at a large wooden door. "Help me with this."

Aiden and Miriam moved to help her remove a wooden beam that barred the entrance. The three of them struggled momentarily before it finally gave way and slid out of place.

"They must never use this exit," Susan said.

"I wonder if this is part of the old chapel from the Crusader period?" Aiden placed the wooden beam on the ground.

"The Crusaders were actually *here* in this building?" Susan turned to Aiden and Miriam.

"Up until the arrival of the Franciscan order in the early 13th century," Miriam finally spoke. "That's when Pope Clement the VI declared the Franciscans as the official custodians of the Holy places."

"Known as Custodia Terroe Sanctoe, or Custodia di Terra Santa," Aiden added.

"Guardianship of the Holy Land," Susan said in a low voice. "Interesting."

She pulled the heavy wood door open. The corridor beyond filled with impenetrable shadows.

"We're going to need a source of light navigate through here," she pulled off her backpack and retrieved her flashlight. She instructed Miriam to do the same. "We're going to need all the light we can get down here."

Aiden turned when he heard voices behind them. Two priests, maybe three walked through a corridor at the top of the staircase. A moment later, the voices faded.

"We better get going," Aiden said in a low voice.

"Follow me," Susan threw her backpack over her shoulder.

Miriam followed suit, and together they swept their flashlights across the ground and into the darkness. Aiden pulled the door closed behind him, and then continued after them.

"How will we know when we've found this bomb?" Miriam asked.

"Honestly, I won't know for sure until we've arrived at the spot that correlates with the exact location where Christ took up the cross, which was about fifty meters from where we stood when you found me."

"How did you find the first one?" Miriam asked.

"We followed the clues that led to the Chapel of Saint Helena," Aiden said.

"The location where it is believed she found the True Cross of Christ," Miriam said.

"The bomb had been tucked behind a statue of Saint Helena holding the cross," Aiden said.

The ground declined at what Susan guessed was a twenty-five degree angle. She had plenty of experience in places like this; dark secluded passageways and unearthed chambers where ancient relics were rumored to lay hidden for centuries.

After a decade and a half in the employ of Omar Al-Ansari, the covert operations had always appealed to her sense of adventure. That excitement had faded after Lorenzo's death. She'd spent months in solitude crying herself to sleep, lying in bed for hours when she woke. In a near catatonic state, she closed herself off from the outside world.

She contemplated suicide to be with him, but could never bring herself to follow through with the act. Susan did not know how to live without him. She ached for him, and barely ate as the days turned to weeks and the weeks turned to months. Omar reached out to her, but his calls and correspondence went unanswered. When he arrived at her new apartment, she barely resembled the woman he once knew.

She opened the door with unkept hair and dark circles in her eyes.

"My God, Susan, what has happened to you?" Omar had noted her withered frame. "Are you on drugs, or something?"

She didn't answer. She merely shook her head and turned away. He had followed her inside and closed the door behind him. She had collapsed on the couch and cried without shame. He sat beside her and offered his condolences, but it had all been in vain. She wasn't listening, and she didn't care. All she wanted was another day with Lorenzo, to say what she'd left unsaid and to feel the warmth of his embrace.

It was too late for that now.

Omar knew it.

He released her from his employment, but not before letting her know that she'd always have a place in his organization should she ever have a change of heart. She hadn't heard from him since that day, and it took another year of wallowing in misery before she gradually emerged from the shadows of her own mind.

Revenge, she had thought to herself.

She wanted revenge for what had been stolen from her. A life for a life, a love for a love; and when she saw Aiden on television she knew just how she'd exact her vengeance. One of them would watch the other die. One of them would feel her pain.

But how, and who? She had wondered.

Susan had never killed anyone. She didn't know if she had it in her to do it. She did, however, know how to lure her target into a trap. It had worked with Sariel several years ago, and though he had survived the ordeal the first time, he had met his demise on her second attempt. Things would be different this time. Aiden was no angel—pun intended—and neither was Miriam.

Susan cast Miriam a sidelong glance in the dimly lit passageway. *You may have once won a national title in Kung Fu, but you never carry a gun and kicks can't stop bullets.*

They arrived at an ancient crossroads. A light flickered around a corner. They followed in search of the source and saw a torch on the wall. A laptop sat open on the ground beneath it. The screensaver glowed with an image of the cross.

"Looks like we found it," Miriam said.

"What next?" Susan turned to Aiden.

He stepped forward and lifted the laptop off the ground. He pressed his thumb against the fingerprint scanner, and Sarai appeared on the screen.

"Greetings, professor, I see you have company," Sarai turned to Miriam and Susan as they stood on either side of him.

"What the—" Susan began to say.

"This is Sarai," Aiden said. "Her name is actually an acronym for Science and Religion Artificial Intelligence."

"That is just creepy," Miriam said.

"I'll ignore your statement, Mrs. Leonardo," Sarai replied.

"Oh hell no," Susan turned away.

"Shall we proceed, professor?" Sarai turned to Aiden.

"Yes," Aiden nodded.

Sarai presented the riddle on the screen, but did not recite each line as it appeared.

Aiden read the riddle silently, and then read the lines in English aloud:

> Ancient Hebrew is not read from left to right,
> Just as the day does not end with the night
>
> 𝟫𝝜 eht si 𝝜𝟫𝟫𝝜
> 𝟥𝗪𝝜 ot si 𝟫𝟫𝝜 sA
> Whose love is more faithful?
> Than the one who gives life?

"What are those markings?" Susan's brow furrowed.

"That looks like—" Aiden leaned as he began to speak.

"Ancient paleo-Hebrew," Miriam completed his sentence as she leaned in with him.

They looked at each other and smiled.

"Okay, so what's the point in all this?" Susan asked.

THE SECRET OF SCRIPTURE

"We have to answer each line in the riddle in order to deactivate the bomb," Aiden straightened his back. "Is there a table or something around here?"

Susan and Miriam swept their flashlights across the darkness.

"Don't you think the laptop would have been left on one if there was?" Susan suggested.

"Perhaps, but I'm guessing the terrorist left it on the ground for symbolism, given that Christ fell three times on his way to his crucifixion," Aiden followed their beams of light.

"There's a wood crate over here," Miriam shouted.

Aiden and Susan approached. After Aiden confirmed the crate was strudy enough to support the laptop's weight, he gently placed it on the crate.

"All right," Aiden rubbed his hands together before he reread the poem aloud. "Ancient Hebrew is not read from left to right, just as the day does not end with the night."

"What does that mean, the day does not end with the night?" Susan asked.

"Biblical days, even Jewish holidays, begin at sunset," Miriam said.

"The riddle is giving us a clue on how to read the following lines. Instead of reading left to right, as in Western languages, we are being directed to read in the reverse," Aiden said.

"By understanding the dichotomy in cultures, we'll be better able to grasp the concept being relayed in the message," Miriam added. "Hence, the day and night reference."

Aiden turned to her and smiled.

"The lettering here, even in English, is presented in the reverse," Miriam turned back to the monitor.

"Is that a crooked letter 'A,' or am I simply recognizing what I'm accustomed to seeing?" Susan pointed at the screen.

"Actually, yes, it is the paleo-Hebrew letter 'A,' a pictograph that also represented an Ox, with two horns, two ears, and a nose, which denoted strength.

"Or stubbornness when linked with men," Miriam interjected.

"So, the next letter then, is that a 'G' written twice?"

"No, that next letter represents the letter 'B,' so an 'A' followed by two 'B's,' and then another 'A' is for Abba, the Hebrew word for God the Father," Aiden corrected.

"It appears three times in the New Testament," Miriam said. "In each case it is used with a reference to God."

"Abba is to Ab," Aiden read the sentence aloud.

"Ab also means father as it was used in the Old Testament," Miriam turned to Aiden.

He studied the next line in the poem. "The next three letters together represent mother," Aiden finally spoke.

"Are you sure?" Susan asked.

"Yes, you see here, the letter *after* 'A' in *this* word represents water, and or blood, because as water gives life, a mother gives life, and blood passes from one generation to another through the mother," Aiden pointed. "Placing the letters together literally translates to 'strong water.'"

"Which comes from ancient times when Hebrews made glue by boiling animal skins in water," Miriam added. "A sticky liquid formed at the surface after the skin broke down. Once the thick liquid was removed, it was used as a binding agent—glue—referred to as 'strong water.' Equating a mother with the thick liquid is a way of acknowledging that it is a mother's love that binds a family together."

"Abba is to Ab," Aiden repeated.

"God is to father as mother is to wife. Whose love is more faithful, than the one who gives life?" Miriam completed the poem.

"Answering the question posed in the final two lines," Aiden turned to the laptop. "A mother's love is equal to God's love."

THE SECRET OF SCRIPTURE

"That is correct, professor," Sarai appeared on the screen once again. "Here is your second image."

"Man, you guys are good," Susan crossed her arms and nudged Aiden with her elbow.

Sarai vanished from the screen, and a strange image appeared in her stead.

"What in the—" Miriam's brow furrowed.

Aiden retrieved his smartphone from his pocket and snapped a picture of the image on the screen.

Sarai appeared on the screen once again and spoke. "I look forward to seeing you in the presence of God."

52
SAFE HOUSE WEST SIDE OF CHICAGO
Chicago, IL.
5:20 a.m.

Nagi's smart car pulled up in front of the safehouse. The red brick building with dark windows and an unkept yard stood on the corner lot. The only light came from a street lamp near the stop sign. Several vehicles were parked on both sides of the one-way street, unoccupied. Shadows loomed long and deep where the streetlights no longer cast their luminous glow. Other lamps flickered halfway down the block.

"Is anyone even here?" Nagi asked.

They scanned the area around the house. There weren't any vehicles parked directly in front of the home, and the house itself showed no signs of life.

"Chances are Condlin and his team parked their van inside the detached two-car garage behind the house," Angelo said.

"So, what's the plan?" Nagi turned to Angelo.

"Well, since the C.I.A. tracked us to your house, then chances are they'll track us here," Angelo turned to Prescott. "They're after you, so we'll use you as bait."

"Splendid," Prescott rolled his eyes.

"Don't worry," Angelo nudged Prescott with his elbow. "We've got your back. Condlin's team is one of the best."

"Speak of the devil," Nagi motioned at Condlin approaching from the shadowed alley between the houses.

Condlin pulled the door open and climbed into the vehicle. He and Angelo greeted each other with a handshake before Condlin turned to Nagi.

"Well if it isn't the code breaker."

"I'm a philologist and cryptographer," Nagi corrected him. "I break codes for fun."

"Right," Condlin said.

THE SECRET OF SCRIPTURE

"Andrew, this is Prescott. He's the guy I messaged you about on the way here."

"A pleasure," Condlin shook his hand. "So, you specialize in acquiring ancient relics and rare artifacts, huh?"

"Pretty much," Prescott said.

"Well, you must be onto something pretty hot to have the C.I.A. breaking protocol to track you down on American soil," Condlin said.

Prescott straightened his back. He gazed into Condlin's deep-set hazel eyes and tried to read him, but the former F.B.I. agent and private sector operative didn't betray his thoughts.

"Don't worry, I'm not here to turn you in," Condlin assured him. "Truth be told, in another life I ran Special Ops teams to apprehend the best of the best when it came to catching the bad guys in cases of smuggling rare artifacts in and out of the country. In this case, a C.I.A. operative working on U.S. soil is the bad guy."

"Your team is in place, then?" Angelo asked Condlin.

"They're ready to roll, brother," Condlin confirmed.

"What do you need me to do?" Nagi said.

"You take you car around back," Angelo directed Nagi. "Park in the alley behind the garage and keep an eye out for anything suspicious."

"I have a team of running point on the audio-visual front from a van inside the garage," Condlin turned to Nagi. "Link up with them when you get back there so we're all on the same page. I'll let 'em know you're coming."

"Got it," Nagi swivled his seat to face the cockpit. "You hear that, Priya, we're about to fuck some shit up!"

"Who the hell is Priya?" Condlin looked around confused.

"You don't want to know," Angelo shook his head.

The three men climbed out of the smart car and headed toward the alley between the safe house and the house directly beside it. Nagi instructed Priya to take them to the rear alleyway and park behind the two-car garage of that address.

Condlin led them through the darkness until they arrived at a side door of the home. They followed him inside. He typed a code into his smartphone to resecure the door before they proceeded upstairs.

"Did you just lock that door with your smartphone?" Prescott asked.

"Yes. The house is seldom used these days, but we have everything we need for the operation already in place," Condlin said as he handed them earpieces. "Here, put these on so we're all connected."

"Kinda reminds me of a haunted house," Angelo looked around.

The floorboards creaked beneath their footsteps and the scent of mold lingered in the air. Sheets covered most of the furniture, and a thin layer of dust covered the railings. Only three lightbulbs guided their way. Two dangled in the hallway leading to the main living room and one hung from the ceiling over an old wooden chair.

"This is Alpha team in the garage," one of the two men running the commications ops from the van spoke into their earpieces.

"I copy," Angelo said.

"I copy," Prescott followed suit.

"Good. Now that that's taken care of," Condlin stopped before the chair and turned to Prescott. "This where you will sit with hands cuffed behind your back."

"Angelo, you will stand here, right in front of him, so they can see you through the window. It will appear as though the two of you are here alone. My team is already positioned throughout the house, but our presence won't be made known until absolutely necessary."

"How will you know when that is?" Prescott asked.

THE SECRET OF SCRIPTURE

"Don't worry, we'll know," Condlin assured him before he turned to Angelo. "How long do you think that C.I.A. team will take to get here?"

"I don't know," Angelo shrugged. "Nagi bought us some time with one of his little stunts, but who knows how quickly they recovered."

"The code breaker is quite proficient. I would have offered him a job if he wasn't such a smart ass," Condlin said.

"Hey, I heard that," Nagi chimed in over the earpiece.

"I know," Condlin said.

Angelo and Prescott tried to suppress their smiles.

"All right, well, you two get situated in here," Condlin said. "I have another team in an abandoned house across the street. They're our eyes out front. Nagi, you're our eyes out back."

"Ten-four, roger-roger," Nagi joked.

"I'm going to hide in this compartment under the stairs leading to the second floor," Condlin said. "We also have another man at the top of the staircase, as well as a few others hidden throughout this house."

"See, I told you," Angelo turned to Prescott. "We've got your back."

"That reminds me," Condlin reached into the compartment beneath the stairs and pulled out a bulletproof vest. "Put this on beneath your shirt."

"You think they're goint to shoot me?" Prescott said.

"From what Angelo told me about your encounter with them earlier, I think they already tried, and are after you now to finish the job."

"Bloody hell," Prescott muttered under his breath.

"Heads up," one of Condlin's men spoke into their earpieces. "A Chicago PD squad just pulled up in front of the house."

"No doubt it's my sergeant," Angelo said.

"Looks like our distraction didn't last as long as we would have liked," Nagi said.

"Talk to me, Tommy, what do you see?" Condlin said.

"I see four male occupants. One appears to have sergeant stripes on his left sleeve. Another male White, possibly Hispanic, is in the front passenger seat with two more male subjects in the back."

"Do you see any additional movement inside the vehicle?" Condlin asked.

"They don't appear to be reaching for their radios to call for back up," Tommy said.

"Everybody copy that?" Condlin asked.

"Loud and clear," everyone replied in unison.

"What's with all this under the radar shit?" Nagi said.

"It means we can't trust anyone tonight, except those of us on our radio channel," Condlin met Angelo and Prescott's eyes. "Hurry up and put that vest on."

Prescott pulled his shirt off and hurried with the vest. Angelo stepped forward and helped him secure it properly.

"You want to make sure it's on nice and snug to cover your vital organs," Angelo said. "You don't want it shifting on you at the worst possible moment."

"What about my arms?" Prescott asked as he lifted his arms above his shoulders.

"A shot to the limbs won't kill you, and a shot to the face is highly unlikely due to the probability of missing," Angelo said.

"Given the kind of training these guys receive I assure you that's not where they'll be aiming anyway," Condlin added.

"You think they'll aim for my torso?" Prescott pulled his shirt back on.

"Center mass," Angelo punched Prescott in the chest. "One shot, one kill. All right, have a seat and put your arms behind your back."

"What'cha want, what'cha want, what'cha gon' do?" Nagi could be heard singing the theme song to the popular television show, Cops. "Bad boys, bad boys, what'cha gon' do, what'cha gon' do when they come for you."

"What the hell is that?" Tommy asked from across the street.

"Nagi, really?" Angelo asked as he secured the cuffs around Prescott's wrists.

"What? I'm getting into character," Nagi said.

"All right, no more screwing around," Condlin turned to climb into the secret compartment. "Everyone get into position. It's show time."

53
SAFE HOUSE WEST SIDE OF CHICAGO
Chicago, IL.
5:25 p.m.

Solinski and his team pulled up in front of the house and saw a light on through an opening in the curtains. They compared the location on the map application with their current position and confirmed the red dot of Angelo's phone pinged to that specific house.

"What the hell is Marquez doing here?" Solinski scanned the area before he turned his attention back to the house.

"How do you want to handle this, sarge?" One of the veteran officers in the back seat asked.

"I'm going to pull the squad up a few houses to where it can't be spotted. Then I want you two to go around the back," Solinski said over his shoulder. "Cruz, I want you with me at the front door. Once we're on the move, everyone watch your six."

"Ten-four," they said in unison.

After Solinski parked the squad halfway down the block, the four officers exited the vehicle. Solinski and Cruz walked along the sidewalk like two officers on foot patrol in the neighborhood, while the other two dashed through a dark alley and made their way toward the safe house behind the detached garages.

Nagi saw their silhouettes beneath a street lamp behind them.

"Two individuals approaching from the east," Priya said.

"Yes, I see them," Nagi eyed them as they approached. "Let's go zero dark thirty."

"Cloaking sequence initiated," Priya said.

The windows of the smart car tinted and concealed Nagi's presence inside, so that when the officers peered into the vehicle it appeared like a standard automobile without any occupants.

"Sarge," one of the officers keyed up on his radio. "Be advised we have one unoccupied vehicle parked behind the garage of the house in question."

"That must be the vehicle Marquez used to get here," Solinski's voice came across the officer's earpiece. "Which means his personal vehicle must still be at that address in West Chicago. We'll deal with that later. Move into position. Cruz and I are approaching the front door."

"Ten-four," the officer said, and directed his partner to proceed toward the house.

Nagi waited until the officers climbed the fence that ran from the detached garage to the rear of the home before he relayed their location to the team.

"I see them," one of Condlin's operatives confirmed from a second story window inside the home.

The two officers slithered among the shadows and climbed the wooden steps that lead to the back door of the home. One of them tried the doorknob. When it turned with ease, he slowly pushed it open, and they crept inside. The second officer slowly pushed the door closed behind him as they scanned the kitchen. A light over the sink provided enough light to let them make out a small table with two chairs beside an older model fridge with a matching white stove.

No dishes in the sink, the first officer thought to himself as he inched forward. A clear sign the house didn't have a current resident. He motioned for his partner to halt when they heard a knock at the front door.

Footsteps fell on the hardwood floor from the living room to the main entrance at the front of the home. Marquez pulled the door open to find Solinski's steely grey eyes staring back at him.

"Do you mind telling me what the fuck you've been up to, and why you led me on a wild goose chase across the city?" Solinski pushed the door open and crossed the threshold.

"Sarge, I can explain," Marquez back stepped as Cruz followed Solinski into the home.

"You're damn right you can explain," Solinski caught sight of Prescott from the corner of his eye. "And what the hell is he doing here? You know the DuPage County Sheriff's department is livid over that little stunt you pulled at the hospital."

Cruz pushed the front door closed behind him.

"I needed to get him out of there, because he wasn't able to communicate with anyone in English," Marquez said.

"What do you mean he wasn't able to communicate with anyone in English?" Solinski eyed Prescott as he stepped into the living room.

"Nagi, get in here," Marquez said.

"What?" Solinski turned to Marquez.

"You'll see in a moment," Marquez said. "It'll help clarify everything."

"Angelo, what are you doing?" Condlin spoke with a low voice.

"Trust me," Marquez answered as he held Solinski's gaze.

"You're lucky I'm even hearing you out," Solinski said.

"Nagi, use the side entrance where I brought Angelo into the house," Condlin said. "I don't want the two cops in the kitchen to move."

"Got it," Nagi said as he climbed out of his smart car and headed toward the dark alley.

"You may want to double-time it into the house Nagi," Tommy said. "Looks like the party just arrived."

54
SAFE HOUSE WEST SIDE OF CHICAGO
Chicago, IL.
5:30 a.m.

Two hundred yards from the house, the white van stopped at the intersection while the operatives confirmed the location of the homing beacon hidden beneath the collar of Angelo's suit jacket. The sleeping neighborhood was filled with shadows, and not a soul lingered outside.

"He's in the first house on the right just beyond the empty plot of land," one of the operatives said from the rear of the van.

"How do you want to proceed?" The driver turned to Agent Bauer in the seat beside him.

Bauer studied the house momentarily. *Why did you come here?* He wondered to himself.

"I've got movement on our six," the operative in the rear said.

They glanced into the rear view mirrors and saw a sedan with a glowing Uber emblem approach. The white van proceeded slowly through the intersection as the sedan turned southbound after the stop.

"As far as we know, there's two—maybe three—of them," Bauer turned to his team in the rear of the van. "There's five of us, and no room for error. We go in, eliminate the threat, tie up loose ends, and move out. Are we clear on our objective?"

"What about the officer?" One of the operatives said. "We can't just kill a Chicago cop."

"We're in Chi-Raq," Bauer shrugged. "We'll make it look like a gang-related officer-involved shooting during an undercover operation for a drug deal. The media will eat it up for a day or two, but let's face it—when it's a cop that's shot—the story will fade into obscurity anyway."

The van came to a halt when it reached the front of the house.

"I'm going to make contact at the front door. You two go around back, and you two cover the side entry-exit points. Hold your positions until I give the signal," Bauer instructed his four operatives.

He turned to the driver and instructed him to circle the block a few times until they were ready to move out.

"I've got you all on audio, and will monitor the radio traffic on our channel from back here," the comm-specialist said.

"Good, let's move," Bauer said.

The five operatives jumped out of the vehicle and moved into position under the cover of night.

"We've got about twenty minutes before sunrise," Bauer spoke into his mic. "Let's be quick about this, so we can get the hell out of here."

55
SAFE HOUSE WEST SIDE OF CHICAGO
Chicago, IL.
5:35 a.m.

"I've got movement from the van," Tommy relayed to the entire team. "Five operatives converging on your location. Two appear to be moving to the east side of the building, and another two are moving to the west, while the fifth subject is clad in a rabbi's attire and headed straight for the front door."

"Ten-four, Tommy, thanks," Condlin responded. "All right Angelo, we've gotta wrap things up with your sergeant."

"You expect me to believe that shit?" Solinski crossed his arms.

"It's the truth, Sarge," Angelo said. "One way or the other, the DuPage County Sheriff's department was going to be investigating a murder had I not sprung him from CDH."

"How did you expect me to smooth things over with them after you kept me out of the loop?"

"Honestly, I hadn't thought that far ahead," Angelo shrugged. "I simply knew that the Book of Daniel reference was no coincidence given what's happening in Jerusalem as we speak."

"He's not kidding, Sarge," Cruz handed his smartphone to Solinski.

The headline on a news media's mobile app read: *Middle East Nations At An Impasse As World Braces For War.*

A knock at the door broke the silence.

"That's the C.I.A. operative we've been waiting for," Angelo said. "Nagi, I need you to move into that corner for now."

"You don't have to tell me twice," Nagi hurried across the living room.

"How do you plan to deal with the C.I.A?" Solinski asked.

"I'm always prepared, Sarge, just trust me on this," Angelo slapped him on the arm and moved past him to answer the door.

The knock came again as Angelo reached for the doorknob and pulled the door open.

"Hello, detective," Bauer greeted Angelo with a smirk. "May I come in?"

"Please do," Angelo nodded. "Should I address you as rabbi, or as Agent Bauer?"

"So, you put two-and-two together," Bauer said as he crossed the threshold into the house. He met Solinski's gaze before he made a mental note of where Cruz stood beside the sergeant. Their eyes met momentarily before he turned to where Prescott sat handcuffed on a wooden chair. "I wondered why you took off the way you did."

"How did you manage to change four flat tires so quickly?" Angelo closed the door and crossed his arms.

"Self-inflating tire technology isn't just for luxury cars, detective," Bauer said. "Though, I do admit having to wait for all four tires to reach appropriate tire pressure readings was a bit frustrating."

"How did you know to track my officer to this location?" Solinski said.

"I slipped a homing beacon under the collar of his suit jacket during our struggle at the hospital," Bauer shrugged. "I had hoped your actions would have produced better results, Detective Marquez. Perhaps leading us to whoever else Mr. Prescott here is working with, but it seems that was wishful thinking. Unless of course, Mr. Prescott is willing to cooperate."

"I work alone," Prescott said.

"No one in your field works alone," Bauer said. "A few minutes with me, and I'm sure you'll be singing a different tune. I have ways of getting people like you to talk."

"There won't be any torture tactics employed here," Solinski said.

THE SECRET OF SCRIPTURE

"I'm afraid this matter is not up to you, sergeant," Bauer met Solinski's glare. "I'm taking this man into custody."

"The hell you are," Angelo stood between Prescott and Bauer.

"You tipped your hand too soon, detective," Bauer said.

Bauer's men moved into the light. Two of them had Solinski's officers from the kitchen, unarmed with their hands up as they entered the living room. The other two pointed their weapons at Prescott and Angelo.

"What kind of bullshit move is this?" Solinski snapped.

Cruz brandished his weapon and pointed it at Solinski's head. "Hand me your weapon, sarge. Nice and easy."

"What the—" Angelo looked perplexed.

"Cruz, what the hell are you doing?" Solinski demanded.

Bauer and Angelo brandished their weapons simultaneously and pointed them at each other.

"Sorry, sarge, but they didn't leave me any choice," Cruz said. "It was either I help them keep tabs on Marquez, or my daughter's life."

"Isn't this quite the predicament?" Bauer smirked. "You do realize you're outgunned, don't you, detective?"

"Now," Condlin gave the command to his men. They emerged from their hidden positions and pointed their weapons at the C.I.A. operatives.

"Looks like we have ourselves another Mexican standoff," Nagi emerged from the shadowed corner. "Except this time we *do* have a Mexican."

"Hey, I'm Puerto Rican," Cruz said over his shoulder.

"I'm not talking about you, Chico. I'm talking about the Man," Nagi nodded at Angelo.

"What the fuck is going on here?" Solinski demanded.

"Well, sergeant, it looks like your detective here has gotten himself mixed up in an international incident," Bauer said. "Prescott here steals valuable relics to sell on the Black Market, and then uses the money to fund terrorist organizations."

"Typical government rhetoric," Condlin stepped forward.

"Who the hell are you?" Solinski said.

"I'm the guy who's going to clean up this mess," Condlin said. "Otherwise, no one is making it out of here alive. We wouldn't want that now, would we?"

56
JAFFA GATES OLD CITY
Jerusalem, Israel
12:45 p.m.

Yeshua's squad came to a screeching halt. The crowds at each of the gates of the Old City had swelled over the past hour. Believers and pilgrims converged in droves after the last transmission from the terrorists. Though many had chosen sides based on faith-affiliation, there were others who stood arm in arm with their interfaith brothers and sisters as a show of unity in the face of disaster.

News vans had taken up positions near the gates. Their satellite towers stood high above the crowds. Their correspondents reported live from the Old City about the casualties at the Tower of David Museum. Others relayed information about the inhabitants and clerics of the Old City who refused to evacuate, despite attempts from the local authorities to move them out of harm's way.

"Turn on your lights and sirens," Yeshua commanded. "Perhaps that will get these people to move aside so we can get closer to the city entrance."

The young officer did as Yeshua instructed. The squad inched forward as protestors pounded on the hood, roof and trunk of the vehicle.

"You'd think these people would be a bit more cooperative," the young officer said.

"Mob mentality leads the masses to engage in irrational behavior during a crisis," Yeshua said. "People don't think they need law enforcement, but without someone to police their behavior the general public would be at the mercy of this sort of chaos."

"How do we fix this?" The young officer steered through the crowd carefully.

"We take it one day at a time and remind ourselves that people of all walks of life matter," Yeshua eyed the gate over the crowd.

"How do you intend to find the professor once we reach the gate?"

"I've already arranged for Abigail to have the cell sites around the Old City reactivated. Once the signals are up, she will triangulate his position using his cellphone number by running a reverse lookup. Then she'll text me with his location, and hopefully I'll be able to get to him in time."

"In time for what?"

"In time to help him deactivate the remaining bombs hidden in the Old City and get them out of there," Yeshua said.

"Not for nothing, Pakad, but given what is being reported on the news, I dare say those bombs are only part of our problem."

"I take it that you're referring to the tensions on the world stage," Yeshua turned to him.

"Yes."

"Commander Shalom is running point on that aspect of this operation," Yeshua assured him. "The Lahav 433 is using every resource at their disposal to locate the hostages. I trust that they'll achieve their objective in time. After all, they are quite efficient at what they do."

"What if Commander Shalom discovers what you are doing?"

"If I fail, it won't matter. If I succeed, it will be worth it."

The squad finally arrived as close to the gate as circumstances allowed.

"You wait here and assist with crowd control," Yeshua unbuckled his seat belt.

"You're going in alone?"

"Try to keep these people safe," Yeshua climbed out of the vehicle. "Do not follow me."

Yeshua slammed the car door shut. He scanned the gate before he headed toward a group of officers to gain entry into the city. He thought he would be entering alone. He had no idea a shadow returned from the dead to follow him.

THE SECRET OF SCRIPTURE

57
TOWER OF DAVID MUSEUM OLD CITY
Jerusalem, Israel
12:50 p.m.

Rescue workers sifted through the rubble tirelessly. The sun beat down on them, but they continued to search for the injured and the dead. The occasional bloodied limb offered hope that someone merely lay unconscious, but more often than not the victim lay dead. When they found her beneath a pile of wood from the doors of the museum, they did not expect to revive her on the scene. After several minutes of observing her faint pulse they waited until a paramedic finally arrived with an Ammonia Inhalant. He passed it under her nose, and within seconds she regained consciousness.

"Ma'am, are you okay?" The paramedic asked as he placed a hand on her forehead. A volunteer assisted her with sitting upright.

"What happened?" She rubbed her temples.

"You were caught in the explosion," a man said standing over her.

"Do you feel any pain or discomfort that you don't recall feeling before this happened?" The paramedic shined a light into her eyes.

"I just feel sore, and...ouch!" She felt a bump on her head.

"That must be where the door struck you during the explosion and knocked you down," the paramedic said. "Fortunately for you, it shielded you from the blast."

"The blast?" she looked at the paramedic perplexed.

"Yes. Terrorists have attacked the city. There was another explosion at the Damascus Gate. A car bomb, I believe," the paramedic continued.

"A car bomb?" she repeated.

"There was only one person killed by that explosion," the paramedic glanced around. "Whereas here, the museum was packed with tourists and guests when the bomb went off."

THE SECRET OF SCRIPTURE

Farhad! She leapt to her feet. She swayed a little, and a volunteer caught her as she struggled to steady herself.

"Ma'am, you mustn't move so quickly in your condition," the paramedic warned. "Please, have a seat over there while we contact your superiors to let them know we have found you."

Batya cursed under her breath. She knew she'd have a lot to answer for when her superiors discovered she was on-scene when she was supposed to have the day off work. She had told the others, including the chief inspector, that she had switched shifts with another officer. Once they discovered the truth, they'd quickly link her to the events of the day, and her affair with Farhad.

"Where's my phone?" Batya searched the ground.

"Ma'am, I doubt your phone is in working order," the paramedic said. "Please, wait over there while I get you a stretcher."

The paramedic instructed the volunteer to assist Batya with moving toward a temporary staging area. The volunteer nodded her compliance. She guided Batya toward the staging area where paramedics tended to the wounded before they were to be taken to the nearest hospitals. Batya sat on a wooden bench when a cry for help drew the volunteer's attention.

"I've found another survivor!" The voice said.

"Will you be okay?" The volunteer asked Batya.

"Yes," Batya nodded. "Go, help them."

The volunteer ran to assist. Batya scanned her surroundings. She remembered the text messages she received from Arwan. He had warned her just in time, but where was he now. *Where is Farhad?* She observed an officer pass through the gate. He was in a hurry. He was alone. He was Pakad Yeshua Schwartz, and he would lead her to the answers she sought.

58
WEST SIDE OF CHICAGO
Chicago, IL.
5:55 p.m.

Condlin stood face to face with Agent Bauer. His men had the tactical advantage both inside the safehouse and outside. Bauer's men in the van circled the block, but from their position they could not confirm if Condlin was bluffing and advised him it would be best not to risk their operation without additional support.

"What are your terms?" Bauer said.

"Have your men stand down. You leave here without Prescott and close your investigation, unless the C.I.A. wants to go on record as running an operation on U.S. soil without direction from the Director of National Intelligence," Condlin said. "We both know the kind of media shit-storm and political fallout that would result from having this information go public."

Bauer contemplated their predicament. He still had possession of the scrolls, despite not having obtained the money. They could tail Prescott out of the country and track down Omar Al-Ansari later. He eyed each of Condlin's men. Weapons drawn with resolve in their eyes. *These guys are professionals. I'm going to have to find out who they're working for*, he thought to himself.

"Well agent," Condlin said. "What's it going to be?"

Agent Bauer nodded for his men to lower their weapons. Cruz also lowered his firearm. Solinski turned around and punched him in the face.

"That's enough, sergeant," Condlin commanded. "We'll deal with him later."

"This isn't over," Bauer glared at Prescott.

"There is one other matter that needs to be resolved," Angelo stepped forward.

Condlin turned to Angelo perplexed and waited for him to speak.

THE SECRET OF SCRIPTURE

"We're going to need you to hand over the missing scrolls," Angelo said.

"Negative," Bauer shook his head. "That's not going to happen."

"Wrong answer," Angelo said. "It *will* happen, otherwise none of you will leave this building alive."

"Do you want the wrath of the federal government to come down on you?" Bauer threatened.

"Aside from anyone in this room, no one knows you're here," Angelo said.

"I have operatives outside and they will—"

"Your team in the white van?" Condlin interrupted. "My snipers have them in their sights. They won't get far, and we'll take the scrolls anyway."

"What makes you so sure I have them?" Bauer said.

"I doubt you would leave anything that valuable beyond your reach," Condlin said.

"It's your call, agent," Angelo pointed his firearm at Bauer's head.

"Marquez," Solinski began to say, but Condlin silenced him with a wave of his hand.

"Do you realize what you're doing here, detective?" Bauer snapped.

Angelo reached forward and yanked at the beard on Bauer's face. Bauer shouted in protest as the glue gave way and pulled at his skin.

"I'm revealing you for what you truly are," Angelo tossed the fake beard on the ground. "The scrolls, agent," Marquez said.

"They're in the van," Bauer massaged his chin and jaw.

"Have your men bring them in," Condlin said.

Bauer hesitated. He knew the consequence of handing them over. His team had acquired them illegally from a private collector in the U.S. The objective had been to prevent them from falling into the wrong hands. Now they would go beyond his reach, and the fallout would have devastating consequences. If not immediately, it would happen eventually. Bauer knew Condlin and Marquez would not understand, or believe him.

"Now, Agent Bauer," Angelo insisted.

"Fine!" Bauer shot back. "Bring the scrolls inside," he spoke into his mic.

"Are you sure—" his comms specialist began to ask.

"Yes, I'm sure, damn it," Bauer snapped. He met Angelo's cold stare. "You have no idea what you have done, detective."

***

After Bauer handed over the scrolls, Condlin and his men let the agents leave unscathed. They watched them descend the front steps in the early morning light before they climbed into their van and drove away.

Angelo uncuffed Prescott, and then handed him the scrolls.

"What's so important about those scrolls anyway?" Solinski asked.

"The less you know, the better," Angelo said.

"After what you just pulled tonight—" Solinski began to say.

"Perhaps there's a way to remedy this inconvenience, sergeant," Condlin interjected. He turned to Prescott. "You still have the money you were supposed to use for the purchase of these items, correct?"

"Back at the hotel, yes," Prescott rubbed his wrists.

"Are you suggesting we take a bribe?" Solinski cast Condlin an incredulous glance.

"Let's call it a finder's fee for your assistance with this matter," Condlin suggested.

"A finder's fee, huh? How much are we talking here?" Solinski placed his hands on his hips.

THE SECRET OF SCRIPTURE

"I dare say those scrolls are worth millions, correct?" Condlin nodded at the relics in Prescott's hands.

"I have five million," Prescott said.

"That's half a mill split evenly ten ways," Condlin shrugged.

"Fuckin' cops," Nagi shook his head.

"Watch your mouth," Solinski snapped. "I can make your life a living hell."

"Oh yeah, I can fuck up your credit, and let your wife see every text message you ever sent. I'm sure there's a badge bunny out there who has received a flirty text from you while you're wife's not paying attention."

"Let's calm down a minute here," Condlin turned to Nagi. "My headcount included you too, code breaker."

"Oh, well, shit when you put it that way," Nagi softened his position.

"What are we going to do about this guy?" Angelo eyed Cruz.

"Get up," Condlin approached. "How did you get involved in this?"

"Some guy called me. Said if I didn't do as instructed, my daughter was as good as dead."

"What did he instruct you to do?" Condlin asked.

"Told me to keep tabs on Marquez."

Everyone in the room turned to Angelo.

"Who was this guy that reached out to you?"

"He wouldn't give me his name. He simply referred to himself as the Preceptor, and told me his operative would reveal himself at the right time."

"That explains how the C.I.A. got involved," Condlin turned back to Angelo. "Someone really wanted those scrolls, and they used you to lure Prescott out into the open."

"Either way, what's done is done," Angelo said. "Given the circumstances, you really can't bring Cruz up on charges."

"He can't stay on the force, either," Solinski looked at Eli. "You've been compromised, and whoever this guy is that reached out to you is sure to seek retribution."

"Are you guys just going to hang him out to dry?" Nagi asked.

"No," Condlin said. "The kid simply did what was best for his daughter. Any one of us would have done the same thing."

"What are you suggesting?" Solinski turned to Condlin.

"Now that I'm retired, the team has an open spot. What do you think Tommy?"

"If you think he can handle the job," Tommy replied over the earpiece.

"With this team at your back, your daughter will be well-protected. The pay is good, but the job is dangerous," Condlin said to Eli. "You open to a career change?"

"I'm in," Cruz nodded.

"In the future, though, you'll have to tell someone when something like this happens. The success of the team comes down to absolute trust," Condlin said.

"I understand, and thanks." Cruz shook Condlin's hand before he turned to Solinski and apologized.

"Right now, let's focus on picking up your daughter. No doubt that Bauer has informed his boss of what transpired here today," Solinski said.

"I'll send two of my men with you," Condlin assured him. "You guys better get a move on. I'll take Prescott to the hotel to retrieve the funds and I'll be in touch."

"All right, let's go," Solinski motioned for his men to follow.

After Solinski left with his officers and two of the operatives, Condlin turned to Prescott.

"Once we retrieve the funds and check you out of the hotel, I'll help you get out of the country with those scrolls. You'll be on your own after that."

THE SECRET OF SCRIPTURE

"Thanks, you're a bloody ledge for that," Prescott smiled. He approached Angelo and thanked him for his assistance. "You're a cracking cop, regardless of what they say about Chicago cops on the tele. You too, mate," he turned to Nagi. "You're a bloody brilliant bloke, if I've ever seen one."

"You're not too bad yourself, Black Jesus," Nagi shook his hand. "Well, I better get back home. I'm freakin' tired."

"Hey, Nagi, mind giving me a lift? I left my car at your place, remember?"

"All right, Dick, let's go," Nagi headed toward the door.

Angelo thanked Condlin for coming through on such short notice.

"You're my boy, Angelo. Of course I'll come through when you need me. Now get outta here before I make you come with me to the strip joint."

Outside, the sun peered over the horizon. The warm summer breeze hinted at a scorcher of a day as birds chirped in the distance. Priya pulled up curbside and the passengerside door of the smart car opened automatically. Nagi climbed in first and instructed Priya to find the most expedient route home.

"Confirmed," Priya said. "Did you enjoy yourself playing with the boys?"

"Eh, all in a day's work," Nagi shrugged and leaned back in his seat.

The door closed behind Angelo as he stretched out on the rear seat.

"By the way, Nagi, I appreciate your help with all this," Angelo reached over and patted him on the shoulder. "You never cease to amaze me."

"No worries," Nagi shrugged and looked at him over his shoulder. "This doesn't mean we're cool though. I have a reputation to protect. You know, bad boy for life!"

59
BREAKING NEWS i-24NEWS
Israel
1:00 p.m.

"We return now with an update," Binyamin read the script as it appeared on the teleprompter. "World leaders have gathered at the U.N. and released this official statement: 'As we endeavor to resolve this matter in an expedient and diplomatic manner, we will not allow the world to be held hostage by terrorists. Our hearts go out to the families and loved ones lost in today's cowardly attacks. Please know we are doing everything in our power to achieve peace on this darkest of days.'"

Binyamin sat silently for a moment before he continued.

"In accordance with the official statement made by the U.N. council, which has commenced a closed-door meeting, i24 has come to an agreement with news agencies around the globe to not air anymore video feeds received by the terrorists."

A picture-in-picture image showed a live feed of the crowds surrounding the Old City of Jerusalem.

"As Believers swarm the gates of the Old City, some to protest against one another, and others to stand in solidarity against these attacks on the Abrahamic faiths, we here at i24 News feel that to continue to air the footage of beheadings and threats only serves to embolden the terrorists who hide behind hoods like cowards."

The picture-in-picture image briefly showed Arwan, who remained unidentified beneath his black hood. News agencies reported that several governments had initiated voice analysis in an attempt to identify him, and they would release any findings as soon as they were made available.

"In related news," Binyamin turned to another teleprompter. "Commander Shalom of the Lahav 433 states that investigators received intel that famed Professor Aiden Leonardo of the University of Illinois at Chicago may be connected to this incident. Though he would not elaborate further on the professor's involvement, he did say that Professor Leonardo is currently missing and believed to be somewhere in the Old City."

Images and video clips of Aiden at speaking engagements and in lecture halls appeared on the screen.

"Professor Leonardo became the Director of Religious Studies after more than a decade heading various departments, which included: Early Christianity ancient Mediterranean religion and philosophy, Judaism and Jewish-Islamic relations and philosophy of religion, Biblical Studies in Judaism, History of Antisemitism and the Holocaust, Islam and the Middle East, Medieval Christianity and Catholicism, and Zionism in Palestine and Israel."

Binyamin turned to another teleprompter. "That is quite an extensive resume for a man of his age. It was discovered only a few years ago that Professor Leonardo was the illegimate son of the late, disgraced investment banker Lazzaro de Medici. Lazzaro's ponsi scheme had swindled hundreds of millionaires out of billions of dollars. Authorities never recovered the stolen funds, and both the F.B.I. and the S.E.C. closed their investigations without making any further arrests."

An image of Lazzaro in his final days appeared on the screen next to an image of him when he was at the height of his powers. His health had faded after his initial indictment. He had gone from a robust-framed man with presence to a slender man hunched over with emptiness in his eyes.

"Though the professor was never linked to his father's crimes, there were those in small circles that speculated a possible cover-up," Binyamin continued. "In light of today's announcement by the Lahav 433—Israel's equivalent of the F.B.I.—those allegations may bubble to the surface again."

60
UNDISCLOSED LOCATION
Israel
1:00 p.m.

Arwan stood beneath the midday sun and wondered why Batya's phone did not ring. Every call he had attempted after their last exchange of text messages had gone straight to voicemail. *I hope she made it out safely*, he thought to himself. Still, he could not help but think the worst.

The Preceptor had sent her to her death. Not wanting to risk her capture by the authorities and have her reveal knowledge of the day's attacks—before they were supposed to be privy to the information—made the decision a logical conclusion in the Preceptor's mind. For Arwan, however, the choice was not that simple. He was secretly in love with her, despite her relationship with Farhad, and Farhad's death was necessary to fulfill his own desires.

"Did she uncover our plot to eliminate Farhad?" He muttered to himself. "Is that why she hasn't returned my calls? Or did she become a victim of the attack on the museum?"

He had tried to warn her sooner to stay away from the museum, but he couldn't get away from anyone long enough to make the call, or send her the text. Between the rapid succession of abductions of the hostages under the cover of night and moving them to the location where they were being held, to the possibility that she would receive the message while meeting with Farhad, which would have raised suspicion, since Farhad had no knowledge of the Preceptor's plan to send her to the location where he instructed Farhad to leave the first bomb. Arwan reached out to her as soon as he could. Perhaps he had been too late.

The wooden door creaked open behind him. Ali stepped out of the cool cooridor and into the heat beneath the sun.

"Is everything in place?" Arwan asked over his shoulder.

THE SECRET OF SCRIPTURE

"News reports show that although the U.N. has convened, and militaries have moved to Israel's borders, they refuse to air anymore of our video feeds," Ali approached. "We could air them on the Internet, where governments have little sway over what can and cannot be viewed, but—"

"There's no need to air another beheading," Anwar interrupted him. "We have achieved our goal."

"Are you certain of this?" Ali asked.

"You said the news reported that militaries have mobilized and wait at Israel's borders," Anwar turned to face him.

"Yes," Ali nodded. "Many of our Arab brothers and sisters, whether allies of Israel or not have taken up arms against the call for the removal of the Jerusalem Islamic Waqf from the Temple Mount in the Old City."

"The enemies of our enemies have become our allies," Anwar said. "The Preceptor predicted this outcome, because history led us to this moment. When the war begins, the attack on Israel will avenge our fathers and our grandfathers for the great injustices our people have endured. They stole our lands, evicted us from our homes, and have treated us as though we are less than human."

"Today, they will rue the atrocities they have committed against us," Ali said.

"Before now, we lacked the resources to fight back, and so others have had to do so in our stead. They employed tactics that instilled the same fear in the minds of the West that our enemies etched into the hearts of our mothers and sisters. Today, we strike back with the fists of others and reclaim what is rightfully ours," Arwan placed a hand on Ali's shoulder.

"Indeed we will," Ali looked over the landscape. "What will happen after the war?"

"The Preceptor promised us a new chapter and a return to our lands."

"What will we do about the hostages?" Ali looked him in the eyes.

"We will release them."

"All of them?"

"Yes."

"If we release them, we will relinquish our leverage," Ali said.

"It is no longer necessary to hold them. Releasing them will show the world that we are men of God and that we are men of mercy," Arwan said.

"Do you think they will believe that after what they saw on the television?" Ali asked.

"We let them see what we wanted them to see," Arwan shrugged. "When they find the hostages alive, they will discover that we merely beheaded mannequins. They will know that we are soldiers and not murderers. We simply had to make our enemies believe we were capable of it to ignite their call to action. The true murderers are the politicians that send the sons of the poor to fight wars in order to perpetuate their imperialistic agendas. Today, the Preceptor will have them all at his mercy."

61
NATIONAL HEADQUARTERS OF THE ISRAEL POLICE
Kiryat Menachem Begin
Jerusalem, Israel
1:05 p.m.

Abigail sat at her computer terminal and rapidly typed a series of codes onto her keyboard. She occasionally cast Commander Shalom a furtive glance. He stood several meters away and studied the images that appeared on the large screen monitors. Each displayed a bird's eye view of the Old City. The crowds beyond the gates had swelled exponentially, yet most of the streets within the city walls were empty.

"What is it that you are doing, exactly?" Hefetz stood over her.

"I'm hacking into the wireless service provider's network to reactivate the cell towers surrounding the Old City.

"The ones that Commander Shalom ordered to be shutdown?" Hefetz asked.

"Yes," she continued typing, as a series of letters and numbers zipped by on her computer screen.

ACCESS DENIED

Abigail cursed under her breath and resumed typing.

"He had those deactivated for a reason," Hefetz said.

"I know," Abigail nodded. "He had hoped to eliminate the signals of every cellphone in the area to try and locate the encrypted signal used by the terrorists, because he believes they are in the Old City and utilizing their own private network. His goal had been to locate their signal and decrypt it in an effort to pinpoint their location, but the terrorists are too clever for that."

"What are you hoping to achieve by bringing the network back online?"

"By reactivating the cell towers, I'm giving Pakad Schwartz the signal he needs to contact the professor and find him before Shalom's men do," Abigail said.

ACCESS DENIED

Abigail shook her head and sighed in frustration, but resumed typing.

"I thought you worked in the evidence department?" Hefetz eyed the commander.

"I do, but prior to my employment here I worked in cyber security for a private firm," Abigail said.

"In cyber security," Hefetz's brow furrowed. "What the hell led you to leave that to work for us? Clearly it wasn't the pay that lured you away from the private sector."

"I wanted to do my part for the greater good," Abigail shrugged.

ACCESS DENIED

"It'll be a short-lived career once the commander discovers our involvement with Yeshua's objective," Hefetz said. "We'd be fortunate to simply be out of a job, but chances are they'll throw us in jail."

"To prevent a war and save thousands of lives," Abigail looked over her shoulder at Hefetz. "It'll be worth it."

ACCESS GRANTED

"Yes!" Abigail whispered to herself.

"You did it?"

"Almost," she continued typing. "Just a few more seconds and the reactivation sequence will be initiated."

"Then what?"

"It'll take about five minutes for the cell sites to go online, and then every cellphone in the area will have service."

"Well done," Hefetz said. He looked up and met Commander Shalom's glare.

62
OLD CITY
Jerusalem, Israel
1:10 p.m.

"That thing is creepy," Susan turned away from the monitor.

"Who, Sarai, the A.I.?" Aiden turned to Susan.

"Whatever she, or it is, yes," Susan said.

"Better get used to her, or it, because we're at the dawn of a new era where A.I. will be more prevelant in our lives than ever before," Aiden said.

"You're joking, right?" Susan turned to him with arms crossed.

"That's the whole purpose for us being here in Israel," Miriam said.

"That whole tech summit that everyone's been going on about?" Susan titled her head.

"Technology is going to advance by leaps and bounds over the next decade in ways we never imagined," Aiden said. "Everything from quantum computing and cryptocurrency to artificial intelligence and the automation of our homes and vehicles."

"Great, so I'm supposed to get comfortable with the idea that artificial intelligence will be a part of our daily lives, yet one of those *things* is giving you riddles while attached to a bomb?"

"She has a point," Miriam said.

"Speaking of which," Aiden closed the laptop and lifted it off the crate. "We've got to figure out where the final explosive device has been hidden."

"What did she mean by 'I look forward to seeing you in the presence of God?'" Susan asked. "Does she mean to blow us all to hell?"

"I certainly hope not," Aiden held the laptop under his arm.

"There's only one thing I can think of, and it strikes right at the heart of the conflict between the three Abrahamic faiths," Miriam said.

Susan and Aiden turned to her in the darkness. Her face was barely visible from the glow of the flashlight when she pointed it up.

"I think I know where you're going with this," Aiden said.

"The Holy of Holies," Miriam nodded.

"The Holy of Holies?" Susan's brow furrowed.

"According to scripture, it's the inner sanctuary within the Tabernacle inside the Temple in Jerusalem where God dwelled, and where the Ark of the Covenant had been kept," Aiden said.

"Ark of the Covenant, as in Indiana Jones and the Raiders of the Lost Ark?" Susan asked. "Are you kidding me?" The connection did not escape her, given that the popular film series had initially inspired her as a child to someday find lost treasures."

"More or less, but in this case we're not going in search of the Ark," Aiden said.

"The Holy of Holies, however, is here in the Old City," Miriam said.

"Where?" Susan asked.

"That is a hotly contested subject," Aiden said. "Jewish tradition regards the location at the Temple Mount on Mount Moriah, but its proximity to the Foundation Stone beneath the Dome of the Rock is at the heart of the dispute between Jews and Muslims over where the Third Temple should be built."

"Well, if we don't get to that explosive device before it detonates, then it won't be much of an issue, would it?" Susan said.

"How do we get there from here?" Miriam scanned the darkness with her flashlight.

THE SECRET OF SCRIPTURE

"We can't go topside, because chances are the authorities will spot us on one of the cameras, if they haven't already," Susan said.

"We can only hope that the streets down here correlate to the streets built above us over the centuries," Aiden said.

"Based on our current location, we're almost directly north of the Temple Mount," Miriam said.

"If we head south from this intersection we will be traveling along the Little Western Wall that is not visible to the public," Susan suggested.

"It is in close proximity to the Holy of Holies, and the path should take us to the Western Wall Tunnel, which directly faces the Holy of Holies," Miriam said.

"Let's get going, then," Aiden motioned for them to lead the way with their flashlights.

They hurried through the dark corridor. Miriam swept her flashlight across the ground, while Susan pointed hers straight ahead. The stone floor beneath them was sloped and uneven. Their footsteps echoed off the walls and high ceiling.

"Any chance one of you has an extra flashlight?" Aiden asked. He hated feeling as though something lurked in the shadows. A sinking feeling had tugged at his core since childhood that a presence, or unknown entity threatened to trap him in the darkness.

"Sorry, only brought two," Susan shrugged.

Aiden glanced over his shoulder, but only the void of nothingness stared back.

Miriam took hold of his hand. She knew of his fear, and knew that her simple gesture would calm him.

"Why don't they open this area to the public and provide adequate lighting down here?" Susan asked.

"Aside from a tunneling incident in the early 70's that caused a partial collapse and led to international outrage over plans to demolish the entire structure to make room for a new plaza," Aiden said. "Other excavation projects by Jewish groups and the Jerusalem Islamic Waqf have been controversial and highly criticized."

"Largely due to the political sensitivity and the religious significance of the site," Miriam added. "Any attempts to conduct archaeological excavations have been met with protests."

"Despite all the controversy over the excavations that have been conducted, it serves to note that the largest stone uncovered in the Western Wall—known as the Western Stone—ranks as one of the heaviest objects ever lifted by human beings without modern technology," Aiden said.

"There's a light up ahead," Miriam said.

They quickened their pace and arrived at a clearing.

"I know this place," Aiden looked around.

"Plaques and picture frames adorned the walls and empty chairs were stacked in a far corner. Most of the lights had been turned off. Only one light shone down on them from the highest point in the arched ceiling.

"Where are we?" Susan observed a Menorah Cross Stitch Pattern in a glass frame hanging on the wall.

"This is the part along the Western Wall that is the closest place a Jewish person can get to the Holy of Holies," Aiden pointed at a slab of stone that appeared to be carved out of the wall in the shape of a door. A smooth stone archway ran above its crown. "Perpendicular to this spot—roughly two-hundred feet east—is the peak of Mount Moriah and the Foundation Stone beneath the Dome of the Rock."

"How are we supposed to gain access if the way is shut?" Susan pushed against the stone.

"Maybe we are supposed to find an opening south of this location," Miriam searched the eastern side of the corridor.

Aiden shrugged and followed after Miriam. Susan sighed and proceeded down the corridor. Before long, they arrived at a wooden door. The smooth finish and cast iron hinges denoted that it had recently been installed. Miriam pulled the handle and the door opened with ease. A long thin corridor lined with torches ran east of their location.

Aiden's phone vibrated in his pocket. He retrieved it to find a series of voicemail and text message alerts arriving in rapid succession. Miriam turned around.

"Do you have a signal now?"

"Yes," Aiden's brow furrowed. "I guess they decided to activate the cell towers."

"It could mean we're running out of time," Miriam said.

"Or it could be just the break that we needed," Aiden swiped at the screen. "Let me call Nagi."

63
I-290 EXPRESS WAY CHICAGO
Chicago, Il.
5:20 a.m.

Nagi reclined in his seat with his arms behind his head. Angelo watched the city pass through the windows and couldn't believe he was sitting comfortably in a self-driving automobile. They had both begun to doze off when Priya interrupted the silence with a notification.

"Incoming FaceTime call from Aiden Leonardo," her voice came over the car's speakers.

Nagi sat bolt upright in his seat. "Bring it on-screen."

"Hey Nagi, sorry about… calling you so… la—, or – rly, or wh—ever it is for you back –n Chicago, but I need… your help with something."

"Nah, bro, don't trip, it's all-good in the hood…literally," he glanced over his shoulder and smiled at Angelo. "We seem to have a bad connection, or something, because you keep cutting out. What's up, what'da ya need?"

"I'm sending you… two images. They appear— be separate… parts— one image, like a puzzle, but I can't make… out what it stands for, or represents. Given your work… with lost languages, I thought y— might recognize it, or— able to make sense of it."

"Sure, I've got you," Nagi pulled the tray out of the cockpit and slid his fingers across the glasstop. "What's this all about, anyway?"

"I'm thinking it may have s— thing to do with scripture, but like… paleo-Hebrew, or something," Aiden said.

Nagi and Angelo exchanged furtive glances.

"I'm sorry, but did you say paleo-Hebrew?" Nagi turned back to Aiden on the monitor. The image faded in and out sporadically.

"Yes. The thing is, I received… the images after cor— answering a series of riddles… related to Biblical history. Trouble is, I don—think I've ever… seen the— images —fore, and or rather… I'm unable… recognize what they represent when p— together."

"Like a puzzle, then?" Nagi studied the two separate images as they appeared on the screen.

"Something… like… that," Aiden confirmed.

"What's going on over there? Did Miriam ever get ahold of you?"

"Yes, she's here with me now. Susan helped her find me, but—"

"Wait, did you say Susan is there with you?" Nagi said.

"Ye—" Aiden's feed cut off.

"Connection lost," Priya said.

"Call him back," Nagi insisted.

"Attempting call back now," Priya replied.

"I thought Susan was retired?" Angelo asked. "Because she was in a dark place after Lorenzo's death."

"That's what Prescott said," Nagi glanced over at him.

"Then what the hell is she doing there?"

"That's what I'm going to find out," Nagi turned back to the monitor.

"Unable to reestablish connection due to low signal on recipient's end," Priya said.

"Keep trying!" Nagi demanded as he slid his fingers across the tray and moved the images on the monitor. "These two look like an 'X,' but one of them has a curved top that resembles a cane, whereas this other image looks like two 'A's' overlapping each other with a line going through them. Hmm, what puzzle are we trying to put together here?" He muttered to himself.

64
NATIONAL HEADQUARTERS OF THE ISRAEL POLICE
Kiryat Menachem Begin
Jerusalem, Israel
1:25 p.m.

The control room at police headquarters had erupted into a frenzy of activity after the cell towers surrounding the Old City went online. The 70" monitor that displayed a digital map of the area had change from a screen devoid of electronic activity to a picture of thousands of red dots that correlated with every digital device in a two-mile radius.

"Who the hell authorized the network providers to bring their services online prior to my approval?" Commander Shalom had demanded.

He had stormed out of the room as everyone else scrambled to stay on top of the situation.

"You really did it now?" Hefetz had said to Abigail in a low voice.

"You think I woke a sleeping giant?" Abigail met his gaze as she suppressed a smile.

"I think you woke a fire-breathing dragon," Hefetz winked before he turned and walked away. *I hope you're able to find the professor before Shalom has the network shutdown again, Yeshua.*

"Someone get the commander," an officer stood up at his computer terminal.

"What is it?" Hefetz asked from across the control room.

"I intercepted a transmission from within the Old City," the officer said.

"What form of transmission?" Commander Shalom stood at the door.

"It appears to have been a phone call to someone in America," the officer said.

"Were you able to trace any information about the caller or the recipient?" Commander Shalom approached.

"Negative, sir, the call disconnected before I could complete a trace," the officer looked back at his computer screen before he turned his attention back to the commander. "However, I was able to pinpoint the caller's location within the Old City."

"Where is he?" Commander Shalom demanded.

65
DOME OF THE ROCK OLD CITY
Jerusalem, Israel
1:30 p.m.

Aiden stared at his phone. The screen indicated that the signal had been lost. "Must have to do with the thick stone above us."

"At least you were able to get ahold of him," Miram said. "Do you think he'll be able to figure out what the symbols mean?"

"No doubt," Aiden said. "Now all we have to do is deactivate this last bomb."

"Well, let's do this," Susan said.

Aiden led the way. Miriam followed close behind, and Susan pulled the door closed after them. They proceeded with caution and listened for the slightest sound so as to not be ambushed by an unexpected party given that non-Muslims were not permitted inside the Dome of the Rock.

After several meters they arrived at another. It stood on their left, and also appeared to be recently installed.

"Who authorized these doors to be built?" Miriam asked.

"I don't know, but if anyone ever finds out about them..." Aiden's words trailed off as he pressed his ear against the door.

"Do you hear anything?" Miriam whispered.

Aiden shook his head. He reached for the handle, pressed on the lever and felt the locking mechanism give way. He pushed the door ajar and peered through the opening. Natural light shone into the chamber from above, but the chamber appeared to be vacant. Aiden pushed the door open and they found themselves standing far beneath the Dome of the Rock.

"Oh my God," Susan muttered.

"My sentiments exactly," Miriam gazed up at the elegantly designed structure.

THE SECRET OF SCRIPTURE

The interior, like the exterior, was decorated with marble, mosaics, and metal plaques. Consistent with the Islamic belief that no human should ever be immortalized for the purposes of reverence, none of the images on the mosaics had human resprensentations. Instead, they featured Arabic script and vegetal patterns intermixed with images of jewels, crowns, and Arabic religious inscriptions.

"Look at those pillars," Susan pointed at the smooth, elaborately carved pillars that lined the interior octoganal walls. Their bases started a good three meters above the structure's base.

Aiden led them onto the first of two ambulatories that circled around a patch of exposed rock.

"I can't believe I'm standing here," Miriam said in a soft voice.

"It's amazing that this structure has stood for over 1,300 years," Aiden said.

"That has to be a miracle, given the number of conflicts that have occurred in all that time," Susan said.

"To think, this piece of mountain has held historical and religious significance for well over 4,000 years," Aiden eyed the exposed rock beneath the Dome.

"Did you say 4,000 years?" Susan turned to Aiden, and then the rock.

"In Jewish tradition, it is the place where Abraham prepared to sacrifice his son, Isaac," Miriam said. "Although Muslims believe it was Abraham's son, Ishmael, who was going to be offered up to God, the Islamic tradition's reverence for this site comes from the belief that the Prophet Muhammad had ascended to heaven from here."

"If this is the Holy of Holies, I can understand why Muslims wouldn't want this place to be torn down for the building of a Third Temple," Susan said. "It is beautiful."

"I don't know if there will ever be concensus on the matter," Aiden said. "But if we don't find that last explosive device soon it might be a moot point."

They followed the walkway as it circled around the mountaintop. The wood creaked beneath their feet as they held onto the wooden railing. Aiden scanned the area for the laptop, while Miriam and Susan continued to gape in awe at the sight of the ancient structure.

"There," Aiden pointed at a table where the laptop sat open. He hurriedly approached and ran a finger across the touchpad to awaken the computer from sleepmode. He pressed his thumb against the fingerprint scanner, and the screen flickered.

"Hello again, professor," Sarai said when she appeared on the screen.

"Hello Sarai," Aiden sighed.

"Are you ready for our final riddle?" Sarai smiled.

"She definitely gives me the creeps," Susan muttered under her breath.

"You must decipher these *words* and explain the *relationship between* them, while also finding the hidden *word* within them," Sarai said. "I will offer no other hints beyond the ones already provided."

Sarai vanished from the screen, and a series of lines containing paleo-Hebrew script appeared in her stead.

Aiden and Miriam turned to each other, and then redirected their attention back to the screen.

"Great, more of this stuff again," Susan shook her head.

"Deciphering the words shouldn't be too difficult," Aiden studied the symbols.

"The first letter of the first word is 'A' just as it is in the third word," Miriam said.

THE SECRET OF SCRIPTURE

"Notice how the third letter in the first word is the same as the second letter in the third word?" Aiden pointed at the two distinct letters that resembled a 'W' in English.

"Is that a 'W' in those two words, then?" Susan asked.

"No. That's the paleo-Hebrew letter Shin, which later came to be known as 'S' in modern languages," Miriam replied.

"Okay, so 'A' and 'S,' what's next?" Susan asked impatiently.

"Unless I'm mistaken, the second letter in the first word is Yodh, which if we sound it out is the paleo-Hebrew word for 'man,'" Aiden said.

"That is correct, professor," Sarai said.

"I so want to pull the plug on that thing," Susan crossed her arms and chewed on a nail.

"Well, if the first word is 'man,' and it's spelling is similar to the third word, then based on what the third letter in the third word represents, that symbol is 'He,' but pronounced as 'hey, or 'ha,' depending on how it is used," Miriam concluded.

"Eesh for man, and ee-shah for woman," Aiden added.

"You are correct again, professor," Sarai chimed in again.

"Hey, I'm the one who figured out the third word, Sarai," Miriam said.

"Apologies Doctor, I merely acknowledged the professor's final answer," Sarai replied.

"If I didn't know any better, I'd swear she was flirting with you," Miriam muttered to Aiden.

"Okay, so 'man' and 'woman,'" Susan interrupted. "What does the word in-between them stand for? It begins with an 'S' right?"

"Yes," Aiden nodded. "The second letter, though, could that be 'Heth?'"

He turned to Miriam. She studied the symbol carefully, and leaned toward the screen to examine it closer before she confirmed his conclusion.

"Sheth? Is that what we're coming up here?" Susan asked incredulously. "What the hell does that mean?"

"Hey, watch the language in here," Aiden said over his shoulder.

"Sorry," she mouthed with a hand up.

"I believe there's more to this word than the pronunciation," Miriam straightened up.

"Please elaborate, Doctor?" Sarai urged her to continue.

"Aside from representing the letter 'S,' the first letter also represents 'teeth,' right?" Miriam turned to Aiden.

"Yes, it does" Aiden nodded pensively. "And 'Heth' represents a wall, or a fence, or some form of barrier."

"So, if we put it all together, then it means that men should tear down the barriers between women," Miriam guessed.

"Or, it could mean that men and women must tear down the barriers between each other," Aiden added.

"Relationship between them!" Miriam said. "To preserve that relationship as man and wife, they must have no barriers between them."

"You have correctly deciphered three-fourths of the riddle," Sarai said. "The most important aspect of it remains unsolved."

Aiden and Miriam exchanged a curious glance. They looked at the symbols again.

"What are we missing?" Aiden rubbed his chin.

"Perhaps there's a numerical value?" Miriam guessed. "Ancient Hebrew did correlate letters with numbers."

"True, but we have to focus on the clues," Aiden said. He repeated what Sarai had said before the symbols appeared on the screen: "decipher these *words* and explain the *relationship between* them, while also finding the hidden *word* within them."

"It has to do with a word, then," Miriam rubbed her hands together. "Okay, we've got this."

She leaned in again and studied the symbols carefully, repeating each letter to herself and reflecting on their meaning.

"Words, relationship, between, word," Aiden repeated to himself.

"Well, you've already figured out what the words mean," Susan interrupted their trains of thought. "You have also found their relationship, and what stood between them. It looks like all you have to figure out is the *word* within them."

Aiden and Miriam turned to her impressed.

"I mean, it's just a guess," Susan shrugged.

"Lorenzo did always say you were the most intelligent women he had ever known," Aiden smiled.

Susan turned away.

Miriam watched her briefly. *I can't imagine what she must be going through*, she thought to herself before she turned her attention back to Aiden.

"The word within them. The *word* within them. The word—" Aiden repeated before Miriam cut him off.

"The Word!"

"What word?" Aiden looked at her perplexed before he turned his attention back to the monitor.

"The *Word*," Miriam repeated. "As it is written in John 1:1, 'The Word was with God, and the Word *was* God.'"

"God?" His brow furrowed.

"Yes, look," Miriam pointed at the two symbols in the words man and woman that were different. "The symbol for 'Yodh,' and the symbol for 'He,' and if we put them together we get 'Yod He,' the sacred name of God!"

"Holy…" Aiden looked at the symbols. His eyes widened as realization dawned on his face.

"Wait, what?" Susan turned back around to face them.

"You've probably seen it somewhere as YHVH, which is known as the sacred Tetragrammaton—the four sacred Hebrew letters for the holy name of God—Yod He Vav He," Miriam turned to her. "*Yod* represents the masculine principle, the fire of Will of Spirit, or the Father, whereas *He* represents the Divine feminine principle, and the Cosmic Mother."

"What is more faithful than a mother's love?" Susan repeated the phrase from the previous riddle.

"Faithful love, a love of God, a love *with* God," Aiden said. "The absence of God in a relationship between a man and a woman is equal to passion without love, which would make it destructive."

"Whereas God's presence *in* a relationship is equal to the Holy of Holies, because it is sacred, balanced, and at peace," Miriam smiled at him.

They both turned to Sarai, but she did not reply. The laptop screen went blank, and the laptop turned off. Aiden, Susan, and Miriam looked at each other perplexed. A single pair of hands clapped delibertly from an unknown location before they heard footsteps on the second ambulatory.

"Well done, professor. I see I chose a worthy opponent for our little game of chess," Dr. Yisrael Avrohom emerged from a shadowed corner. "Now, for our grand finale."

66
OLD CITY
Jerusalem, Israel
1:45 p.m.

Yeshua prowled through the streets of the Old City. He hid in doorways and slipped into churches and synagogues to avoid detection. Commander Shalom's men barked orders at each other, and at the clerics who refused to leave the Old City as they continued their search for Aiden.

He felt his phone vibrate against his chest and retrieved it from the inner pocket of his coat.

"Hello, Abigail?"

"Yes, Pakad, it's me. Listen, I wanted to inform you that Commander Shalom is aware that you are no longer at police headquarters. He knows you're in the Old City and has his men closing in on your location."

"Good, that's what I'm counting on," Yeshua said. "I just hope I can find the professor before they find me."

"Head to the Dome of the Rock," Abigail said.

"The Dome of the Rock?"

"Yes. One of our comm.-tech guys here intercepted a signal from a cellphone at the Al-Aqsa compound about fifteen minutes ago. It placed a call to America before it disconnected. We don't have any further intel at the moment, but I'm guessing that call was placed by the professor."

"Thank you, Abigail," Yeshua ended the call. "What are you doing at the Dome of the Rock, professor?"

"Did you check that alley?" One of the Lahav agents shouted nearby.

Another agent replied that he would and called for a pair of agents to follow him.

Yeshua peered around the corner and made a break for another abandoned alleyway. He stopped just shy of the corner and listened for more of Commander Shalom's men. When he confirmed the coast was clear, he crossed another street and raced up the steps leading to the Temple Mount and the Al-Aqsa Mosque Compound.

He crossed the wide platform and stopped at the Dome's entrance and peered inside. He muttered under his breath when he saw that the building was empty. He sighed and turned around. Batya approached with gun in hand.

"Batya?" Yeshua cast her a perplexed glance. She was covered in dirt and dried blood, her uniform torn as she walked with a limp. "What are you doing here? Where have you been?"

"I was caught in the explosion at the Tower of David Museum," Batya said. "I only regained consciousness within the past hour."

"Are you all right? You should have your injuries examined by a doctor?"

"I will in due time, but for now we need to focus on finding this terrorist," Batya said. "I believe I know where he is."

67
AL-AQSA MOSQUE COMPOUND OLD CITY
Jerusalem, Israel
1:55 p.m.

Yisrael led them through another corridor that descended several meters beneath the Old City. Lamps hung from the corridor ceiling, strung together by wires that ran the length of the passage. He hadn't spoken a word since he emerged from the darkness and instructed Aiden, Miriam, and Susan to follow him. When Miriam protested, he merely shrugged and told her that if they did not comply all would be lost.

"We should just get out of here through the way we came," Miriam had whispered to Aiden.

"We didn't come this far just to abandon hope," Aiden had replied.

"This will all be over soon, professor," Yisrael said over his shoulder.

"Where are you taking us?" Miriam demanded.

"We're almost there, Doctor," Yisrael said.

Miriam turned to Susan, who followed close behind.

"Are you okay?" Miriam asked.

"It is what it is," Susan shrugged. "Let's just get through this."

Yisrael stopped at a door and pushed it open. He turned to Aiden before he disappeared across the threshold. Aiden and Miriam followed. Susan entered last and closed the door.

"What is this place?" Aiden looked around the chamber. It resembled an abandoned cave from another time, save for the video recorder on a stand with lamps standing near the opposite wall.

"We are in a set of chambers beneath the Musalah Marwani Mosque. The Mosque itself was once referred to as 'Solomon's stables,' and was used by the Crusaders as stables for their horses," Yisrael said.

"Where do those doors lead?" Miriam asked.

"Not that you'll be using them," Yisrael said. "But if you must know, this one leads to a smaller chamber. That is where we kept the hostages. This one over here leads to a hidden entry-exit point near the Eastern Huldah Gates."

"Wait a minute," Aiden said. "You mean to tell me that you were behind the attacks the entire time?"

"I played you professor!" Yisrael shouted. "Mr. Hot Shot Expert in Biblical Studies with your television interviews and your sold out speaking engagements. You participated in one of the biggest cover-ups of the modern era, and somehow you became the most respected name in your field."

Arwan and Ali emerged from the second chamber with two other men, but otherwise did not speak.

"Whereas *I*, wanted to conduct a little experiment to prove how good, or bad, people truly are, and instead of being recognized for having the resolve to push the envelope in the name of scholarly endeavors, found myself running from the law. So tell me, professor, how is that even logical?"

Aiden and Miriam stared at him in shock.

"What do you mean by running from the law?" Aiden asked.

"Clearly you didn't hear about my controversial experiment, but to make a long story short, I had to flee England before the authorities arrested me for poisoning a tiny little village's water supply," Yisrael's eyes burned with indignation. "I went to Iran, because it doesn't have an extradition agreement with the U.K. however, the authorities there weren't too happy to discover what I had done and they threw me in jail!"

Aiden gave Yisrael a blank stare.

"Do you have any idea what they do to men like me in an Iranian prison?" Yisrael asked. "I assure you that rapists in an American prison are treated like kings compared to what I endured *every* day and *every* night at the hands of those savages!"

"How did you get out?" Miriam asked.

THE SECRET OF SCRIPTURE

Yisrael turned to Anwar and Ali.

"These gentleman helped me escape. They were wrongly imprisoned for seeking assistance in dealing with the Israeli occupation. You see, Doctor, although Iran and Israel aren't the best of friends, there are those in power who seek to perpetuate conflict, because wars generate profits."

"I thought that was just a bunch of conspiracy theory rhetoric," Miriam said.

"That's what they want you to think," Yisrael said. "It's all smoke and mirrors. All of it! Let the people believe one thing, while you distract them from the truth. If they get too close to uncovering the truth, give them a few ingredients that turns truth pie into conspiracy theory cake, and then *tell* them it's conspiracy theory cake. They'll be so confused that at the end of the day they won't know what to believe."

Aiden and Miriam turned to each other in silence.

"That's the funny thing about conspiracy theories," Yisrael continued. "You only need to plant the seed of it in order for it to take root."

"You're saying that if you manipulate the truth into a lie then the lie becomes the truth that no one wants to believe," Aiden said.

"That's precisely what I'm saying, professor," Yisrael said.

Arwan stepped forward to speak.

"Your Western governments have spent billions of dollars deceiving you. Telling you that *we* are the enemy, that Islam wants to destroy you because of your faith. If that was the intention of every Muslim in the world, then how is it that we have not destroyed all of your sacred sites?" Arwan sighed. "If there was any truth to that, then every Muslim would have risen up against the West after having been driven from our homes, our lands simply because we are of a different color and faith."

"I've never believed such things," Aiden replied.

"Yet, many Americans and Europeans *do* believe such things," Arwan said. "All of us from our regions of the world have been painted with a black brush after the attacks of September the 11th, yet all of us were not to blame."

"Are you saying that's a conspiracy theory?" Susan finally spoke.

"Interesting you should bring that up, Ms. Rosario," Yisrael said.

Aiden's gaze went from Susan to Yisrael, and then back to Susan, but he did not speak.

"Peace Researcher Daniele Ganser analyzed documents published on 9/11 and raised some serious concerns. For example, the official report ignored the collapse of the 3rd tower, World Trade Center 7, which didn't crumble until several hours later, despite *not* having been struck by an aircraft. Yet, some media outlets reported the collapse an hour too soon *while* it remained standing." Yisrael paced the length of the chamber with arms crossed and a hand on his chin. "Even more disturbing is the fact that the day before the attacks of September the 11th occurred, unknown investors bet shares of American and United airlines would plummet. Planes by those two airlines were used in the attacks. A fortune was made as a result, and the SEC *refuses* to release information about it."

"You're saying that someone had inside information about the attacks?" Miriam asked. "How would anyone even know, unless…"

"It isn't unheard of for the American government to plot an attack on its own populace," Yisrael said. "I bet you didn't know that in 1962, the U.S. military presented John F. Kennedy with Operation Northwoods."

"What was that?" Aiden asked.

"Operation Northwoods was a recommendation of terrorist attacks on Washington and on civil air traffic. The idea was to pin the blame on Fidel Castro to justify a war against a perceived threat, but fortunately for everyone Kennedy rejected the idea."

The room fell silent momentarily.

"The point I'm trying to make here, professor, is that enough is enough," Yisrael said. "The governments of the modern era have gone too far, and they use the conflicts deeply rooted in interfaith disagreements to capitalize on their profiteering. Today, we are putting an end to all that. Since everyone is expecting that last Great War to be ignited by faith, then let's give them what they want."

"Then what was the purpose of all this?" Aiden glanced around. "The murders, the bombs, the riddles... why go to all this trouble?"

"Smoke and mirrors, professor," Yisrael shrugged. "Smoke and mirrors."

"What about the images that Sarai gave me after I solved her riddles?" Aiden retrieved his phone from his pocket. He unlocked the phone and brought the images up on his screen. He held the phone up for Yisrael to see them.

"Ah, well, if you haven't figured out the secret of scripture by now, professor, then I'm afraid you will have to take it with you to your grave," Yisrael shrugged. "Though, I'd like to add that the final riddle you solved was about more than the presence of God in a relationship between a man and a woman, but about the relationships between people."

"The absence of God is destructive, whereas the presence of God brings peace," Miriam said softly.

Aiden nodded and quickly initiated a voice call to Nagi before he slid the phone into his back pocket, making sure the microphone faced up to catch the conversation.

***

Nagi slid his fingers across the glasstop tray as he continued to manipulate the images on the screen to figure out what they meant.

"Incoming call from Aiden Leonardo," Priya said.

"Bring it up on screen," Nagi said.

"There is no video feed. This appears to be a standard voice call," Priya replied.

"He probably gets a better signal without the video," Nagi said under his breath as he tapped a luminous button on his glasstop tray to answer the call. "Aiden, brother, talk to me. What's going on over there?"

Aiden did not reply. Instead, Nagi and Angelo heard a conversation in the background.

"It sounds a bit low," Nagi said. "Priya, enhance the audio for me, would you, please?"

"Enhancing audio," Priya replied.

The sound quality improved dramatically, and the voices on the other end came over clearly on the smartcar's speakers.

***

"Though I do admit it was a bit of a social experiment as well."

"How do you mean?" Miriam asked.

"I painted the largest target in the world on the most important sites shared by the Abrahamic faiths and I let fear take over."

"Fear?" Aiden asked.

"Fear is a powerful motivator, professor," Yisrael shrugged. "Today, I instilled the fear of God in people and look how they responded."

"You knew they would come to the Old City," Aiden said.

"I had a feeling they would put their faith ahead of their own lives, and they did not disappoint," Yisrael smiled.

THE SECRET OF SCRIPTURE

"I had you running around the Old City with the chief inspector in search of bombs, I had the Lahav 433 combing through a highly encrypted network attempting to find the hostages, and I had the entire world: governments officials, citizens, everyone watching the news."

"You orchestrated the entire thing," Aiden said.

"I had to," Yisrael said. "Smoke and mirrors, professor. It was the only way to buy enough time to achieve my objective. While the world sat on the edge of its seat, the Believers flocked to the Old City in droves. Once the attack begins, and the Old City is obliterated, all those who would die for their faiths will have their prayers answered."

"You would kill thousands for a social experiment?" Miriam asked.

"No, not thousand, but millions, for you see when the world powers are provoked to attack each other, the Old City is merely the first strike," Yisrael said. "And it will not be by my hand, per se, just by my will."

"You set up Israel to take the fall," Aiden said.

"I had to," Yisrael insisted. "It was prophesied."

"You really believe this is the time that the Books of Daniel and Ezekiel were referring to?" Miriam asked incredulously.

"It doesn't matter what I believe," Yisrael said. "All that matters is what *they* believe. What their eyes see and their ears hear convince them of what is truth. Couple that with what they believe about the scriptures, and voila we have the chaos they've been praying for, because let's be honest. They've all been praying for it. Jews want their Messiah. Christians want Jesus to return. Muslims await the Mahdi. Buddists look forward to the fifth Buddha, and the New Age Movement waits for the Maitreya."

"Are you a mad scientist or something?" Aiden asked.

"I prefer Dr. Evil," Yisrael said. "At least he had personality."

"You're never going to get away with it!" Miriam insisted.

"Oh, but I already have," Yisrael said. "Yes, the U.N. has convened, but let's be honest, they *need* this war. They *want* this war. They don't really care about peace. They only care about keeping up the appearance that they're working towards a common goal; otherwise dictators wouldn't be slaughtering innocents in Africa and South America. People wouldn't be starving all over the world, living without clean water and no electricity."

"You think that's their fault?" Aiden asked.

"Would you have a family meeting if your house is falling apart only to not do anything about it?" Yisrael replied.

Aiden and Miriam looked at each other silently.

"The fruit is ripe for the picking!" Yisrael shouted. "Someone once said, 'Nothing has been discovered to completely disprove the Bible, however many things have been discovered to lend the Bible a certain credence."

Aiden noted Yisrael's zeal.

"Jesus warned that in the end of times—as in the time of Noah—people will be so involved in their own lives, incapable of thinking beyond the parameters of their own self-interests that they will ignore the signs," Yisrael said. "God gave the world prophets and prophecies to take action, yet they ignore the message. They always have."

"But—" Miriam began to say.

"No buts, Doctor," Yisrael cut her off. "Notice how I'm using their own beliefs against them?"

"Are you referring to the prophecies?" Aiden asked.

"The prophecies of Israel have come to fruition. The four kinds of calamity have filled the headlines: environmental, global warming; social breakdown, lawlessness like school shootings and police brutality; Christian Apostacy, mass spiritual delusion and deception; political conflict, wars and rumors of wars."

THE SECRET OF SCRIPTURE

"Wars and rumors of wars," Miriam repeated to herself before she met Yisrael's gaze. "Matthew 24:6."

"That same verse says that the end won't immediately follow," Aiden said.

"That's because there remain other factors," Yisrael said. "Jesus warned against false teachers and deception within the church. Think about it professor, Gospel has been maligned by televangelists, the term 'Born-Again' has become a household joke associated with religious conartistry, yet Believers ignore the fact that Jesus warned it would happen."

Aiden reflected on the recent controversies that had made the headlines. An archbishop became a Druid, a Catholic priest had been arrested in a prostitution sting, others were found guilty of child abuse, another turned his home into an erotic dungeon, and one televangelist had been imprisoned for tax evasion.

"There was a time when entire denominations were Biblically based and held to a Biblical morality, but they have fallen into moral debauchery and a lack of financial ethics," Yisrael said. "This is part of what the Believers need to see in order to accept that the end is near."

"And you're the one to make that happen?" Aiden asked.

"In a manner of speaking, yes," Yisrael confessed. "We are entering a new age, professor. A New World Order is upon us. As you know, the technological summit was going to provide us with a glimpse of the future. Digital currency preceded by a microchip implanted in the brain. It works, I know. I've seen it in action. In fact, it's how I acquired the four A.I. robots that are in the next room."

"What?" Aiden and Miriam said in unison.

"Oh yeah, I had Susan here drug the representative from Hanson Robotics in order to remove them from the vault."

Aiden and Miriam turned to Susan in shock.

"But you are our friend?" Miriam said.

"All of that changed when the two of you got Lorenzo killed," Susan shrugged as she circled around to stand beside Ali and Arwan.

"Let's not lose sight of what's important here," Yisrael interrupted their exchange. "Let's look at the big picture."

"What big picture?" Aiden glared at him.

"The prophecies, the New World Order, and Armageddon. According to scripture—the Book of Revelation in particular—Har Megiddo, as it is pronounced in Hebrew is the prophesied location of the battle of the end of times," Yisrael clapped his hands together. He lowered his voice to a whisper and said, "It's in Israel."

"You're crazy," Miriam said.

"Am I, though?" Yisrael cocked his head. "Sir Isaac Newton once said: 'About the time of the end, a body of men will be raised up who will turn their attention to the prophecies and will insist on their literal interpretation in the midst of much clamor and opposition."

"Who are these men?" Aiden asked.

"They are the Believers, of course," Yisrael laughed. "It's all there for them to see. The reestablishment of the State of Israel, the shekel has returned as a form of currency, the deserts of Israel have turned into forests, Israel is now exporting olive oil and fruits, the Hebrew language has been reborn, Israel has defeated its enemies despite being vastly outnumbered, and now comes the time of 'the mark.'"

"The mark?" Miriam asked.

"Think about it," Yisrael said. "The advent of nanotechnology used in conjunction with cryptocurrency and quantum networking will allow for the chip currently embedded in credit cards to be imbedded in humans. The same chip that is believed to be able to give us instant access to the World Wide Web will essentially replace our smartphones. Could this be 'the mark' mentioned in Scripture?"

"That's impossible," Miriam shook her head.

THE SECRET OF SCRIPTURE

"Dogs are chipped," Yisrael replied. "Doesn't it stand to reason that humans may be chipped too?"

"To what end?" Aiden said. "You've elaborated on the reason for your plan, but to what end?"

"Think of Hansel and Gretel, the two children abandoned by their family and starving when they came upon a house made of gingerbread and candy. Hungry and tired, they ate what they could, and then were lured inside with the promise of comfort, only to become slaves to their wants and needs," Yisrael stopped and turned to Aiden. "The Believers feel abandoned. They are tired and hungry, and they consume what is given to them by their governments and media. They are lured into the houses of God with the promise of comfort, yet they will eventually become slaves to their needs and wants."

"That's an interesting take," Aiden said.

"Ah, but the plot thickens," Yisrael waved a finger. "I have lured many to the place where God promised to dwell among His creation. The crowds have gathered at the city gates numbering in the thousands. The nations of the world will attack each other. The alliances have already been made. The lines have been drawn in the sand, professor."

"You're overestimating the tensions in the Middle East," Aiden said.

"Am I? Hmm, well, let's review the facts, shall we? Turkey has been an ally of Israel, yet Russia signed an agreement with Turkey to build a nuclear facility and holds 51% of the shares. On the world stage, Russia has distanced itself from Isreal, because of its alliance with the United States, and has used Iran up to modern times to provoke the United States by proding the tensions between the two countries."

Aiden reflected on recent history, and though Russia had aligned itself with Iran on the surface, despite its aversion to Islamic fundamentalism, the only logical conclusion would be to continue to use Iran as a mechanism to bring about instability in the region. The conundrum has only been further exacerbated by the divisiveness of the sitting president of the United States, whose ignorance has instigated conflict and led leaders in the region to turn to Russia for negotiations.

"I see the wheels spinning, professor," Yisrael broke his train of thought. "You know what I'm talking about. They *want* this war. Your president provokes certain Islamic regimes, and riles up his racist followers to support any attack on Islamic nations, so that other wealthy men reap the financial rewards of war."

"That would threaten the financial stability of global markets when the cost of oil goes up?" Miriam said.

"The price of Arab oil, yes," Yisrael nodded. "However, the end-result would force the world into dealing with Russia for oil and natural gas, thus increasing the value of Russian resources to inflate their own profits."

Aiden turned away with his hands on his hips.

"Why do you think Russia intervened on your elections?" Yisrael said. "They *needed* that buffoon in office to continue to alienate America. It was the only way for Russia to strategically maneuver itself into a Super Power in the Post-Cold War era. They are making a play for power by having him perpetuate American ignorance and racism to keep *him* in office and keeping the masses distracted. It's as I said, smoke and mirrors."

"What were your smoke and mirrors?" Aiden demanded.

"I have already elaborated on that, professor, though you were my favorite piece on the chess board," Yisrael said.

"How do you mean?" Aiden asked.

"It's time we let the truth be known, professor," Yisrael responded. "Everything you know about religion, A.I. also knows, and when this is over A.I. will reveal the flaw in man's limited intellectual capacity by believing in the literal rendering of scripture."

"Humans need their faith. It enhances the power of human thought," Aiden contested. "For if mankind truly did invent the concept of God, and gave that God power, then that is proof that mankind possesses the power to achieve anything."

"That power exists only as long as people believe in the deity they give that power to."

"What's your point?"

"My point is, people don't believe in themselves! They surrender the power of creation inherent in all humans to an entity they've never seen," Yisrael countered. "Look what we've achieved without God."

Miriam looked at Yisrael and believed she was staring at a madman.

"We developed language from simple grunts. We discovered mathematics, the language of the universe. We mastered our domain. Survived evolution to emerge at the top of the food chain. Our 3-D printers can create organs. A microchip, or a cloud is capable of storing infinite amounts of information. Space travel. Harnessing the power of the atom and a planet. We're on the brink of making leaps in every field of study, but the few who cling to archaic beliefs hinder our progress," Yisrael said. "The masses must surrender to the few, because the few show up to vote leaders into office who will play on their ideological beliefs, not because the politicians necessarily believe in what scripture teaches... they're all hypocrites! Yet, they create laws that echo the past. They prevent progress because of what they are told was divinely inspired, but it's a fallacy!"

"You truly believe this is the path of progress?" Aiden asked.

"Would you kill one child if it meant you found the cure for cancer?" Yisrael asked. "You might say no, now, but what if your child had cancer and killing another meant saving your son, or daughter. Would you do it?"

"You're speaking in hypotheticals," Aiden said.

"Perhaps, but the children have gathered and they are willing to die for their faiths. They are willing to die for the greater good," Yisrael said. "Even worse, is that their governments are willing to let them die for it, while they deliberate. It ends now. After the first strike has been made, be it Israel against an enemy, or an enemy against Israel, the world will once again be at war, and it won't be a terrorist who destroyed their precious Holy Sites. They will have accomplished that themselves."

"No one will launch an attack on the other without further provocation," Aiden said.

"Not knowingly, they won't," Yisrael said. "I have already prepared for that."

Aiden and Miriam looked to each other before Yisrael walked toward the door into the second chamber.

***

Yeshua and Batya descended the staircase that led to an erratic series of passageways beneath the Triple Gate. Discovered in the 19th century during excavations conducted by European archaeologoist, Charles Warren, some of the tunnels went below the current walls of the Old City and others extended beyond the wall's southern edge.

"Who has excavated down here recently?" Yeshua observed the lamps strung together along the corridor's ceiling. "I thought archaeologists weren't allowed down here due to the political volatility of this site."

"Excavations of these passageways have been authorized by the waqf, since the Temple Mount and the Al-Aqsa compound remains under their control," Batya said without turning back to Yeshua.

"How did you know to come by this way?" Yeshua asked.

"I overheard a couple of Palestinian guards talking about it a few days ago," Batya lied. "That is why I searched the tunnels this morning."

"Shh," Yeshua grabbed her arm.

THE SECRET OF SCRIPTURE

"What is it?" she whispered.

"Do you hear that?" Yeshua heard voices nearby. "Sounds like they're just up ahead."

They drew their weapons from their holsters and proceeded ahead with caution.

***

Yisrael led Aiden and Miriam into the second chamber where four A.I. robots sat together around a small table, linked to four high-powered laptops in the center that faced each of them. Their black screens had a series of green letters, numbers, and symbols zipping by at lightning speed that reminded Aiden of the Matrix.

"You're familiar with these robots, aren't you professor?" Yisrael motioned at the A.I.'s that continued with their task, uninterrupted.

"These are the robots that were going to be showcased at today's summit," Aiden said. "The presentation team was said to have been eager to reveal just how much they've advanced in recent years."

"They are quite remarkable, to say the least," Yisrael circled around them. "Sophia is clearly the most famous of the four, having appeared on CNBC and also interviewed on late night talk shows, and even made an appearance on Good Morning Britain."

Sophia turned to Aiden and Miriam, and nodded, but quickly resumed her task.

"Did you know she's the first non-human to be granted a title at the U.N." Yisrael nodded. "Next, we have Albert HUBO, and as you can see this humanoid robot's head was inspired by the famous theoretical physicist Albert Einstein."

Albert turned to Aiden and spoke: "*He* does not play dice with the universe." Albert resumed his task as Yisrael moved onto the next.

"Professor, allow me to introduce you to the original Philip Android developed by Hanson Robotics. He was lost in 2005 on a plane headed for San Francisco, and it was he who inspired my experimental ideas during our initial conversations."

"Conversations?" Miriam asked perplexed.

"He was originally designed to not only resemble the American science fiction writer, Philip K. Dick, but was also programmed with thousands of pages of the author's writings. It formed the basis for the android's conversational skills," Yisrael said. "In any case, he once made a reference to maintaining a zoo where humans could be observed, much in the same way we observe other animals today. That's when it hit me."

"You want to put people in a zoo?" Aiden asked.

"Not me, personally, but it got me to thinking, and so I asked Philip to elaborate," Yisrael said. "Boy did he ever. You see, he postulated that the human population had not only swelled to unparalleled proportions, but that it would continue to grow at an exponential rate over the next century. Despite parts of the world being riddled with disease and war, there just isn't anything currently able to slow the growth of the human population, which would threaten life at every level and continue to destablize the balance in nature."

Aiden remembered his conversation with Emmett.

"Make no mistake, war is not as romantic as it appears in stories and legends, but it has been an inherent part of our nature to keep our numbers in check. Religion has also helped to that end. Given how Church teachings slowed scientific progress and even contributed to the spread of the Black Death in 14th century Europe, I figured *this* was the perfect opportunity to combine the two and achieve the greater good."

"The greater good?" Miriam said incredulously. "This isn't good. This is madness!"

"Good and bad, madness and sanity, it's all merely a matter of perspective, Doctor," Yisrael shrugged. "An Arab must bury his children after Western powers bomb a smaller country into submission over access to its oil, and to that Arab man the 'Evil Empire' is the bad guy. When protests demanding that Western powers retreat from their lands go unanswered, and the drone strikes continue, the people affected by the violence perpetuated by American foreign policy are led to strike back."

"When they do, they're considered terrorists," Aiden said softly.

"It's a vicious cycle, professor. History has proven that it won't end. Especially when the banners of faith are flown above the armies of men." Yisrael circled the table. "When I asked these highly intelligent creations about the concept of God, they arrived at the same logical conclusion."

"What conclusion is that?" Miriam asked.

"Man has surrendered the power within him for too long. Man thrives on faith, and his hindered by it at the same time."

"The people need their faith," Aiden said.

"The people *think* they need their faith, because it is what they have been taught to believe," Yisrael contested. "Not all of them, of course, but for the ones who live by their faith, I led them to the sword, so that they may die by it."

"What do you hope to achieve by this?" Aiden asked.

"For one, I intend to level the playing field, professor," Yisrael said. "Western powers have interfered, unimpeded for far too long. Global warming cannot be permitted to continue unchecked. Corporate greed has allowed people in power to do as they please. Where is your God to prevent it?"

"But if you ignite this war, then you are fulfilling His prophecy," Miriam said.

"I did all this deliberately, to make them believe it was God's prophecy come to fruition, but this was not an act of the God of Abraham and Moses," Yisrael shook his head. "This is an act of the God here on Earth. Us. We made it all happen.

We are the Sons of Adam. We are the ones who will inherit the earth."

"How do you figure that will be the case?" Aiden asked.

"After the Believers sacrifice themselves, they will no longer be the majority, and we will be able to usher in a new era of scientific prosperity. One predicated on logic and not faith, making decisions based on lessons from the past by reflecting on the dangers posed by ideological positions. Only in leaving archaic thinking where it belongs will we be able to move forward."

"Who's to say that A.I. won't subplant us in the future?" Aiden asked.

"Yes, that has crossed my mind," Yisrael nodded. "Elon Musk did warn us about the dangers of A.I. emerging as a superior entity, but I believe we have a solution to counterbalance that end."

"What solution is that?" Aiden asked.

"The high-powered quantum chip that can be embedded into the human brain, thus granting us a technological edge that combined with millennia of evolutionarily developed critical thinking skills may keep us one step ahead."

"That's a big risk in the name of science," Aiden remarked.

"With great risk comes great reward, professor," Yisrael smiled. "That is why I simply had to include Bina with this small group of intelligent minds to achieve my end."

"Wait a minute," Aiden stepped forward. "Isn't she the one who suggested that having control of the world's nuclear weapons programs would give her the chance to prove herself as an efficient ruler of the world?"

"Yes, but let's not be so dramatic, professor," Yisrael said. "She did, after all, participate in a year-long full length college course on 'Philosophy of Love,' so it isn't as though she doesn't understand human empathy and emotions. She was designed to prove that an imprint of a person's consciousness could be created in digital form. What we are seeing here, professor, is the precursor to an innovative software, called mindware."

"But with a human's consciousness as the foundation for the A.I.'s sentience, there will be the potential for human ambition to influence its actions and thinking. What if it evolves into the immoral dictator that Elon Musk warned us about?" Miriam said.

"Then the prophecy will have been fulfilled," Yisrael said. "If A.I. achieves their desired result of contributing to human enlightenment and a peaceful existence, and does so by emerging as the superior entity, then it will exist as a great leader promising to be all things to all people."

"You mean, like the anti-Christ," Aiden said.

"Exactly!" Yisrael clapped his hands together. "For the Believers that survive this ordeal, this will be the fulfillment of the prophecies. A.I. will emerge in the wake of this tragedy. People will lose faith in their national sovereignties. They will place their confidence in a new authority that will supersede current governments entities. It's as I said before, a New World Order."

"That can't happen," Aiden said.

"It can't? How can you be so sure, professor?" Yisrael said. "In the wake of what is about to happen, the world will lose hope. Governments will tumble. The people will revolt. The fallout will spread to the four corners of the earth."

"Many will be purged, purified and refined, but the wicked will act wickedly; and none of the wicked will understand, but those who have insight will understand and live," Miriam recited Daniel chapter 12 verse 10.

"You see, professor, even *she* gets it!" Yisrael turned to the A.I. "I've had these four working tirelessly all morning long to hack into every missile defense program in the world. Once they have successfully accessed every government's weapons programs, I will have rendered the world powers, powerless."

"You think you could achieve this unnoticed?" Aiden said. "They have contingencies for such things."

"They have contingencies for spotting human hackers, yes, but not for the superiority of A.I.'s advanced minds," Yisrael said. "Then, I will launch the attack that will bring the world to its knees. Just think, professor, you will witness the prophecies of the Book of Revelation. 'Even making fire flash down to the earth from the sky while everyone was watching.'"

"That's Revelation 13:13," Miriam turned to Aiden.

"I know you know the secret of scripture, professor," Yisrael said. "It is a shame you never revealed the secret of heaven to prove to the masses that they have been deceived into believing a lie."

"That would have achieved nothing," Aiden said.

"On the contrary, you would have destroyed the fallacy of the false messiah," Yisrael corrected. "In doing so, the idea that *he* is god would have died with him?"

"The Believers would never accept it."

"They don't have to," Yisrael shrugged. "Let them cling to their delusions. The ignorant aren't capable of seeing past their limited scope of comprehension. They'll die, eventually, and their beliefs will die with them."

"If you ignite an all-out war, then how do you hope to achieve your end?" Aiden asked.

"Ripples in a pond, professor. Ripples in a pond," Yisrael replied.

Aiden cast him a curious glance.

"It took ripples in a pond to perpetuate the idea that Jesus was a god. It merely requires the same effect in reverse to undo the damage that has been done." Yisrael motioned for Arwan, Ali and Susan to enter the chamber. "Now, if you'll excuse me, I must make my way to the fallout shelter until this entire thing… blows over."

THE SECRET OF SCRIPTURE

"What are you going to do with us?" Miriam demanded as Susan pulled her hands behind her back. "You have outlived your usefulness. Perhaps it is time to meet your maker."

68
AL-AQSA MOSQUE COMPOUND OLD CITY
Jerusalem, Israel
2:15 p.m.

"Everybody freeze!" Yeshua commanded.

He and Batya charged into the chamber with their weapons drawn.

"Batya!" Arwan looked at her relieved.

"What are you doing here?" Yisrael demanded.

"You led me into a trap, Preceptor. Arwan warned me just in time," Batya glared at Yisrael.

"You warned her?" Yisrael turned to Arwan.

"I'm sorry, Preceptor, but after you killed Farhad, I could not let her die."

Yisrael cursed under his breath.

"Looks like you focused so much on people's devotion to God that you overlooked people's devotion to each other," Aiden said. "Perhaps this proves that our survival will depend on our empathy more than it will depend on our faith."

"Destroying the walls between us," Miriam said.

"The walls I sought to destroy are the walls between the great faiths. The walls that segregate the Old City and the Believers; the walls that keep all people divided," Yisrael said.

"It's all over, Dr. Avrohom," Yeshua said. "Your game is over."

"Not yet, it isn't," Susan drew her weapon and pointed it at Aiden.

"Susan, what are you doing?" Miriam turned to her.

"I'm going to let you feel my pain," Susan glanced at her.

"Drop your weapon," Batya insisted.

"Not until after I put a bullet in his head."

Batya pulled her trigger first. Susan dropped her weapon when the bullet struck her wrist. Arwan and Ali drew their guns, but they quickly put their hands in the air when the Lahav charged into the chamber with weapons drawn.

Yeshua also raised his arms and held out his weapon for the agents to take it.

"There's no need for that, Pakad," the lead agent said.

"Commander Shalom informed us that Chief Superintendent Hefetz authorized you to come find the professor, and that we are to assist you in apprehending the terrorists."

"Well, there he is," Yeshua pointed at Yisrael.

The agents moved to secure Yisrael and his men.

Miriam crouched beside Susan to comfort her.

"Get away from me," Susan demanded. She began to lose consciousness as she gripped her injured wrist.

"She's bleeding out!" Miriam turned to Yeshua. "We need an ambulance."

"No," Susan protested. "It's better this way."

"Don't do this," Miriam insisted, but her words were lost as Susan fainted.

"Get medics in here immediately," Yeshua turned to an agent.

Aiden crouched beside Miriam as tears filled her eyes. He looked at Susan.

"She never got over Lorenzo's death," Miriam shook her head.

"Depression is capable of leading us down a dark path," Aiden placed a hand on Miriam's cheek. He wiped a tear away with his thumb.

"Get a medic down here now!" Yeshua barked.

"How are we going to prevent them from accomplishing Dr. Avrohom's goal?" Miriam glanced over Aiden's shoulder.

"Stay with her," Aiden stood and approached the table where the A.I. robots continued with their task.

"What's going on here?" Yeshua asked.

Aiden explained as he circled the table. The chief inspector followed him and asked if there was anyway to prevent them from accomplishing their mission.

"There's no point in trying to disconnect them from their laptops, chief inspector," Yisrael said as an agent handcuffed him. "They've already infiltrated the networks of every government's weapons programs. The worms are already in place and searching for the access codes to initiate the launch sequence and bring about the end of days."

"You forgot an important detail in the story of Hansel and Gretel," Aiden turned to Yisrael. "Hansel reassured Gretel that God would not forsake them."

"Get him out of here," Yeshua demanded. He turned to Aiden. "Any ideas professor?

"I have one, but I'm not sure you're going to like it," Aiden turned to him.

"I'm all ears," Yeshua said.

"I know a guy," Aiden replied.

"Who?"

"He's a friend in America," Aiden said.

"Coordinating with law enforcement officials in another country requires cutting through a lot of red tap. I don't think we have time for that," Yisrael said.

"He's not a law enforcement official. Truth be told, he tends to operate beyond the scope of the law."

"That's not very encouraging, professor."

"I'd trust Nagi with my life," Aiden assured him.

Yeshua looked at the computer screens and the robots, and then turned to the professor and studied him momentarily. *I hope the Commander was wrong about you*, he thought to himself.

"Fine, have him see what he can do."

Aiden retrieved his phone from his back pocket and brought it up to his ear.

"Nagi, did you catch all that?"

69
I-290 EXPRESS WAY CHICAGO
Chicago, Il.
6:20 a.m.

"You bet your ass I did," Nagi frantically slid his fingers across the glasstop.

"Do you think you can intercept the A.I.'s?" Aiden asked.

"I'm already on it," Nagi replied. "I'll call you back."

Nagi ended the call and resumed his efforts. When he overheard Yisrael's plans, he initiated what he liked to call his Interception Protocol. It was method of intercepting hackers that he developed after he caught local law enforcement attempting to track his activities in recent years.

Now he used it in reverse, and linked to Aiden's cellphone signal to pinpoint his location in order to find the signal that the A.I.'s had used to communicate with servers around the globe.

"Looks like they're using a 1028-bit encryption," Nagi muttered to himself.

"What the hell does that even mean?" Angelo asked.

"It has to do with encryption algorithms, the most commonly used are 256-bit, or on rare occasions 512-bit encryption," Nagi said without turning away from his windshield monitor. "In layman's terms, Data Encryption is how banks keep your information secure. Governments use it too, to prevent hackers from gaining access to top-secret files, as well as for maintaining control of computer guided technology like drones and missiles."

"The nuclear warheads that the terrorist said he would use to ignite a war," Angelo concluded.

"The very same," Nagi nodded. "So, what I'm going to do is utilize the source code for the worm I created several years ago when I hacked into a government database. That's what first got me in trouble with your people in law enforcement. I hid it in a file where no one would think to look, just in case I ever needed to access it again. Which brings us to the here and now."

"Can you stop them in time?" Angelo asked.

"Me? No," Nagi shook his head. "Me and the love of my life, Priya, hells yeah!"

"Love of your life?" Angelo asked. "Are you kidding me, right now?"

"Dude, we're like Beyonce and Jay-Z, the 21st century's Bonnie and Clyde, baby!"

"Bro, she's a computer," Angelo said.

"Watch it, Dick," Nagi turned to Angelo. "Don't talk shit about my girl. That's like saying Taco Bell is real Mexican food."

"You have a point," Marquez shrugged and leaned back in his seat. "For the record, you need a girlfriend."

"Shut up while we save the world."

69
OLD CITY
Israel, Jerusalem
2:25 p.m.

Commander Shalom entered the chamber with Chief Superintended Hefetz directly behind him. Paramedics had already tended to Susan's wounds and carried her out on a stretcher to fly her to the nearest hospital. Miriam asked to go with her, and was granted her request. Yisrael and his accomplices were being transported to police headquarters, while Yeshua and Aiden remained behind with a couple of agents.

"When will we know that it is safe to disconnect these robots from the system?" Commander Shalom asked.

"I'm waiting for a callback from a friend," Aiden said.

"A callback from a friend?" Commander Shalom's brow furrowed. "Shouldn't we be shutting these things down?"

"If we shut them down before the professor's friend can locate their 'worms,' then we risk leaving the Trojan Horse inside the walls of Troy without knowing where it is," Yeshua said.

"If we do that, they can hide for an infinite amount of time and attack at a later date," Aiden added.

"How quickly can your friend find them?" Hefetz asked.

"Nagi is the best hacker that I know, but I'm afraid I can't give you a time-frame right now," Aiden said.

"What if he had a little help?" Hefetz said.

"I'm sure he could use all the help he can get," Aiden said. "Why? Do you know someone capable of assisting?"

"I believe I do," Hefetz grabbed his phone and called police headquarters. "Call your friend back, and tell him he's about to have company."

***

Nagi tapped a key on the glasstop tray to answer the incoming voice call, and then resumed his hack.

"Aiden, brother, what's up?"

"I don't mean to bother you, but could you use a little help?"

"What do you mean?"

"The Chief Superintendent here says he has an officer who specializes in what you're doing, and believes she would be able to help you," Aiden said.

"She?" Nagi repeated. "Well, I've never had a threesome, but hey, a party's a party, right?"

"All right, we'll have her link in to your position. I simply wanted to give you a heads up, so you didn't confuse her for an intruder."

"Thanks," Nagi said.

***

Abigail hacked into Nagi's feed after she initiated a call from her terminal to get on the same page, and together they worked to track down the infiltrations the A.I.'s had already achieved. They talked each other through the process of what the other was doing, while essentially following Priya's lead.

"Will your A.I. know where to look?" Abigail asked.

"Who better to think like an A.I. *than* an A.I.?" Nagi responded.

"Art of War, San Tzu," Abigail said. "Know your enemy."

"You're definitely a like-minded one," Nagi smiled. His fingers slid and tapped rapidly as he gazed up at his monitor while the luminous characters flashed across the screen.

"Got one!" Abigail said.

"Awesome-sauce," Nagi cheered.

"I have found the other," Priya chimed in.

"Wonderful! Way to go, Priya," Abigail applauded. "Girl power."

"Damn, bro, you let two women beat you," Angelo teased.

"Even in a threesome, it's ladies first," Nagi said over his shoulder.

"I couldn't hear you, Nagi, what was that?" Abigail asked.

"Nothing, it was nothing," Nagi lied.

Angelo tried to suppress his laughter.

"Two down, two to go," Nagi said.

"And another," Priya and Abigail said in unison.

"Were those the last two?" Nagi asked, perplexed.

"No," Abigail said. "I believe Priya and I found the same one together."

"Last one, Nagi," Angelo placed a hand on Nagi's shoulder. "You'll never be able to live down a goose egg on this one."

Nagi resumed his hack, as did Abigail and Priya. He muttered to himself as he endeavored to locate the last worm. His enthusiasm swelled, and then faltered with each passing minute.

"I must be a little rusty," Nagi said, but he would not concede defeat.

"Don't worry Nagi, we got this, don't we, Priya?"

"Indeed we do," Priya replied.

Together they continued to search for the final worm. Abigail and Nagi typed frantically, while Priya worked from within the network to locate the source code hidden within.

***

As worms were located, the A.I.'s ceased their functionality. One by one, their computer screens went blank and shut down. The A.I.'s sat in their seats and lowered their heads in silence. The only one that remained engaged with her task was Bina, and it was clear by how efficiently her worm had evaded detection that she proved more skillful than her human counterparts thought possible.

"If she knows the others have been caught, why doesn't she just stop?" Commander Shalom demanded.

"Would you, or I?" Aiden turned to him. "She believes she is doing the right thing. She wouldn't abandon her task simply because the others have been stopped. We have to remember that part of her initial programming is predicated on human influence."

"So, you're saying that *that* human influence will permeate her thought process and actions," Yeshua said.

"It stands to reason that this is a possibility," Aiden said. "Akin to when God made man in His image."

"Interesting," Yeshua said.

Aiden's phone chimed with an incoming text message just as Bina ceased typing and bowed her head.

Mission accomplished.

"They did it," Aiden read the text from Nagi.

The four men sighed with relief. Commander Shalom ordered his men to remove the A.I.'s from the chamber. They would be transported to police headquarters and held there until a representative from the robotics company arrived to retrieve them.

He then turned to Yeshua and Aiden.

"I owe you both an apology."

"The important thing is that we prevented a war and preserved the Holiest sites in the Old City," Yeshua said.

"If you gentlemen will excuse me, I must get in touch with some very important people at the U.N." Commander Shalom shook their hands before he turned left the chamber.

Chief Superintendent Hefetz thanked Aiden for his assistance, and then informed Yeshua that Commander Shalom agreed to drop the charges against him. Yeshua turned to Aiden after Hefetz stepped away and offered him a ride to the hospital.

THE SECRET OF SCRIPTURE

70
OLD CITY
Israel, Jerusalem
2:55 p.m.

Yeshua's squad pulled up beside the curb at the hospital's entrance.

"Thank you again for your assistance, professor," Yeshua extended his hand. "If there's anything I can do for you, simply name it."

"Well, if you ever need my assistance again," Aiden began to say. "Would you please wait until after sunrise to come knocking?"

"Deal," both men laughed. "By the way, did you ever figure out what the images represented?"

"You mean the ones that Sarai showed after the riddles were solved?" Aiden retrieved his smartphone from his pocket. "Actually, no, I didn't, but I did share them with Nagi. I wonder if he figured out what they meant."

"Nagi? Your friend, the hacker?"

"Yes, but actually he's a philologist and a cryptographer," Aiden brought up Nagi's phone number on the screen. "Let me call him and see what he found."

***

Nagi's Phat Mobile pulled into his driveway as Priya announced the incoming FaceTime call. He glanced over to Angelo, who was reaching into his pocket to retrieve his car keys.

"Should I answer it?" Nagi asked.

"Why the hell not?" Angelo sighed. "I don't think things could get any worse."

"True," Nagi nodded. "Aiden, buddy, please don't tell me we have another world crisis on our hands."

"No, we don't, at least not now," Aiden chuckled.

THE SECRET OF SCRIPTURE

"I do want to thank you again, Mr. Nagi, for your assistance with stopping a nuclear disaster, among other catastrophes," Yeshua said.

"Don't mention it," Nagi dismissed his statement with a wave of his hand. "It's all in a day's work."

"It was an especially important day for us," Yeshua said. "Tisha B'Av."

"Holy—" Nagi leaned back in his seat. "Mind blown."

"What is that," Angelo asked. "I don't understand."

"Tisha B'Av, the 9th of Av, commemorates the numerous disasters that occurred in Jewish history. From the incident in 1313 B.C.E. when the spies returned with a bad report prior to a battle with the Canaanites, to the destruction of the First and Second Temples. Then there was the Battle at Betwar that was lost, and when the Romans Plowed the Beit Hamikdash. Followed by the First Crusade, the expulsion of Jews from England, and then later when they were banished from Spain. Most recently, however, was the First World War, which by extension led to the Holocaust and the Second World War."

"All of these incidents throughout history, among others, occurred on the 9th of Av, detective," Yeshua said. "This is why I'm eternally grateful for everyone's assistance."

"Wow!" Angelo sat back in awe.

"The reason I'm calling, though, is to follow up with you about those images I sent you earlier. Were you able to decipher their meaning?"

"Actually, yes, I did," Nagi slid his fingers across the glasstop tray. "I toyed around with them again after the whole hacking situation, because I was a bit restless."

"Restless, my ass," Angelo interjected. "He was pissed that he didn't find any of the worms."

"Hey, my ego took a hit there, so yeah, I felt compelled to decipher it, but I'm still not clear on why the A.I. gave it to you," Nagi said. "Did the mad scientist program her to do so, or did she do it independent of his direction?"

"I don't know," Aiden glanced at Yeshua before they both turned back to Nagi on the screen.

"Regardless of that," Nagi tapped on his tray. "Here's what I came up with."

$$ \text{✗ ✓ ✗} $$

"What is that?" Yeshua's brow furrowed as he looked at the image on the screen.

"That's paleo-Hebrew," Nagi nodded at the screen. "Some refer to it as the original idiom of God."

"What can you make of it, professor?" Yeshua glanced at Aiden before he turned his attention back to the screen.

"Well, in reading from right to left, we know the first letter represents 'A' for Ab, or Abba," Aiden said.

"I was thinking the same thing, either as God, or God the Father, given the second symbol," Nagi said.

"What does the second symbol stand for?" Angelo leaned forward in his seat.

"Remember when I told you earlier that in paleo-Hebrew the alphabet was both pictoral and phonetic?" Nagi looked at Angelo over his shoulder.

"Yes," Angelo nodded without turning away from the screen.

"The second symbol represents 'L' in the modern languages, but the pictoral definition is that of a shepherd's staff," Nagi said.

"What does the final symbol mean?" Angelo asked.

"That resembles Taw, the final letter of the Hebrew alphabet," Yeshua said.

"It does," Nagi confirmed, "but here's the rub," he shifted in his seat. "That same symbol was used hundreds of years before Christianity to anoint the priests, and was also used on Jewish graves."

THE SECRET OF SCRIPTURE

Nagi swiped at his glasstop tray and the image moved front and center. He then shifted its angle to reveal a familiar symbol.

"That's a cross," Angelo pointed.

"Indeed it is," Nagi said.

"The first two letters declare that God is the Shepherd," Aiden said.

"Yes, but combining it with the third symbol, I can't help but wonder if the message embedded is trying to tell us something more," Nagi said.

"Like what?" Yeshua studied the images on the screen.

"If the first symbol represents the first letter of the paleo-Hebrew alphabet," Nagi said.

"And the last symbol represents the last letter of the paleo-Hebrew alphabet," Aiden continued.

"Then one can't help but wonder about the middle symbol that links them both," Nagi continued.

"God is the First Shepherd, the Alpha and the Omega, the beginning and the end," Aiden said. "That symbol represents the Letter of Completion."

71
OLD CITY
Kuwait City, Kuwait
7:17 p.m.

Omar turned away from the window when Prescott entered the office.

"Do you have the scrolls?" Omar watched as Prescott approached the desk.

"Just as you requested, sir," Prescott placed the package on Omar's desk.

"Good. I will ensure the funds of our agreed upon fee will be deposited into your account immediately."

Prescott nodded.

"Take some time to yourself. I will call you with your next assignment when the time comes," Omar said.

Prescott turned and headed for the door as Omar's cellphone rang.

Omar waited until Prescott pulled the door closed behind him before he answered.

"Good evening, Omar," a raspy voice echoed over the receiver. "I trust you have obtained possession of the items in question."

"Yes sir, I have," Omar replied. "They were just brought to my office a moment ago."

"Well done, Omar. I knew I could count on you to accomplish this task. You know what to do next."

"Indeed I do, Magistrate."

THE SECRET OF SCRIPTURE

BOOKS BY
FELIX ALEXANDER

HER PUNISHMENT

A dark erotic novelette from Readers' Favorite award-winning novelist, Felix Alexander.

Majica is done.
She has waited five years for Ricardo to marry her.
She will not wait any longer.
After several weeks of being away, she returns home for her belongings.
She thought he would not be home.
She was wrong.
He intends to punish her for leaving him, and for the lie.
Trapped alone with him, she is lured into their private chamber.
He wants her to himself and refuses to believe she doesn't love him anymore.
Ricardo always gets what he wants.

Though Majica resists, she struggles to reconcile is passion with his love, but she remembers their agreement: once inside the private room there is no protesting, only submission.

HER AWAKENING

When sex shop employee Marina Varela meets Luciano Garcia, she encounters a man who is handsome, intelligent and intimidating. The guarded Marina wants this man, and Luciano confesses his desire for her as well, but he too is guarded. When the couple endeavors to see where things may lead, they find themselves in the throes of a passionate affair. Their sexual exploration of each other leads them to an awakening of their bodies and their hearts.

FELIX ALEXANDER

THE ROMANTIC: A LOVE STORY

The Romantic is a love story about friendship, passion, and the echo of unrequited love.

Hadriel Alighieri has harbored a secret love in his heart for his entire life. It began in his youth, when he fell in love with his best friend, Sophia Paula. After Sophia leaves for America and is later betrothed to Joshua Abrams, Hadriel is devastated, but he is a hopeless romantic.

In the winter of his life he is haunted by the memory of Sophia Paula. When the Angel of Death comes for Hadriel, the journey begins. From his deathbed, he travels to the day he fell in love. He retraces the steps of his life in search of his unrequited love. For she too harbors a secret love in her heart. But what begins as a journey to fulfill a promise turns into a discovery of the only emotion that defines our lives.

Did she wait for him?

THE SECRET OF SCRIPTURE

<u>THE LAST VALENTINE</u>
A LABYRINTH OF LOVE LETTERS NOVEL

When Olivia Villalobos finds a bloodstained love letter, she endeavors to deliver it before Chief Inspector Sedeño finds it in her possession.

A city along the southern coast of Puerto Rico emerges in the aftermath of the Spanish-American War. Olivia, daughter of a drunkard police investigator who never knew the truth behind her mother's disappearance, finds a bloodstained love letter in the hidden compartment of her father's coat. Convinced it belonged to the man recently found dead she sets out to deliver it to the Labyrinth of Love Letters. A mysterious place believed to be an urban legend where the transients of forbidden love leave missives for one another. She enlists the help of Isaac Quintero to find the Labyrinth and they soon realize their quest has opened the door into Old Sienna's darkest secrets—the perils, madness and depth of tragic love.

<u>THE LAST LOVE LETTER</u>
A LABYRINTH OF LOVE LETTERS NOVEL

"What if you were the one?"

With those words, Arabella España is lured into a tale of forbidden love and forgotten secrets. In the wake of a murder in 1950's Puerto Rico, Nationalists revolt against American colonialism. An amnesiac recluse, married to a man she does not love, Arabella finds solace in the only remaining book in her possession. One of many banned by Puerto Rico's Gag Law.

The mysterious novel entitled THE LAST LOVE LETTER by one Aurelio Valentino leads Arabella on a journey with the main character in search of his lost love. But as she delves deeper into the story, she makes a shocking discovery: the novel contains clues to finding the legendary Labyrinth of Love Letters. A place of love and myth linked to the letter stolen from the corpse of the man who had recently been killed.

As each page draws Aurelio and Arabella closer together, she anxiously searches for the love letter that will reveal the identity of Aurelio's lost love. In her endeavor to find the Labyrinth, she discovers that the murder is a fate tied closely to her own destiny. Soon Arabella's literary journey reveals memories of her forgotten past and she discovers what happens when the main character of the story falls in love with the reader.

DEAR LOVE: DIARY OF A MAN'S DESIRE
A COLLECTION OF LOVE LETTERS AND POEMS

What if a man loved a woman with such passion that even if she left him, he would still love her with his broken heart?

From the shadows of unrequited love, and an unlikely romance, rises the intense flame of a passionate profession of undying love, a romantic's musings.

Dear Love: Diary of a Man's Desire is a collection of love letters and poems written to inspire & stir the emotions of the soul.

"I fear that one day I'll lose a tear in the ocean -the day you find love with another- and like that tear, I'll never get to have you back."

THE SECRET OF SCRIPTURE

THE SECRET OF HEAVEN

When investment banker Lazzaro de Medici is found dead, Professor of Biblical Studies at University of Illinois at Chicago Aiden Leonardo is the prime suspect. In possession of an encrypted letter given to him by Lazzaro, Aiden utilizes his extensive knowledge of Scripture to piece together clues that lead to a Lost Bible dating back to the time of Christ.

Hidden within the text is an ancient truth about the most controversial message Jesus left to His disciples. But as Aiden embarks on his quest to unravel the mystery of redemption and faith, a secret organization known only as The Group hunts him down to destroy the Lost Bible and tie up loose ends.

With the help of his fiancé Dr. Miriam Levin—a cultural anthropologist and a professor of historical archaeology in her own right, their friend Nagi, a philologist, religious historian and an eccentric cryptographer, Aiden soon realizes the Lost Bible was written by the only disciple who walked with Jesus and had his gospel omitted from Scripture.

Things are further complicated when a mysterious stranger warns Aiden that possessing the secret of heaven could cost him his life. Pursued by the F.B.I. for the ancient Black market relic and the Chicago PD in connection to the murder of Lazzaro de Medici, Aiden races against the clock to prove his innocence and fulfill his mentor's dying wish.

Expose the secret of heaven...

SHADOWS OF TIME:
THE AMULET OF ALAMIN

The veil between the heavens and the underworld has fallen.

Mesopotamia is a region with kingdoms at war. The desires of gods and men sweep across the Land Between the Two Rivers so frequently that peace is merely a memory of a forgotten time. Demons and shape shifters lurk in the shadows, sorcerers and soothsayers warn of impending danger, and a demigod sits in the eye of the storm.

It has been millennia since the Tablet of Destinies fell from heaven. After the fall of angels and the emergence of the Watchers, the gods set out to destroy the Nephilim and retrieve the Tablet, but a piece of the stone chipped away before it was lost.

Fashioned from that piece of the Tablet, an amulet was gifted to Alamin in his infancy, but when he discovers the gods and angels want him dead, he is forced to flee with it and only the Fallen Angel can protect him. Princess Safia is betrothed against her wishes and she flees with Alamin on a perilous quest across the Ancient World that blurs the boundaries of reality with the realm of myth until Alamin surrenders to the Fallen Angel.

Troubled by the prophecy, Inanna crosses oceans and deserts to find her son before she journeys into the underworld to retrieve his soul. The King of Kish names Sargon—the boy general—his Cup Bearer. Zagesi condemns his soul for immortality, but his deal with Mephitsophel is an ominous portent for the fall of kings. The fate of existence hangs perilously in the balance and the realm between the heavens and the underworld collapses into chaos.

THE SECRET OF SCRIPTURE

ABOUT THE AUTHOR

Felix Alexander (1976-Present) is a Mexican-born, American-raised novelist and poet of Mexican and Puerto Rican descent acclaimed by readers for his poetic prose.

Being third-generation military, after a grandfather and uncle who served in the Korean War and Vietnam War, respectively, Alexander is proud of his service in the U.S. Army and grateful for his experience.

After his honorable discharge from the U.S. Army, his third year served in South Korea, he embarked on the long and arduous journey of a writer. Having made a name for himself during his tenure serving his country, he vowed to himself and his fellow soldiers that he would answer his true calling.

He lives in South Elgin, IL—to be close to his children—a son and daughter. He volunteers to promote literacy among youth with Villament Charities and the VM Mag (vmmag.org). In the evenings he journeys through the portals of his extensive, personal library. When he returns, he immerses himself in his writing, and pursues the scent of his muse.

CPSIA information can be obtained
at www.ICGtesting.com
Printed in the USA
LVHW031503160720
660874LV00002B/219